SpongeBob™ COMICS #2

Aquatic Adventurers, Unite!

ALSO AVAILABLE
SpongeBob Comics: Silly Sea Stories
SpongeBob Comics: Tales from the Haunted Pineapple

PUBLISHER'S NOTE:
This is a work of fiction. Names, characters, places, and incidents are either the product of the author's imagination or used fictitiously, and any resemblance to actual persons, living or dead, business establishments, events, or locales is entirely coincidental.

Cataloging-in-Publication Data has been applied for and may be obtained from the Library of Congress.

ISBN 978-1-4197-2320-9

Cover and title page illustrations by Jacob Chabot

Book design by Pamela Notarantonio

The stories included in this collection were originally published in *SpongeBob Comics* no. 3 (June 2011), 7 (February 2012), 9 (June 2012), 10 (July 2012), 17 (February 2013), 19 (April 2013), and 35 (August 2014); *Annual Super-Giant Spectacular 1* (June 2013) and 2 (June 2014); and *Freestyle Funnies* (Free Comic Book Day, May 2013).

Printed and bound in China
10 9 8

Amulet Books are available at special discounts when purchased in quantity for premiums and promotions as well as fundraising or educational use. Special editions can also be created to specification. For details, contact specialsales@abramsbooks.com or the address below.

ABRAMS The Art of Books
195 Broadway, New York, NY 10007
abramsbooks.com

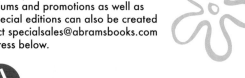

SpongeBob COMICS #2™

Aquatic Adventurers, Unite!

STEPHEN HILLENBURG
EDITED BY CHRIS DUFFY

AMULET BOOKS
NEW YORK

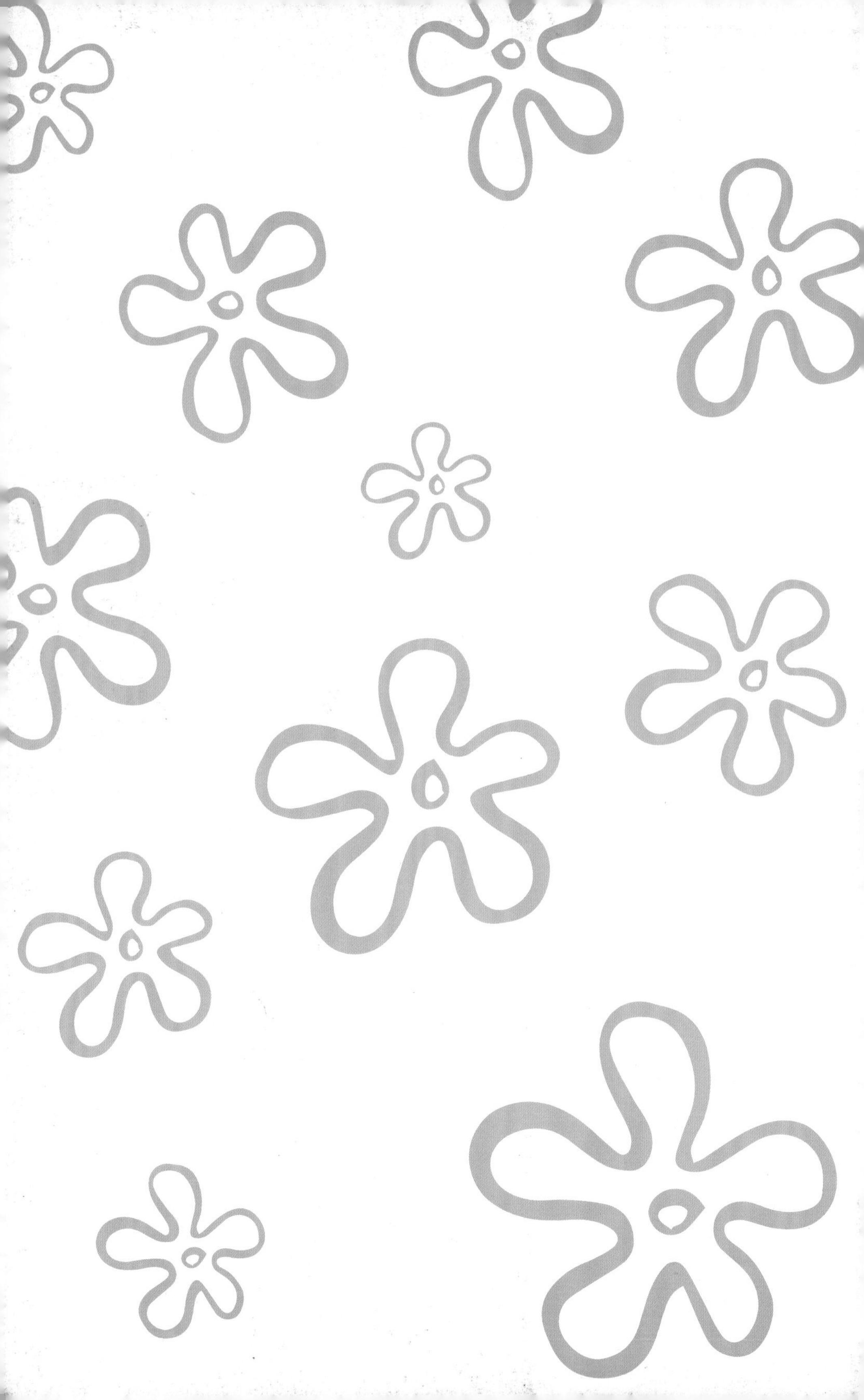

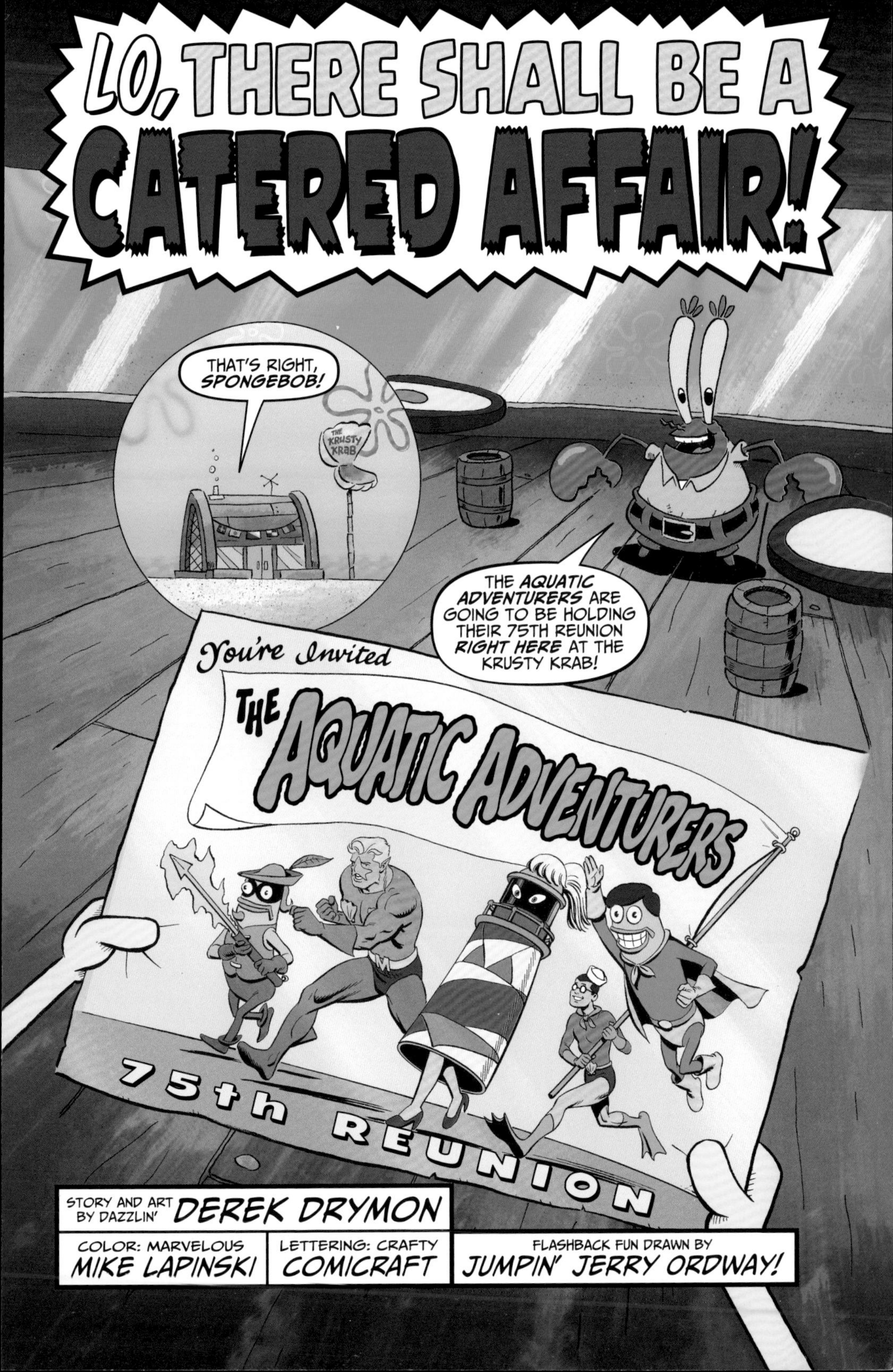
LO, THERE SHALL BE A CATERED AFFAIR!
THAT'S RIGHT, SPONGEBOB!
THE KRUSTY KRAB
THE AQUATIC ADVENTURERS ARE GOING TO BE HOLDING THEIR 75TH REUNION RIGHT HERE AT THE KRUSTY KRAB!
You're Invited
THE AQUATIC ADVENTURERS
75th REUNION
STORY AND ART BY DAZZLIN' DEREK DRYMON
COLOR: MARVELOUS MIKE LAPINSKI
LETTERING: CRAFTY COMICRAFT
FLASHBACK FUN DRAWN BY JUMPIN' JERRY ORDWAY!

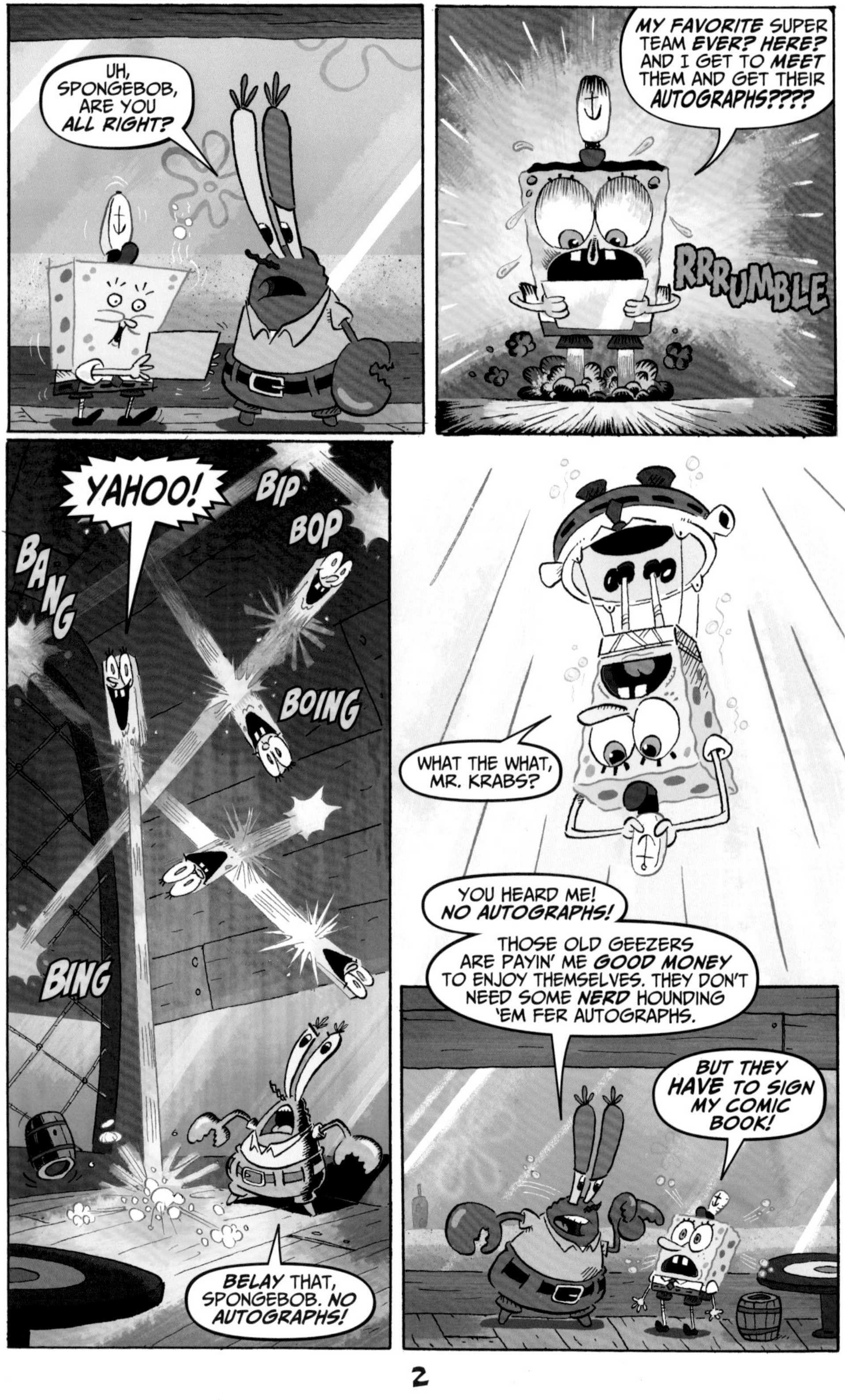
UH, SPONGEBOB, ARE YOU ALL RIGHT?
MY FAVORITE SUPER TEAM EVER? HERE? AND I GET TO MEET THEM AND GET THEIR AUTOGRAPHS????
RRRUMBLE
YAHOO!
BIP
BOP
BANG
BOING
BING
BELAY THAT, SPONGEBOB. NO AUTOGRAPHS!
WHAT THE WHAT, MR. KRABS?
YOU HEARD ME! NO AUTOGRAPHS!
THOSE OLD GEEZERS ARE PAYIN' ME GOOD MONEY TO ENJOY THEMSELVES. THEY DON'T NEED SOME NERD HOUNDING 'EM FER AUTOGRAPHS.
BUT THEY HAVE TO SIGN MY COMIC BOOK!

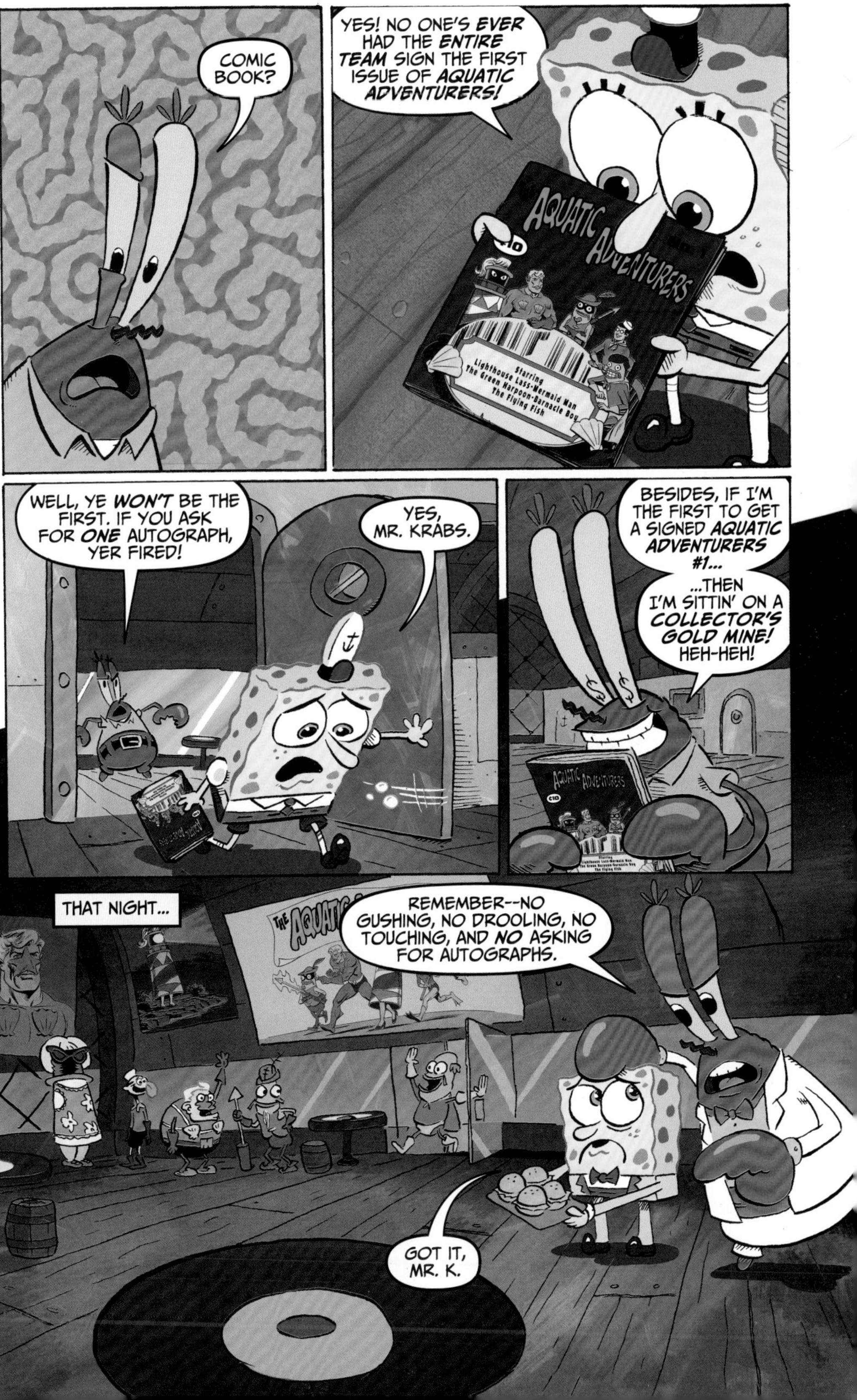
COMIC BOOK?
YES! NO ONE'S *EVER* HAD THE *ENTIRE TEAM* SIGN THE FIRST ISSUE OF *AQUATIC ADVENTURERS!*
AQUATIC ADVENTURERS
Starring
Lighthouse Lass-Mermaid Man
The Green Harpoon-Barnacle Boy
The Flying Fish
WELL, YE *WON'T* BE THE FIRST. IF YOU ASK FOR *ONE* AUTOGRAPH, YER FIRED!
YES, MR. KRABS.
BESIDES, IF I'M THE FIRST TO GET A SIGNED *AQUATIC ADVENTURERS #1...*
...THEN I'M SITTIN' ON A *COLLECTOR'S GOLD MINE!* HEH-HEH!
AQUATIC ADVENTURERS
THAT NIGHT...
REMEMBER--NO GUSHING, NO DROOLING, NO TOUCHING, AND *NO* ASKING FOR AUTOGRAPHS.
GOT IT, MR. K.

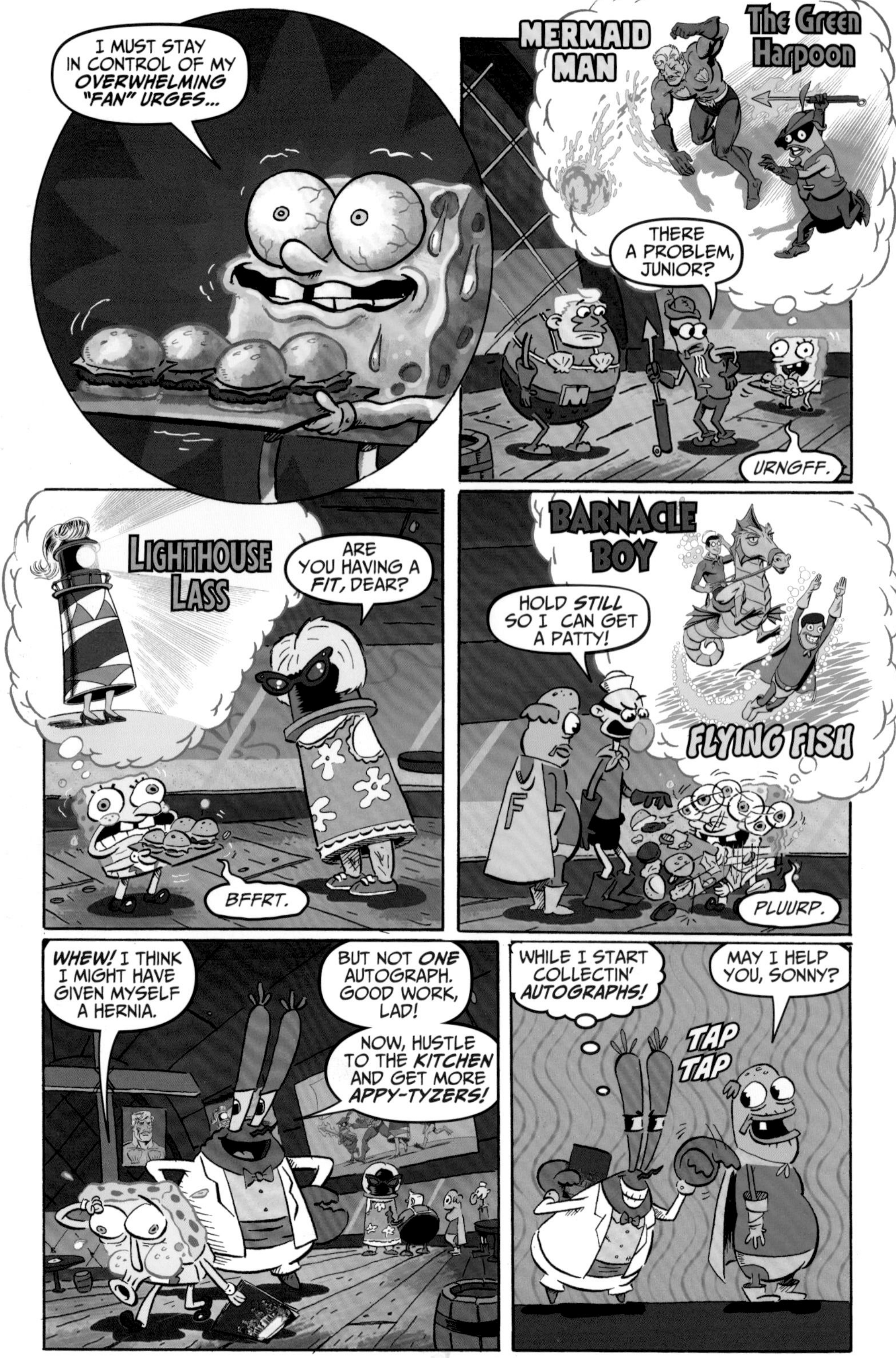
I MUST STAY IN CONTROL OF MY OVERWHELMING "FAN" URGES...
MERMAID MAN
The Green Harpoon
THERE A PROBLEM, JUNIOR?
URNGFF.
LIGHTHOUSE LASS
ARE YOU HAVING A FIT, DEAR?
BFFRT.
BARNACLE BOY
HOLD STILL SO I CAN GET A PATTY!
FLYING FISH
PLUURP.
WHEW! I THINK I MIGHT HAVE GIVEN MYSELF A HERNIA.
BUT NOT ONE AUTOGRAPH. GOOD WORK, LAD!
NOW, HUSTLE TO THE KITCHEN AND GET MORE APPY-TYZERS!
WHILE I START COLLECTIN' AUTOGRAPHS!
MAY I HELP YOU, SONNY?
TAP TAP

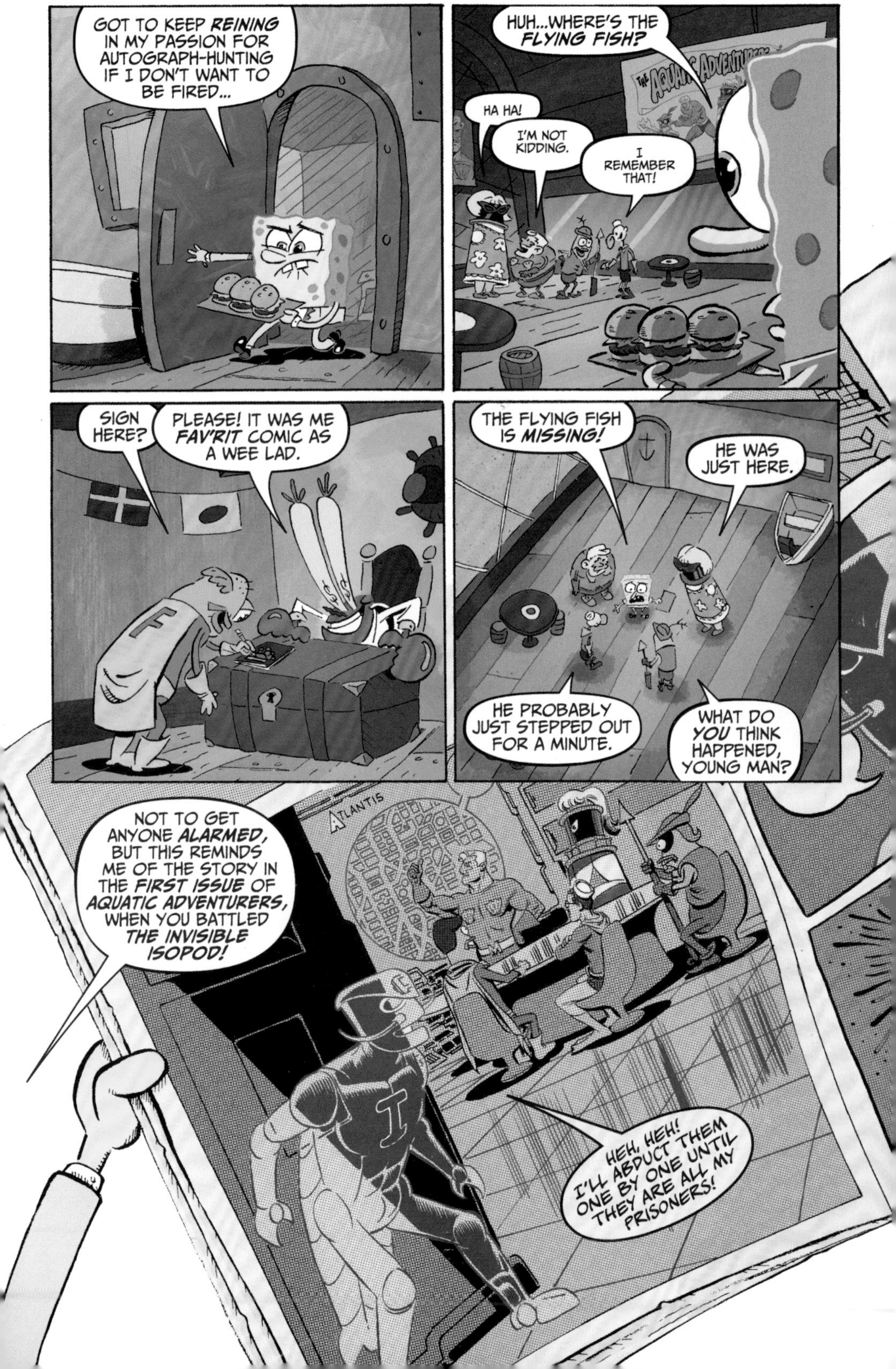
GOT TO KEEP *REINING* IN MY PASSION FOR AUTOGRAPH-HUNTING IF I DON'T WANT TO BE FIRED...
HUH...WHERE'S THE *FLYING FISH?*
HA HA!
I'M NOT KIDDING.
I REMEMBER THAT!
SIGN HERE?
PLEASE! IT WAS ME *FAV'RIT* COMIC AS A WEE LAD.
THE FLYING FISH IS *MISSING!*
HE WAS JUST HERE.
HE PROBABLY JUST STEPPED OUT FOR A MINUTE.
WHAT DO *YOU* THINK HAPPENED, YOUNG MAN?
NOT TO GET ANYONE *ALARMED,* BUT THIS REMINDS ME OF THE STORY IN THE *FIRST ISSUE* OF *AQUATIC ADVENTURERS,* WHEN YOU BATTLED *THE INVISIBLE ISOPOD!*
ATLANTIS
HEH, HEH! I'LL ABDUCT THEM ONE BY ONE UNTIL THEY ARE ALL MY PRISONERS!

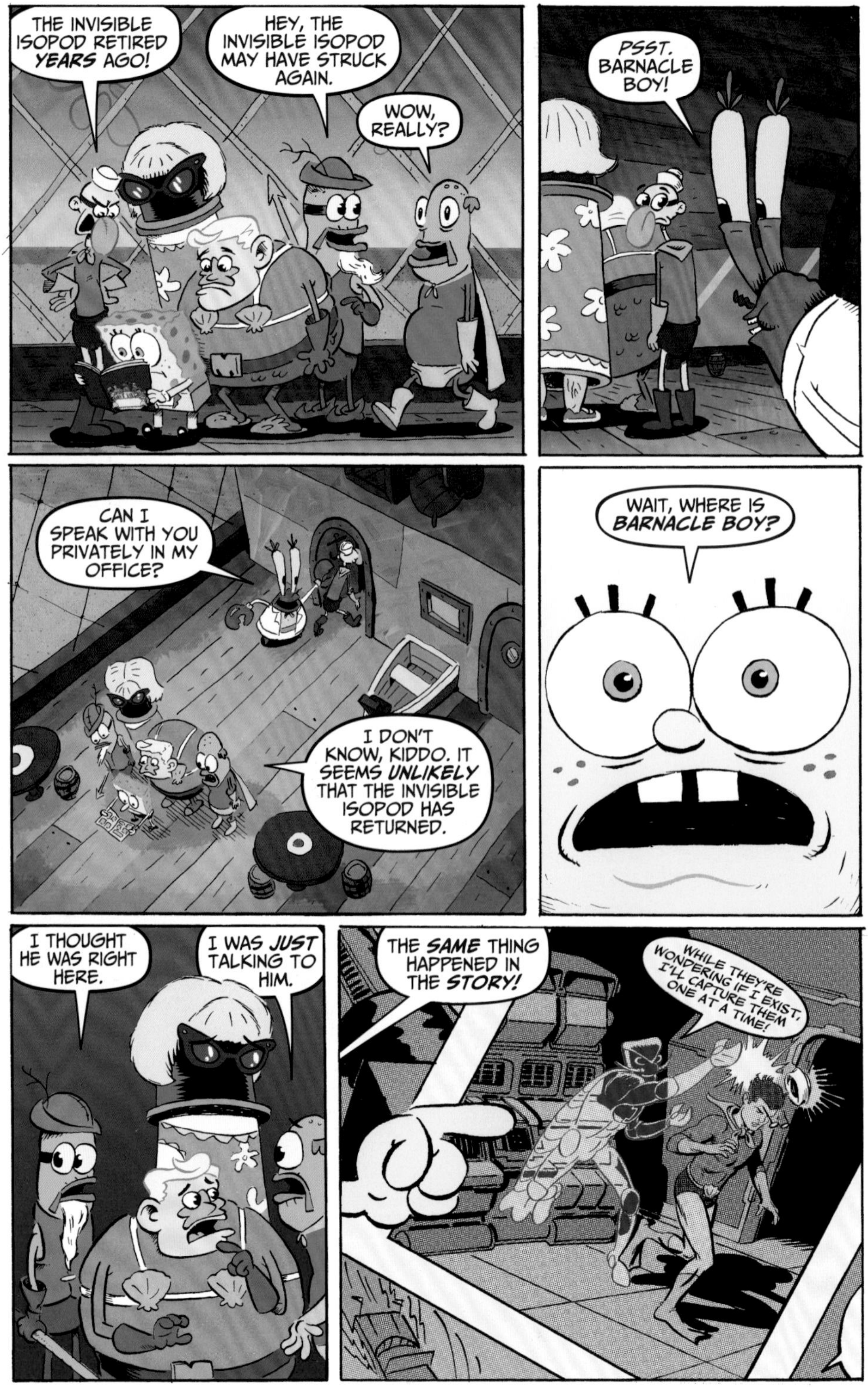
THE INVISIBLE ISOPOD RETIRED YEARS AGO!
HEY, THE INVISIBLE ISOPOD MAY HAVE STRUCK AGAIN.
WOW, REALLY?
PSST. BARNACLE BOY!
CAN I SPEAK WITH YOU PRIVATELY IN MY OFFICE?
I DON'T KNOW, KIDDO. IT SEEMS UNLIKELY THAT THE INVISIBLE ISOPOD HAS RETURNED.
WAIT, WHERE IS BARNACLE BOY?
I THOUGHT HE WAS RIGHT HERE.
I WAS JUST TALKING TO HIM.
THE SAME THING HAPPENED IN THE STORY!
WHILE THEY'RE WONDERING IF I EXIST, I'LL CAPTURE THEM ONE AT A TIME!

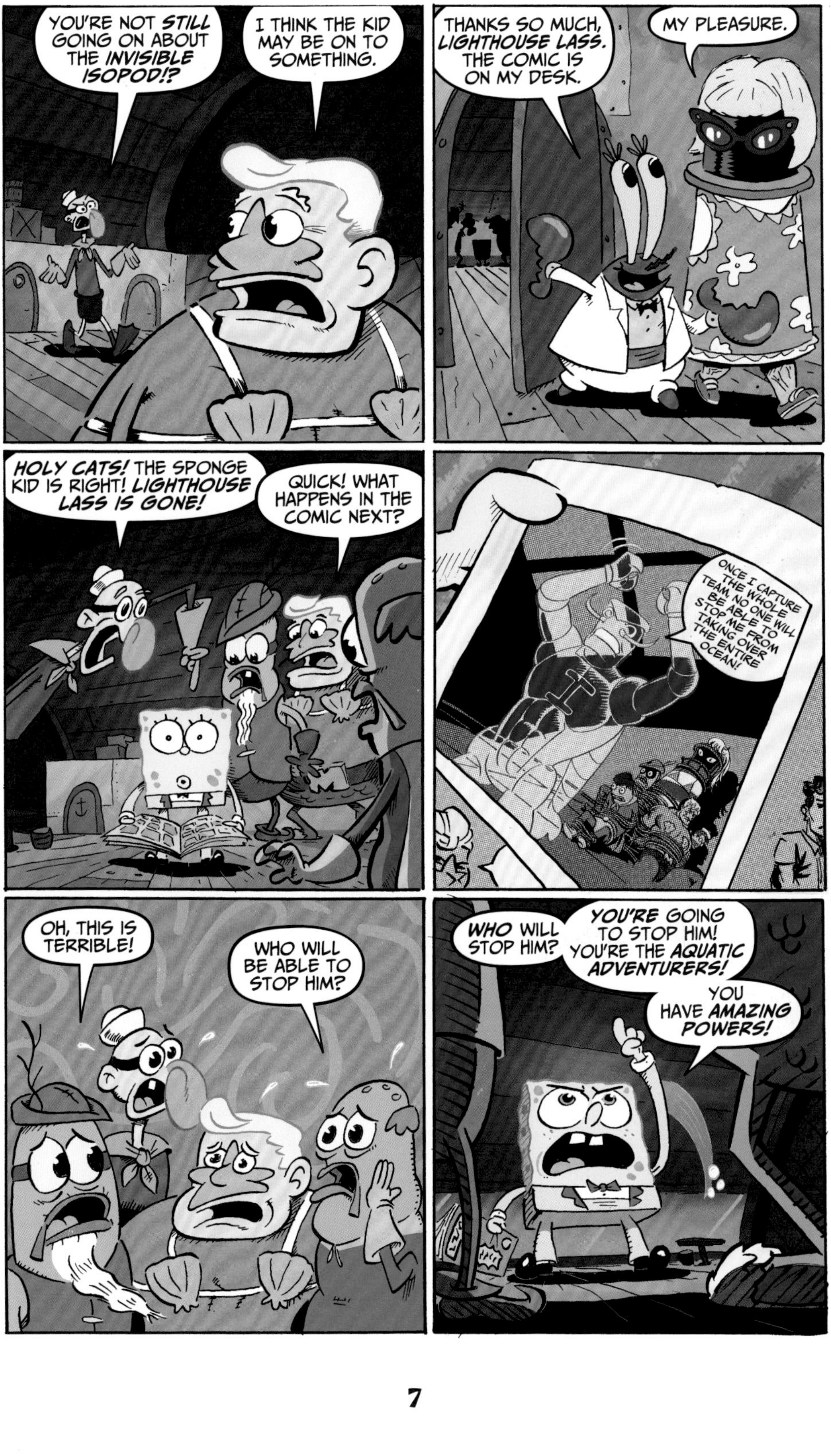
YOU'RE NOT STILL GOING ON ABOUT THE INVISIBLE ISOPOD!?
I THINK THE KID MAY BE ON TO SOMETHING.
THANKS SO MUCH, LIGHTHOUSE LASS. THE COMIC IS ON MY DESK.
MY PLEASURE.
HOLY CATS! THE SPONGE KID IS RIGHT! LIGHTHOUSE LASS IS GONE!
QUICK! WHAT HAPPENS IN THE COMIC NEXT?
ONCE I CAPTURE THE WHOLE TEAM, NO ONE WILL BE ABLE TO STOP ME FROM TAKING OVER THE ENTIRE OCEAN!
OH, THIS IS TERRIBLE!
WHO WILL BE ABLE TO STOP HIM?
WHO WILL STOP HIM?
YOU'RE GOING TO STOP HIM! YOU'RE THE AQUATIC ADVENTURERS!
YOU HAVE AMAZING POWERS!

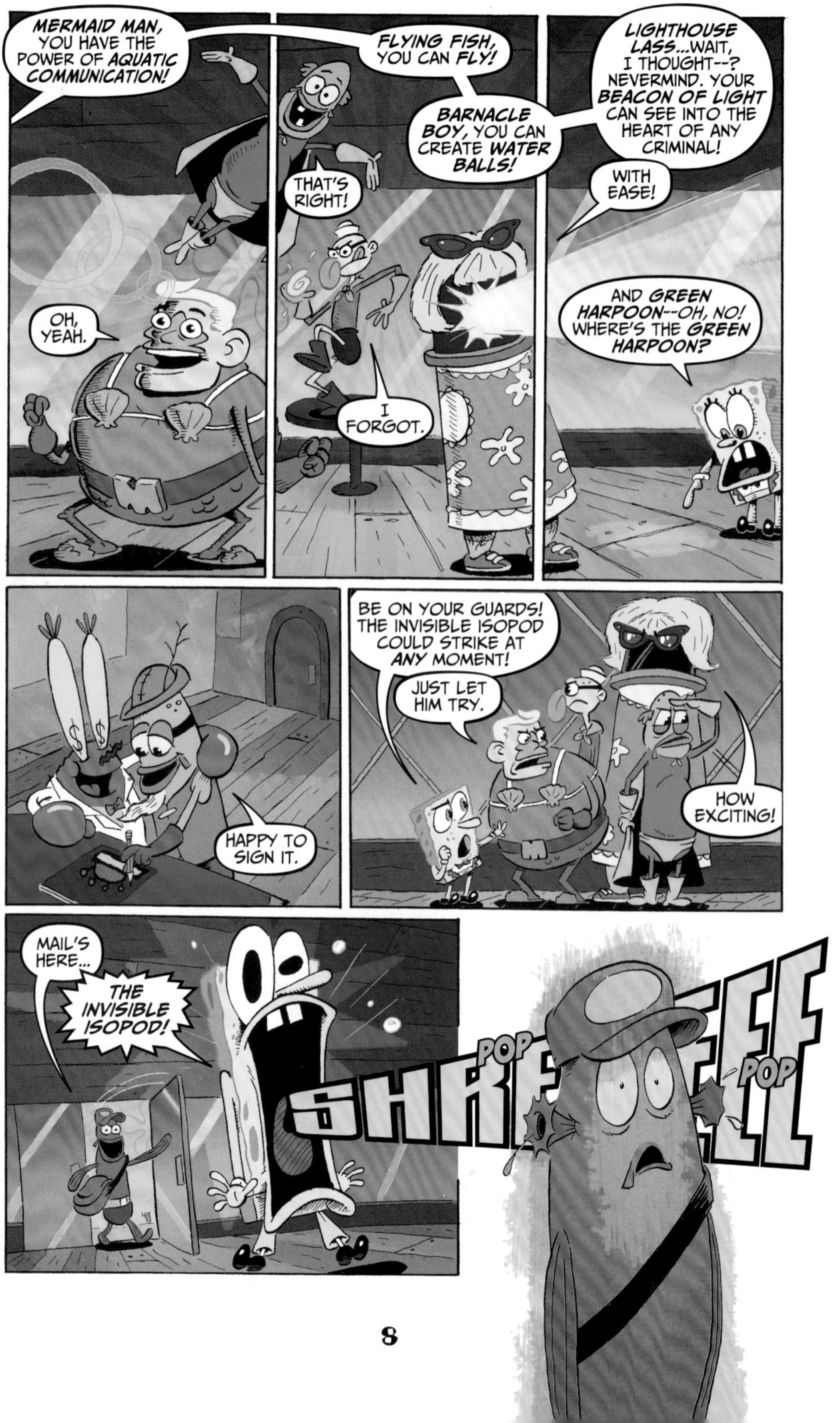
MERMAID MAN, YOU HAVE THE POWER OF AQUATIC COMMUNICATION!
OH, YEAH.
FLYING FISH, YOU CAN FLY!
THAT'S RIGHT!
BARNACLE BOY, YOU CAN CREATE WATER BALLS!
I FORGOT.
LIGHTHOUSE LASS...WAIT, I THOUGHT--? NEVERMIND. YOUR BEACON OF LIGHT CAN SEE INTO THE HEART OF ANY CRIMINAL!
WITH EASE!
AND GREEN HARPOON--OH, NO! WHERE'S THE GREEN HARPOON?
HAPPY TO SIGN IT.
BE ON YOUR GUARDS! THE INVISIBLE ISOPOD COULD STRIKE AT ANY MOMENT!
JUST LET HIM TRY.
HOW EXCITING!
MAIL'S HERE...
THE INVISIBLE ISOPOD!
POP
SHREEEE
POP

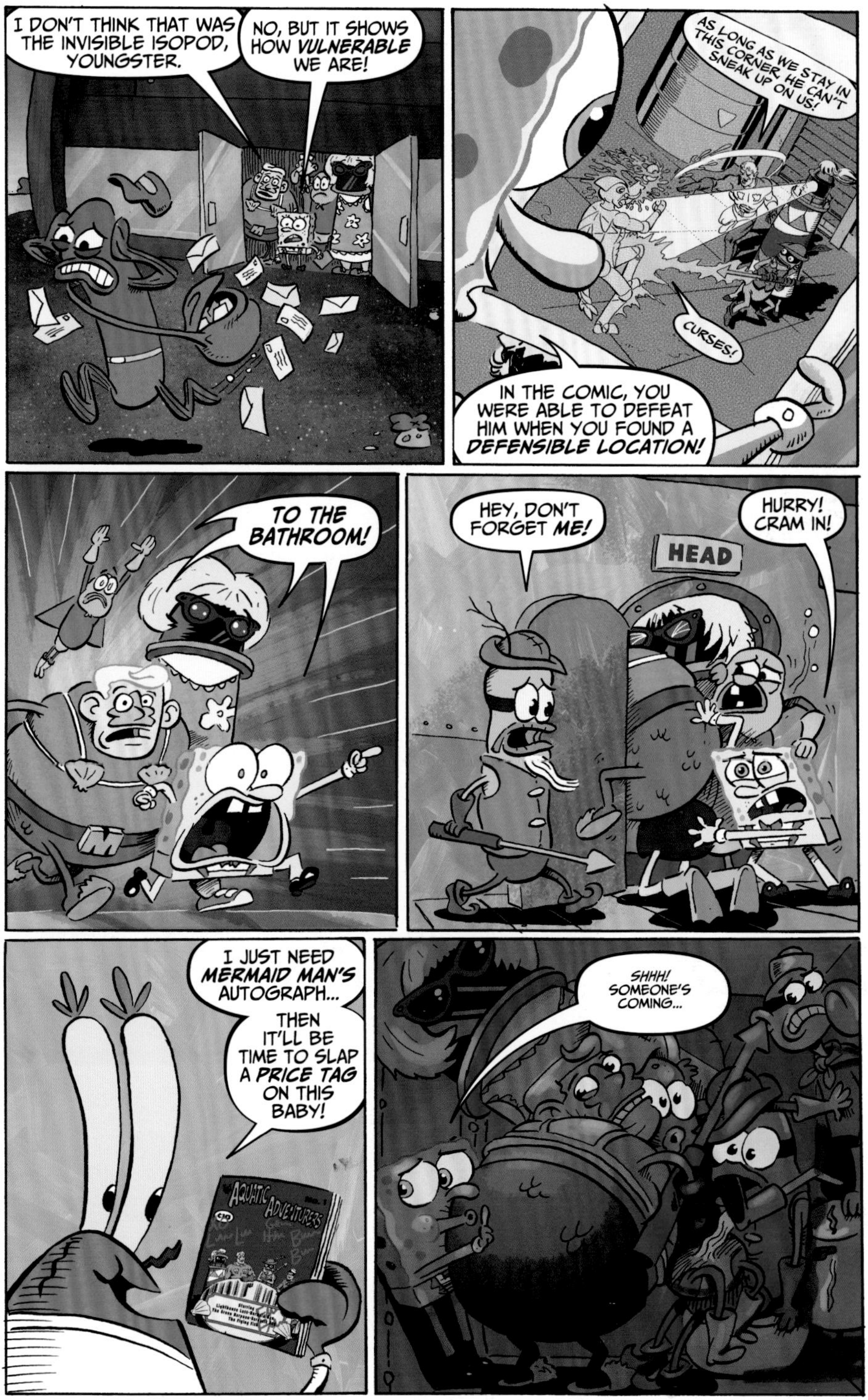
I DON'T THINK THAT WAS THE INVISIBLE ISOPOD, YOUNGSTER.
NO, BUT IT SHOWS HOW VULNERABLE WE ARE!
AS LONG AS WE STAY IN THIS CORNER, HE CAN'T SNEAK UP ON US!
CURSES!
IN THE COMIC, YOU WERE ABLE TO DEFEAT HIM WHEN YOU FOUND A DEFENSIBLE LOCATION!
TO THE BATHROOM!
HEY, DON'T FORGET ME!
HEAD
HURRY! CRAM IN!
I JUST NEED MERMAID MAN'S AUTOGRAPH...
THEN IT'LL BE TIME TO SLAP A PRICE TAG ON THIS BABY!
AQUATIC ADVENTURERS
SHHH! SOMEONE'S COMING...

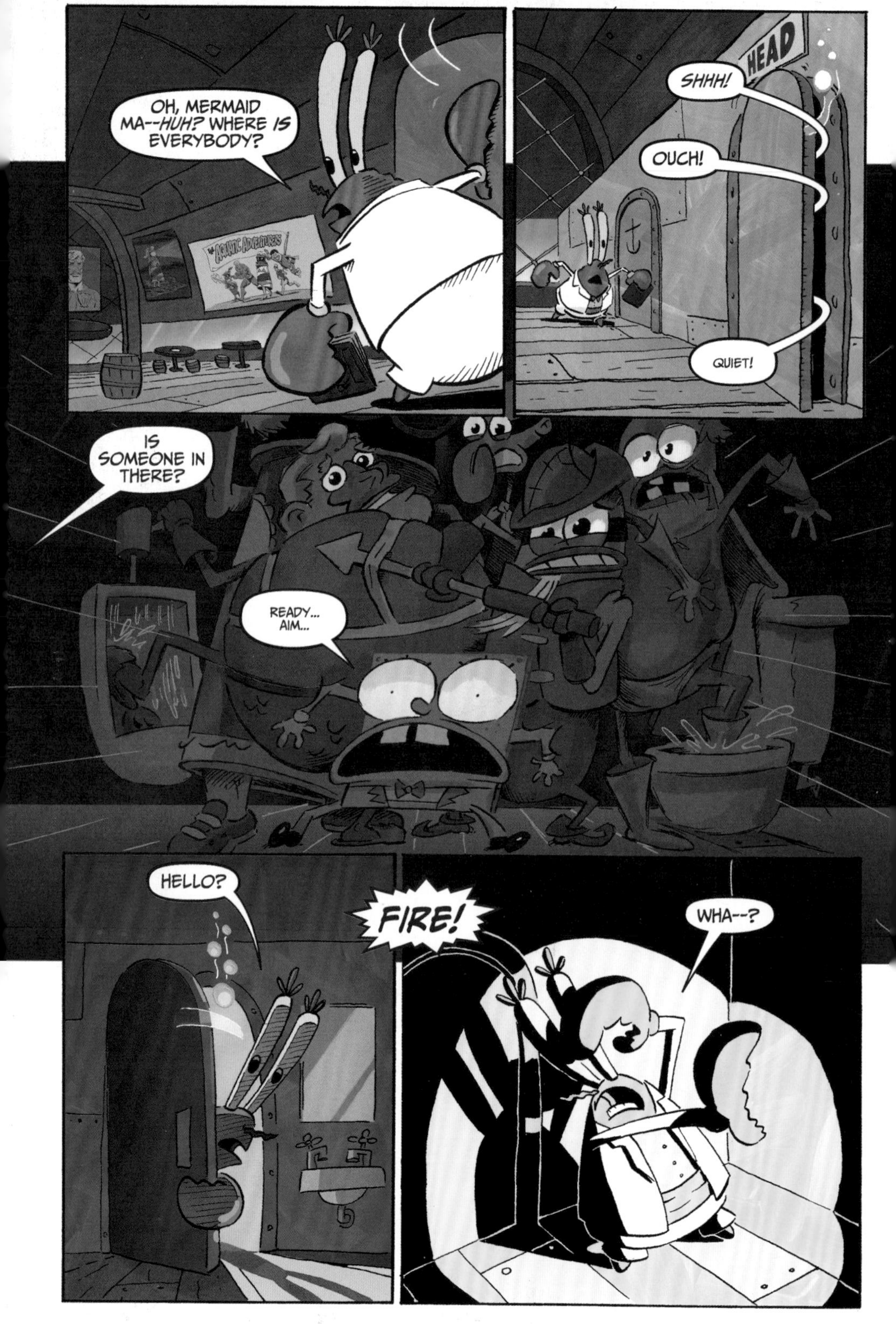
OH, MERMAID MA--HUH? WHERE IS EVERYBODY?
SHHH!
OUCH!
QUIET!
HEAD
IS SOMEONE IN THERE?
READY... AIM...
HELLO?
FIRE!
WHA--?

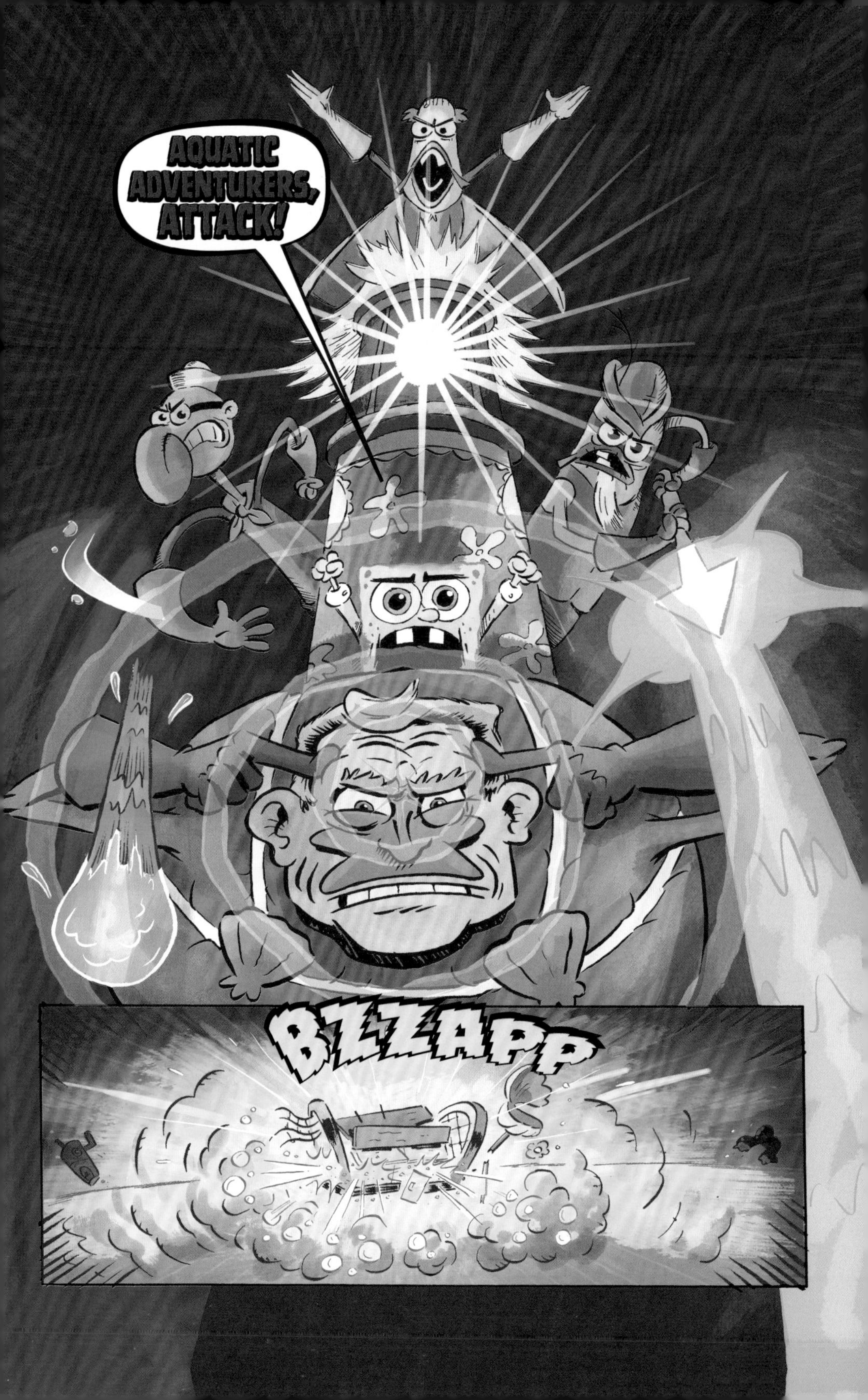
AQUATIC ADVENTURERS, ATTACK!
BZZAPP

IRONIC! THE INVISIBLE ISOPOD LOOKS JUST LIKE MR. KRABS.
THAT AIN'T THE INVISIBLE ISOPOD! IT'S JUST THAT NERD WHO WANTED OUR AUTOGRAPHS!
BUT WHY WOULD MR. KRABS HAVE YOU ALL SIGN THIS VALUABLE COLLECTOR'S EDITION WHEN HE TOLD ME NOT TO, UNLESS HE PLANNED TO...
AQUATIC ADVENTURERS
No. 1
...GIVE IT TO ME AS A SURPRISE! WHAT ELSE?!
OH, THANK YOU, MR. KRABS!
GROAN...
I'M KIND OF DISAPPOINTED TO FIND OUT IT WASN'T THE INVISBILE ISOPOD, AFTER ALL.
YEAH. MOST FUN I'VE HAD IN YEARS!
BACK TO THE RETIREMENT HOME.
PFFT! I KNEW IT THE WHOLE TIME. THE ISOPOD COULD NEVER GET ONE OVER ON US!
OOP!
GASP!
HA, HA! YOU ALWAYS WERE A WEENIE, BARNACLE BOY!
END

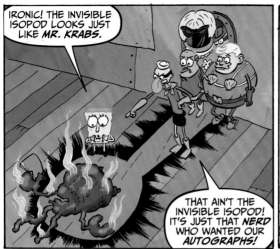

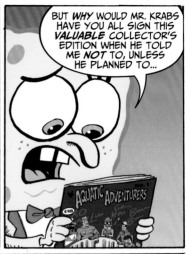

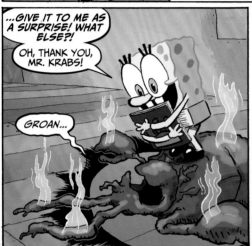

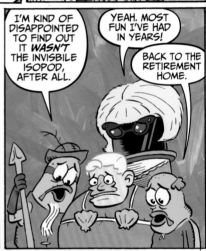

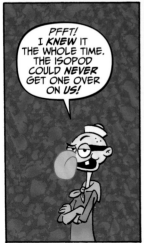

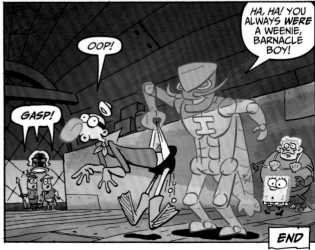

Sufferin' Salesfish! Enjoy FOUR CLASSIC MERMAID MAN-SPONSORED ADS from the BRINEY AGE of comics! Archival research by writer **Robert Leighton** and artist **Mark Martin**.

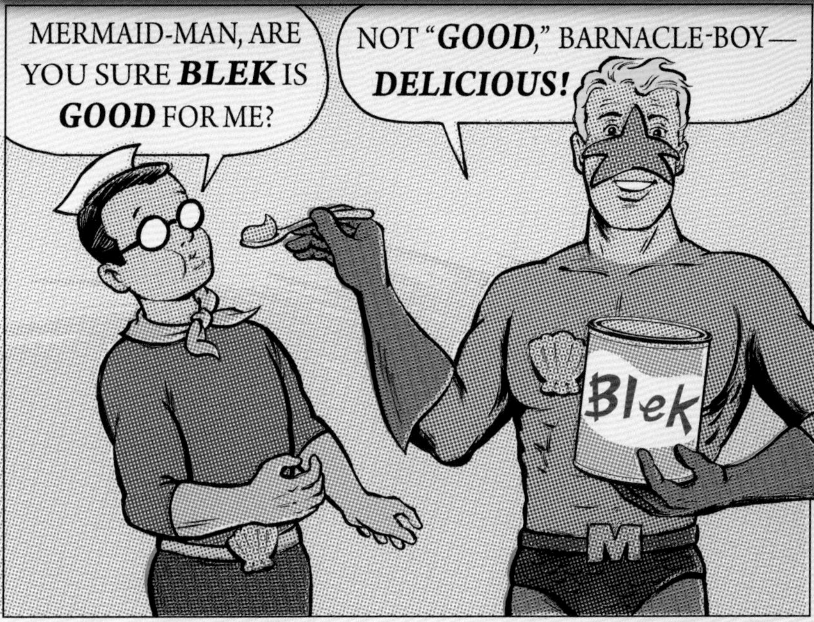
MERMAID-MAN, ARE YOU SURE BLEK IS GOOD FOR ME?
NOT "GOOD," BARNACLE-BOY— DELICIOUS!
Blek
M

MOMS AND SUPER-CHUMS KNOW THAT FOODS ENRICHED WITH CHOLESTEROL SHOULD BE THE CENTERPIECE OF EVERY MEAL!

Don't say "No" when your youngster asks for foods high in cholesterol. Doctors know that cholesterol fortifies kids' arteries so they stand up straight!

Foods deep-fried in BLEK take on a thick shell of crispy yumminess. BLEK is not only smooth on the system, its high schmaltz factor guarantees "It Goes Straight Through!"

Are you a puny guppy? Eat two tablespoons of wholesome BLEK at every meal and watch those pounds add up. That's right–BLEKfast, lunch, and dinner, BLEK should be a part of every suggestion in Mom's recipe basket.

AN IMPORTANT SOURCE OF CHOLESTEROL!

Only BLEK takes unprocessed lard and triple-mills it to remove every drop of harmful vitamins and nutrients. What's left? Just tasty chunks of thick, chewy goodness. When your lad leaves the table after a dinner cooked with BLEK, he'll feel the healthful pull of gravity!

Remember–your family can't enjoy the benefits of BLEK unless it's always on hand! Ask your grocer for the new 22-pound canister!

TAKE IT FROM MERMAID-MAN AND BARNACLE-BOY!

They're not just paid endorsers, they're highly compensated spokesmen! And they know that kids who want to be Heroes of the Deep need that thick, yummy goodness that only comes from BLEK!

KIDS—Check Mom's kitchen cabinet. If BLEK's not there, run out and get some today. DAD WILL THANK YOU AND PAY YOU BACK!

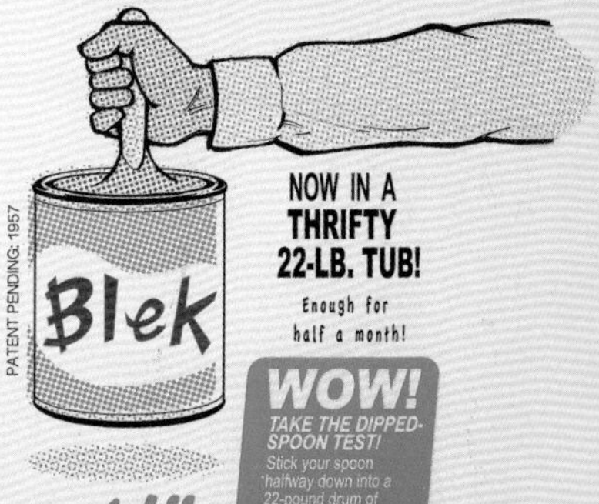
PATENT PENDING: 1957
Blek

NOW IN A THRIFTY 22-LB. TUB!

Enough for half a month!

WOW!

TAKE THE DIPPED-SPOON TEST!

Stick your spoon halfway down into a 22-pound drum of BLEK. You'll need the super strength of MERMAID-MAN to pull it back out!

"It Goes Straight Through!"

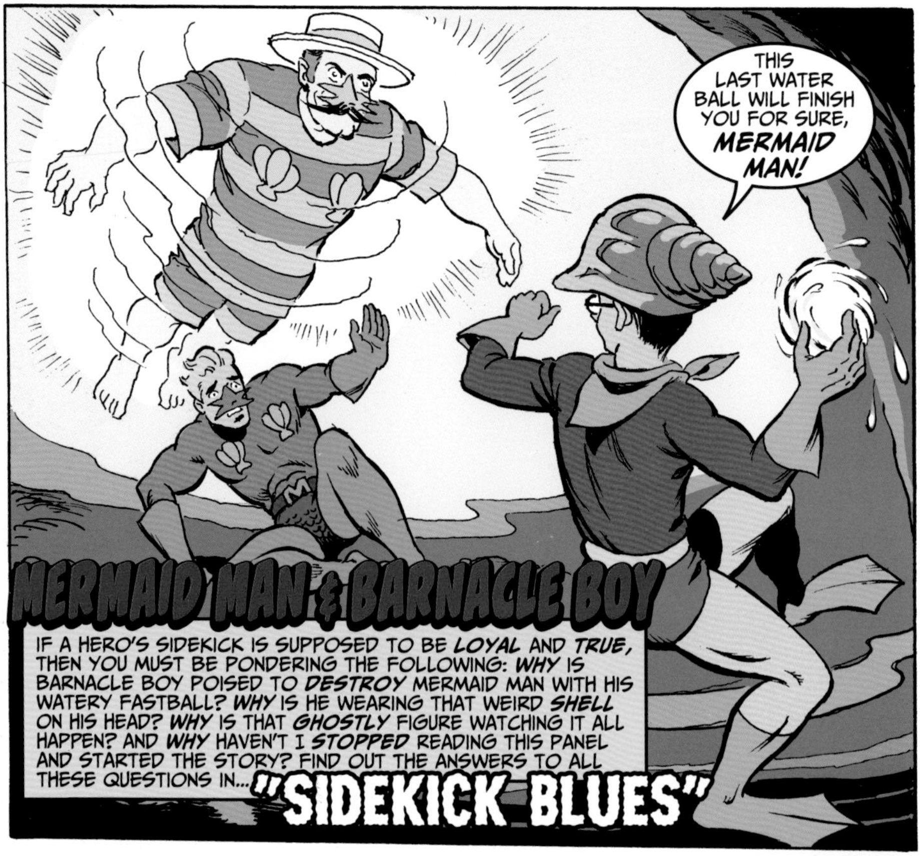
THIS LAST WATER BALL WILL FINISH YOU FOR SURE, MERMAID MAN!
MERMAID MAN & BARNACLE BOY
IF A HERO'S SIDEKICK IS SUPPOSED TO BE LOYAL AND TRUE, THEN YOU MUST BE PONDERING THE FOLLOWING: WHY IS BARNACLE BOY POISED TO DESTROY MERMAID MAN WITH HIS WATERY FASTBALL? WHY IS HE WEARING THAT WEIRD SHELL ON HIS HEAD? WHY IS THAT GHOSTLY FIGURE WATCHING IT ALL HAPPEN? AND WHY HAVEN'T I STOPPED READING THIS PANEL AND STARTED THE STORY? FIND OUT THE ANSWERS TO ALL THESE QUESTIONS IN...
"SIDEKICK BLUES"

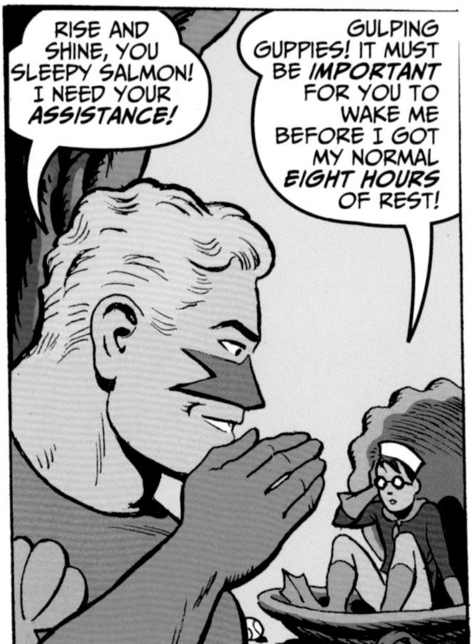
RISE AND SHINE, YOU SLEEPY SALMON! I NEED YOUR ASSISTANCE!
GULPING GUPPIES! IT MUST BE IMPORTANT FOR YOU TO WAKE ME BEFORE I GOT MY NORMAL EIGHT HOURS OF REST!

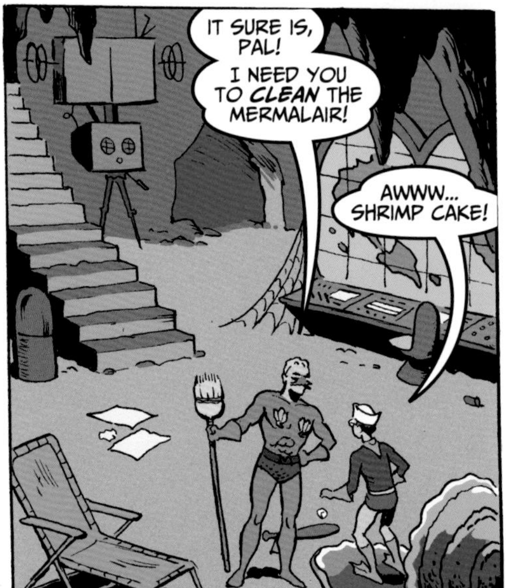
IT SURE IS, PAL!
I NEED YOU TO CLEAN THE MERMALAIR!
AWWW... SHRIMP CAKE!

STORY: DEREK DRYMON ART: RAMONA FRADON COLORING: JIM CAMPBELL LETTERING: COMICRAFT

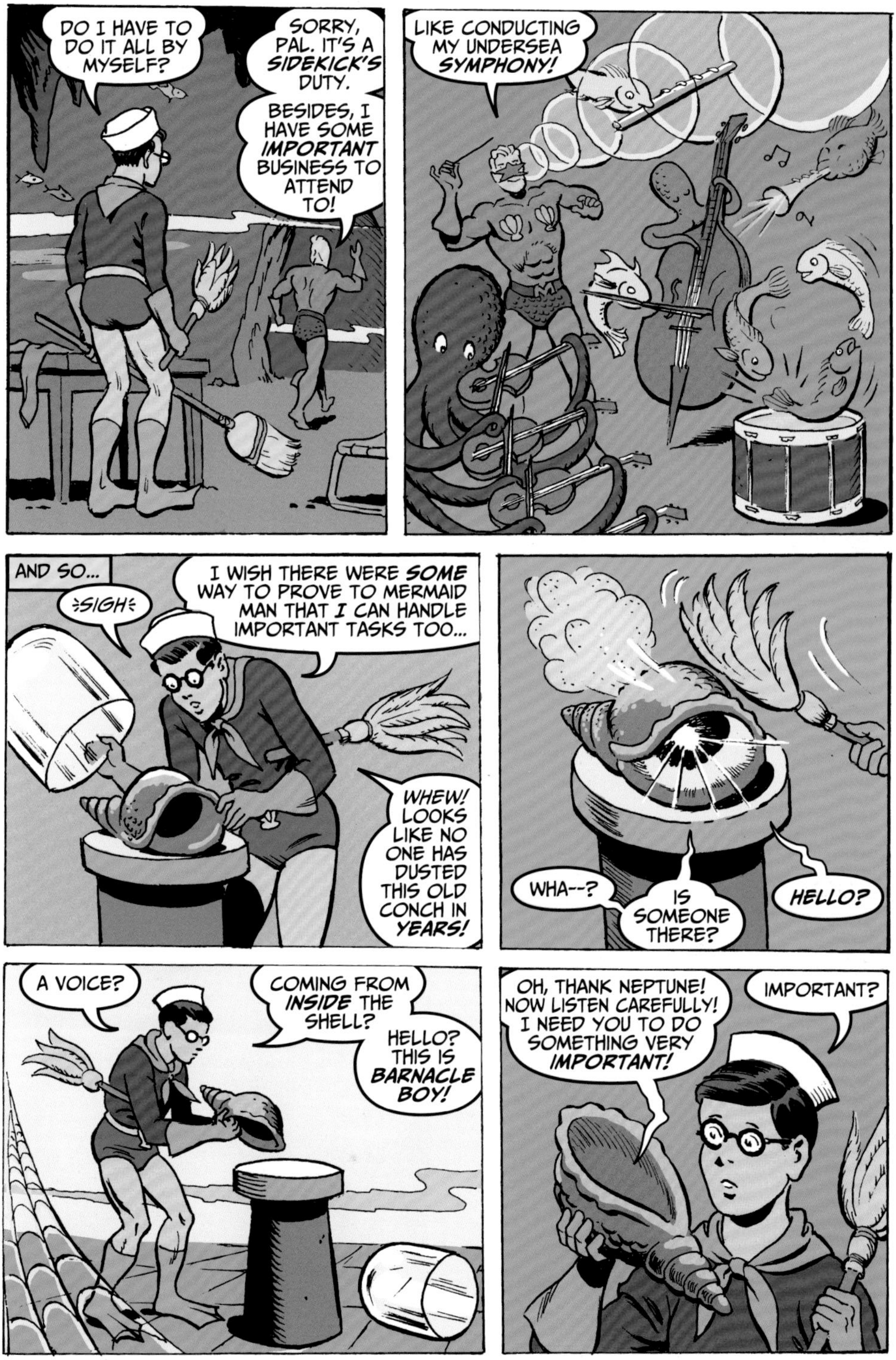
DO I HAVE TO DO IT ALL BY MYSELF?
SORRY, PAL. IT'S A SIDEKICK'S DUTY.
BESIDES, I HAVE SOME IMPORTANT BUSINESS TO ATTEND TO!
LIKE CONDUCTING MY UNDERSEA SYMPHONY!
AND SO...
SIGH
I WISH THERE WERE SOME WAY TO PROVE TO MERMAID MAN THAT I CAN HANDLE IMPORTANT TASKS TOO...
WHEW! LOOKS LIKE NO ONE HAS DUSTED THIS OLD CONCH IN YEARS!
WHA--?
IS SOMEONE THERE?
HELLO?
A VOICE?
COMING FROM INSIDE THE SHELL?
HELLO? THIS IS BARNACLE BOY!
OH, THANK NEPTUNE! NOW LISTEN CAREFULLY! I NEED YOU TO DO SOMETHING VERY IMPORTANT!
IMPORTANT?

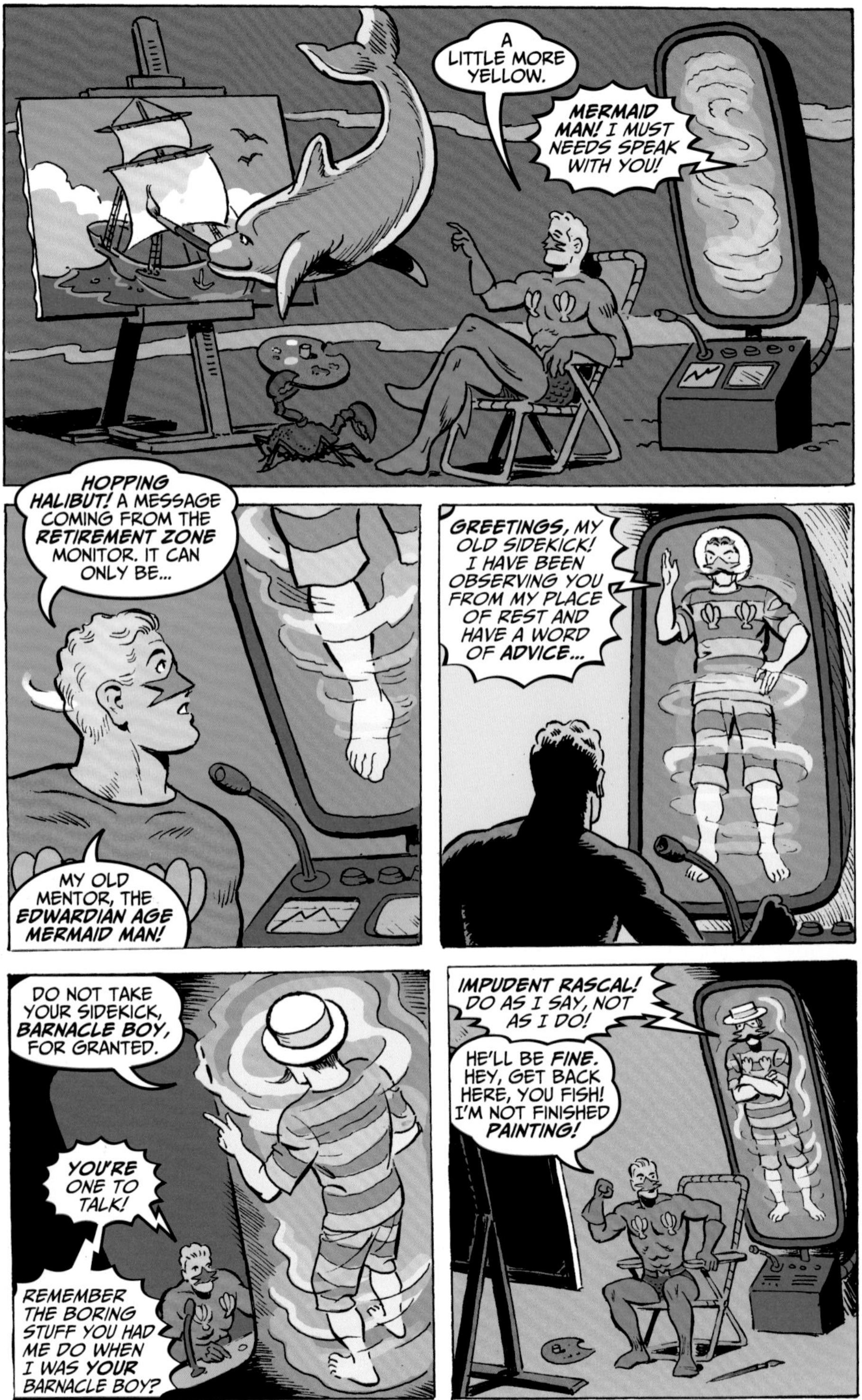
A LITTLE MORE YELLOW.
MERMAID MAN! I MUST NEEDS SPEAK WITH YOU!
HOPPING HALIBUT! A MESSAGE COMING FROM THE RETIREMENT ZONE MONITOR. IT CAN ONLY BE...
MY OLD MENTOR, THE EDWARDIAN AGE MERMAID MAN!
GREETINGS, MY OLD SIDEKICK! I HAVE BEEN OBSERVING YOU FROM MY PLACE OF REST AND HAVE A WORD OF ADVICE...
DO NOT TAKE YOUR SIDEKICK, BARNACLE BOY, FOR GRANTED.
YOU'RE ONE TO TALK!
REMEMBER THE BORING STUFF YOU HAD ME DO WHEN I WAS YOUR BARNACLE BOY?
IMPUDENT RASCAL! DO AS I SAY, NOT AS I DO!
HE'LL BE FINE. HEY, GET BACK HERE, YOU FISH! I'M NOT FINISHED PAINTING!

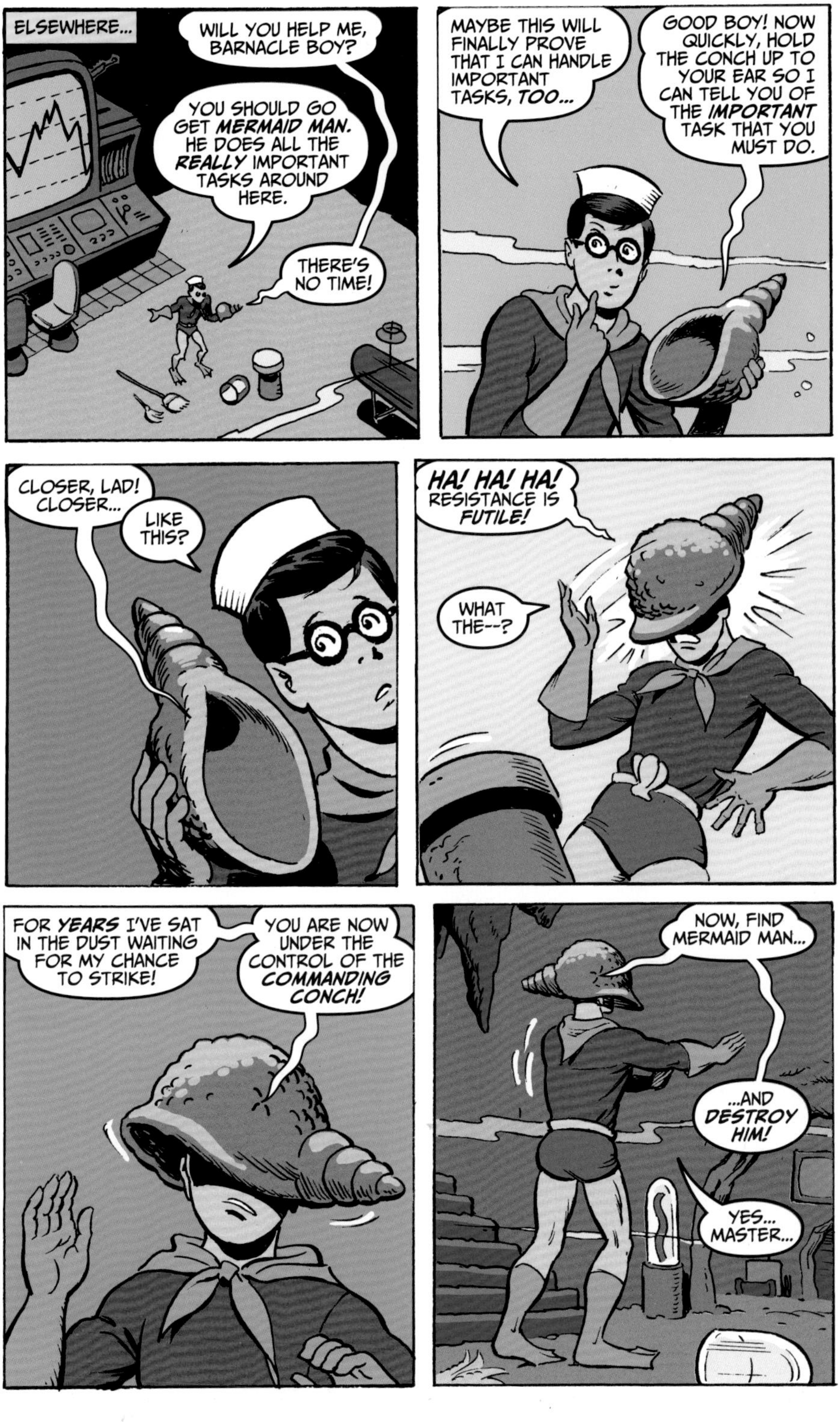
ELSEWHERE...
WILL YOU HELP ME, BARNACLE BOY?
YOU SHOULD GO GET MERMAID MAN. HE DOES ALL THE REALLY IMPORTANT TASKS AROUND HERE.
THERE'S NO TIME!
MAYBE THIS WILL FINALLY PROVE THAT I CAN HANDLE IMPORTANT TASKS, TOO...
GOOD BOY! NOW QUICKLY, HOLD THE CONCH UP TO YOUR EAR SO I CAN TELL YOU OF THE IMPORTANT TASK THAT YOU MUST DO.
CLOSER, LAD! CLOSER...
LIKE THIS?
HA! HA! HA! RESISTANCE IS FUTILE!
WHAT THE--?
FOR YEARS I'VE SAT IN THE DUST WAITING FOR MY CHANCE TO STRIKE!
YOU ARE NOW UNDER THE CONTROL OF THE COMMANDING CONCH!
NOW, FIND MERMAID MAN...
...AND DESTROY HIM!
YES... MASTER...

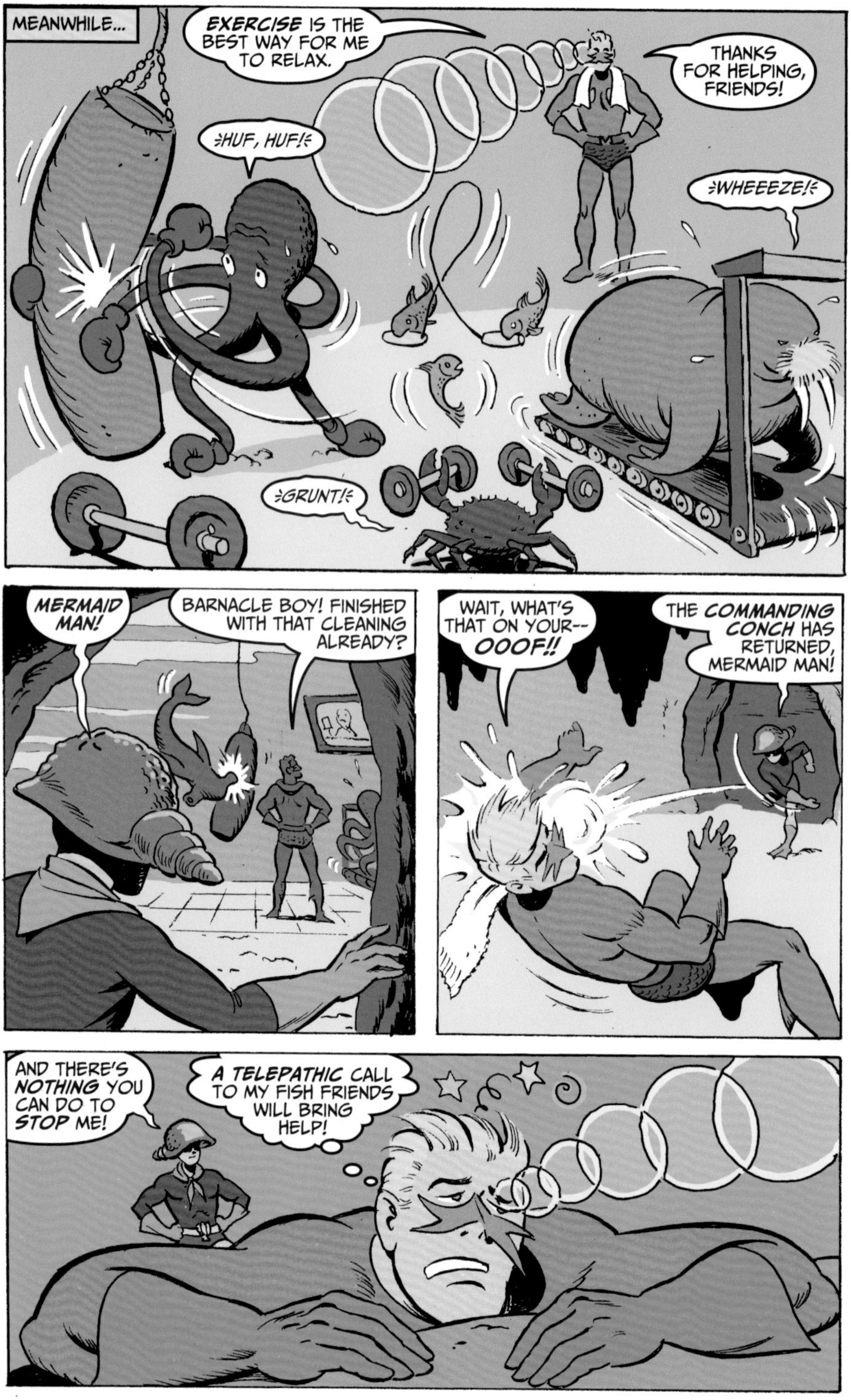
MEANWHILE...
EXERCISE IS THE BEST WAY FOR ME TO RELAX.
THANKS FOR HELPING, FRIENDS!
HUF, HUF!
WHEEEZE!
GRUNT!
MERMAID MAN!
BARNACLE BOY! FINISHED WITH THAT CLEANING ALREADY?
WAIT, WHAT'S THAT ON YOUR-- OOOF!!
THE COMMANDING CONCH HAS RETURNED, MERMAID MAN!
AND THERE'S NOTHING YOU CAN DO TO STOP ME!
A TELEPATHIC CALL TO MY FISH FRIENDS WILL BRING HELP!

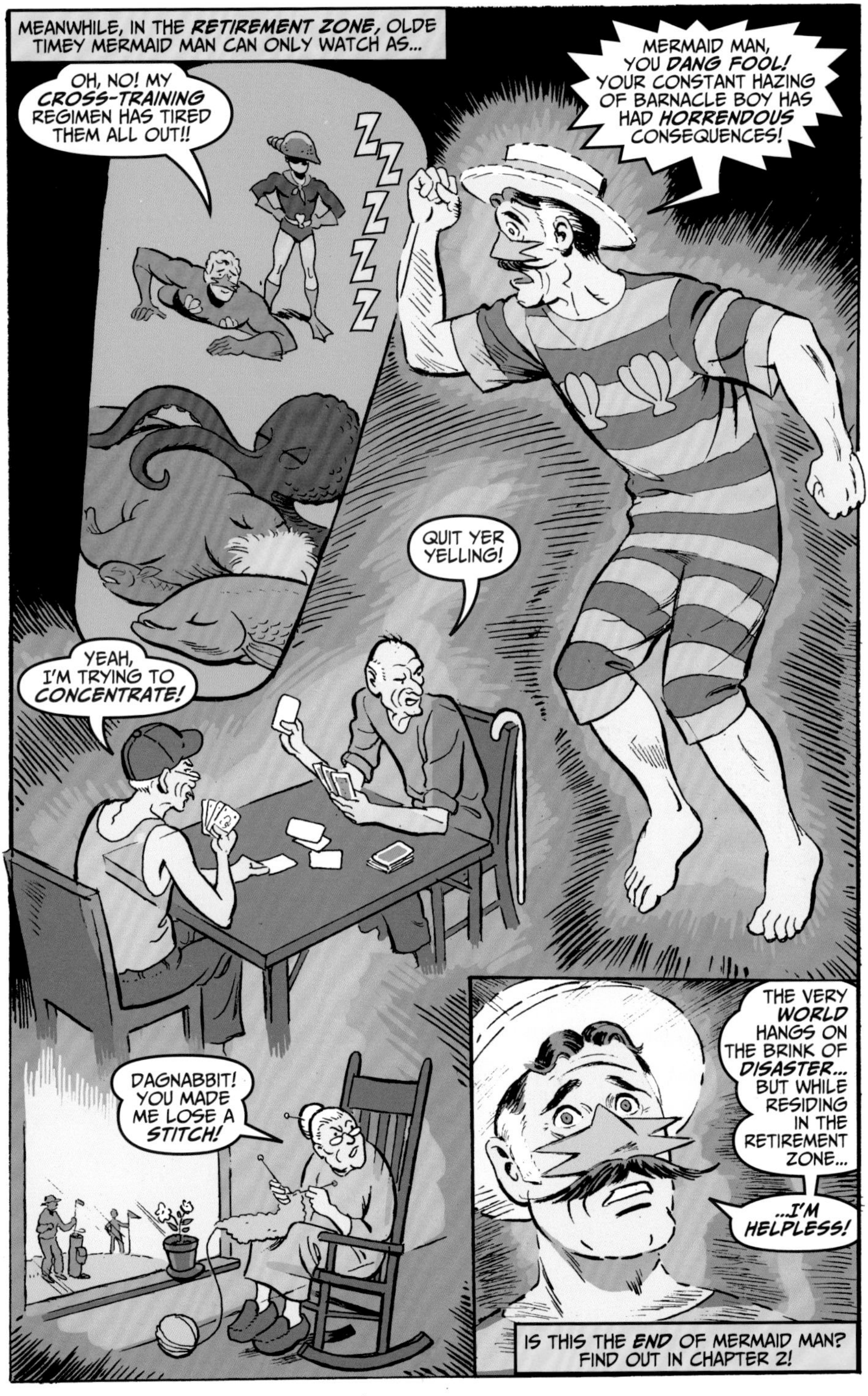
MEANWHILE, IN THE RETIREMENT ZONE, OLDE TIMEY MERMAID MAN CAN ONLY WATCH AS...
OH, NO! MY CROSS-TRAINING REGIMEN HAS TIRED THEM ALL OUT!!
ZZZZZ
MERMAID MAN, YOU DANG FOOL! YOUR CONSTANT HAZING OF BARNACLE BOY HAS HAD HORRENDOUS CONSEQUENCES!
QUIT YER YELLING!
YEAH, I'M TRYING TO CONCENTRATE!
DAGNABBIT! YOU MADE ME LOSE A STITCH!
THE VERY WORLD HANGS ON THE BRINK OF DISASTER... BUT WHILE RESIDING IN THE RETIREMENT ZONE...
...I'M HELPLESS!
IS THIS THE END OF MERMAID MAN? FIND OUT IN CHAPTER 2!

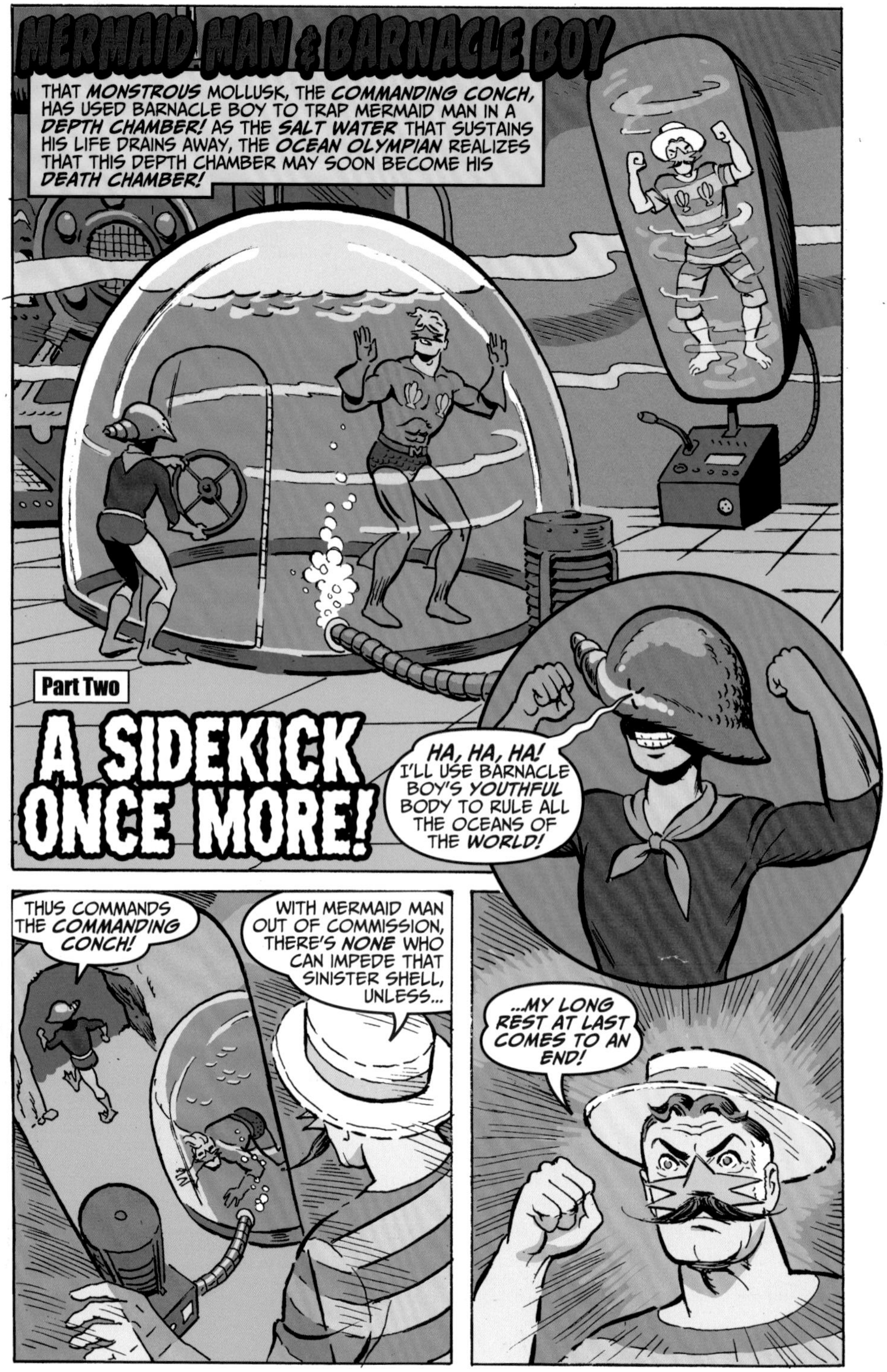
MERMAID MAN & BARNACLE BOY
THAT MONSTROUS MOLLUSK, THE COMMANDING CONCH, HAS USED BARNACLE BOY TO TRAP MERMAID MAN IN A DEPTH CHAMBER! AS THE SALT WATER THAT SUSTAINS HIS LIFE DRAINS AWAY, THE OCEAN OLYMPIAN REALIZES THAT THIS DEPTH CHAMBER MAY SOON BECOME HIS DEATH CHAMBER!
Part Two
A SIDEKICK ONCE MORE!
HA, HA, HA! I'LL USE BARNACLE BOY'S YOUTHFUL BODY TO RULE ALL THE OCEANS OF THE WORLD!
THUS COMMANDS THE COMMANDING CONCH!
WITH MERMAID MAN OUT OF COMMISSION, THERE'S NONE WHO CAN IMPEDE THAT SINISTER SHELL, UNLESS...
...MY LONG REST AT LAST COMES TO AN END!

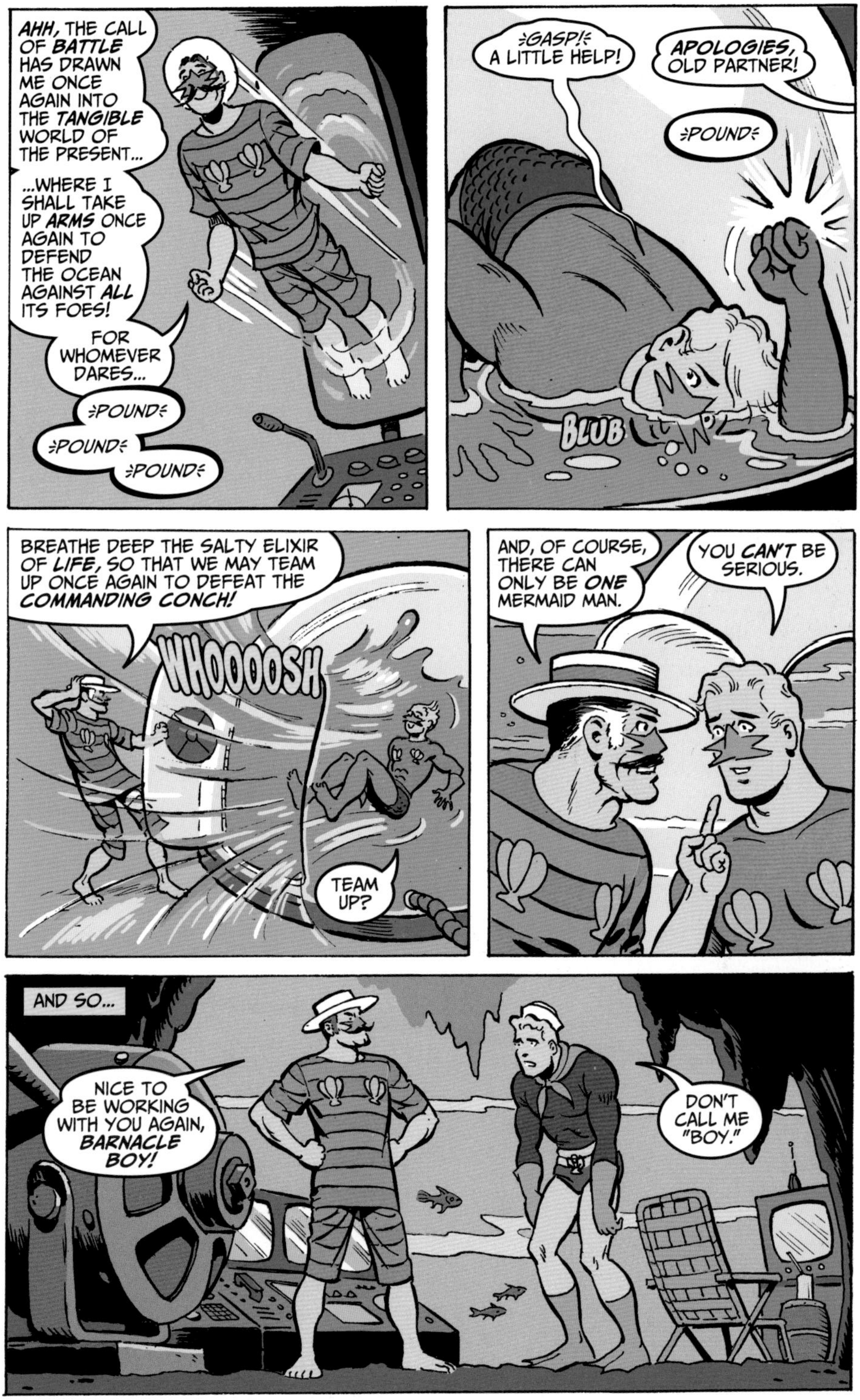
AHH, THE CALL OF BATTLE HAS DRAWN ME ONCE AGAIN INTO THE TANGIBLE WORLD OF THE PRESENT...
...WHERE I SHALL TAKE UP ARMS ONCE AGAIN TO DEFEND THE OCEAN AGAINST ALL ITS FOES!
FOR WHOMEVER DARES...
POUND
POUND
POUND
GASP! A LITTLE HELP!
APOLOGIES, OLD PARTNER!
POUND
BLUB
BREATHE DEEP THE SALTY ELIXIR OF LIFE, SO THAT WE MAY TEAM UP ONCE AGAIN TO DEFEAT THE COMMANDING CONCH!
WHOOOOSH
TEAM UP?
AND, OF COURSE, THERE CAN ONLY BE ONE MERMAID MAN.
YOU CAN'T BE SERIOUS.
AND SO...
NICE TO BE WORKING WITH YOU AGAIN, BARNACLE BOY!
DON'T CALL ME "BOY."

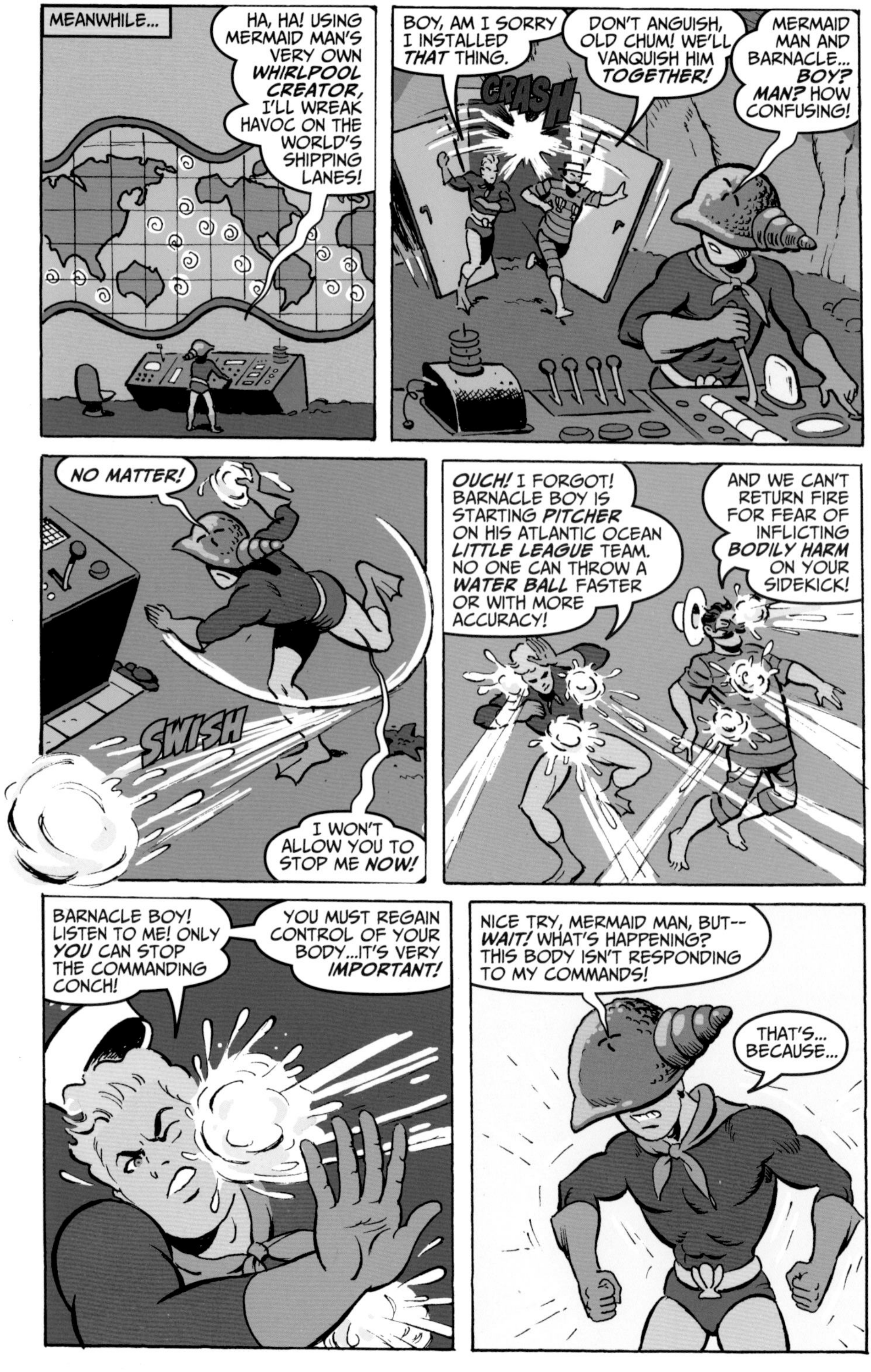
MEANWHILE...
HA, HA! USING MERMAID MAN'S VERY OWN WHIRLPOOL CREATOR, I'LL WREAK HAVOC ON THE WORLD'S SHIPPING LANES!
BOY, AM I SORRY I INSTALLED THAT THING.
CRASH
DON'T ANGUISH, OLD CHUM! WE'LL VANQUISH HIM TOGETHER!
MERMAID MAN AND BARNACLE... BOY? MAN? HOW CONFUSING!
NO MATTER!
SWISH
I WON'T ALLOW YOU TO STOP ME NOW!
OUCH! I FORGOT! BARNACLE BOY IS STARTING PITCHER ON HIS ATLANTIC OCEAN LITTLE LEAGUE TEAM. NO ONE CAN THROW A WATER BALL FASTER OR WITH MORE ACCURACY!
AND WE CAN'T RETURN FIRE FOR FEAR OF INFLICTING BODILY HARM ON YOUR SIDEKICK!
BARNACLE BOY! LISTEN TO ME! ONLY YOU CAN STOP THE COMMANDING CONCH!
YOU MUST REGAIN CONTROL OF YOUR BODY...IT'S VERY IMPORTANT!
NICE TRY, MERMAID MAN, BUT-- WAIT! WHAT'S HAPPENING? THIS BODY ISN'T RESPONDING TO MY COMMANDS!
THAT'S... BECAUSE...

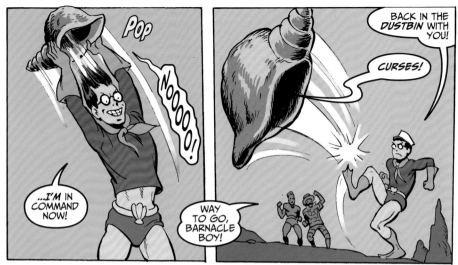

POP

NOOOOO!

...I'M IN COMMAND NOW!

BACK IN THE *DUSTBIN* WITH YOU!

CURSES!

WAY TO GO, BARNACLE BOY!

I'M JUST GLAD I COULD *FINALLY* PULL MY WEIGHT AROUND HERE AND DO SOMETHING IMPORTANT.

UM...

BARNACLE BOY, THE TRUTH IS, BEING A SIDEKICK IS THE *MOST* IMPORTANT JOB OF ALL. AND I'M *SORRY* I FORGOT THAT.

WOW, I'M NOT SURE THAT MAKES SENSE, BUT...THANKS.

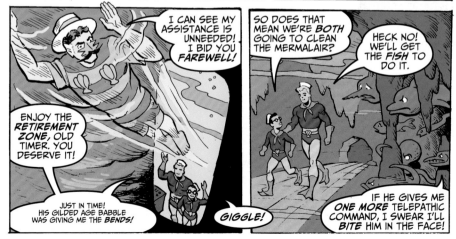

I CAN SEE MY ASSISTANCE IS UNNEEDED! I BID YOU *FAREWELL!*

ENJOY THE *RETIREMENT ZONE*, OLD TIMER. YOU DESERVE IT!

JUST IN TIME! HIS GILDED AGE BABBLE WAS GIVING ME THE *BENDS!*

GIGGLE!

SO DOES THAT MEAN WE'RE *BOTH* GOING TO CLEAN THE MERMALAIR?

HECK NO! WE'LL GET THE *FISH* TO DO IT.

IF HE GIVES ME *ONE MORE* TELEPATHIC COMMAND, I SWEAR I'LL *BITE* HIM IN THE FACE!

END

23

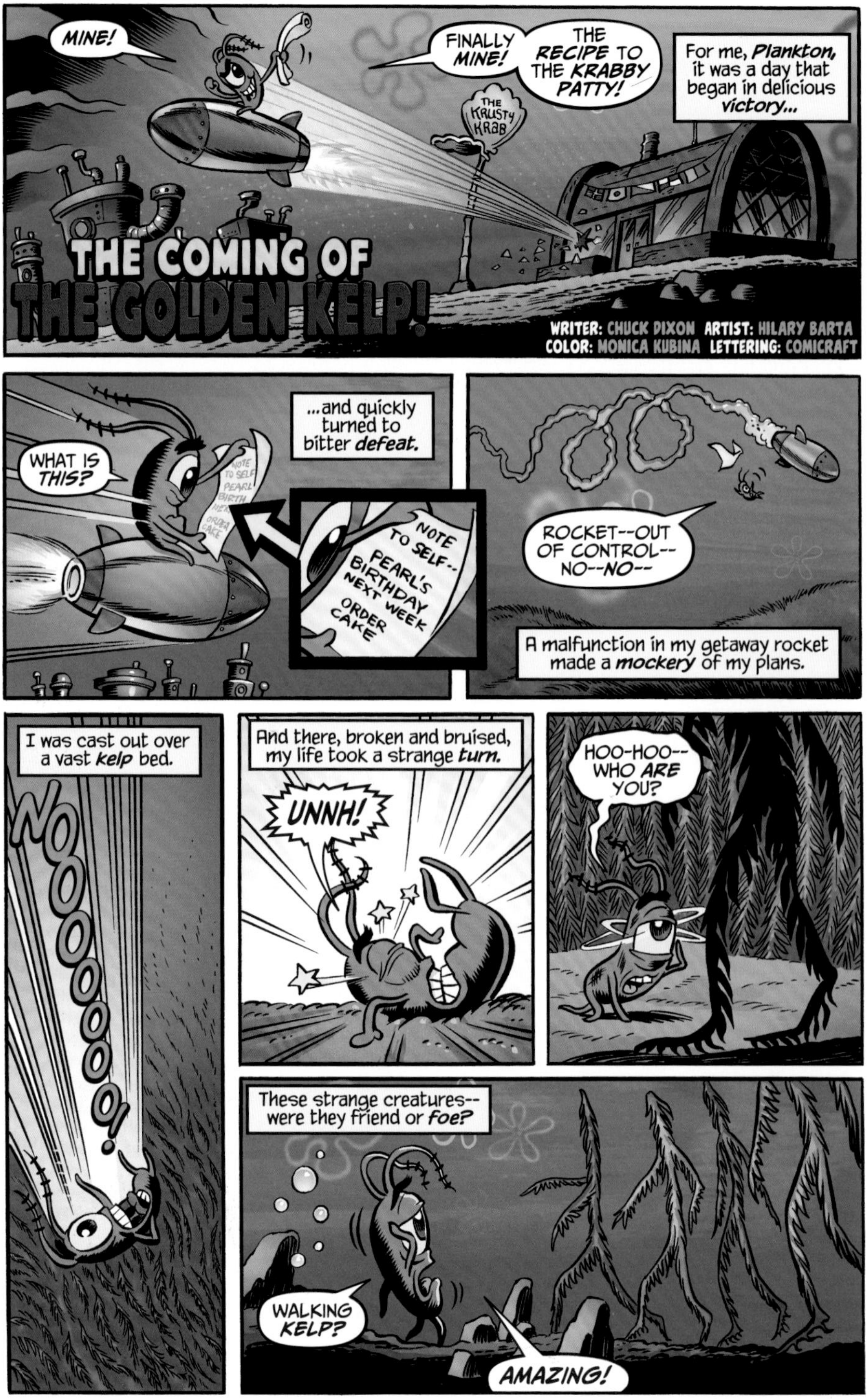
MINE!
FINALLY MINE!
THE RECIPE TO THE KRABBY PATTY!
For me, Plankton, it was a day that began in delicious victory...
THE KRUSTY KRAB
THE COMING OF THE GOLDEN KELP!
WRITER: CHUCK DIXON ARTIST: HILARY BARTA
COLOR: MONICA KUBINA LETTERING: COMICRAFT
...and quickly turned to bitter defeat.
WHAT IS THIS?
NOTE TO SELF-- PEARL'S BIRTHDAY NEXT WEEK ORDER CAKE
ROCKET--OUT OF CONTROL-- NO--NO--
A malfunction in my getaway rocket made a mockery of my plans.
I was cast out over a vast kelp bed.
NOOOOOOOOO!
And there, broken and bruised, my life took a strange turn.
UNNH!
HOO-HOO-- WHO ARE YOU?
These strange creatures-- were they friend or foe?
WALKING KELP?
AMAZING!

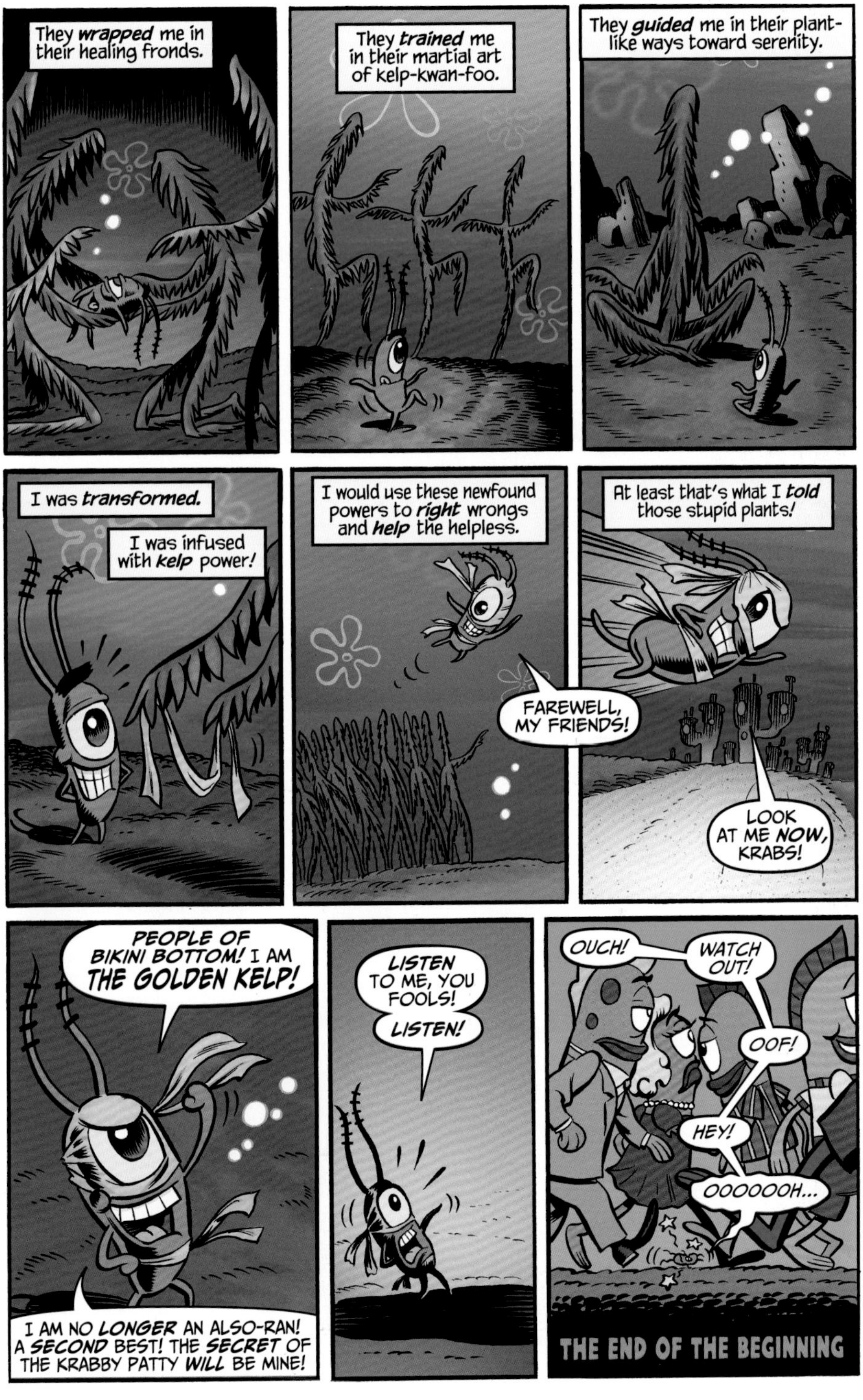
They wrapped me in their healing fronds.
They trained me in their martial art of kelp-kwan-foo.
They guided me in their plant-like ways toward serenity.
I was transformed.
I was infused with kelp power!
I would use these newfound powers to right wrongs and help the helpless.
FAREWELL, MY FRIENDS!
At least that's what I told those stupid plants!
LOOK AT ME NOW, KRABS!
PEOPLE OF BIKINI BOTTOM! I AM THE GOLDEN KELP!
I AM NO LONGER AN ALSO-RAN! A SECOND BEST! THE SECRET OF THE KRABBY PATTY WILL BE MINE!
LISTEN TO ME, YOU FOOLS!
LISTEN!
OUCH!
WATCH OUT!
OOF!
HEY!
OOOOOOH...
THE END OF THE BEGINNING

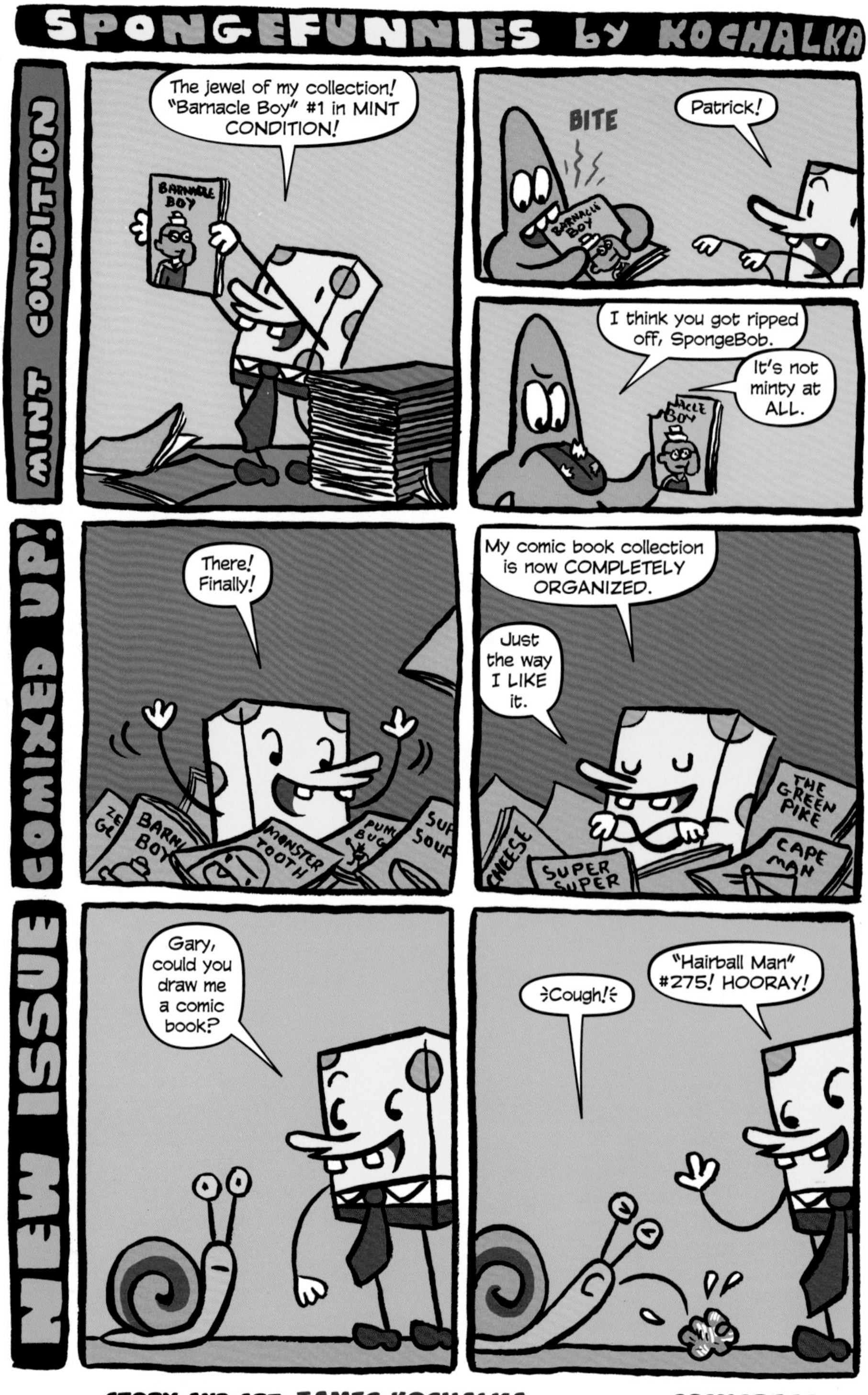

STORY AND ART: JAMES KOCHALKA LETTERING: COMICRAFT

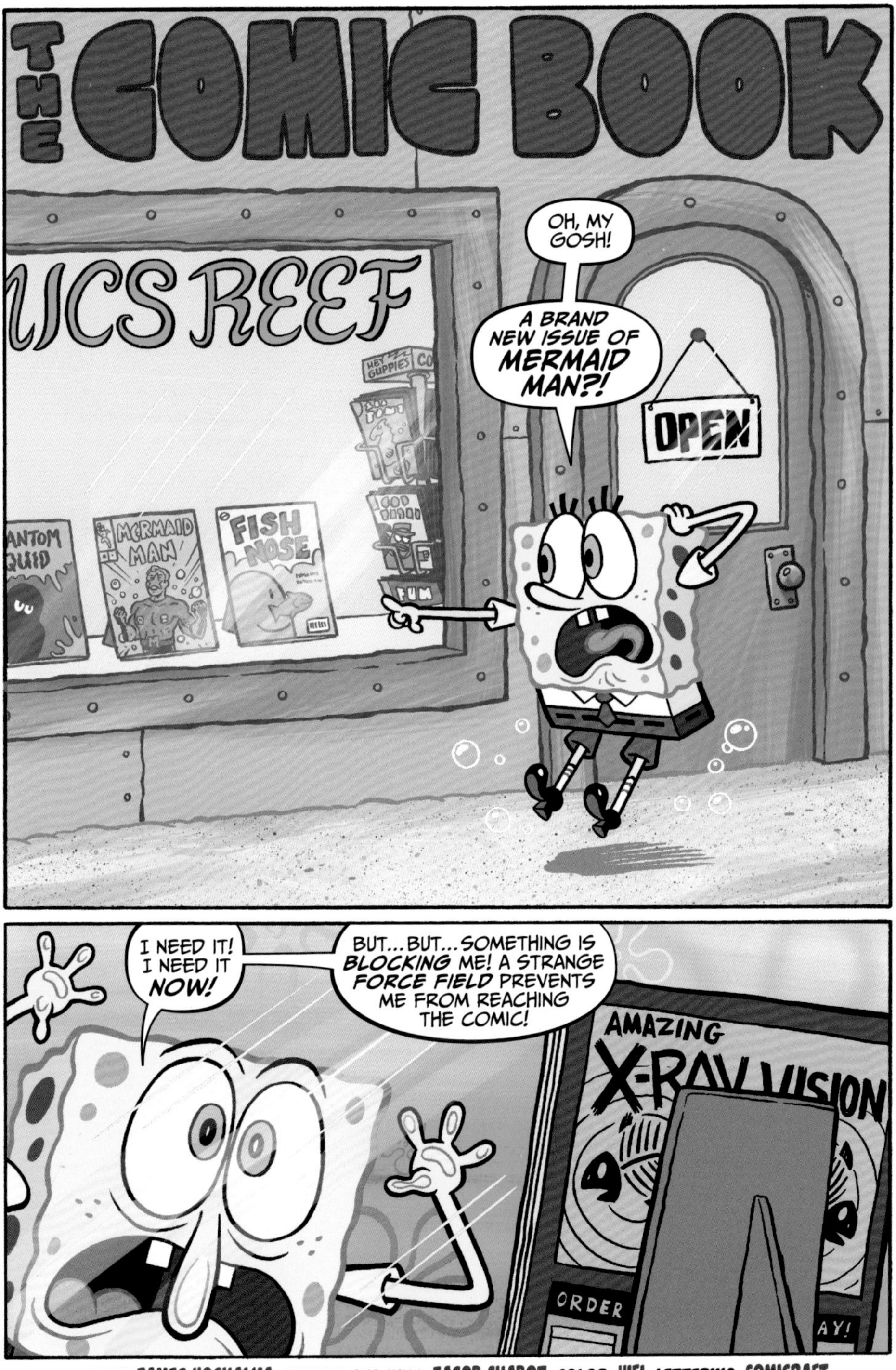
THE COMIC BOOK
UCS REEF
OH, MY GOSH!
A BRAND NEW ISSUE OF MERMAID MAN?!
OPEN
MERMAID MAN
FISH NOSE
I NEED IT! I NEED IT NOW!
BUT...BUT...SOMETHING IS BLOCKING ME! A STRANGE FORCE FIELD PREVENTS ME FROM REACHING THE COMIC!
AMAZING X-RAY VISION
ORDER
AY!

STORY: JAMES KOCHALKA PENCILS AND INKS: JACOB CHABOT COLOR: HIFI LETTERING: COMICRAFT

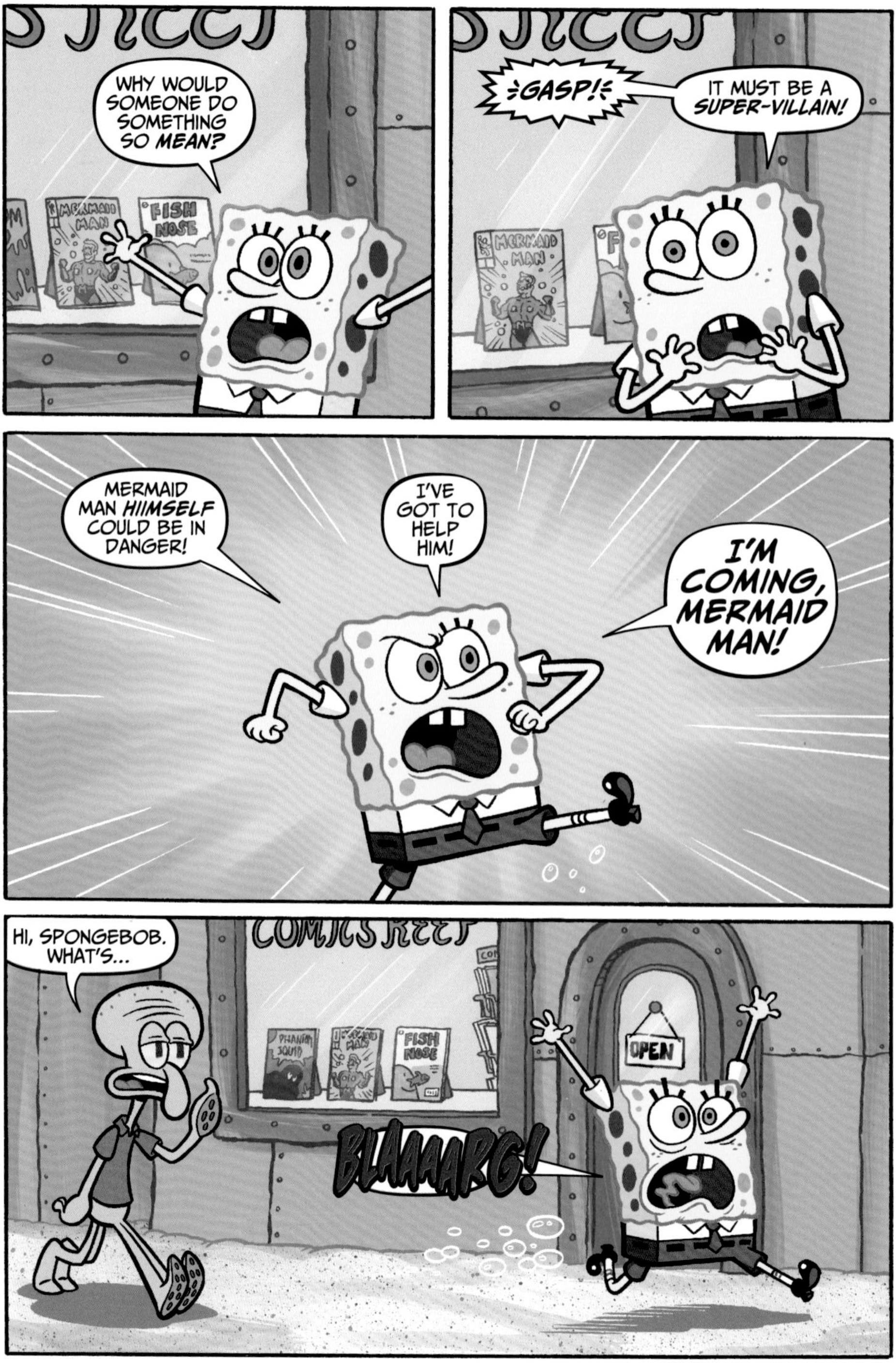
WHY WOULD SOMEONE DO SOMETHING SO *MEAN?*
FISH NOSE
GASP!
IT MUST BE A *SUPER-VILLAIN!*
MERMAID MAN
MERMAID MAN *HIIMSELF* COULD BE IN DANGER!
I'VE GOT TO HELP HIM!
I'M COMING, MERMAID MAN!
HI, SPONGEBOB. WHAT'S...
OPEN
BLAAAARG!

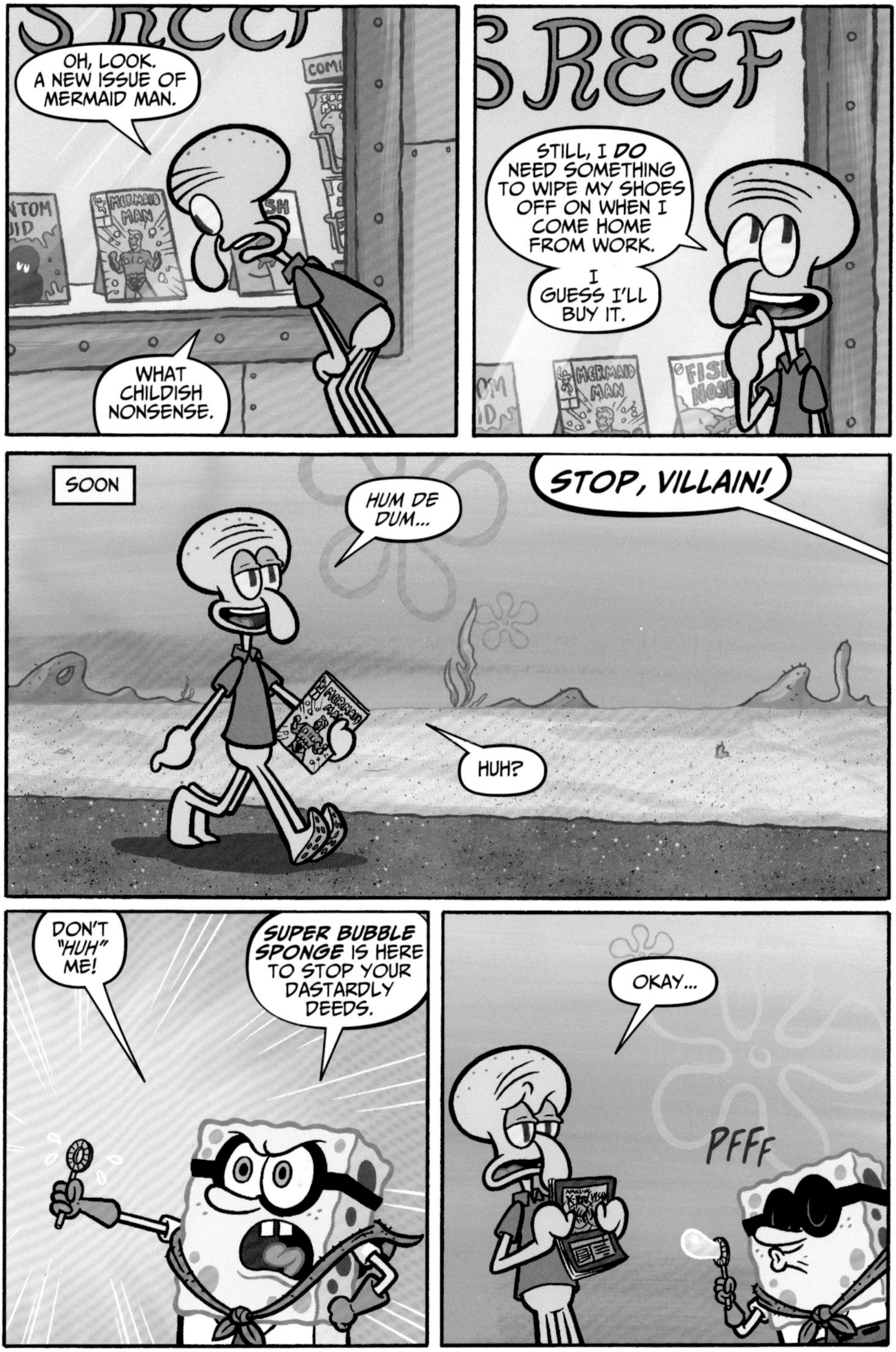
OH, LOOK. A NEW ISSUE OF MERMAID MAN.
WHAT CHILDISH NONSENSE.
STILL, I *DO* NEED SOMETHING TO WIPE MY SHOES OFF ON WHEN I COME HOME FROM WORK.
I GUESS I'LL BUY IT.
SOON
HUM DE DUM...
STOP, VILLAIN!
HUH?
DON'T *"HUH"* ME!
SUPER BUBBLE SPONGE IS HERE TO STOP YOUR DASTARDLY DEEDS.
OKAY...
PFFF

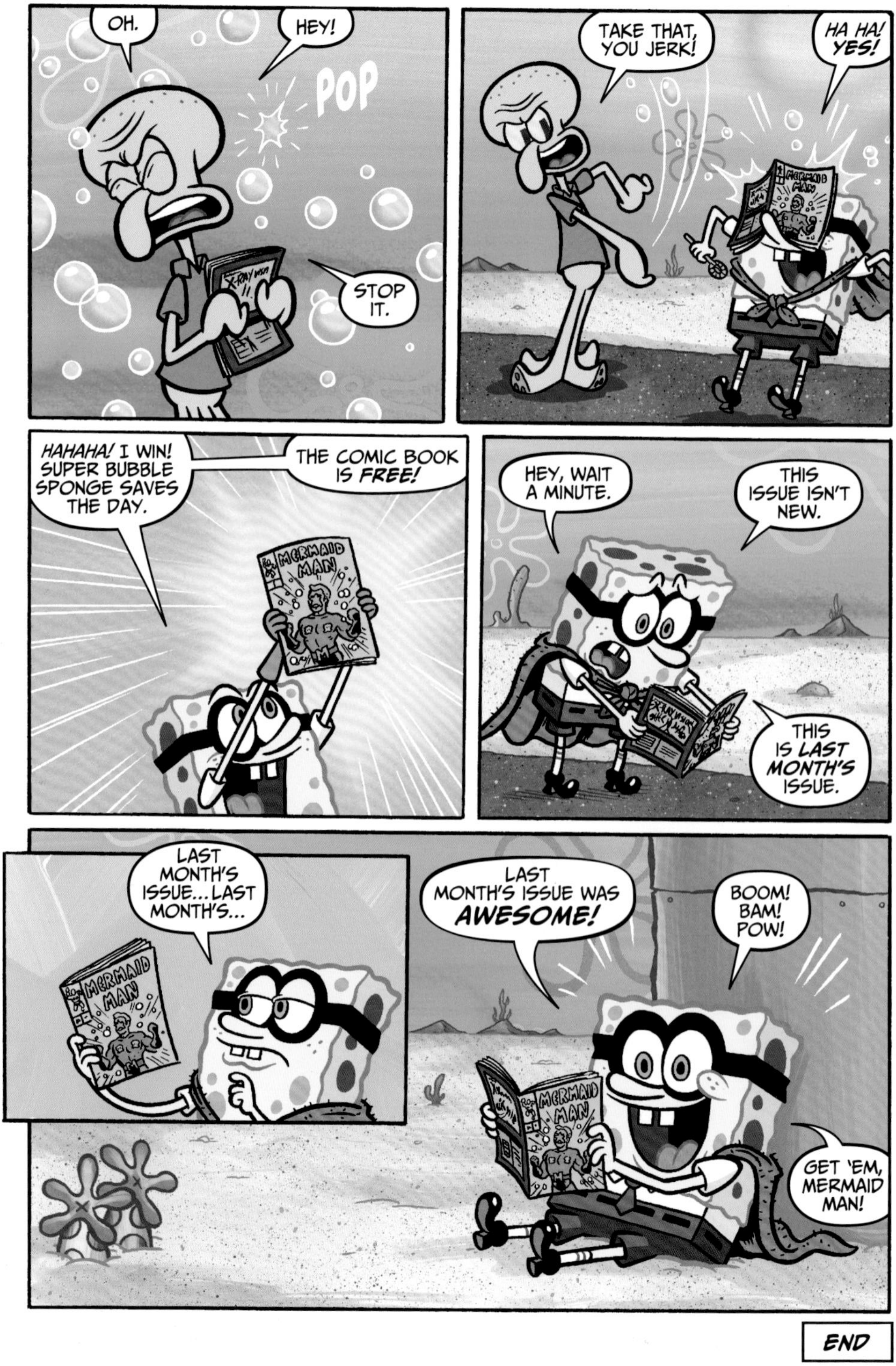
OH.
HEY!
POP
STOP IT.
TAKE THAT, YOU JERK!
HA HA! YES!
HAHAHA! I WIN! SUPER BUBBLE SPONGE SAVES THE DAY.
THE COMIC BOOK IS FREE!
HEY, WAIT A MINUTE.
THIS ISSUE ISN'T NEW.
THIS IS LAST MONTH'S ISSUE.
LAST MONTH'S ISSUE... LAST MONTH'S...
LAST MONTH'S ISSUE WAS AWESOME!
BOOM! BAM! POW!
GET 'EM, MERMAID MAN!
END

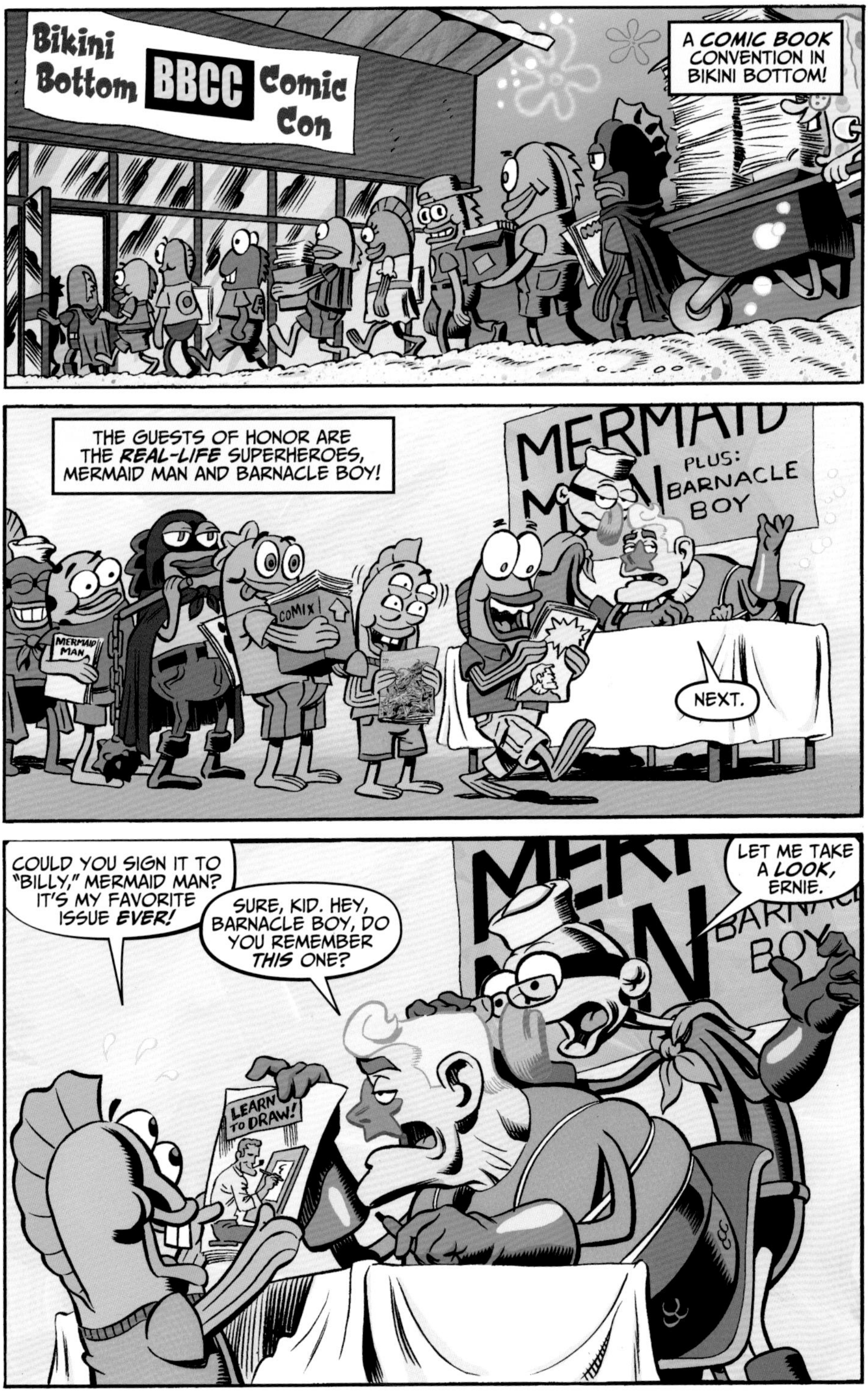
Bikini Bottom BBCC Comic Con
A COMIC BOOK CONVENTION IN BIKINI BOTTOM!
THE GUESTS OF HONOR ARE THE REAL-LIFE SUPERHEROES, MERMAID MAN AND BARNACLE BOY!
MERMAID MAN PLUS: BARNACLE BOY
COMIX
MERMAID MAN
NEXT.
COULD YOU SIGN IT TO "BILLY," MERMAID MAN? IT'S MY FAVORITE ISSUE EVER!
SURE, KID. HEY, BARNACLE BOY, DO YOU REMEMBER THIS ONE?
LET ME TAKE A LOOK, ERNIE.
LEARN TO DRAW!

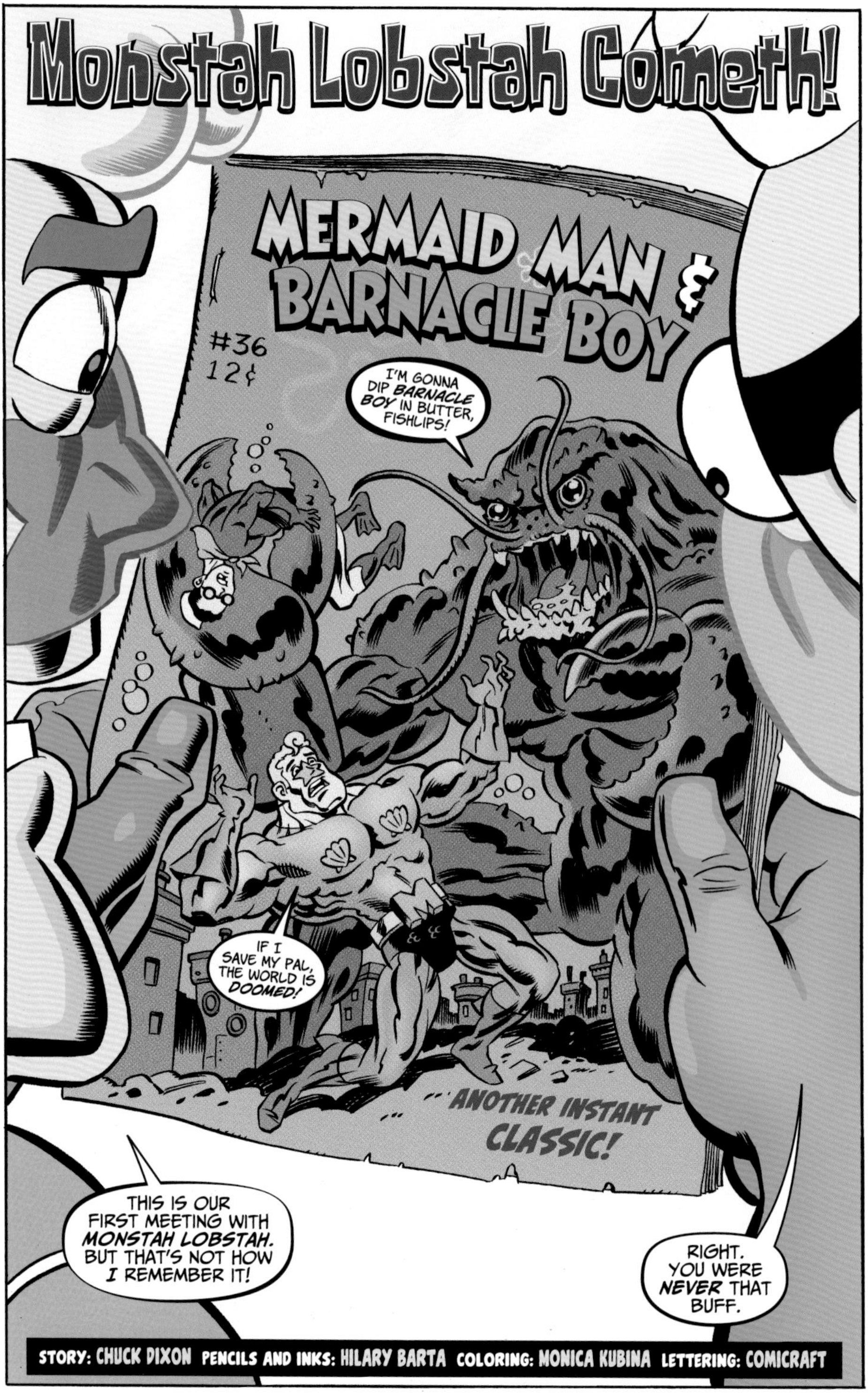

Monstah Lobstah Cometh!
MERMAID MAN & BARNACLE BOY
#36
12¢
I'M GONNA DIP BARNACLE BOY IN BUTTER, FISHLIPS!
IF I SAVE MY PAL, THE WORLD IS DOOMED!
ANOTHER INSTANT CLASSIC!
THIS IS OUR FIRST MEETING WITH MONSTAH LOBSTAH. BUT THAT'S NOT HOW I REMEMBER IT!
RIGHT. YOU WERE NEVER THAT BUFF.
STORY: CHUCK DIXON PENCILS AND INKS: HILARY BARTA COLORING: MONICA KUBINA LETTERING: COMICRAFT

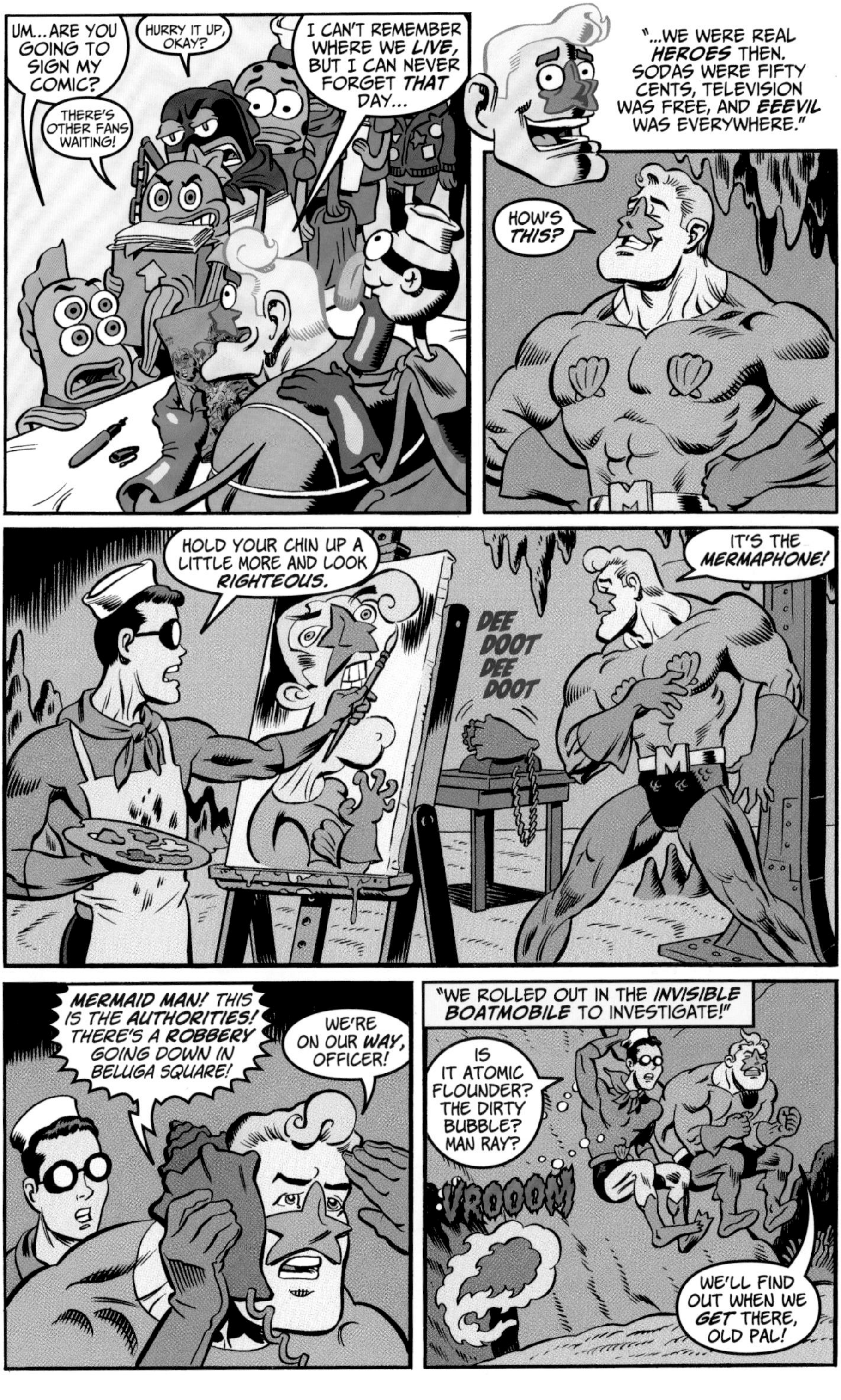
UM...ARE YOU GOING TO SIGN MY COMIC?
HURRY IT UP, OKAY?
THERE'S OTHER FANS WAITING!
I CAN'T REMEMBER WHERE WE LIVE, BUT I CAN NEVER FORGET THAT DAY...
"...WE WERE REAL HEROES THEN. SODAS WERE FIFTY CENTS, TELEVISION WAS FREE, AND EEEVIL WAS EVERYWHERE."
HOW'S THIS?
HOLD YOUR CHIN UP A LITTLE MORE AND LOOK RIGHTEOUS.
DEE DOOT DEE DOOT
IT'S THE MERMAPHONE!
MERMAID MAN! THIS IS THE AUTHORITIES! THERE'S A ROBBERY GOING DOWN IN BELUGA SQUARE!
WE'RE ON OUR WAY, OFFICER!
"WE ROLLED OUT IN THE INVISIBLE BOATMOBILE TO INVESTIGATE!"
IS IT ATOMIC FLOUNDER? THE DIRTY BUBBLE? MAN RAY?
VROOOM
WE'LL FIND OUT WHEN WE GET THERE, OLD PAL!

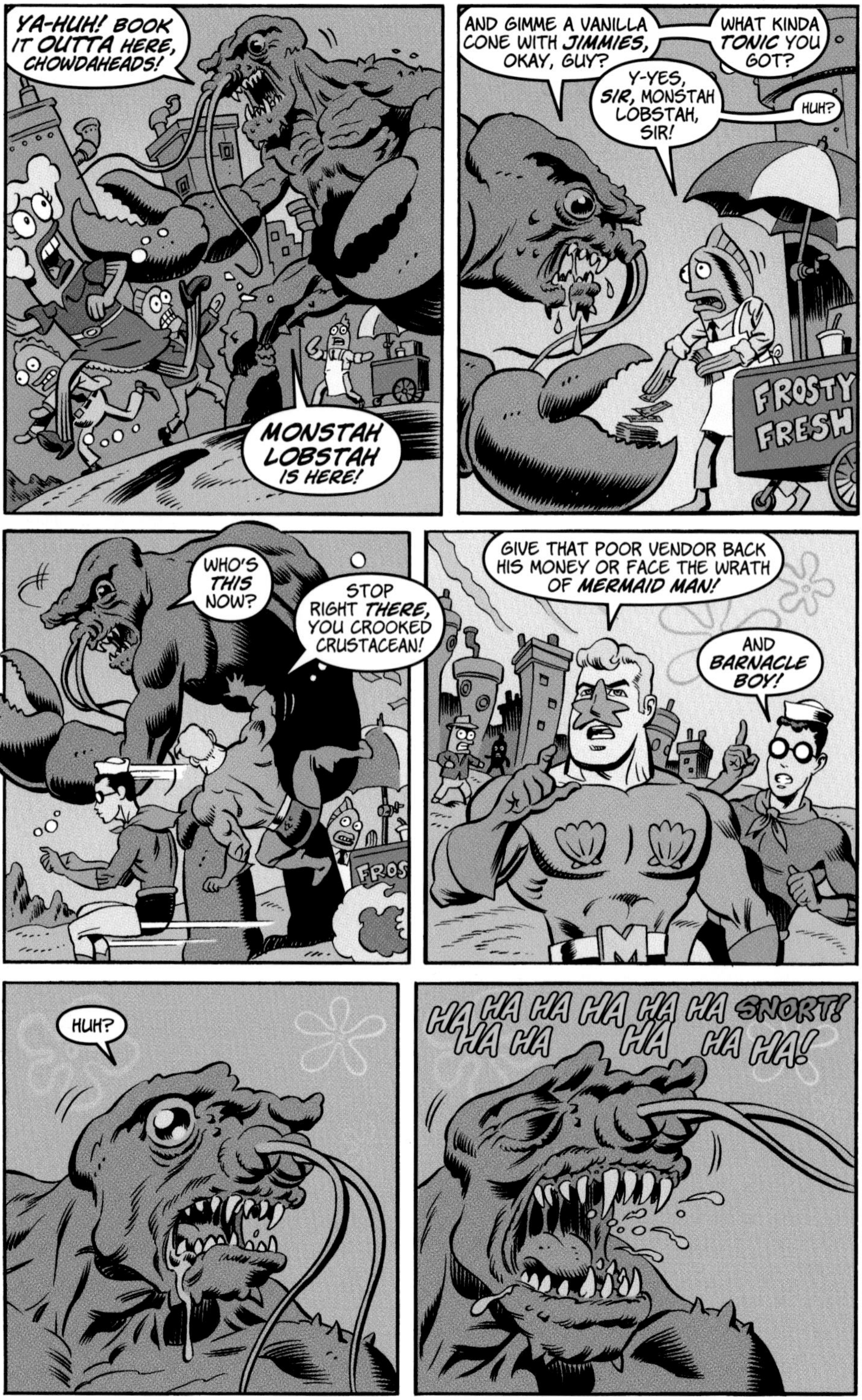
YA-HUH! BOOK IT OUTTA HERE, CHOWDAHEADS!
MONSTAH LOBSTAH IS HERE!
AND GIMME A VANILLA CONE WITH JIMMIES, OKAY, GUY?
WHAT KINDA TONIC YOU GOT?
Y-YES, SIR, MONSTAH LOBSTAH, SIR!
HUH?
FROSTY FRESH
WHO'S THIS NOW?
STOP RIGHT THERE, YOU CROOKED CRUSTACEAN!
FROS
GIVE THAT POOR VENDOR BACK HIS MONEY OR FACE THE WRATH OF MERMAID MAN!
AND BARNACLE BOY!
M
HUH?
HA HA HA HA HA HA HA SNORT! HA HA HA HA HA!

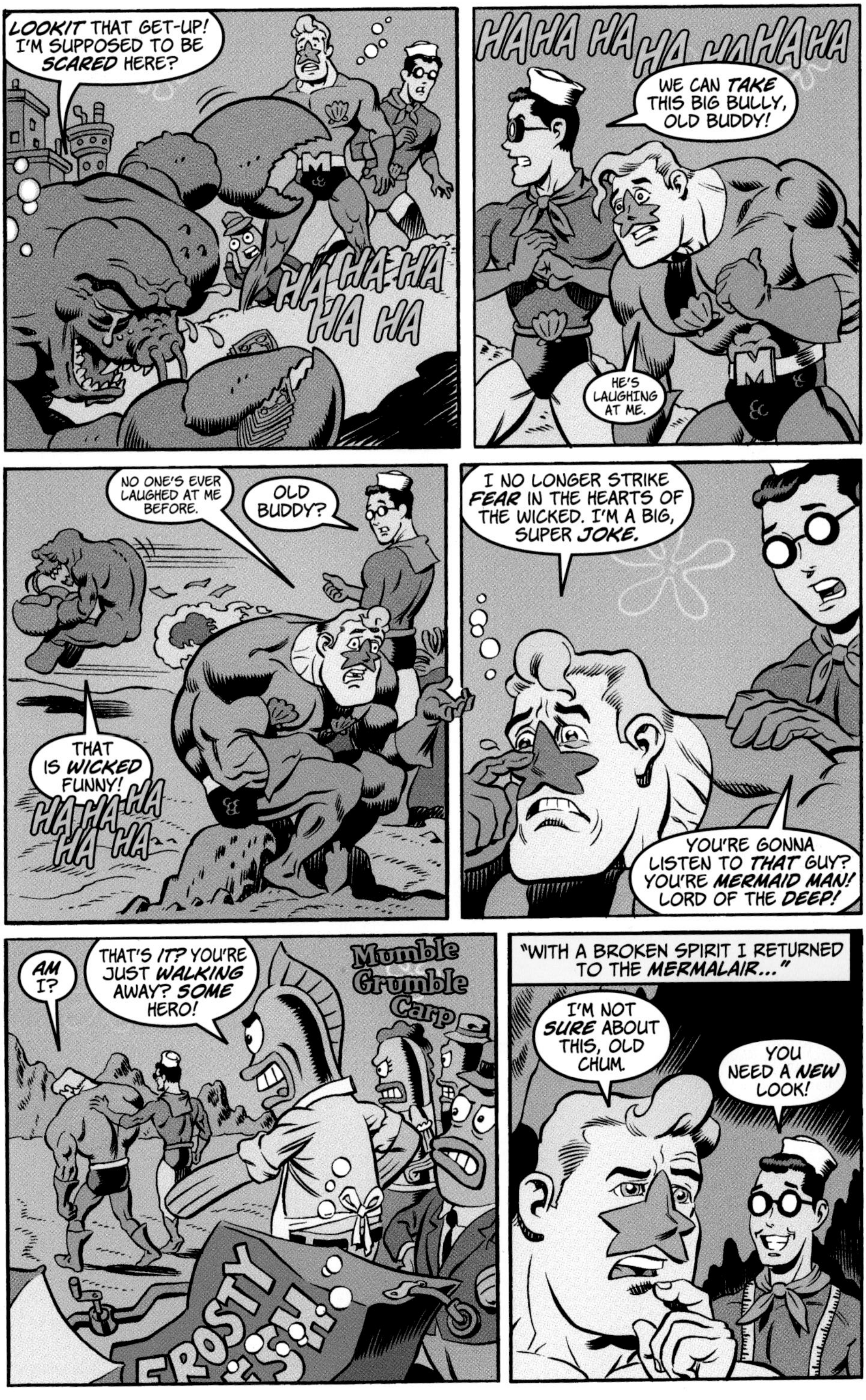
LOOKIT THAT GET-UP! I'M SUPPOSED TO BE SCARED HERE?
HA HA HA HA HA HA
HAHA HA HA HA HA HAHA HA
WE CAN TAKE THIS BIG BULLY, OLD BUDDY!
HE'S LAUGHING AT ME.
NO ONE'S EVER LAUGHED AT ME BEFORE.
OLD BUDDY?
THAT IS WICKED FUNNY!
HA HA HA HA HA
I NO LONGER STRIKE FEAR IN THE HEARTS OF THE WICKED. I'M A BIG, SUPER JOKE.
YOU'RE GONNA LISTEN TO THAT GUY? YOU'RE MERMAID MAN! LORD OF THE DEEP!
AM I?
THAT'S IT? YOU'RE JUST WALKING AWAY? SOME HERO!
Mumble Grumble Carp
FROSTY
"WITH A BROKEN SPIRIT I RETURNED TO THE MERMALAIR..."
I'M NOT SURE ABOUT THIS, OLD CHUM.
YOU NEED A NEW LOOK!

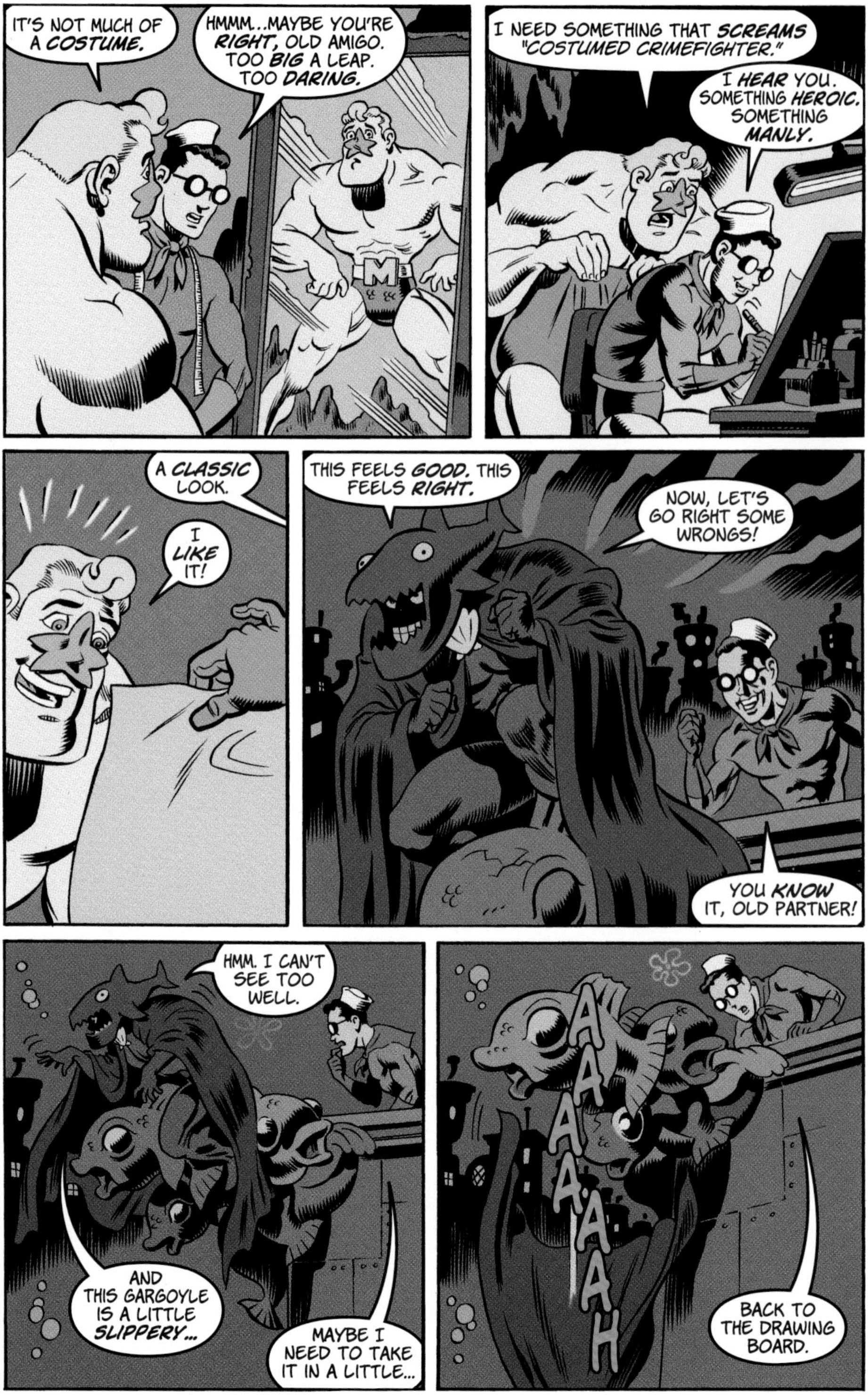
IT'S NOT MUCH OF A COSTUME.
HMMM...MAYBE YOU'RE RIGHT, OLD AMIGO. TOO BIG A LEAP. TOO DARING.
I NEED SOMETHING THAT SCREAMS "COSTUMED CRIMEFIGHTER."
I HEAR YOU. SOMETHING HEROIC. SOMETHING MANLY.
A CLASSIC LOOK.
I LIKE IT!
THIS FEELS GOOD. THIS FEELS RIGHT.
NOW, LET'S GO RIGHT SOME WRONGS!
YOU KNOW IT, OLD PARTNER!
HMM. I CAN'T SEE TOO WELL.
AND THIS GARGOYLE IS A LITTLE SLIPPERY...
MAYBE I NEED TO TAKE IT IN A LITTLE...
AAAAAAH
BACK TO THE DRAWING BOARD.

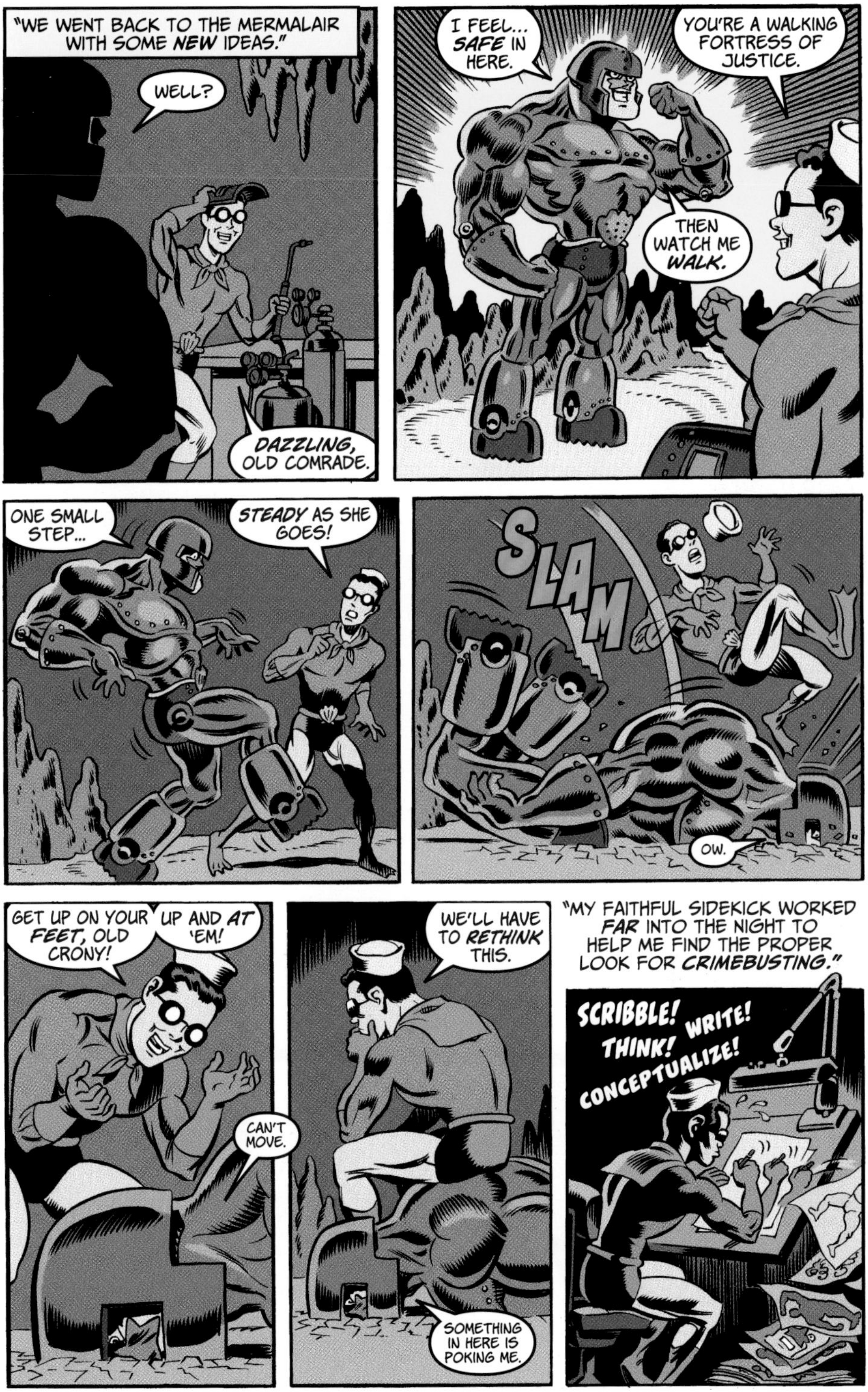
"WE WENT BACK TO THE MERMALAIR WITH SOME NEW IDEAS."
WELL?
DAZZLING, OLD COMRADE.
I FEEL... SAFE IN HERE.
YOU'RE A WALKING FORTRESS OF JUSTICE.
THEN WATCH ME WALK.
ONE SMALL STEP...
STEADY AS SHE GOES!
SLAM
OW.
GET UP ON YOUR FEET, OLD CRONY!
UP AND AT 'EM!
CAN'T MOVE.
WE'LL HAVE TO RETHINK THIS.
SOMETHING IN HERE IS POKING ME.
"MY FAITHFUL SIDEKICK WORKED FAR INTO THE NIGHT TO HELP ME FIND THE PROPER LOOK FOR CRIMEBUSTING."
SCRIBBLE! THINK! WRITE! CONCEPTUALIZE!

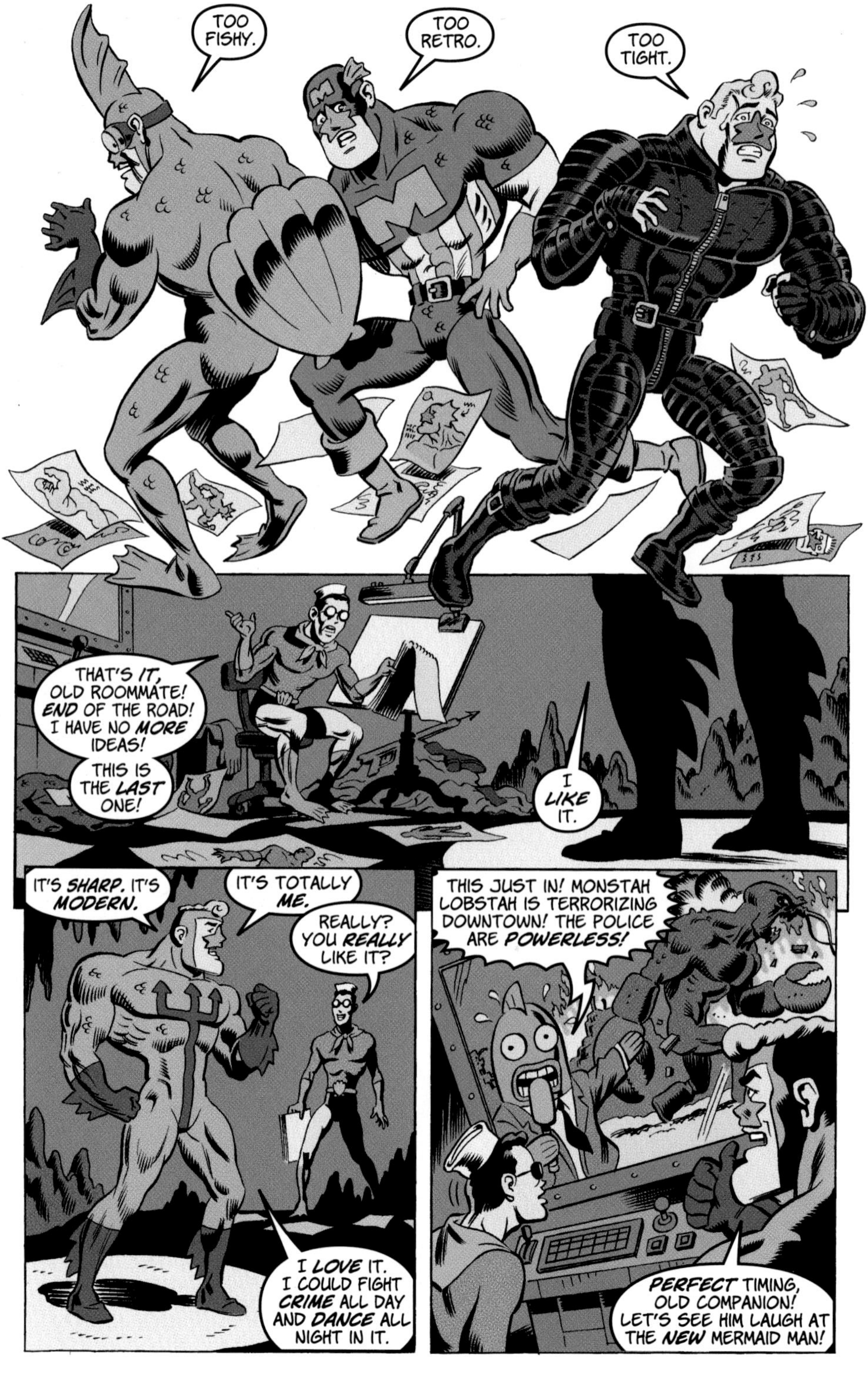
TOO FISHY.
TOO RETRO.
TOO TIGHT.
THAT'S IT, OLD ROOMMATE! END OF THE ROAD! I HAVE NO MORE IDEAS!
THIS IS THE LAST ONE!
I LIKE IT.
IT'S SHARP. IT'S MODERN.
IT'S TOTALLY ME.
REALLY? YOU REALLY LIKE IT?
I LOVE IT. I COULD FIGHT CRIME ALL DAY AND DANCE ALL NIGHT IN IT.
THIS JUST IN! MONSTAH LOBSTAH IS TERRORIZING DOWNTOWN! THE POLICE ARE POWERLESS!
PERFECT TIMING, OLD COMPANION! LET'S SEE HIM LAUGH AT THE NEW MERMAID MAN!

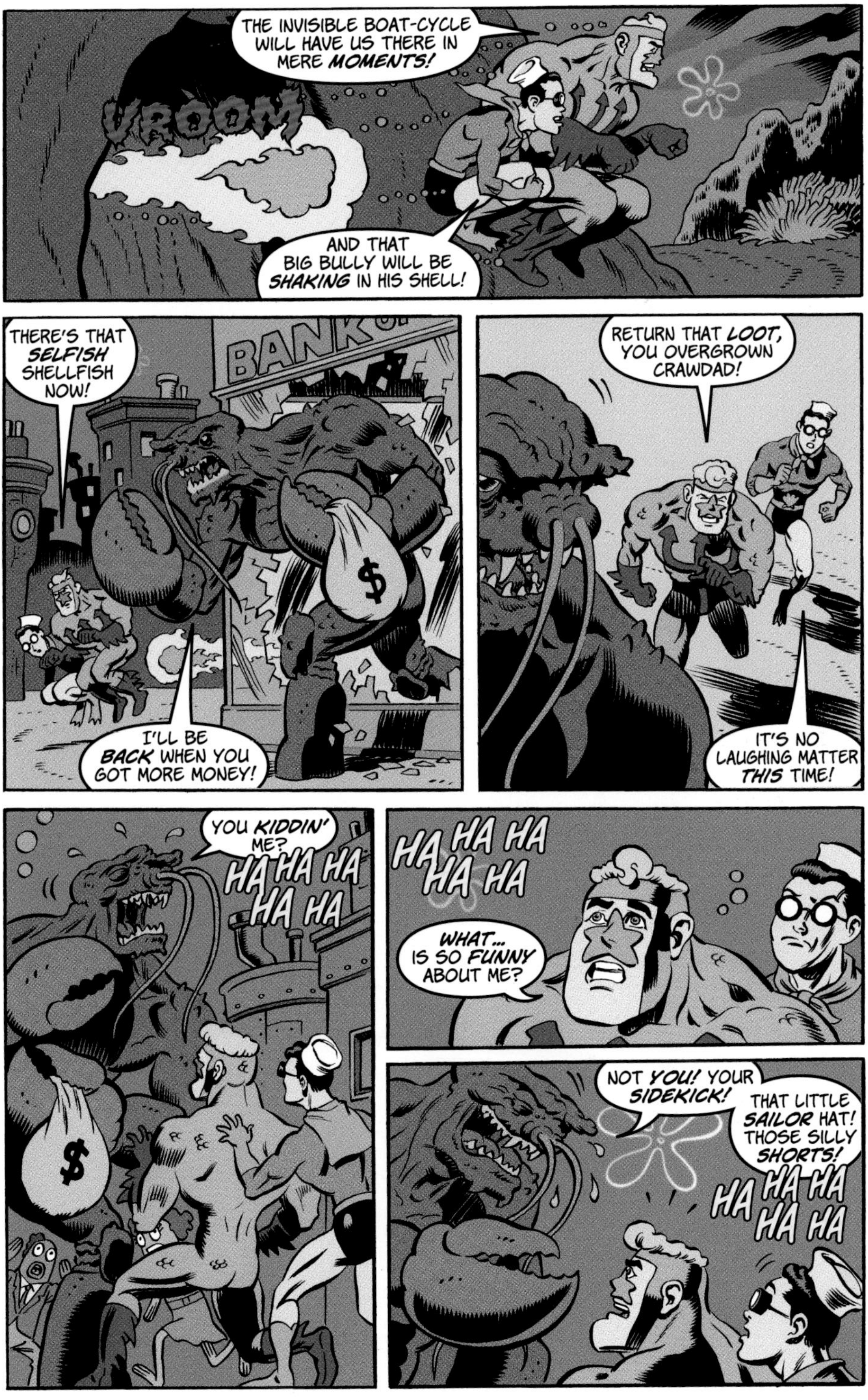
THE INVISIBLE BOAT-CYCLE WILL HAVE US THERE IN MERE MOMENTS!
VROOM
AND THAT BIG BULLY WILL BE SHAKING IN HIS SHELL!
THERE'S THAT SELFISH SHELLFISH NOW!
BANK
I'LL BE BACK WHEN YOU GOT MORE MONEY!
RETURN THAT LOOT, YOU OVERGROWN CRAWDAD!
IT'S NO LAUGHING MATTER THIS TIME!
YOU KIDDIN' ME?
HA HA HA HA HA
HA HA HA HA HA
WHAT... IS SO FUNNY ABOUT ME?
NOT YOU! YOUR SIDEKICK!
THAT LITTLE SAILOR HAT! THOSE SILLY SHORTS!
HA HA HA HA HA

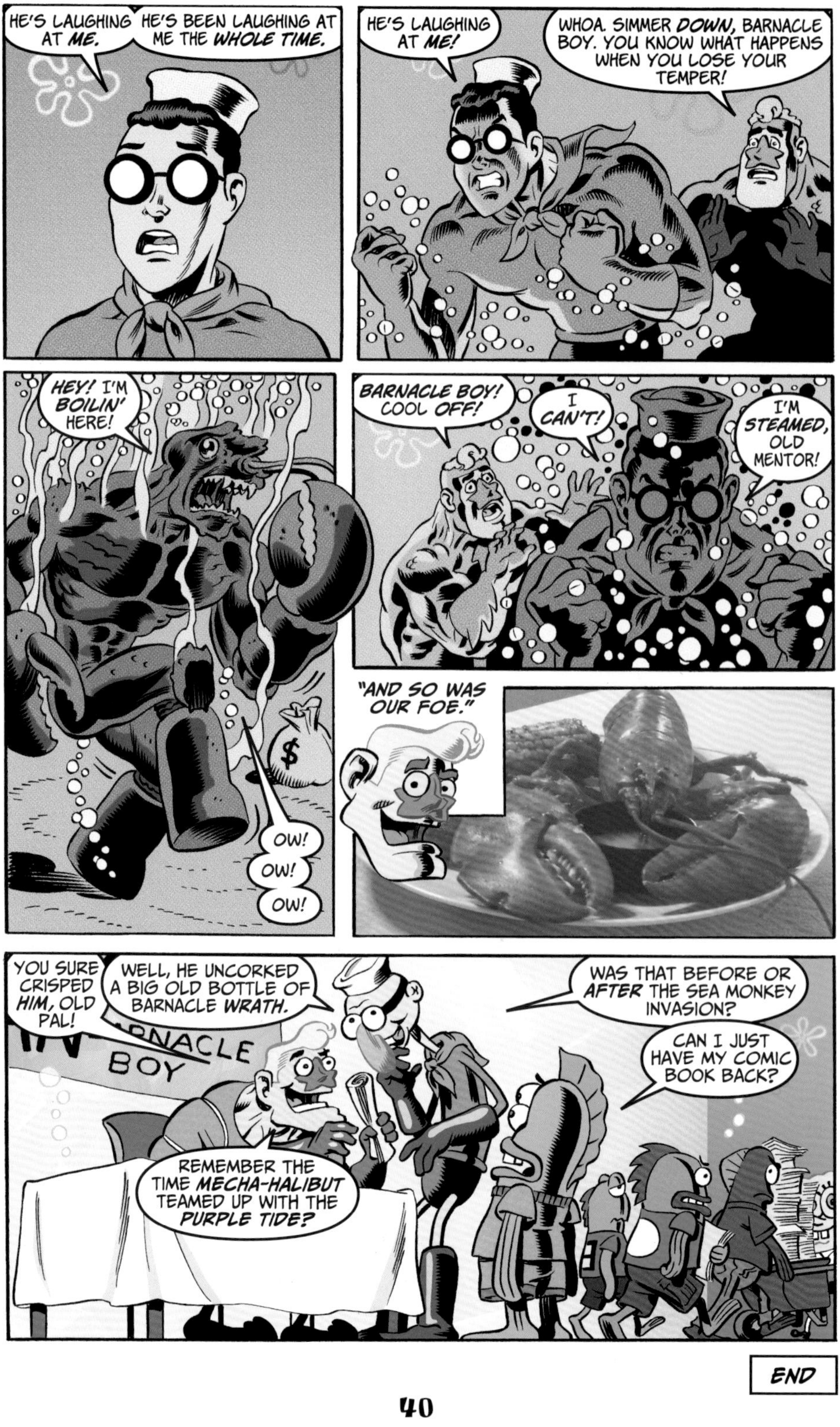
HE'S LAUGHING AT ME.
HE'S BEEN LAUGHING AT ME THE WHOLE TIME.
HE'S LAUGHING AT ME!
WHOA. SIMMER DOWN, BARNACLE BOY. YOU KNOW WHAT HAPPENS WHEN YOU LOSE YOUR TEMPER!
HEY! I'M BOILIN' HERE!
OW!
OW!
OW!
BARNACLE BOY! COOL OFF!
I CAN'T!
I'M STEAMED, OLD MENTOR!
"AND SO WAS OUR FOE."
YOU SURE CRISPED HIM, OLD PAL!
WELL, HE UNCORKED A BIG OLD BOTTLE OF BARNACLE WRATH.
REMEMBER THE TIME MECHA-HALIBUT TEAMED UP WITH THE PURPLE TIDE?
WAS THAT BEFORE OR AFTER THE SEA MONKEY INVASION?
CAN I JUST HAVE MY COMIC BOOK BACK?
END

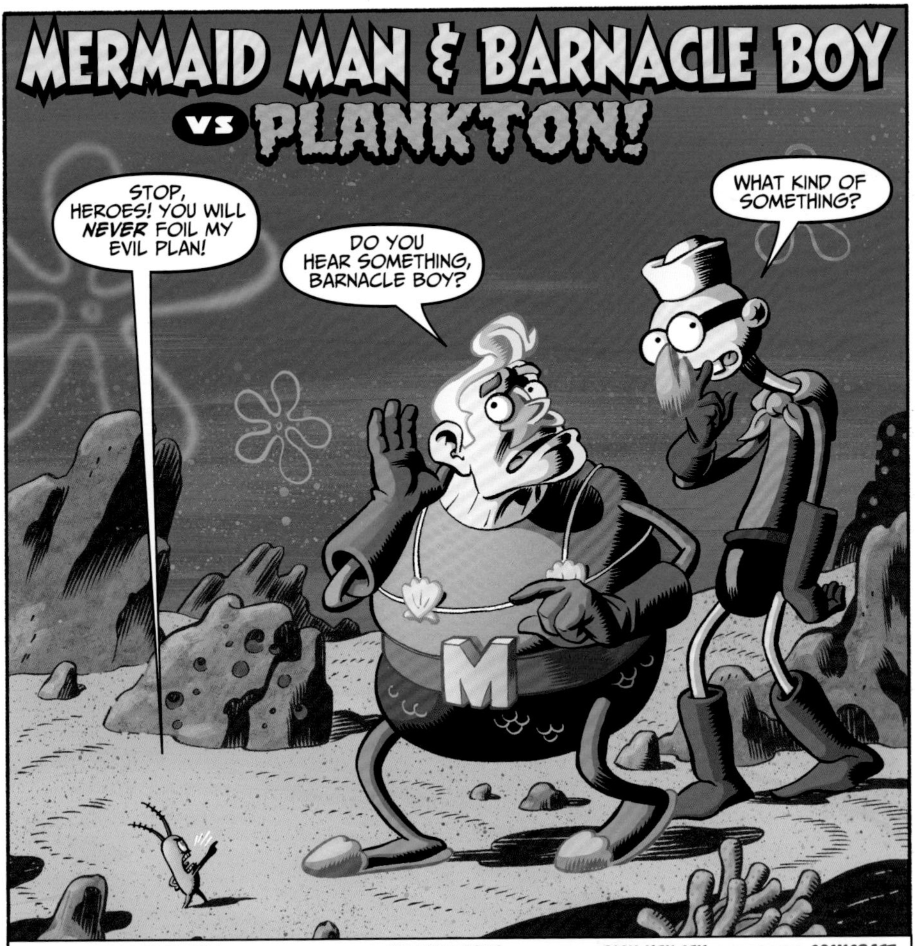
MERMAID MAN & BARNACLE BOY
VS PLANKTON!
STOP, HEROES! YOU WILL *NEVER* FOIL MY EVIL PLAN!
DO YOU HEAR SOMETHING, BARNACLE BOY?
WHAT KIND OF SOMETHING?

STORY: JAMES KOCHALKA **PENCILS AND INKS:** HILARY BARTA **COLORING:** RICK NEILSEN **LETTERING:** COMICRAFT

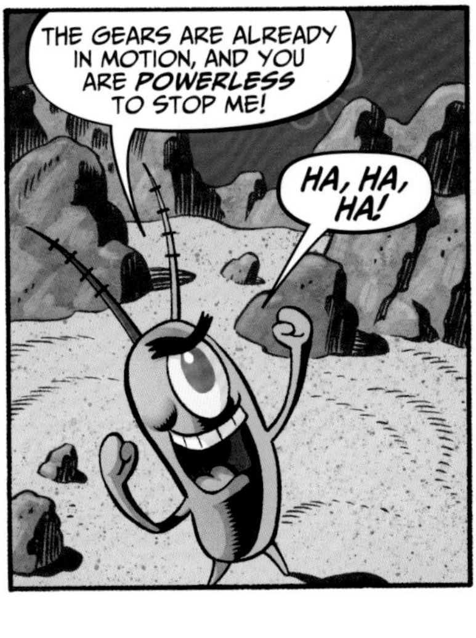
THE GEARS ARE ALREADY IN MOTION, AND YOU ARE *POWERLESS* TO STOP ME!
HA, HA, HA!

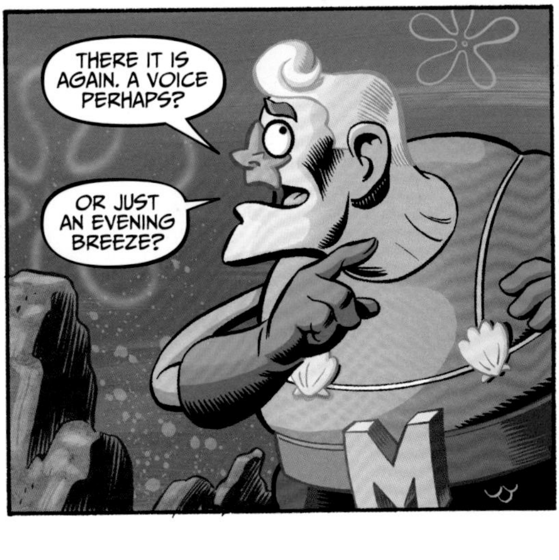
THERE IT IS AGAIN. A VOICE PERHAPS?
OR JUST AN EVENING BREEZE?

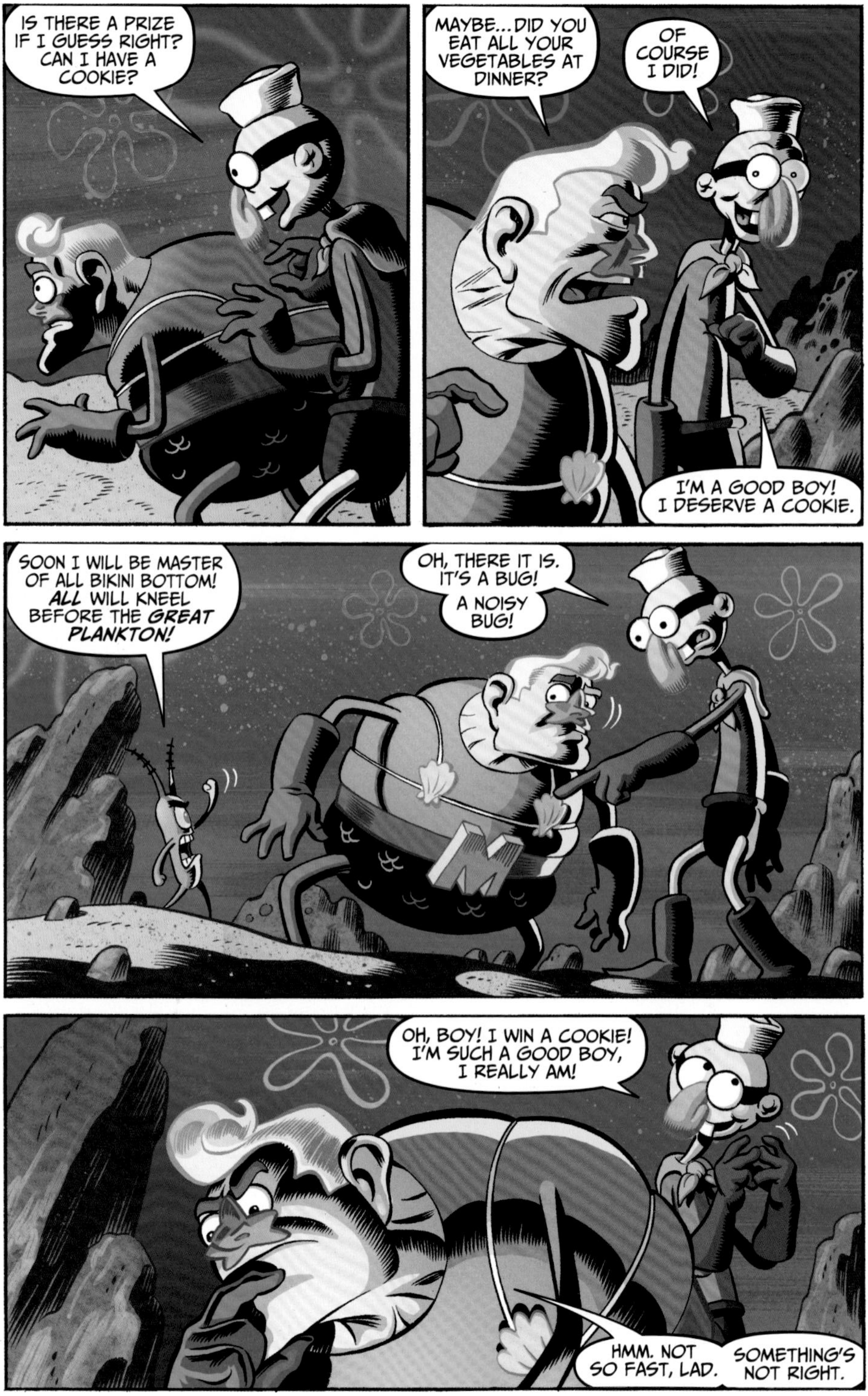
IS THERE A PRIZE IF I GUESS RIGHT? CAN I HAVE A COOKIE?
MAYBE...DID YOU EAT ALL YOUR VEGETABLES AT DINNER?
OF COURSE I DID!
I'M A GOOD BOY! I DESERVE A COOKIE.
SOON I WILL BE MASTER OF ALL BIKINI BOTTOM! ALL WILL KNEEL BEFORE THE GREAT PLANKTON!
OH, THERE IT IS. IT'S A BUG!
A NOISY BUG!
OH, BOY! I WIN A COOKIE! I'M SUCH A GOOD BOY, I REALLY AM!
HMM. NOT SO FAST, LAD.
SOMETHING'S NOT RIGHT.

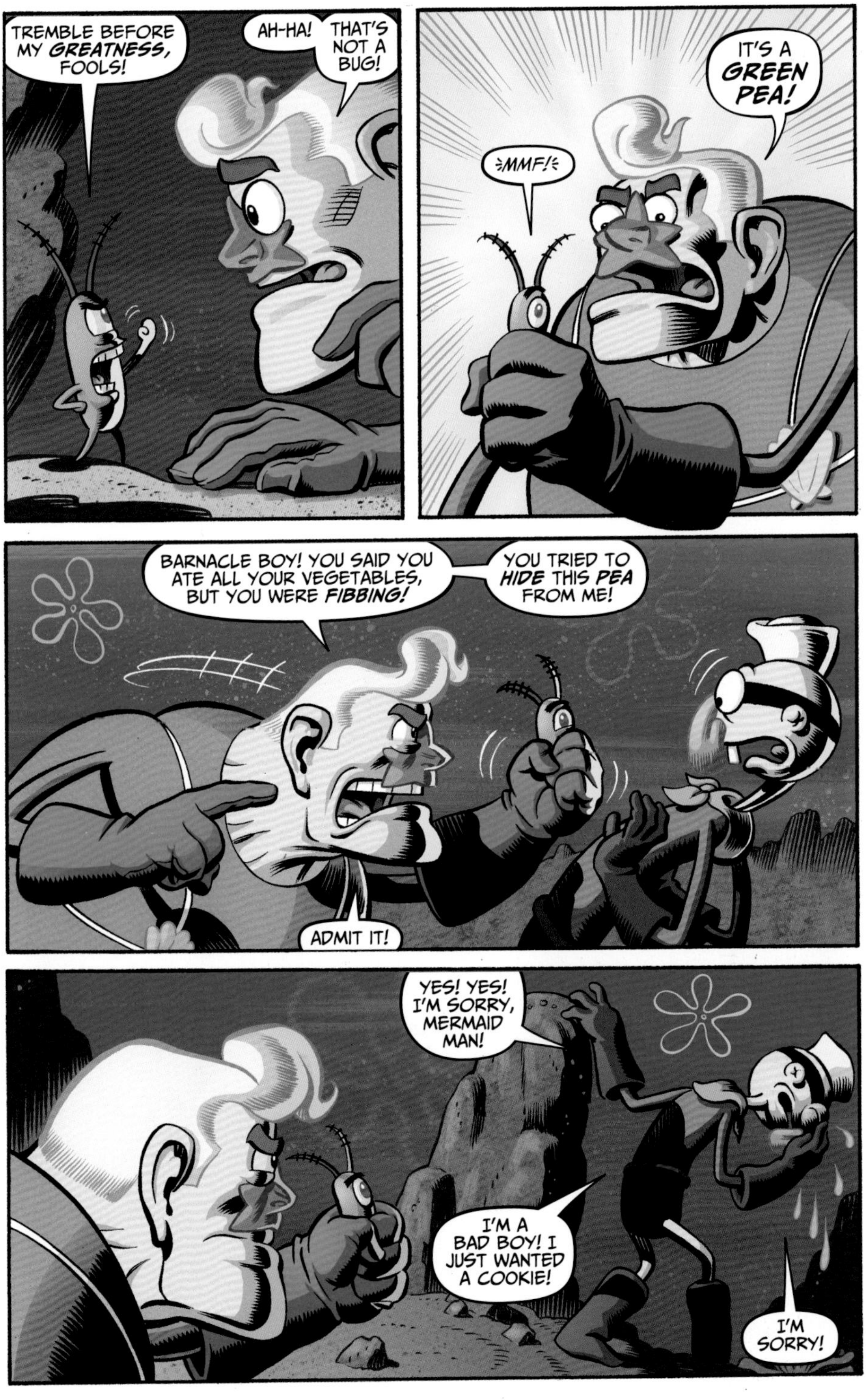
TREMBLE BEFORE MY GREATNESS, FOOLS!
AH-HA!
THAT'S NOT A BUG!
IT'S A GREEN PEA!
MMF!
BARNACLE BOY! YOU SAID YOU ATE ALL YOUR VEGETABLES, BUT YOU WERE FIBBING!
YOU TRIED TO HIDE THIS PEA FROM ME!
ADMIT IT!
YES! YES! I'M SORRY, MERMAID MAN!
I'M A BAD BOY! I JUST WANTED A COOKIE!
I'M SORRY!

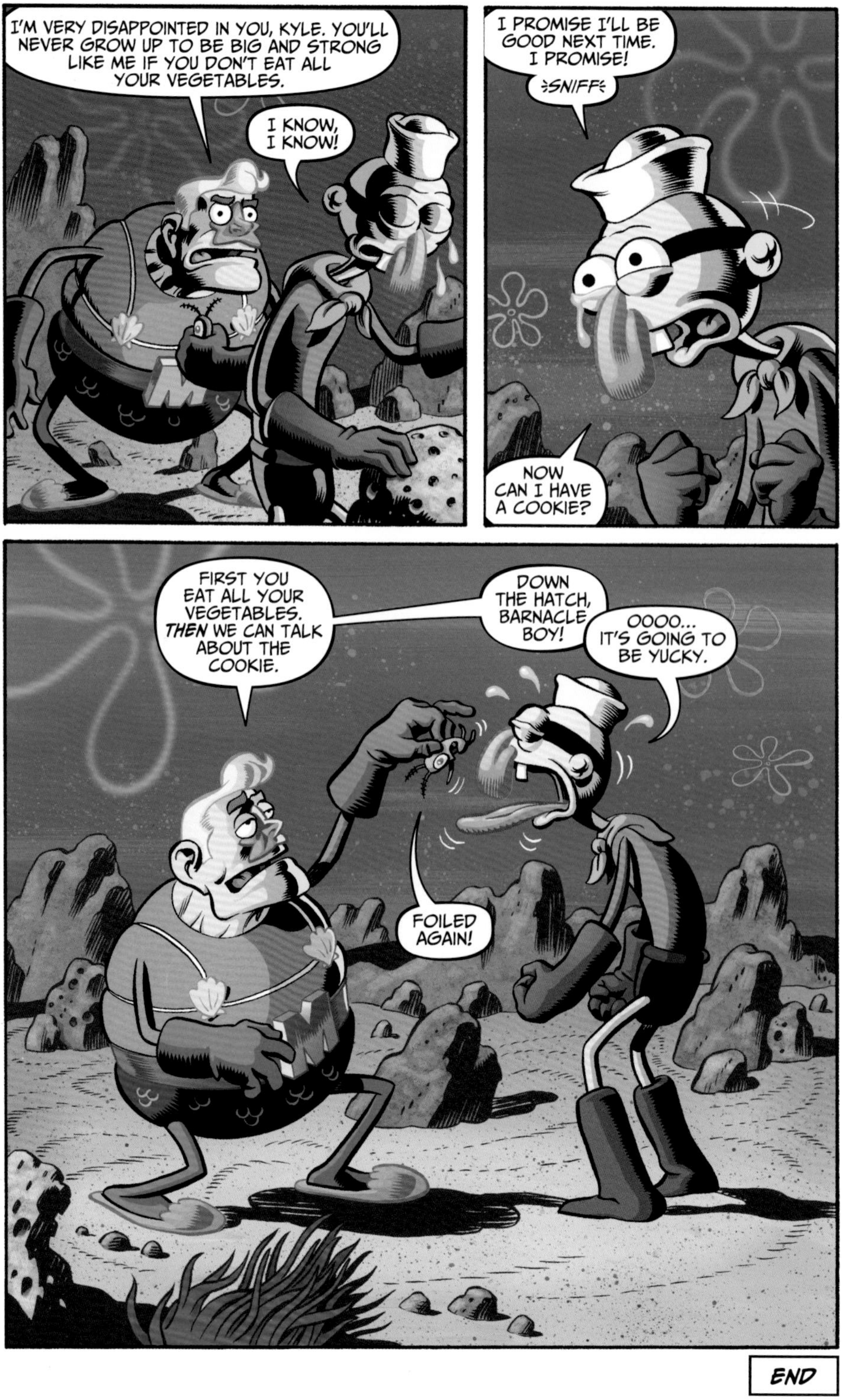
I'M VERY DISAPPOINTED IN YOU, KYLE. YOU'LL NEVER GROW UP TO BE BIG AND STRONG LIKE ME IF YOU DON'T EAT ALL YOUR VEGETABLES.
I KNOW, I KNOW!
I PROMISE I'LL BE GOOD NEXT TIME. I PROMISE!
SNIFF
NOW CAN I HAVE A COOKIE?
FIRST YOU EAT ALL YOUR VEGETABLES. THEN WE CAN TALK ABOUT THE COOKIE.
DOWN THE HATCH, BARNACLE BOY!
OOOO... IT'S GOING TO BE YUCKY.
FOILED AGAIN!

END

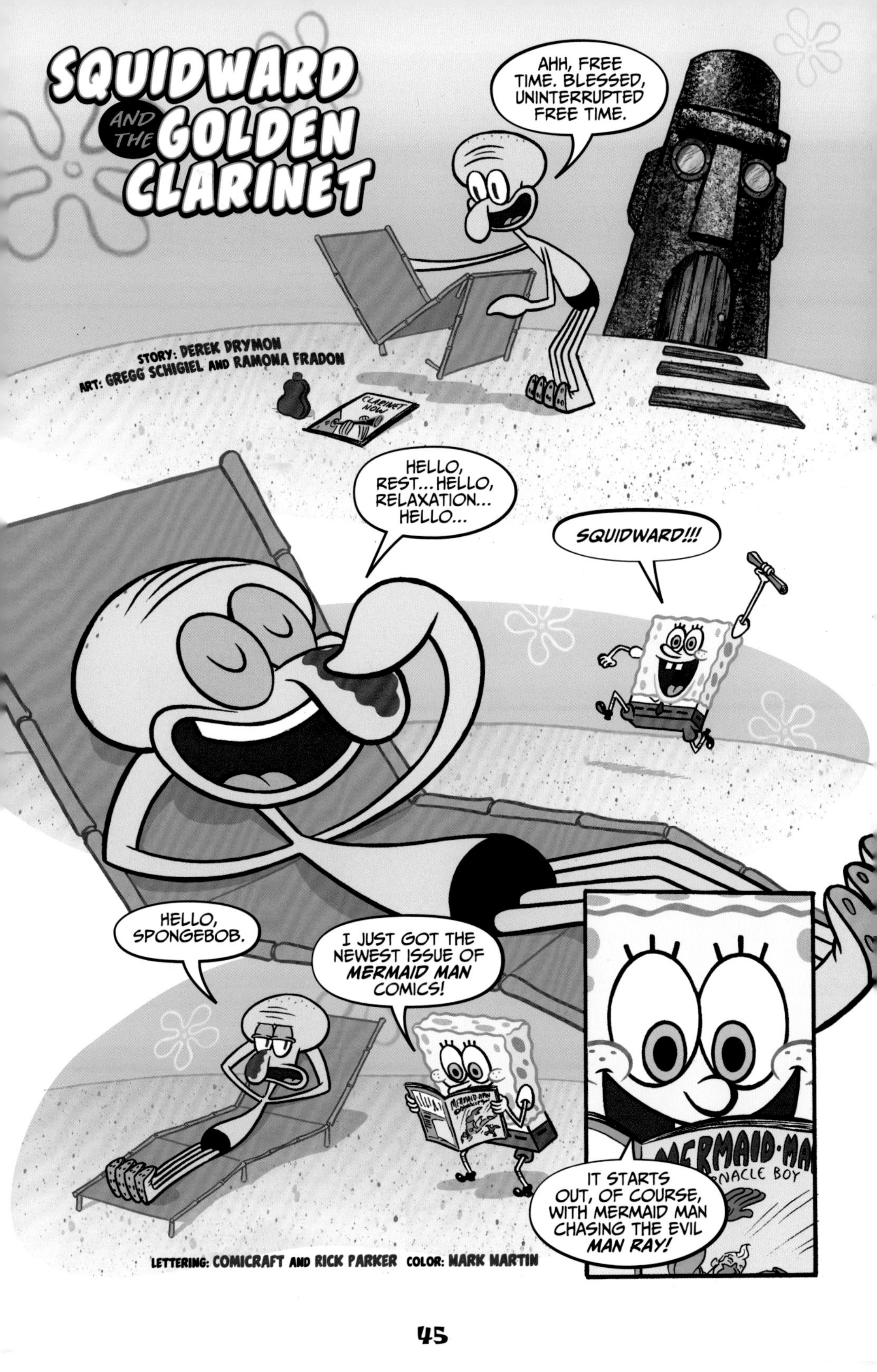
SQUIDWARD AND THE GOLDEN CLARINET
AHH, FREE TIME. BLESSED, UNINTERRUPTED FREE TIME.
STORY: DEREK DRYMON
ART: GREGG SCHIGIEL AND RAMONA FRADON
CLARINET NOW
HELLO, REST... HELLO, RELAXATION... HELLO...
SQUIDWARD!!!
HELLO, SPONGEBOB.
I JUST GOT THE NEWEST ISSUE OF *MERMAID MAN* COMICS!
IT STARTS OUT, OF COURSE, WITH MERMAID MAN CHASING THE EVIL *MAN RAY!*
LETTERING: COMICRAFT AND RICK PARKER COLOR: MARK MARTIN

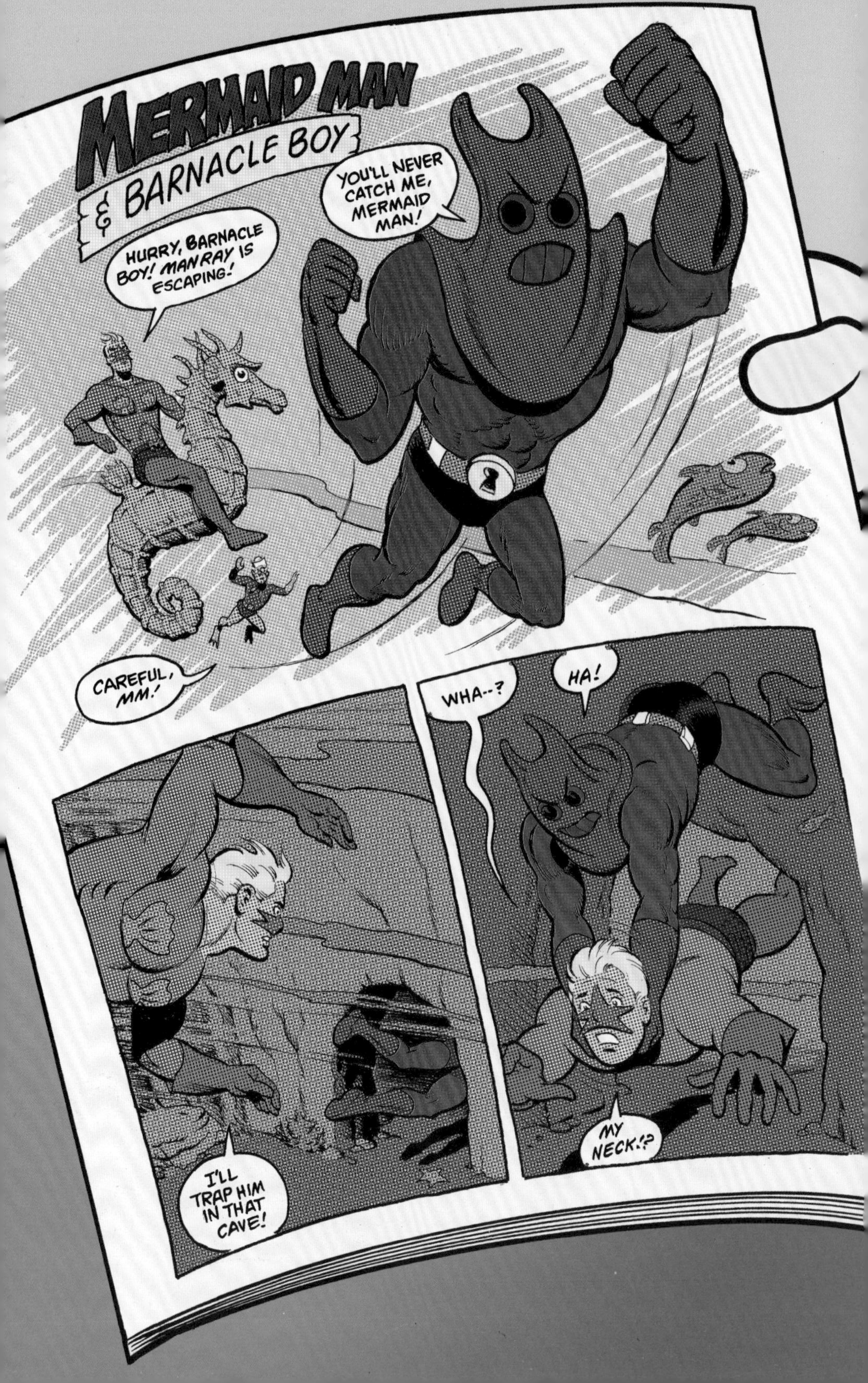
MERMAID MAN
& BARNACLE BOY
HURRY, BARNACLE BOY! MAN RAY IS ESCAPING!
YOU'LL NEVER CATCH ME, MERMAID MAN!
CAREFUL, MM!
I'LL TRAP HIM IN THAT CAVE!
WHA--?
HA!
MY NECK!?

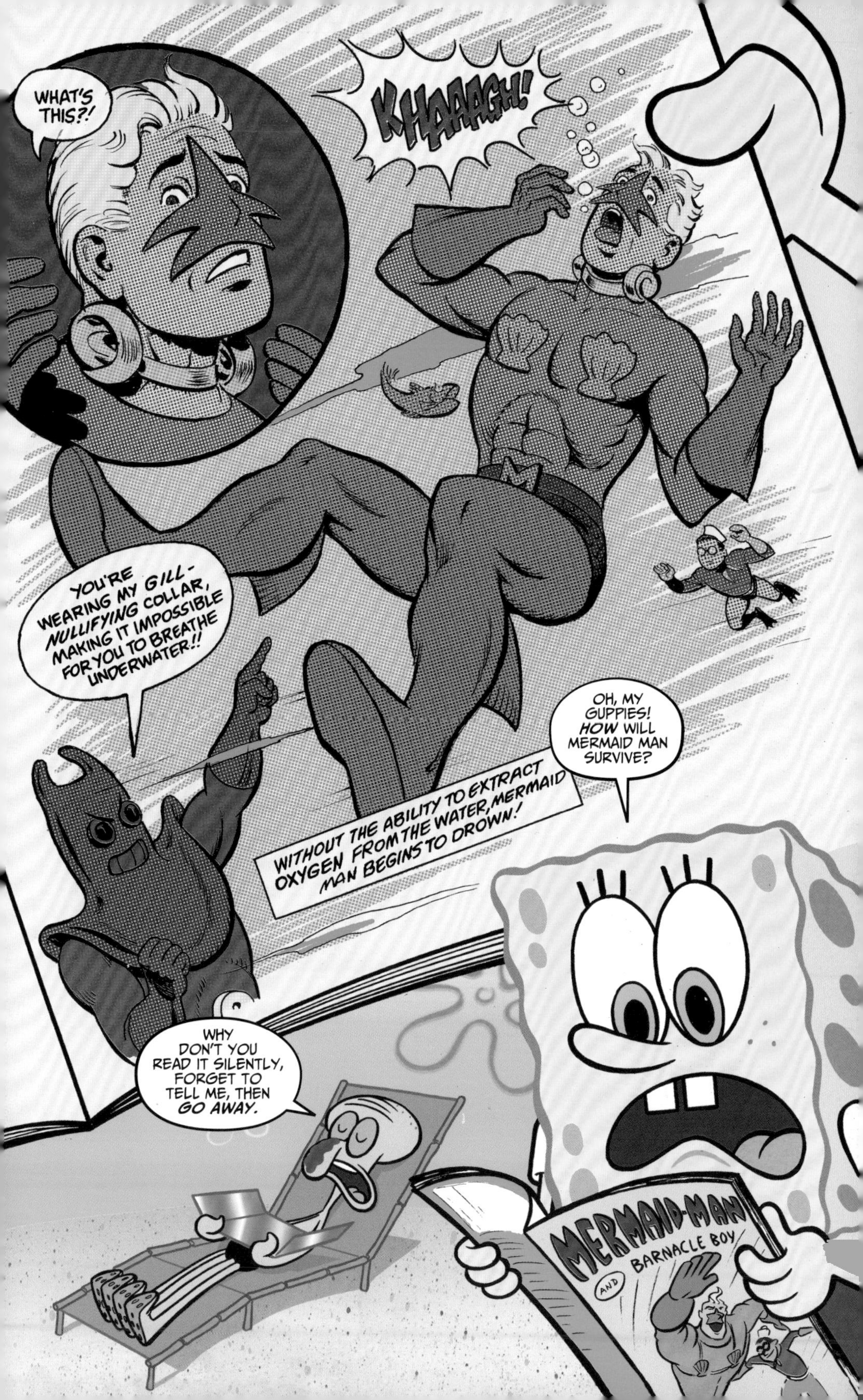
WHAT'S THIS?!
KHAAAGH!
YOU'RE WEARING MY GILL-NULLIFYING COLLAR, MAKING IT IMPOSSIBLE FOR YOU TO BREATHE UNDERWATER!!
WITHOUT THE ABILITY TO EXTRACT OXYGEN FROM THE WATER, MERMAID MAN BEGINS TO DROWN!
OH, MY GUPPIES! HOW WILL MERMAID MAN SURVIVE?
WHY DON'T YOU READ IT SILENTLY, FORGET TO TELL ME, THEN GO AWAY.
MERMAID-MAN AND BARNACLE BOY

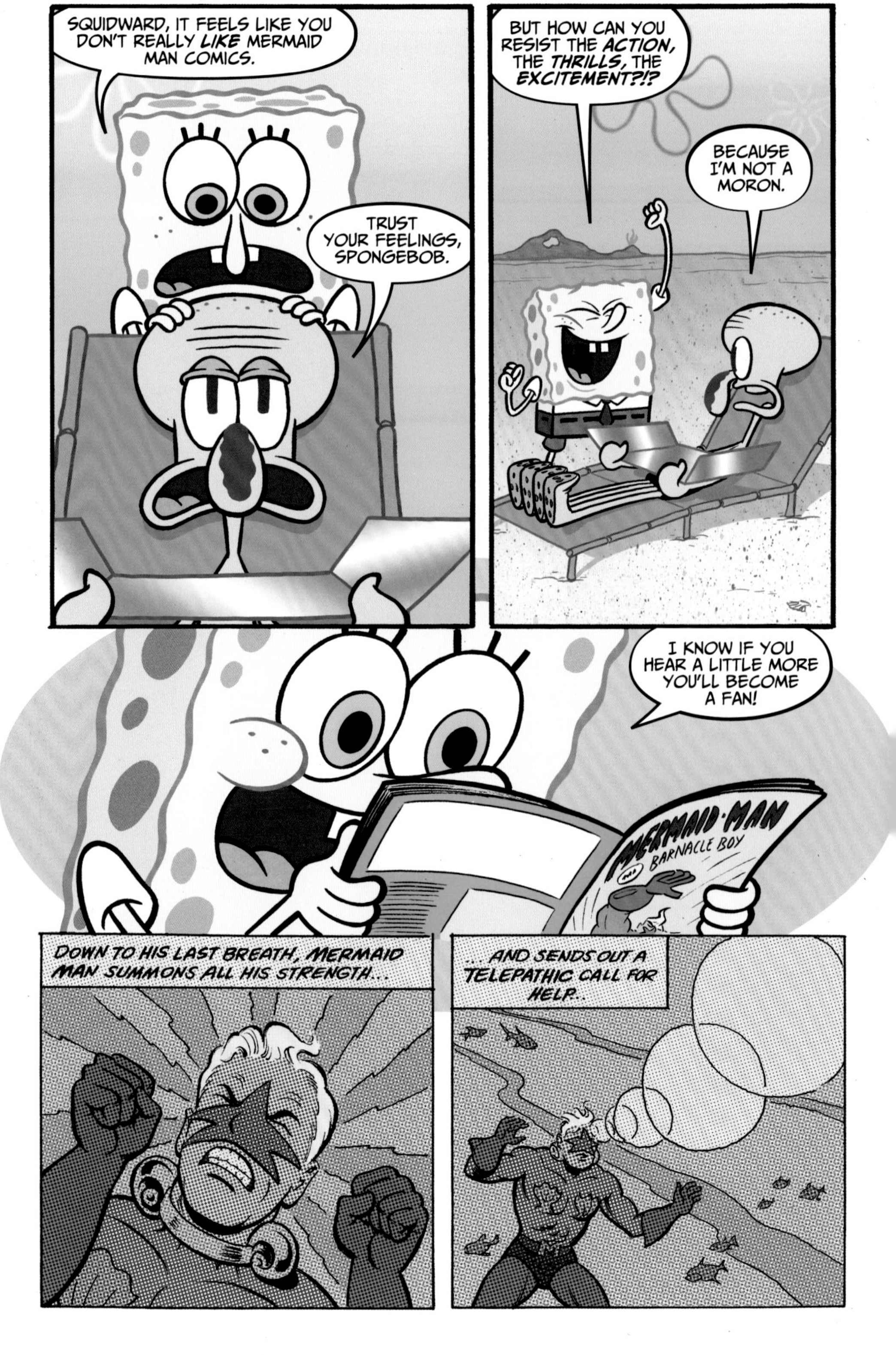
SQUIDWARD, IT FEELS LIKE YOU DON'T REALLY *LIKE* MERMAID MAN COMICS.
TRUST YOUR FEELINGS, SPONGEBOB.
BUT HOW CAN YOU RESIST THE *ACTION*, THE *THRILLS*, THE *EXCITEMENT?!?*
BECAUSE I'M NOT A MORON.
I KNOW IF YOU HEAR A LITTLE MORE YOU'LL BECOME A FAN!
MERMAID·MAN
BARNACLE BOY
DOWN TO HIS LAST BREATH, MERMAID MAN SUMMONS ALL HIS STRENGTH...
...AND SENDS OUT A TELEPATHIC CALL FOR HELP...

...WHICH IS HEARD BY A SCHOOL OF LOYAL BLOWFISH...

...WHO INFLATE THEIR EXPANDABLE BODIES WITH OXYGEN FROM THE SURFACE...

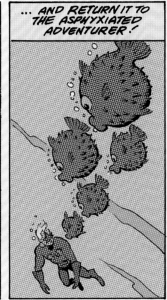

...AND RETURN IT TO THE ASPHYXIATED ADVENTURER!

INHALE

NO FAIR! YOU ALWAYS GET HELP!

POW!!

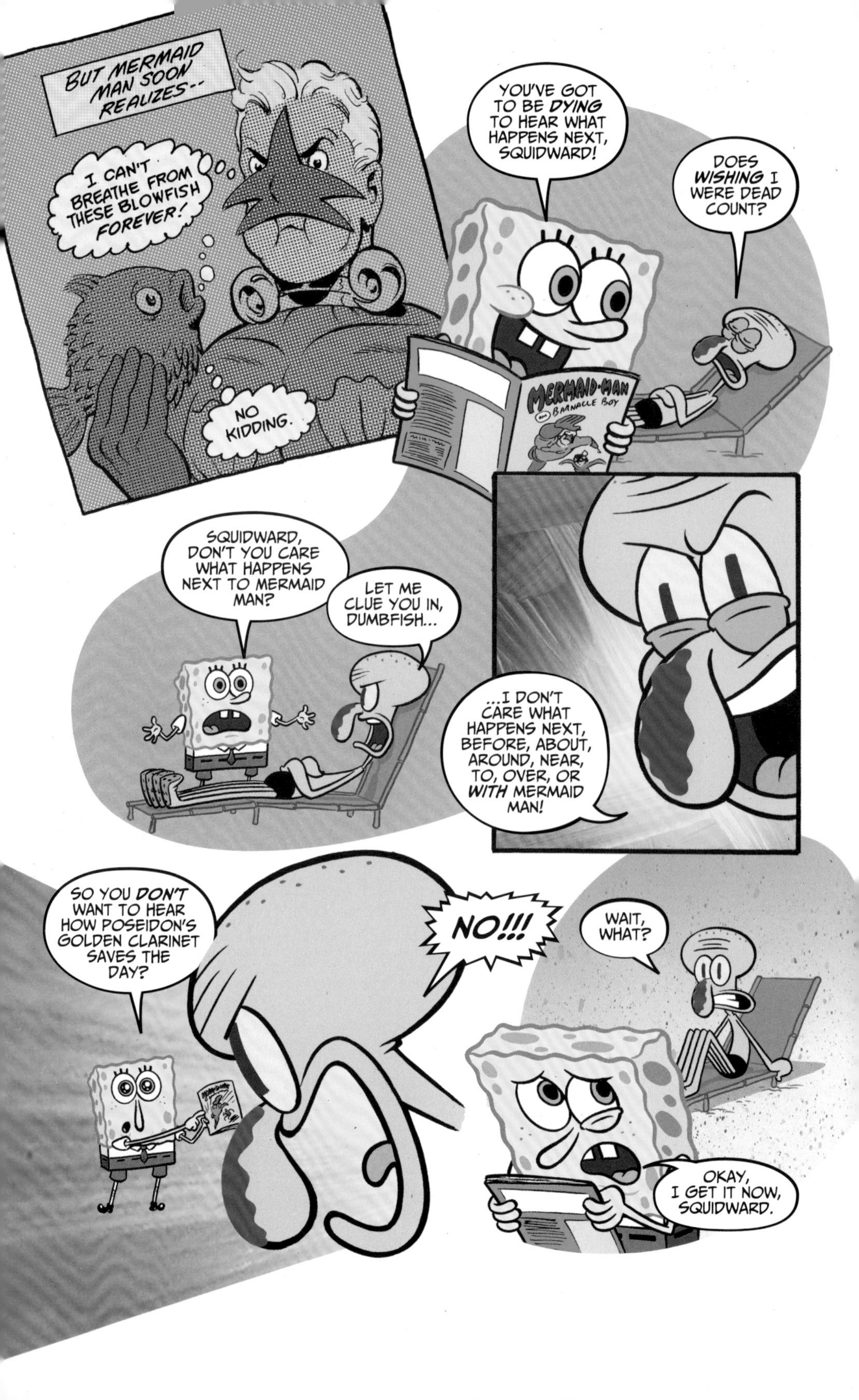

BUT MERMAID MAN SOON REALIZES--
I CAN'T BREATHE FROM THESE BLOWFISH FOREVER!
NO KIDDING.
YOU'VE GOT TO BE DYING TO HEAR WHAT HAPPENS NEXT, SQUIDWARD!
DOES WISHING I WERE DEAD COUNT?
MERMAID-MAN
BARNACLE BOY
SQUIDWARD, DON'T YOU CARE WHAT HAPPENS NEXT TO MERMAID MAN?
LET ME CLUE YOU IN, DUMBFISH...
...I DON'T CARE WHAT HAPPENS NEXT, BEFORE, ABOUT, AROUND, NEAR, TO, OVER, OR WITH MERMAID MAN!
SO YOU DON'T WANT TO HEAR HOW POSEIDON'S GOLDEN CLARINET SAVES THE DAY?
NO!!!
WAIT, WHAT?
OKAY, I GET IT NOW, SQUIDWARD.

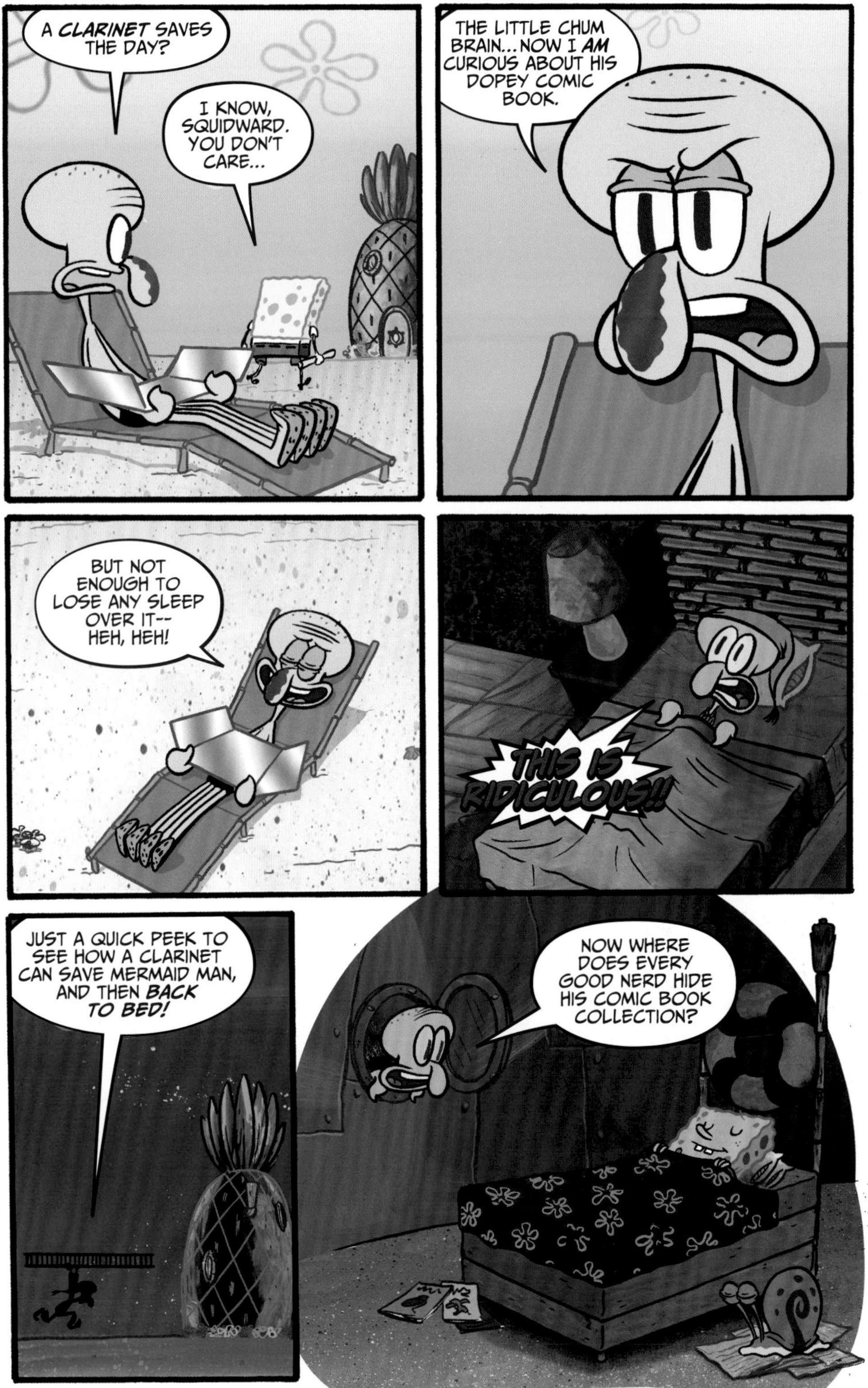
A CLARINET SAVES THE DAY?
I KNOW, SQUIDWARD. YOU DON'T CARE...
THE LITTLE CHUM BRAIN...NOW I AM CURIOUS ABOUT HIS DOPEY COMIC BOOK.
BUT NOT ENOUGH TO LOSE ANY SLEEP OVER IT-- HEH, HEH!
THIS IS RIDICULOUS!!
JUST A QUICK PEEK TO SEE HOW A CLARINET CAN SAVE MERMAID MAN, AND THEN BACK TO BED!
NOW WHERE DOES EVERY GOOD NERD HIDE HIS COMIC BOOK COLLECTION?

UNDER HIS *BED,* OF COURSE!

HERE WE GO...

KLIK

KLANG-ALANG-ALANG-ALANG-ALANG-ALANG-ALANG

KLANG-ALANG-ALANG-ALANG-ALANG-ALANG

KLANG-ALANG-ALANG-ALANG-ALANG

SOMEONE'S STEALING MY MERMAID MAN COMICS!!!!

SQUIDWARD? YOU MUST REALLY LIKE MERMAID MAN COMICS AFTER ALL!

NO I DON'T!

AND WHY IN THE WORLD WOULD YOU PUT AN *ALARM* ON THOSE WORTHLESS THINGS?

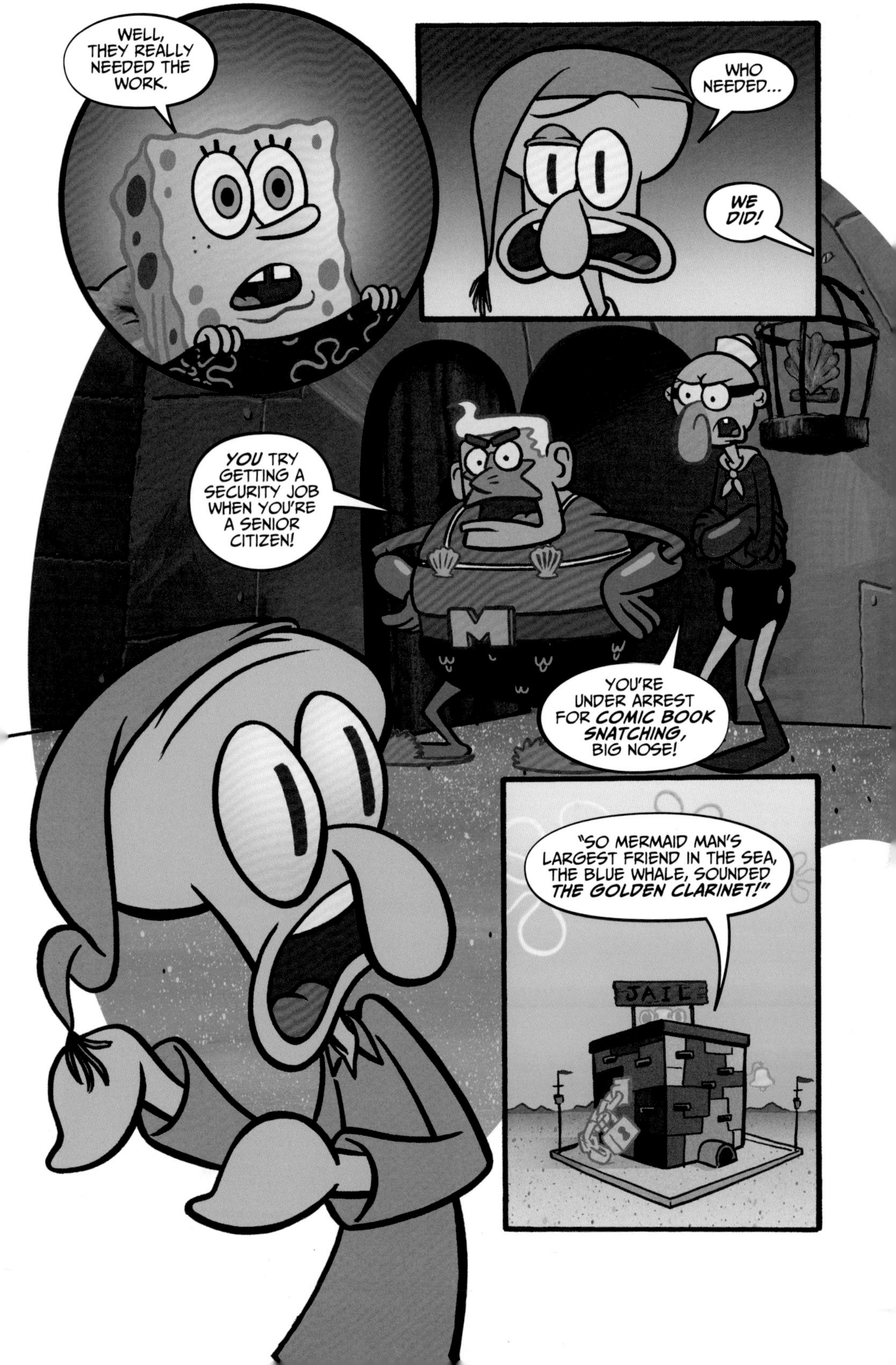
WELL, THEY REALLY NEEDED THE WORK.
WHO NEEDED...
WE DID!
YOU TRY GETTING A SECURITY JOB WHEN YOU'RE A SENIOR CITIZEN!
YOU'RE UNDER ARREST FOR COMIC BOOK SNATCHING, BIG NOSE!
"SO MERMAID MAN'S LARGEST FRIEND IN THE SEA, THE BLUE WHALE, SOUNDED THE GOLDEN CLARINET!"
JAIL

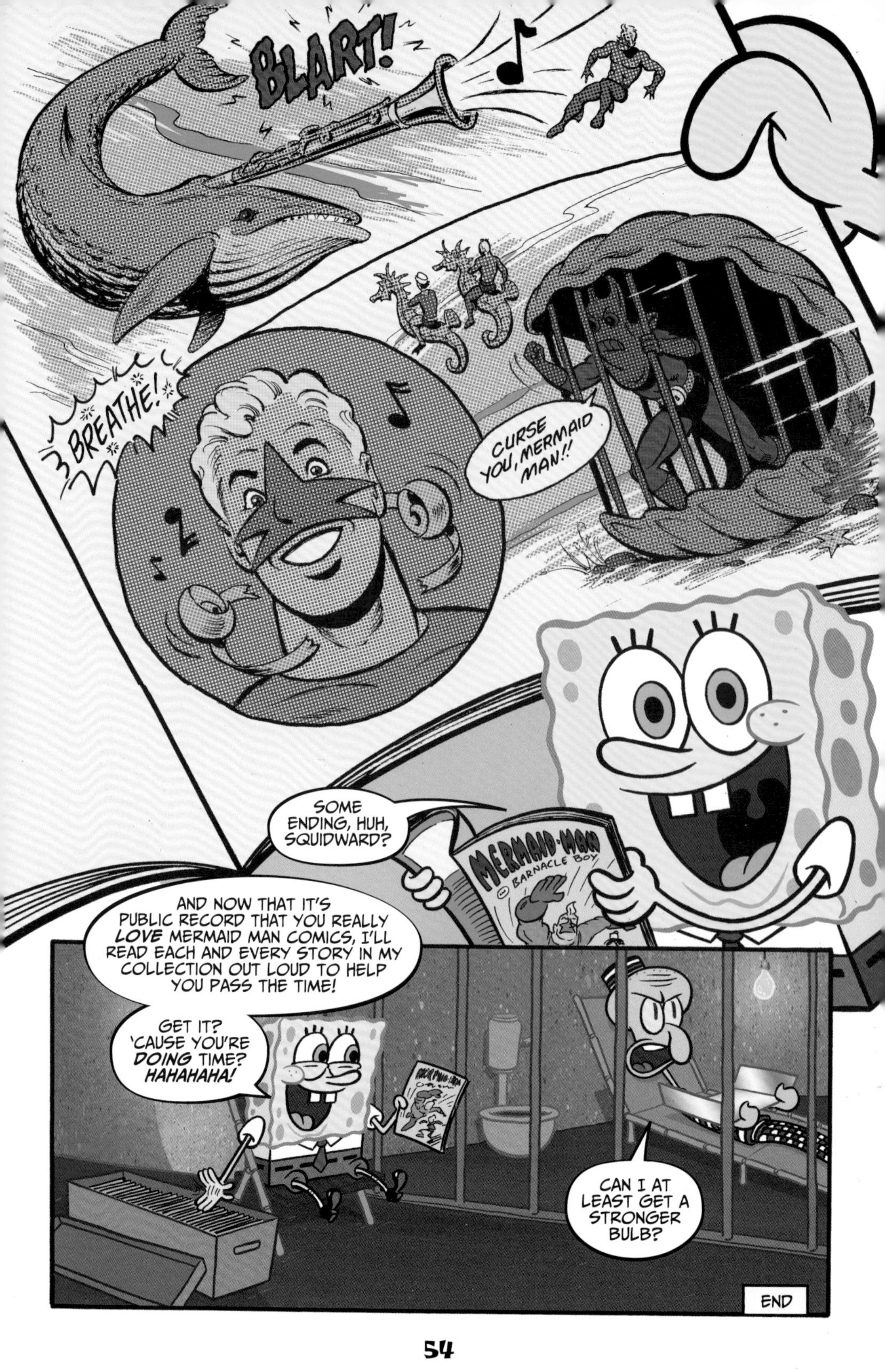
BLART!
BREATHE!
CURSE YOU, MERMAID MAN!!
SOME ENDING, HUH, SQUIDWARD?
MERMAID MAN
BARNACLE BOY
AND NOW THAT IT'S PUBLIC RECORD THAT YOU REALLY LOVE MERMAID MAN COMICS, I'LL READ EACH AND EVERY STORY IN MY COLLECTION OUT LOUD TO HELP YOU PASS THE TIME!
GET IT? 'CAUSE YOU'RE DOING TIME? HAHAHAHA!
CAN I AT LEAST GET A STRONGER BULB?
END

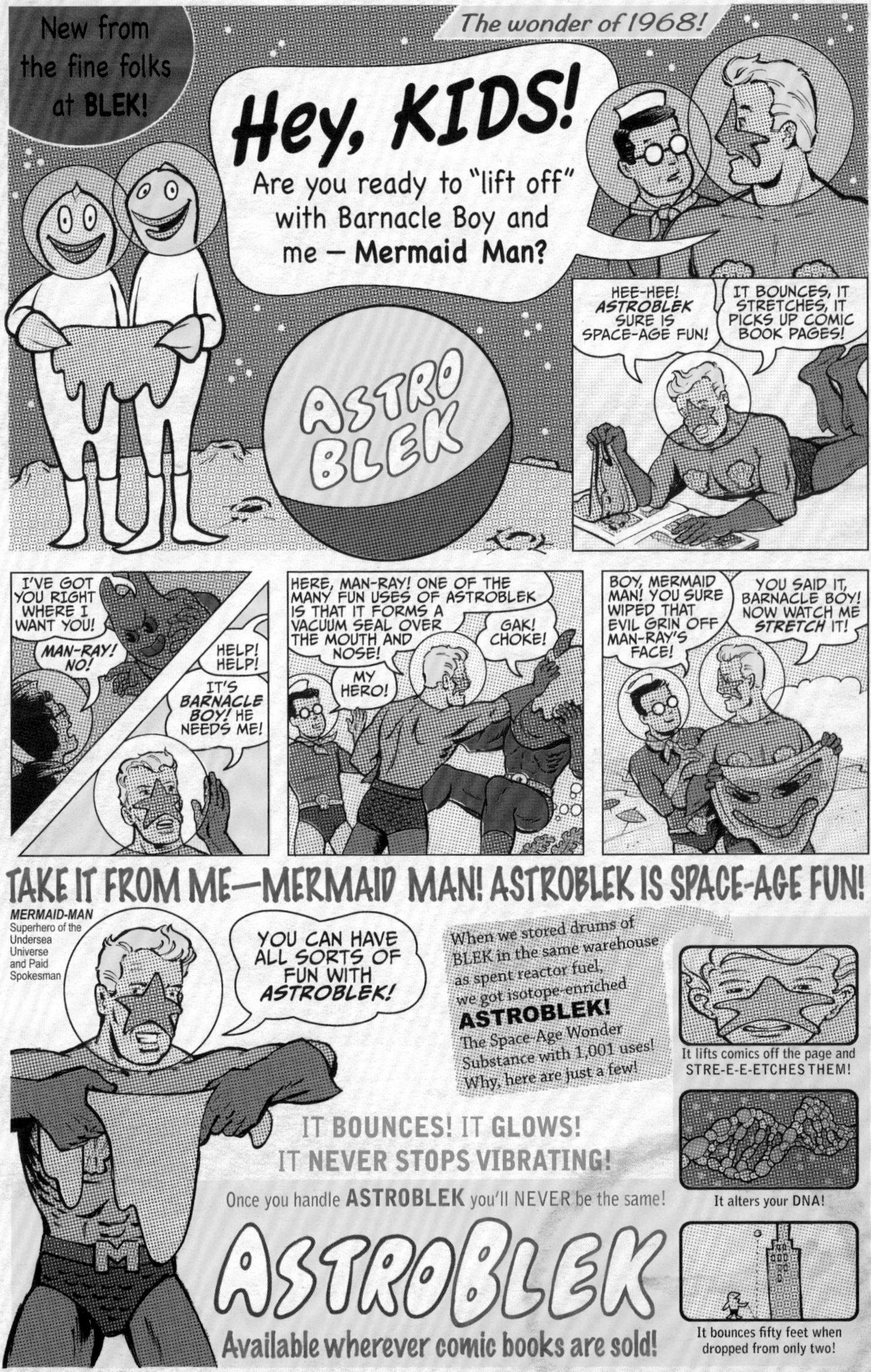

New from the fine folks at BLEK!
The wonder of 1968!
Hey, KIDS!
Are you ready to "lift off" with Barnacle Boy and me — Mermaid Man?
ASTRO BLEK
HEE-HEE! ASTROBLEK SURE IS SPACE-AGE FUN!
IT BOUNCES, IT STRETCHES, IT PICKS UP COMIC BOOK PAGES!
I'VE GOT YOU RIGHT WHERE I WANT YOU!
MAN-RAY! NO!
HELP! HELP!
IT'S BARNACLE BOY! HE NEEDS ME!
HERE, MAN-RAY! ONE OF THE MANY FUN USES OF ASTROBLEK IS THAT IT FORMS A VACUUM SEAL OVER THE MOUTH AND NOSE!
GAK! CHOKE!
MY HERO!
BOY, MERMAID MAN! YOU SURE WIPED THAT EVIL GRIN OFF MAN-RAY'S FACE!
YOU SAID IT, BARNACLE BOY! NOW WATCH ME STRETCH IT!
TAKE IT FROM ME—MERMAID MAN! ASTROBLEK IS SPACE-AGE FUN!
MERMAID-MAN
Superhero of the Undersea Universe and Paid Spokesman
YOU CAN HAVE ALL SORTS OF FUN WITH ASTROBLEK!
When we stored drums of BLEK in the same warehouse as spent reactor fuel, we got isotope-enriched
ASTROBLEK!
The Space-Age Wonder Substance with 1,001 uses! Why, here are just a few!
It lifts comics off the page and STRE-E-E-ETCHES THEM!
It alters your DNA!
It bounces fifty feet when dropped from only two!
IT BOUNCES! IT GLOWS!
IT NEVER STOPS VIBRATING!
Once you handle ASTROBLEK you'll NEVER be the same!
ASTROBLEK
Available wherever comic books are sold!

Moms! AstroBlek is safe when handled with protective gear as shown in this advertisement.

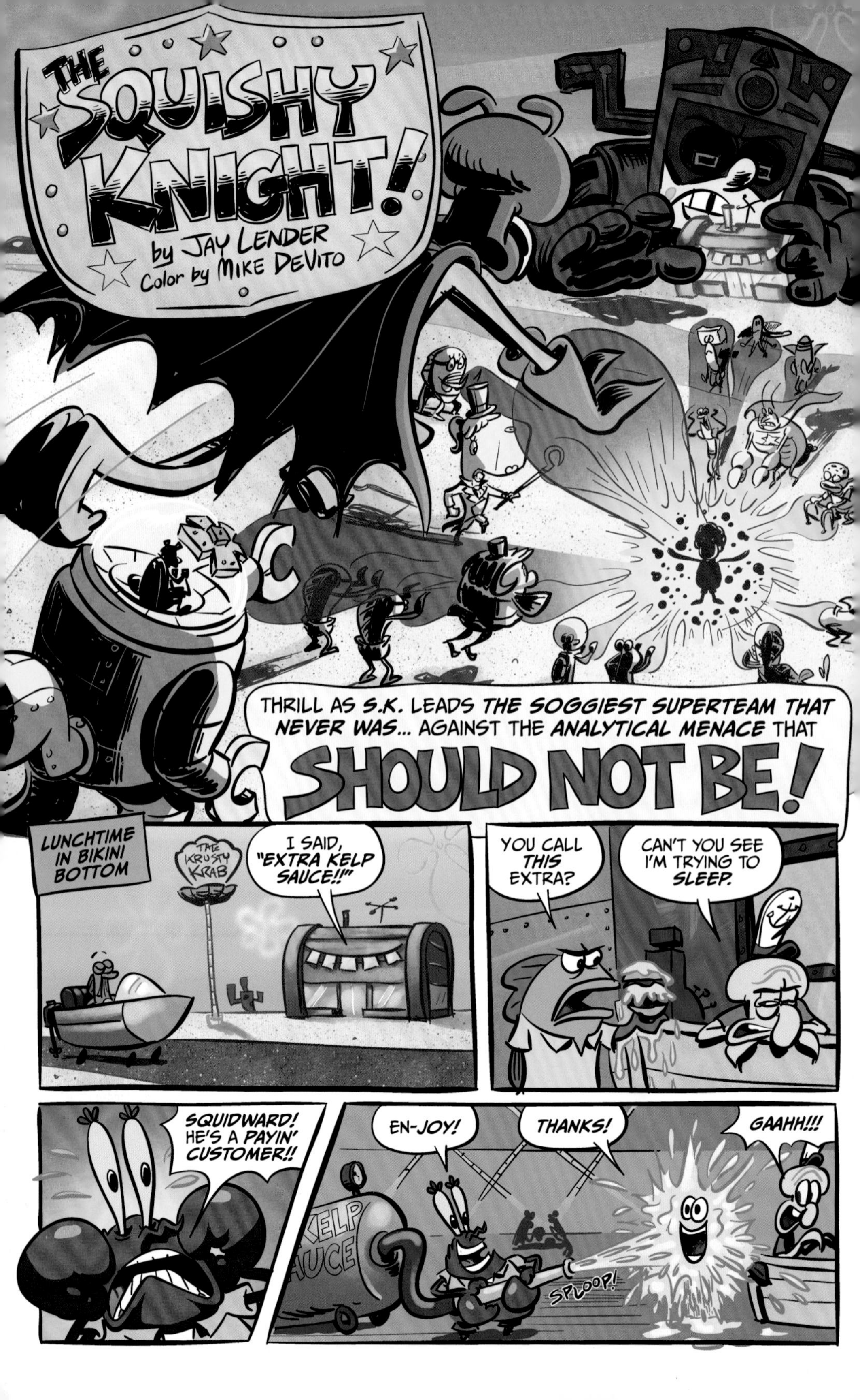
THE SQUISHY KNIGHT!
by JAY LENDER
Color by MIKE DeVITO
THRILL AS S.K. LEADS THE SOGGIEST SUPERTEAM THAT NEVER WAS... AGAINST THE ANALYTICAL MENACE THAT
SHOULD NOT BE!
LUNCHTIME IN BIKINI BOTTOM
THE KRUSTY KRAB
I SAID, "EXTRA KELP SAUCE!!"
YOU CALL THIS EXTRA?
CAN'T YOU SEE I'M TRYING TO SLEEP.
SQUIDWARD! HE'S A PAYIN' CUSTOMER!!
EN-JOY!
THANKS!
GAAHH!!!
KELP SAUCE
SPLOOP!

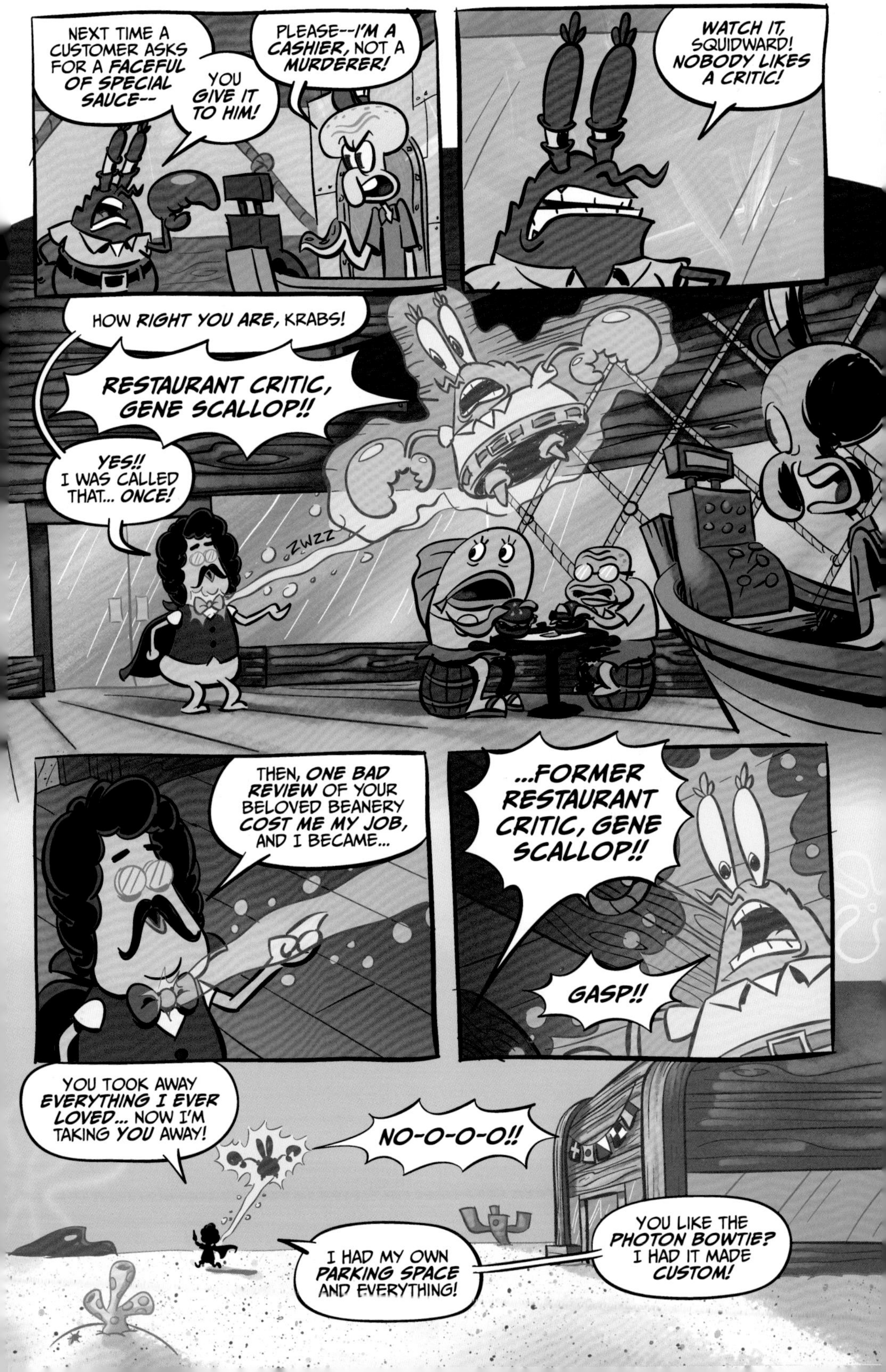
NEXT TIME A CUSTOMER ASKS FOR A FACEFUL OF SPECIAL SAUCE--
YOU GIVE IT TO HIM!
PLEASE--I'M A CASHIER, NOT A MURDERER!
WATCH IT, SQUIDWARD! NOBODY LIKES A CRITIC!
HOW RIGHT YOU ARE, KRABS!
RESTAURANT CRITIC, GENE SCALLOP!!
YES!! I WAS CALLED THAT... ONCE!
ZWZZ
THEN, ONE BAD REVIEW OF YOUR BELOVED BEANERY COST ME MY JOB, AND I BECAME...
...FORMER RESTAURANT CRITIC, GENE SCALLOP!!
GASP!!
YOU TOOK AWAY EVERYTHING I EVER LOVED... NOW I'M TAKING YOU AWAY!
NO-O-O-O!!
I HAD MY OWN PARKING SPACE AND EVERYTHING!
YOU LIKE THE PHOTON BOWTIE? I HAD IT MADE CUSTOM!

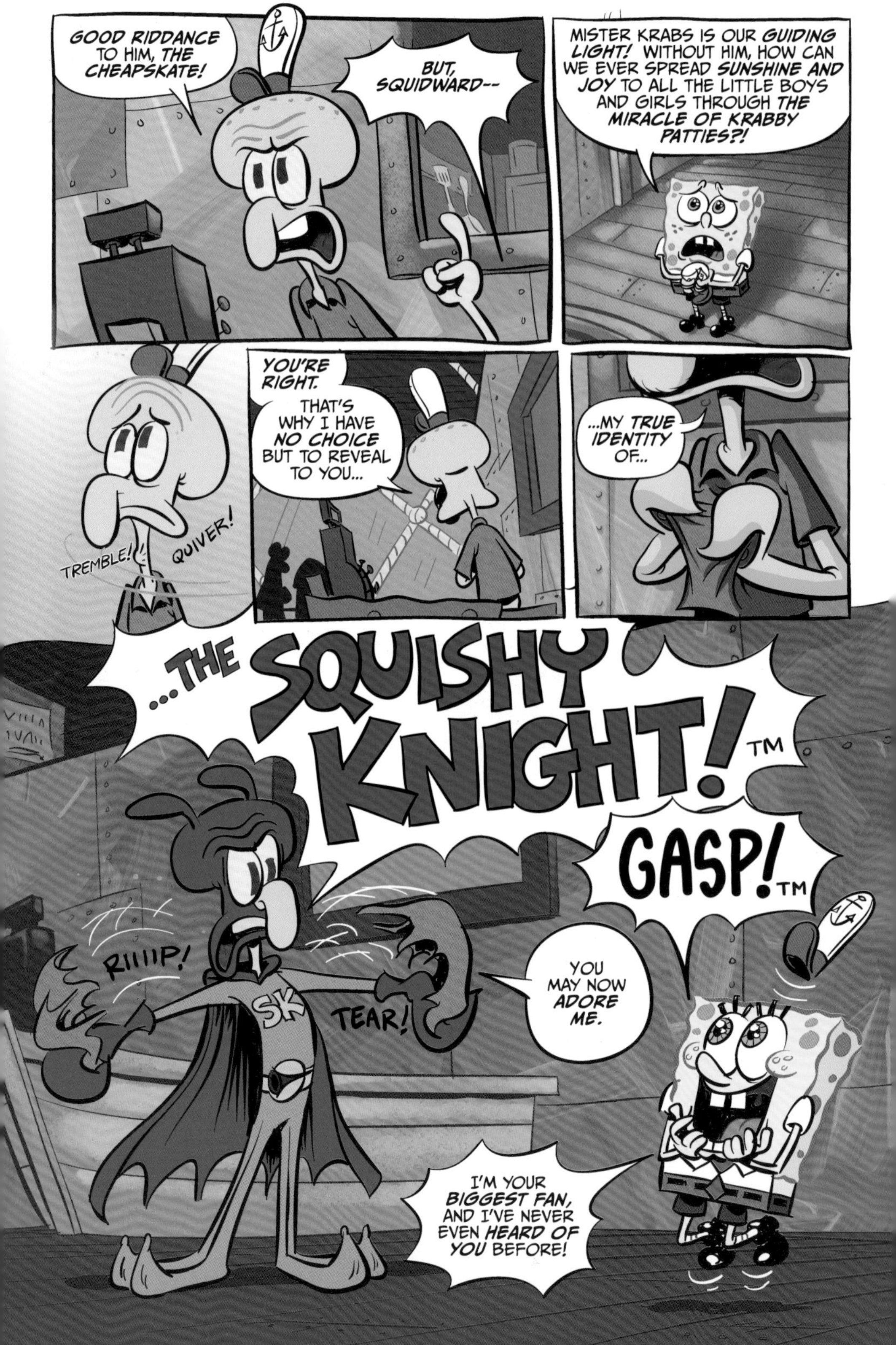
GOOD RIDDANCE TO HIM, THE CHEAPSKATE!
BUT, SQUIDWARD--
MISTER KRABS IS OUR GUIDING LIGHT! WITHOUT HIM, HOW CAN WE EVER SPREAD SUNSHINE AND JOY TO ALL THE LITTLE BOYS AND GIRLS THROUGH THE MIRACLE OF KRABBY PATTIES?!
TREMBLE!
QUIVER!
YOU'RE RIGHT.
THAT'S WHY I HAVE NO CHOICE BUT TO REVEAL TO YOU...
...MY TRUE IDENTITY OF...
...THE SQUISHY KNIGHT!™
GASP!™
RIIIIP!
TEAR!
SK
YOU MAY NOW ADORE ME.
I'M YOUR BIGGEST FAN, AND I'VE NEVER EVEN HEARD OF YOU BEFORE!

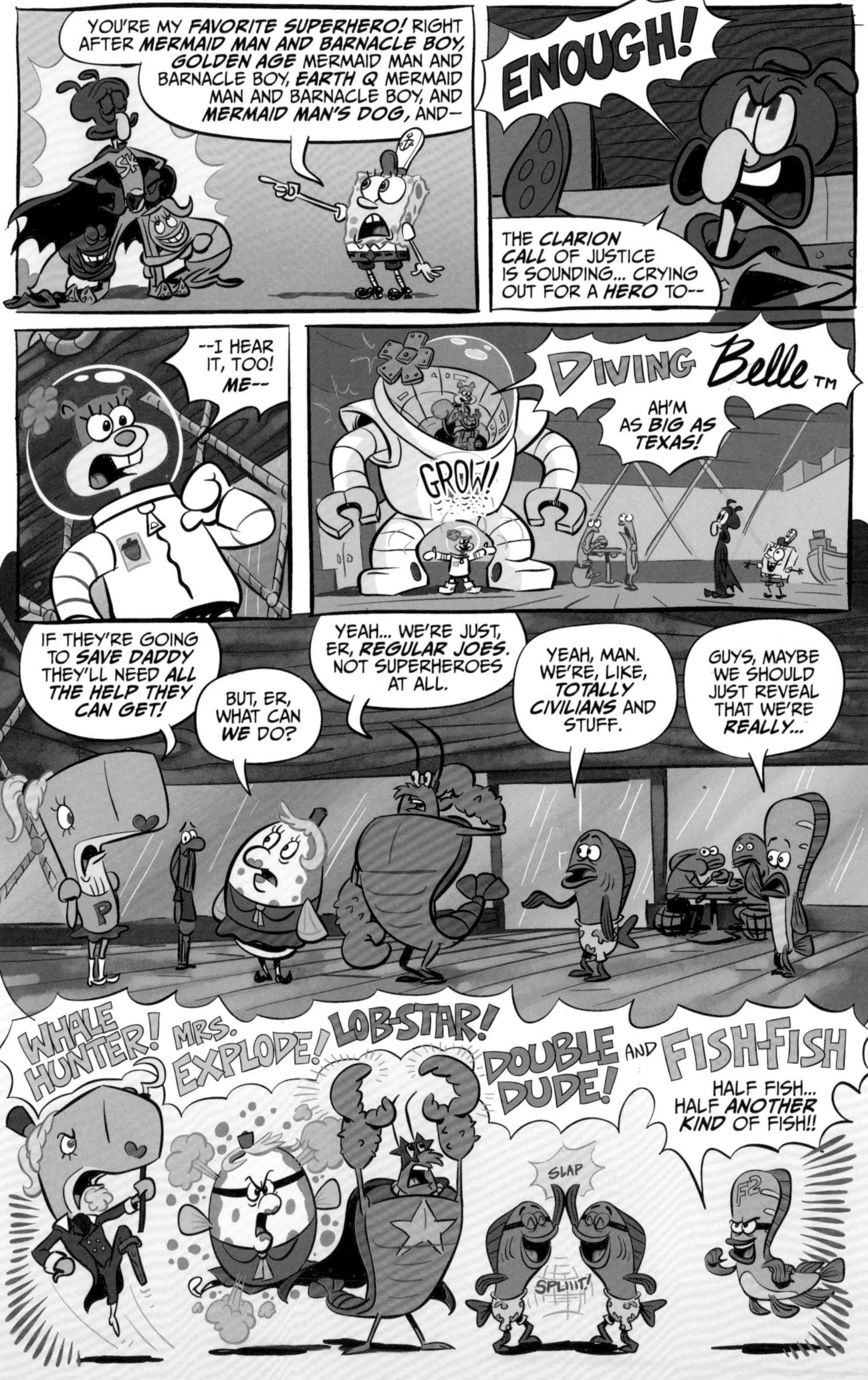
YOU'RE MY FAVORITE SUPERHERO! RIGHT AFTER MERMAID MAN AND BARNACLE BOY, GOLDEN AGE MERMAID MAN AND BARNACLE BOY, EARTH Q MERMAID MAN AND BARNACLE BOY, AND MERMAID MAN'S DOG, AND—
ENOUGH!
THE CLARION CALL OF JUSTICE IS SOUNDING... CRYING OUT FOR A HERO TO--
--I HEAR IT, TOO! ME--
DIVING Belle TM
AH'M AS BIG AS TEXAS!
GROW!
IF THEY'RE GOING TO SAVE DADDY THEY'LL NEED ALL THE HELP THEY CAN GET!
BUT, ER, WHAT CAN WE DO?
YEAH... WE'RE JUST, ER, REGULAR JOES. NOT SUPERHEROES AT ALL.
YEAH, MAN. WE'RE, LIKE, TOTALLY CIVILIANS AND STUFF.
GUYS, MAYBE WE SHOULD JUST REVEAL THAT WE'RE REALLY...
WHALE HUNTER! MRS. EXPLODE! LOB-STAR! DOUBLE DUDE! AND FISH-FISH
HALF FISH... HALF ANOTHER KIND OF FISH!!
SLAP
SPLIIIT!

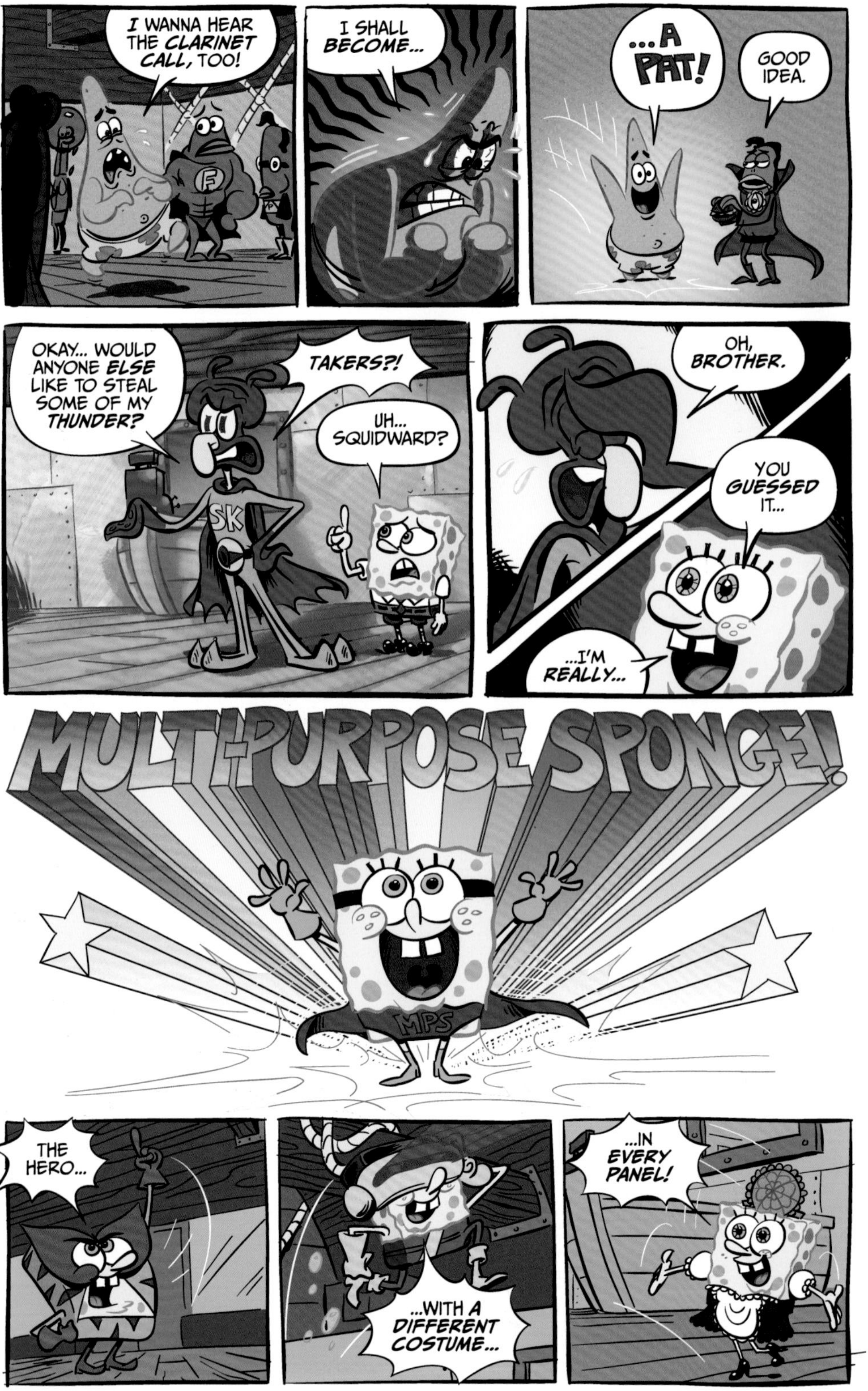
I WANNA HEAR THE CLARINET CALL, TOO!
I SHALL BECOME...
...A PAT!
GOOD IDEA.
OKAY... WOULD ANYONE ELSE LIKE TO STEAL SOME OF MY THUNDER?
TAKERS?!
UH... SQUIDWARD?
OH, BROTHER.
YOU GUESSED IT...
...I'M REALLY...
MULTI-PURPOSE SPONGE!
MPS
THE HERO...
...WITH A DIFFERENT COSTUME...
...IN EVERY PANEL!

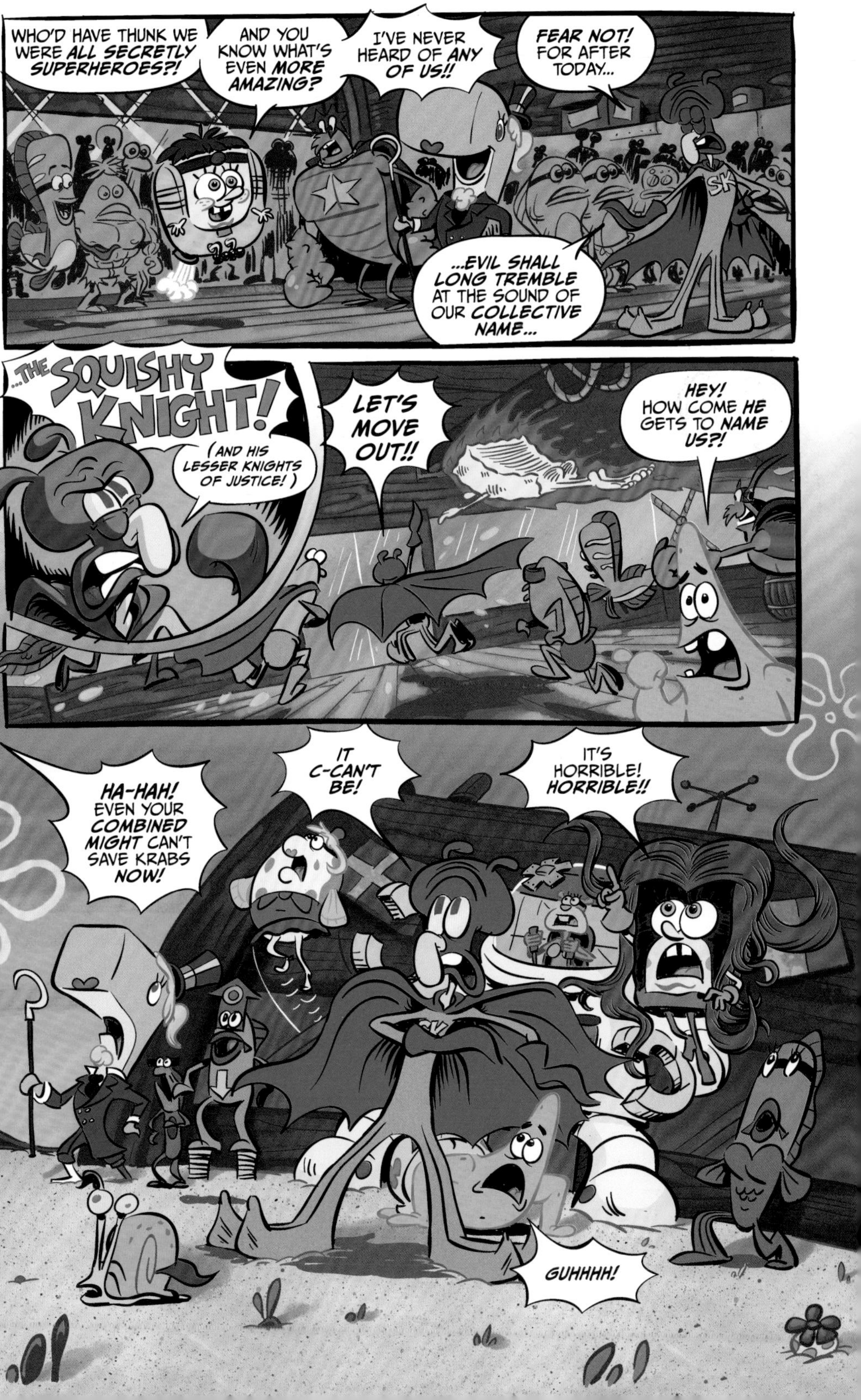
WHO'D HAVE THUNK WE WERE ALL SECRETLY SUPERHEROES?!
AND YOU KNOW WHAT'S EVEN MORE AMAZING?
I'VE NEVER HEARD OF ANY OF US!!
FEAR NOT! FOR AFTER TODAY...
...EVIL SHALL LONG TREMBLE AT THE SOUND OF OUR COLLECTIVE NAME...
...THE SQUISHY KNIGHT!
(AND HIS LESSER KNIGHTS OF JUSTICE!)
LET'S MOVE OUT!!
HEY! HOW COME HE GETS TO NAME US?!
HA-HAH! EVEN YOUR COMBINED MIGHT CAN'T SAVE KRABS NOW!
IT C-CAN'T BE!
IT'S HORRIBLE! HORRIBLE!!
GUHHHH!

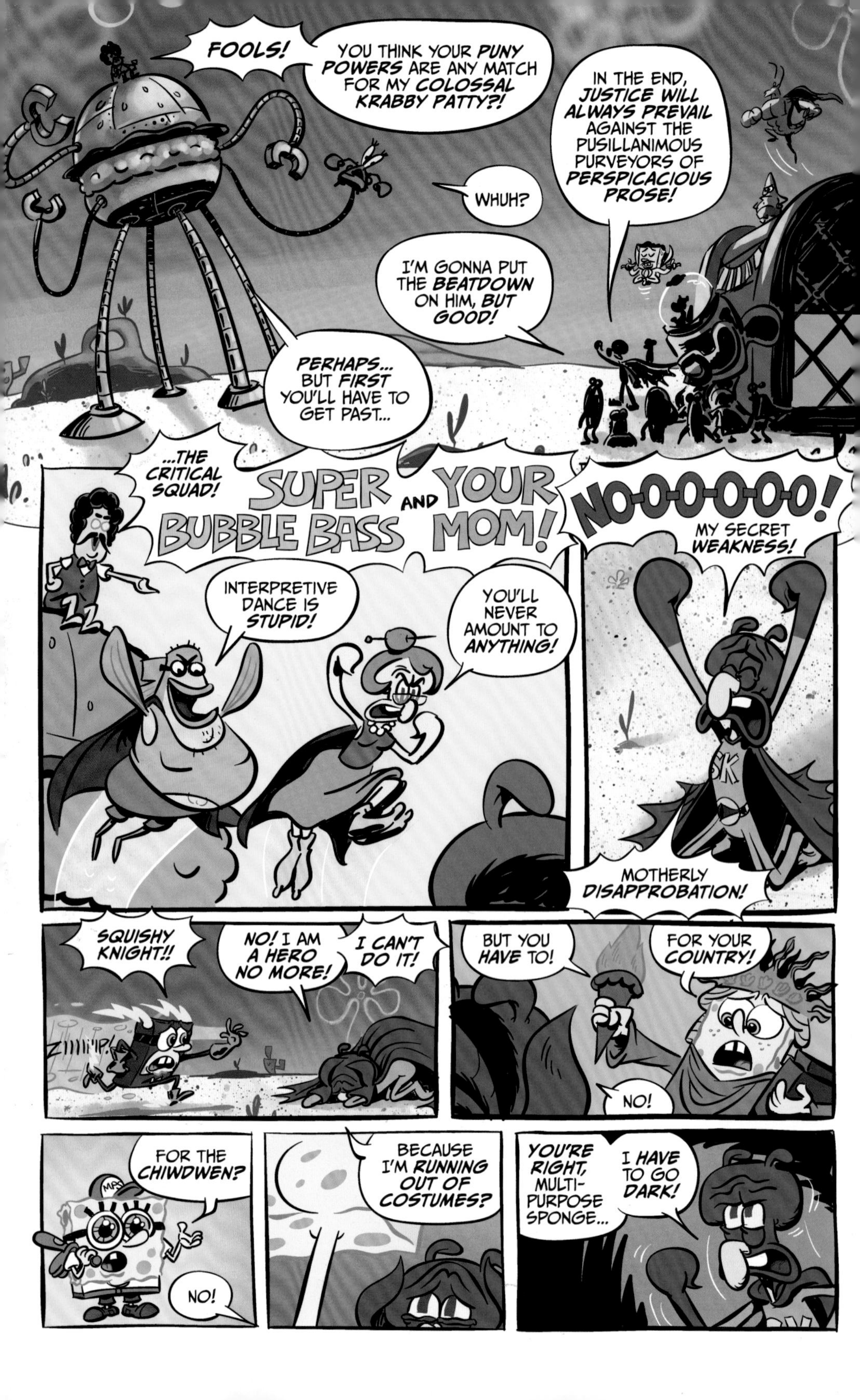
FOOLS!
YOU THINK YOUR PUNY POWERS ARE ANY MATCH FOR MY COLOSSAL KRABBY PATTY?!
IN THE END, JUSTICE WILL ALWAYS PREVAIL AGAINST THE PUSILLANIMOUS PURVEYORS OF PERSPICACIOUS PROSE!
WHUH?
I'M GONNA PUT THE BEATDOWN ON HIM, BUT GOOD!
PERHAPS... BUT FIRST YOU'LL HAVE TO GET PAST...
...THE CRITICAL SQUAD!
SUPER BUBBLE BASS AND YOUR MOM!
INTERPRETIVE DANCE IS STUPID!
YOU'LL NEVER AMOUNT TO ANYTHING!
NO-O-O-O-O-O!
MY SECRET WEAKNESS!
MOTHERLY DISAPPROBATION!
SQUISHY KNIGHT!!
ZIIIIIP!
NO! I AM A HERO NO MORE!
I CAN'T DO IT!
BUT YOU HAVE TO!
FOR YOUR COUNTRY!
NO!
FOR THE CHIWDWEN?
NO!
BECAUSE I'M RUNNING OUT OF COSTUMES?
YOU'RE RIGHT, MULTI-PURPOSE SPONGE...
I HAVE TO GO DARK!

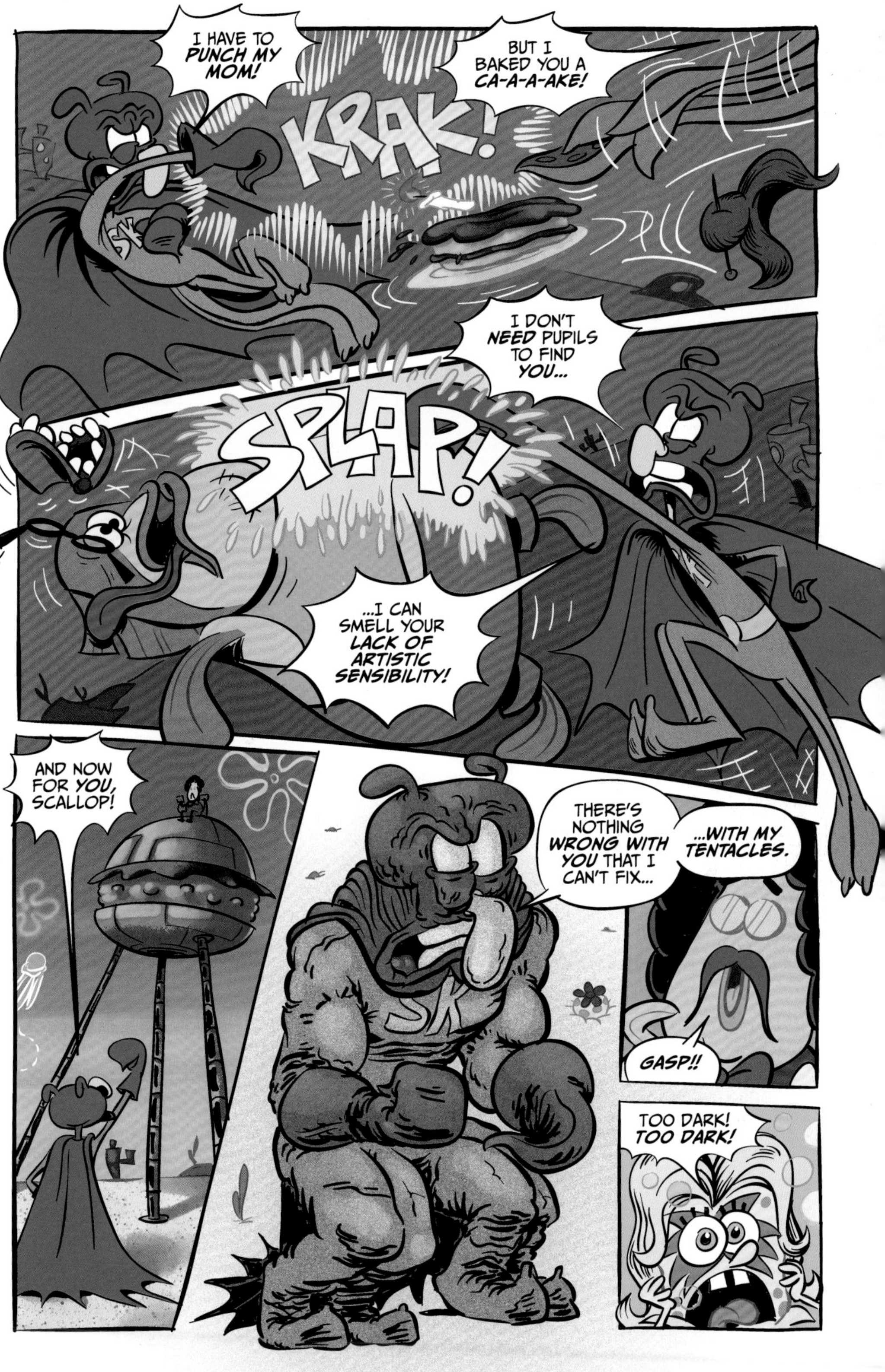
I HAVE TO PUNCH MY MOM!
BUT I BAKED YOU A CA-A-A-AKE!
KRAK!
I DON'T NEED PUPILS TO FIND YOU...
SPLAP!
...I CAN SMELL YOUR LACK OF ARTISTIC SENSIBILITY!
AND NOW FOR YOU, SCALLOP!
THERE'S NOTHING WRONG WITH YOU THAT I CAN'T FIX...
...WITH MY TENTACLES.
GASP!!
TOO DARK! TOO DARK!

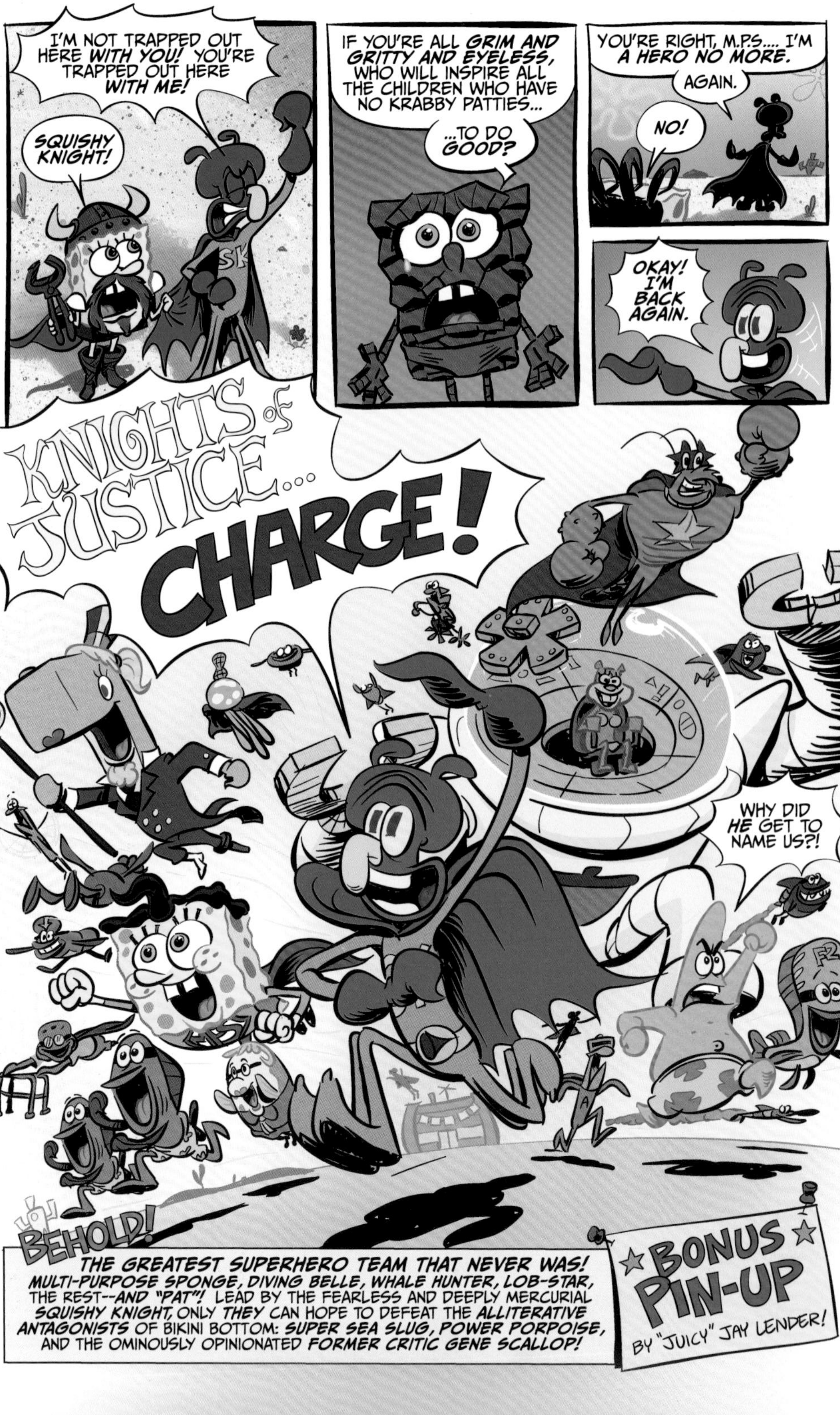
I'M NOT TRAPPED OUT HERE WITH YOU! YOU'RE TRAPPED OUT HERE WITH ME!
SQUISHY KNIGHT!
IF YOU'RE ALL GRIM AND GRITTY AND EYELESS, WHO WILL INSPIRE ALL THE CHILDREN WHO HAVE NO KRABBY PATTIES...
...TO DO GOOD?
YOU'RE RIGHT, M.P.S.... I'M A HERO NO MORE.
AGAIN.
NO!
OKAY! I'M BACK AGAIN.
KNIGHTS of JUSTICE... CHARGE!
WHY DID HE GET TO NAME US?!
BEHOLD!
THE GREATEST SUPERHERO TEAM THAT NEVER WAS! MULTI-PURPOSE SPONGE, DIVING BELLE, WHALE HUNTER, LOB-STAR, THE REST--AND "PAT"! LEAD BY THE FEARLESS AND DEEPLY MERCURIAL SQUISHY KNIGHT, ONLY THEY CAN HOPE TO DEFEAT THE ALLITERATIVE ANTAGONISTS OF BIKINI BOTTOM: SUPER SEA SLUG, POWER PORPOISE, AND THE OMINOUSLY OPINIONATED FORMER CRITIC GENE SCALLOP!
BONUS PIN-UP
BY "JUICY" JAY LENDER!

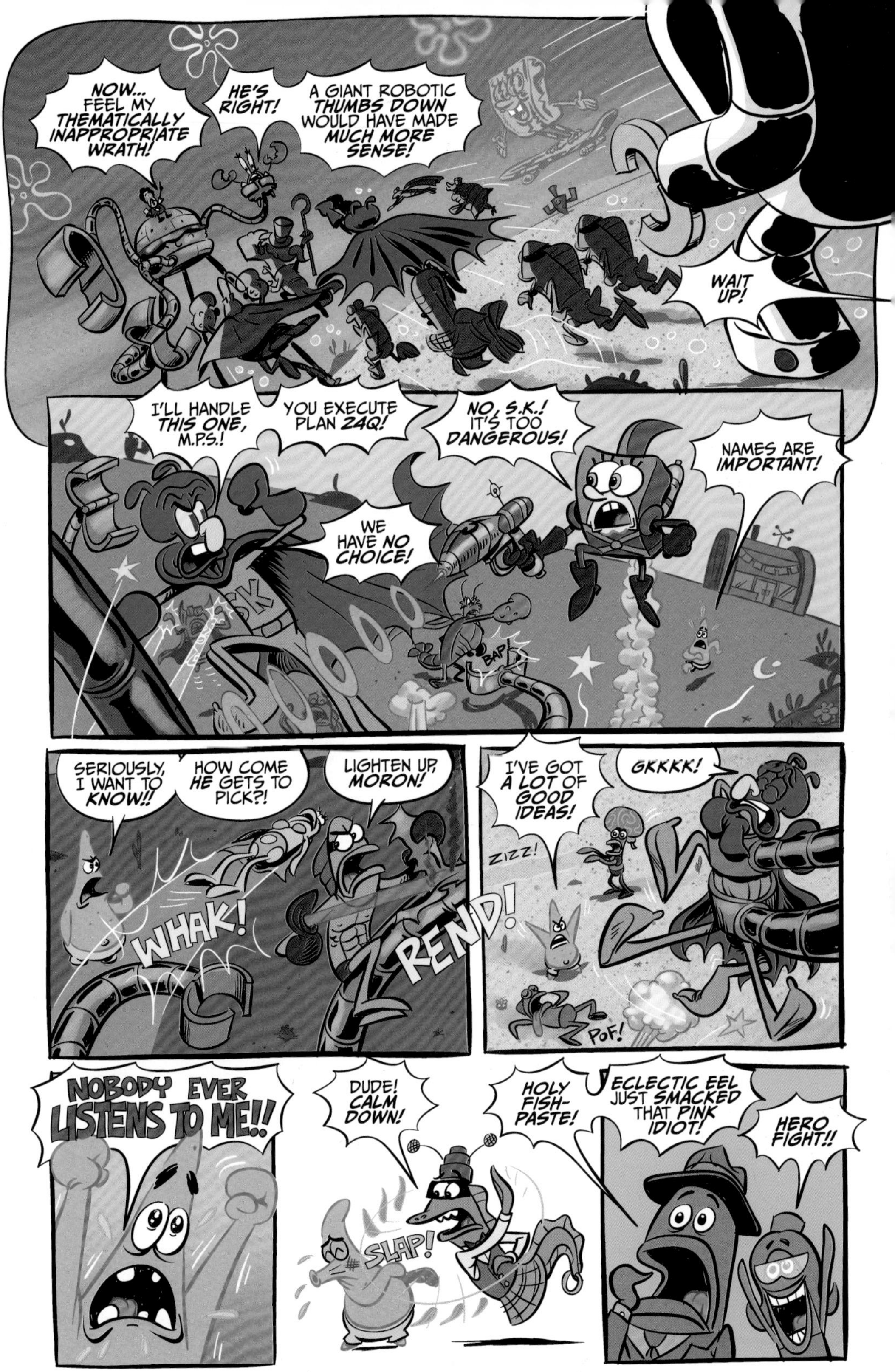
NOW... FEEL MY THEMATICALLY INAPPROPRIATE WRATH!
HE'S RIGHT!
A GIANT ROBOTIC THUMBS DOWN WOULD HAVE MADE MUCH MORE SENSE!
WAIT UP!
I'LL HANDLE THIS ONE, M.P.S.!
YOU EXECUTE PLAN 24Q!
NO, S.K.! IT'S TOO DANGEROUS!
WE HAVE NO CHOICE!
NAMES ARE IMPORTANT!
SK
BAP
SERIOUSLY, I WANT TO KNOW!!
HOW COME HE GETS TO PICK?!
LIGHTEN UP, MORON!
WHAK!
REND!
I'VE GOT A LOT OF GOOD IDEAS!
GKKKK!
ZIZZ!
POF!
NOBODY EVER LISTENS TO ME!!
DUDE! CALM DOWN!
SLAP!
HOLY FISH-PASTE!
ECLECTIC EEL JUST SMACKED THAT PINK IDIOT!
HERO FIGHT!!

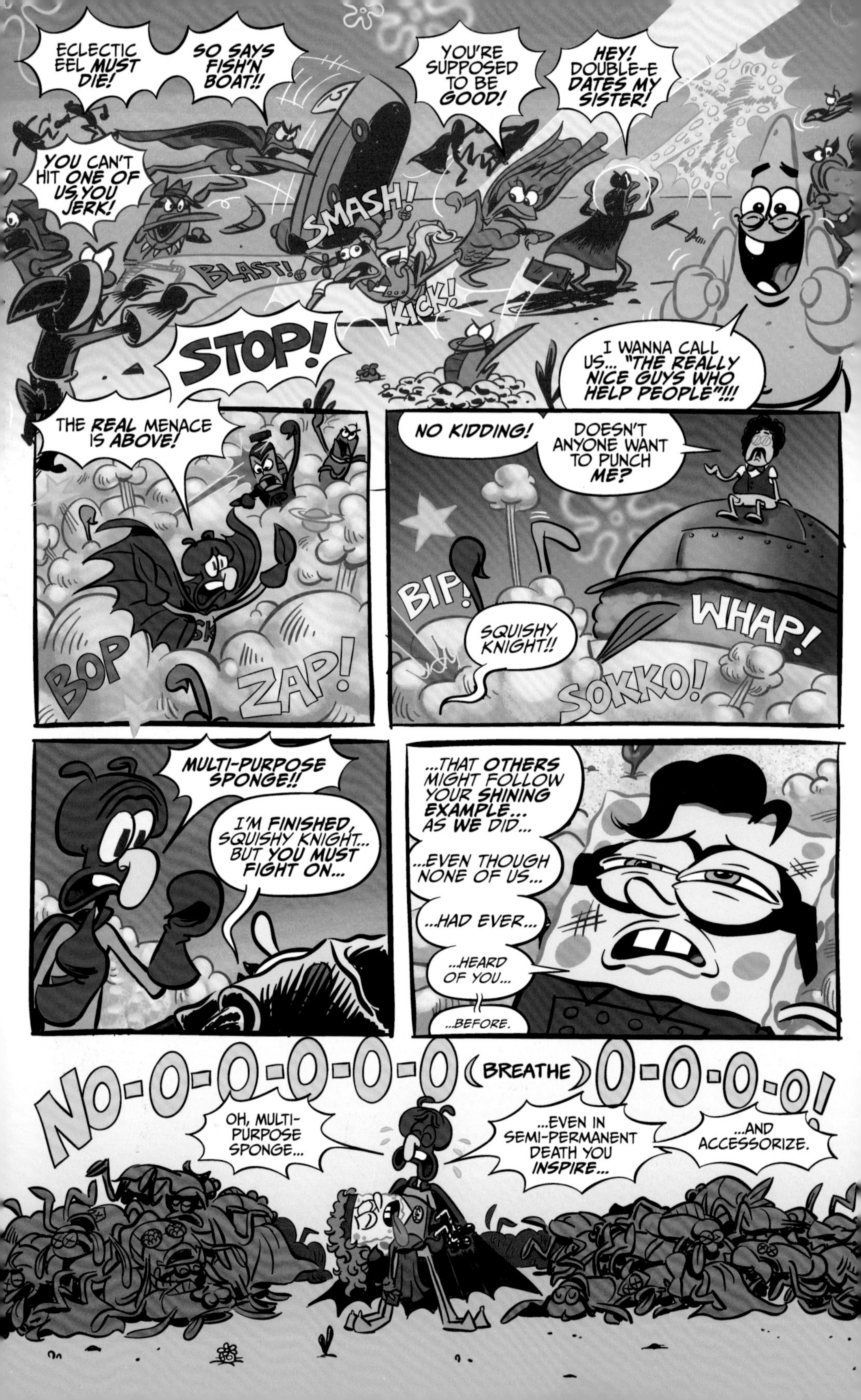
ECLECTIC EEL MUST DIE!
SO SAYS FISH'N BOAT!!
YOU'RE SUPPOSED TO BE GOOD!
HEY! DOUBLE-E DATES MY SISTER!
YOU CAN'T HIT ONE OF US, YOU JERK!
SMASH!
BLAST!
KICK!
STOP!
I WANNA CALL US... "THE REALLY NICE GUYS WHO HELP PEOPLE"!!!
THE REAL MENACE IS ABOVE!
BOP
ZAP!
NO KIDDING!
DOESN'T ANYONE WANT TO PUNCH ME?
BIP!
SQUISHY KNIGHT!!
WHAP!
SOKKO!
MULTI-PURPOSE SPONGE!!
I'M FINISHED, SQUISHY KNIGHT... BUT YOU MUST FIGHT ON...
...THAT OTHERS MIGHT FOLLOW YOUR SHINING EXAMPLE... AS WE DID...
...EVEN THOUGH NONE OF US...
...HAD EVER...
...HEARD OF YOU...
...BEFORE.
NO-O-O-O-O-O-O (BREATHE) O-O-O-O!
OH, MULTI-PURPOSE SPONGE...
...EVEN IN SEMI-PERMANENT DEATH YOU INSPIRE...
...AND ACCESSORIZE.

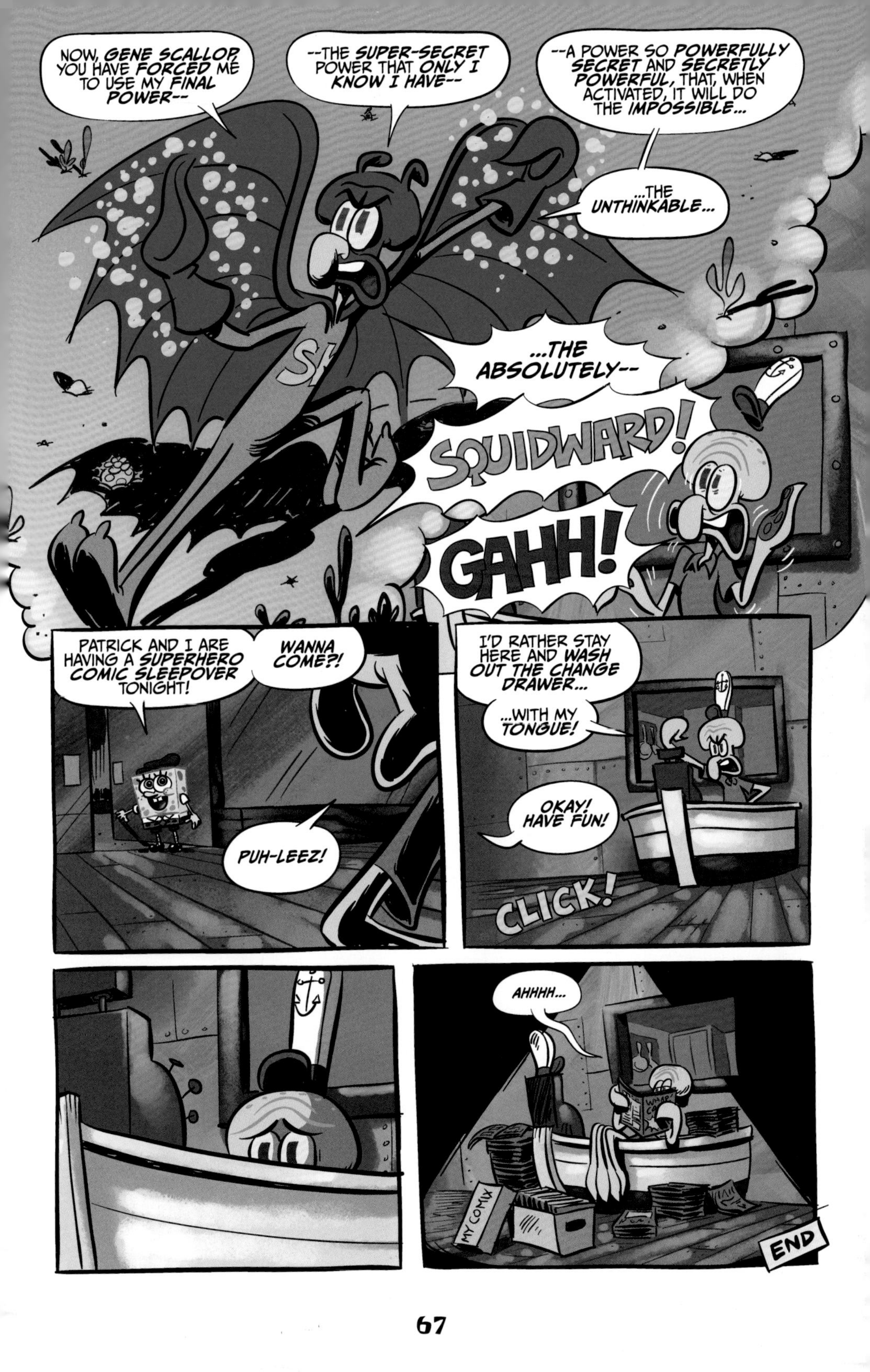

NOW, GENE SCALLOP, YOU HAVE FORCED ME TO USE MY FINAL POWER--
--THE SUPER-SECRET POWER THAT ONLY I KNOW I HAVE--
--A POWER SO POWERFULLY SECRET AND SECRETLY POWERFUL, THAT, WHEN ACTIVATED, IT WILL DO THE IMPOSSIBLE...
...THE UNTHINKABLE...
...THE ABSOLUTELY--
SQUIDWARD!
GAHH!
PATRICK AND I ARE HAVING A SUPERHERO COMIC SLEEPOVER TONIGHT!
WANNA COME?!
PUH-LEEZ!
I'D RATHER STAY HERE AND WASH OUT THE CHANGE DRAWER...
...WITH MY TONGUE!
OKAY! HAVE FUN!
CLICK!
AHHHH...
MY COMIX
END

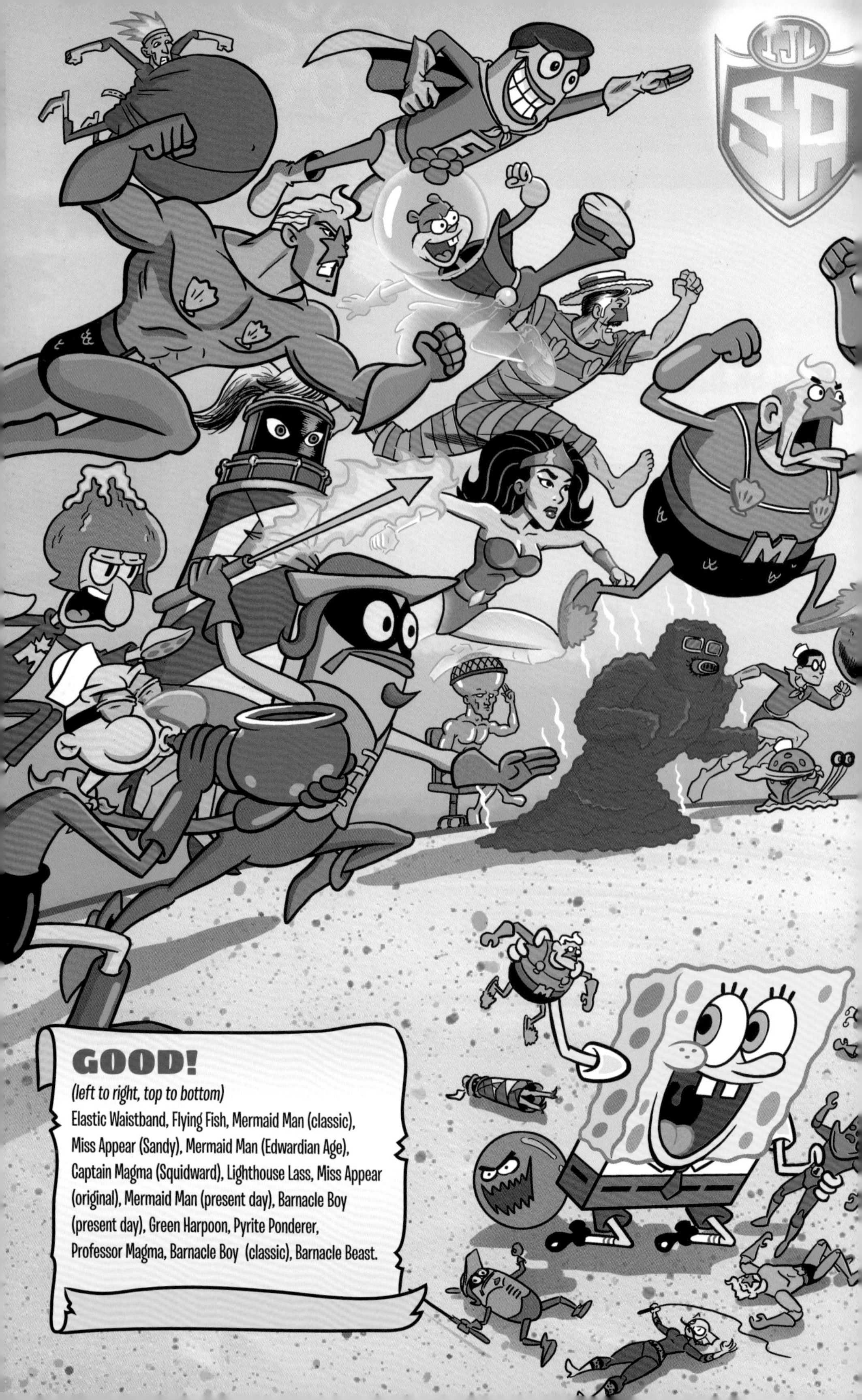

GOOD!

(left to right, top to bottom)

Elastic Waistband, Flying Fish, Mermaid Man (classic), Miss Appear (Sandy), Mermaid Man (Edwardian Age), Captain Magma (Squidward), Lighthouse Lass, Miss Appear (original), Mermaid Man (present day), Barnacle Boy (present day), Green Harpoon, Pyrite Ponderer, Professor Magma, Barnacle Boy (classic), Barnacle Beast.

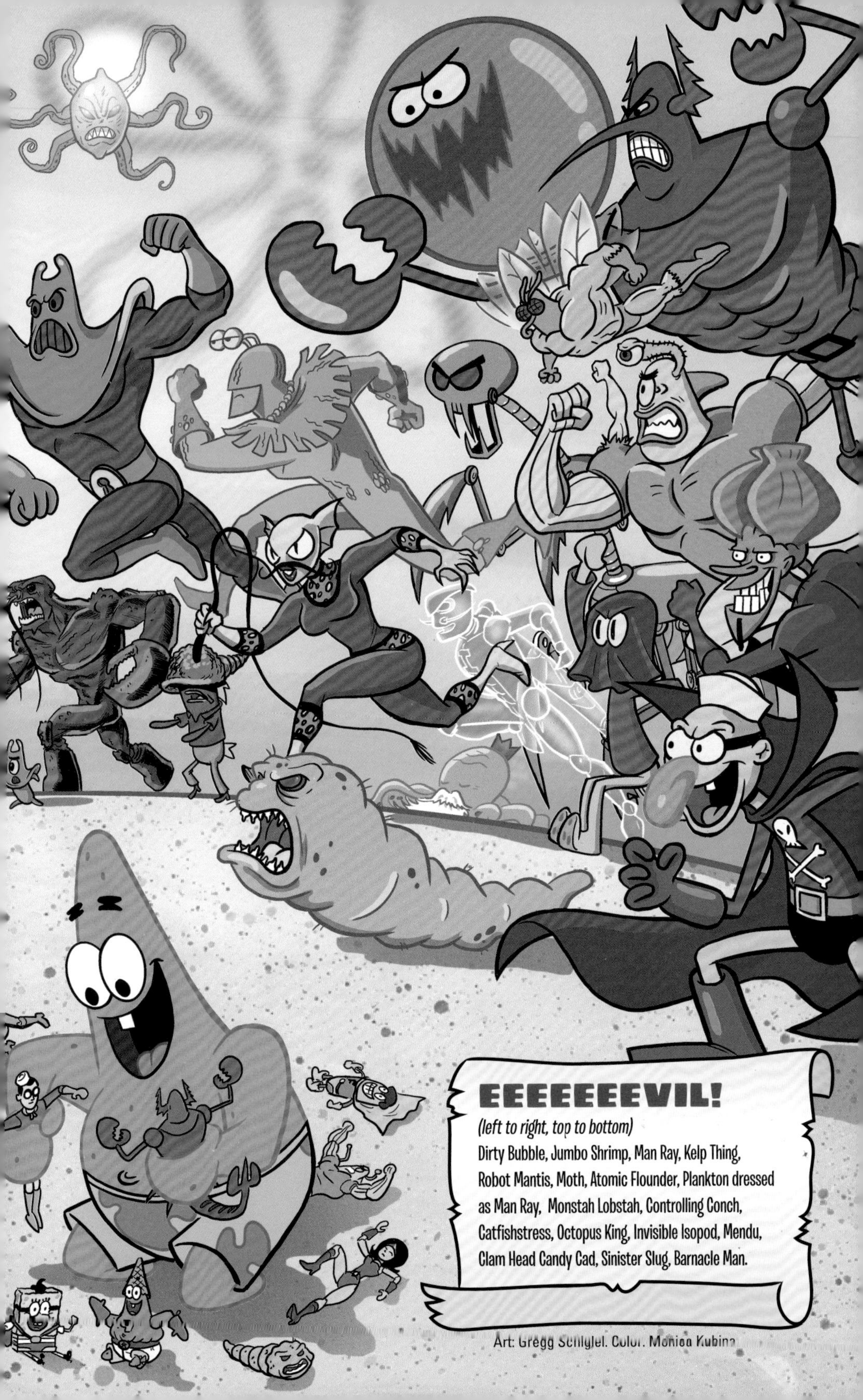

EEEEEEEEVIL!

(left to right, top to bottom)

Dirty Bubble, Jumbo Shrimp, Man Ray, Kelp Thing, Robot Mantis, Moth, Atomic Flounder, Plankton dressed as Man Ray, Monstah Lobstah, Controlling Conch, Catfishstress, Octopus King, Invisible Isopod, Mendu, Clam Head Candy Cad, Sinister Slug, Barnacle Man.

Art: Gregg Schigiel. Color: Monica Kubina

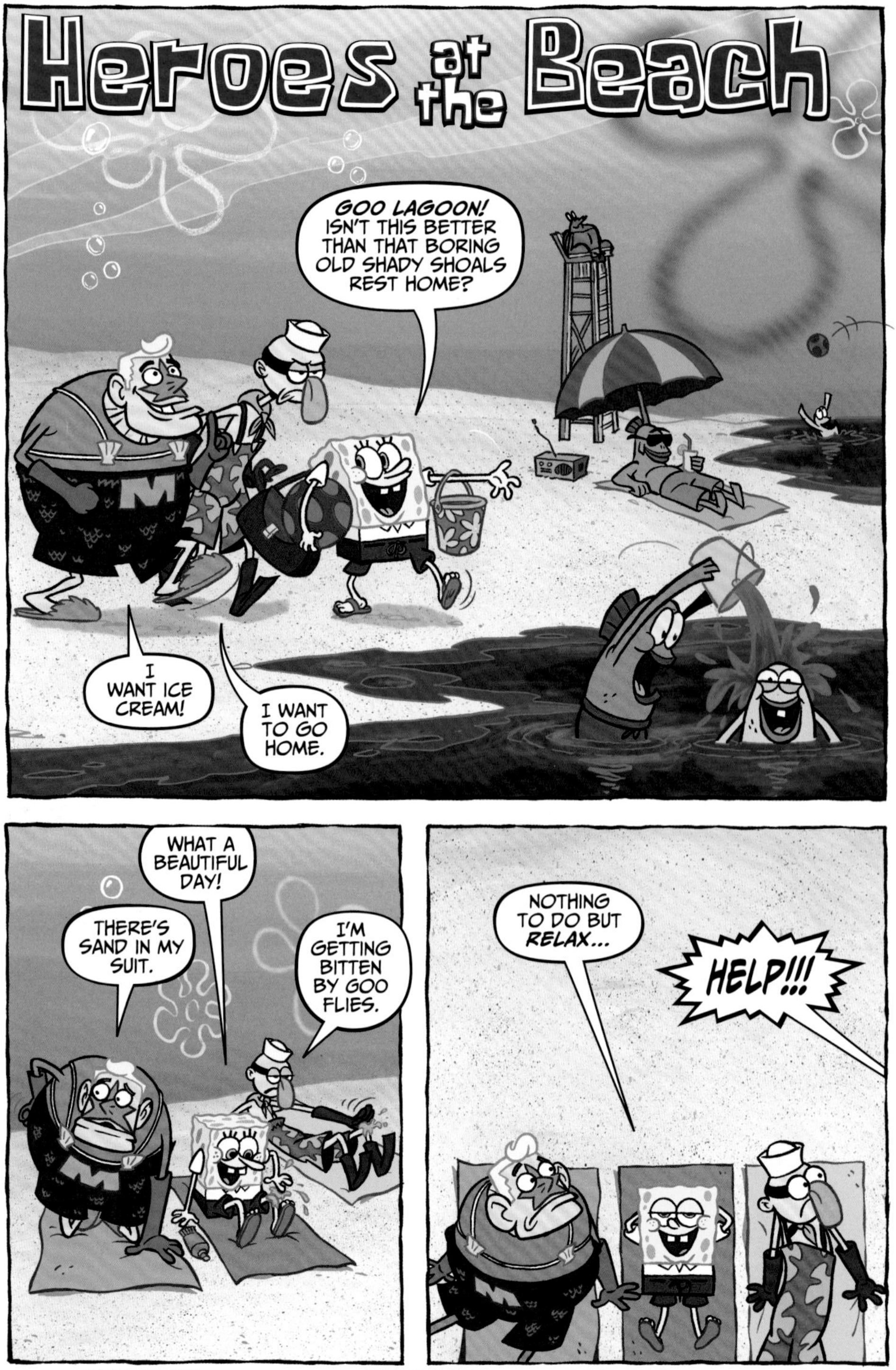
Heroes at the Beach
GOO LAGOON! ISN'T THIS BETTER THAN THAT BORING OLD SHADY SHOALS REST HOME?
I WANT ICE CREAM!
I WANT TO GO HOME.
WHAT A BEAUTIFUL DAY!
THERE'S SAND IN MY SUIT.
I'M GETTING BITTEN BY GOO FLIES.
NOTHING TO DO BUT RELAX...
HELP!!!

STORY: DAVID LEWMAN PENCILS AND INKS: VINCE DEPORTER COLORS: MOLLY DOLBEN LETTERS: COMICRAFT

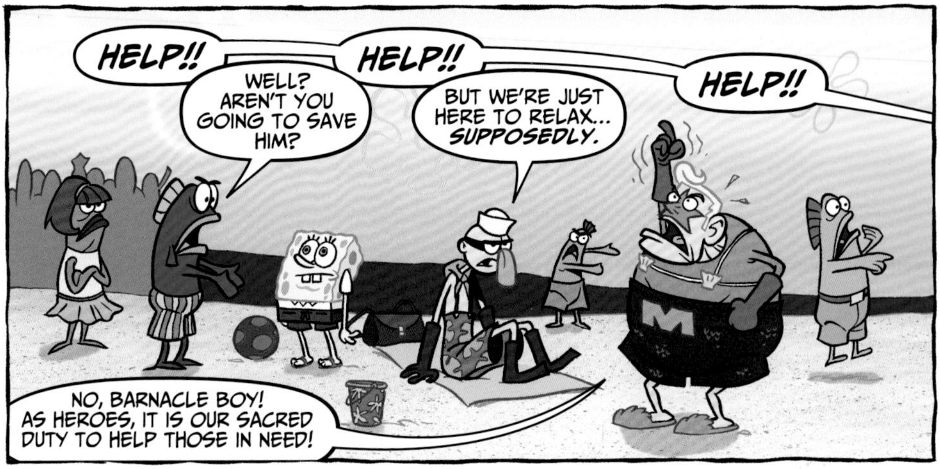
HELP!!
WELL? AREN'T YOU GOING TO SAVE HIM?
HELP!!
BUT WE'RE JUST HERE TO RELAX... SUPPOSEDLY.
HELP!!
NO, BARNACLE BOY! AS HEROES, IT IS OUR SACRED DUTY TO HELP THOSE IN NEED!

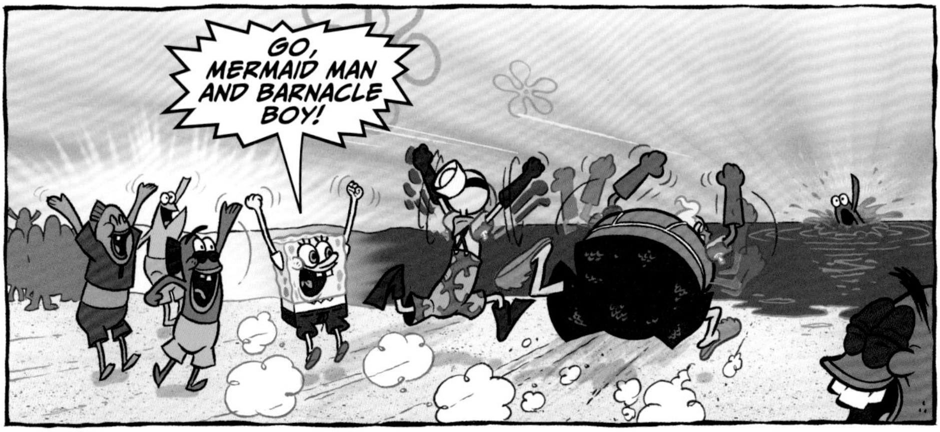
GO, MERMAID MAN AND BARNACLE BOY!

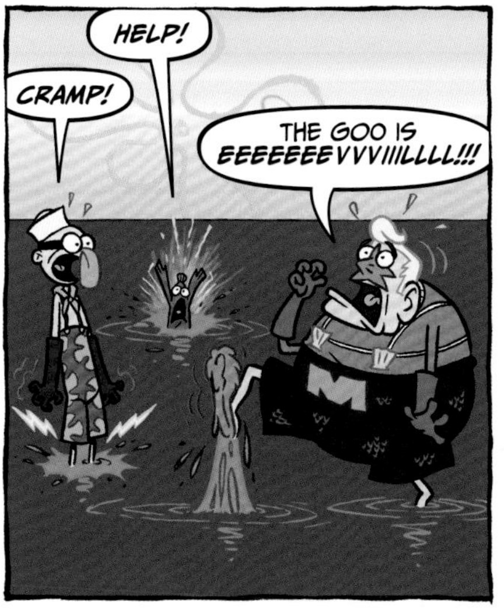
HELP!
CRAMP!
THE GOO IS EEEEEEEVVVIIILLLL!!!

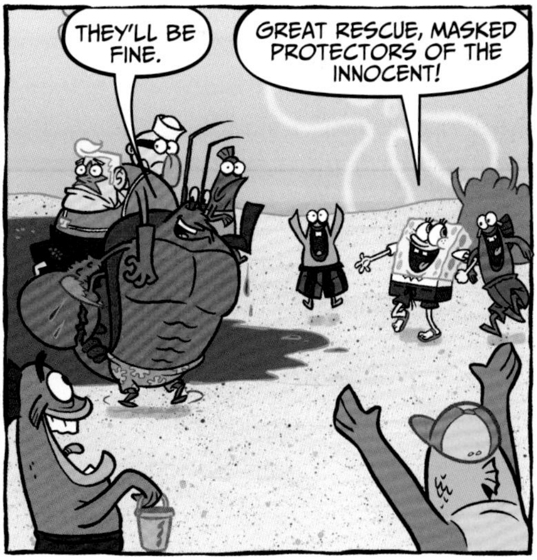
THEY'LL BE FINE.
GREAT RESCUE, MASKED PROTECTORS OF THE INNOCENT!

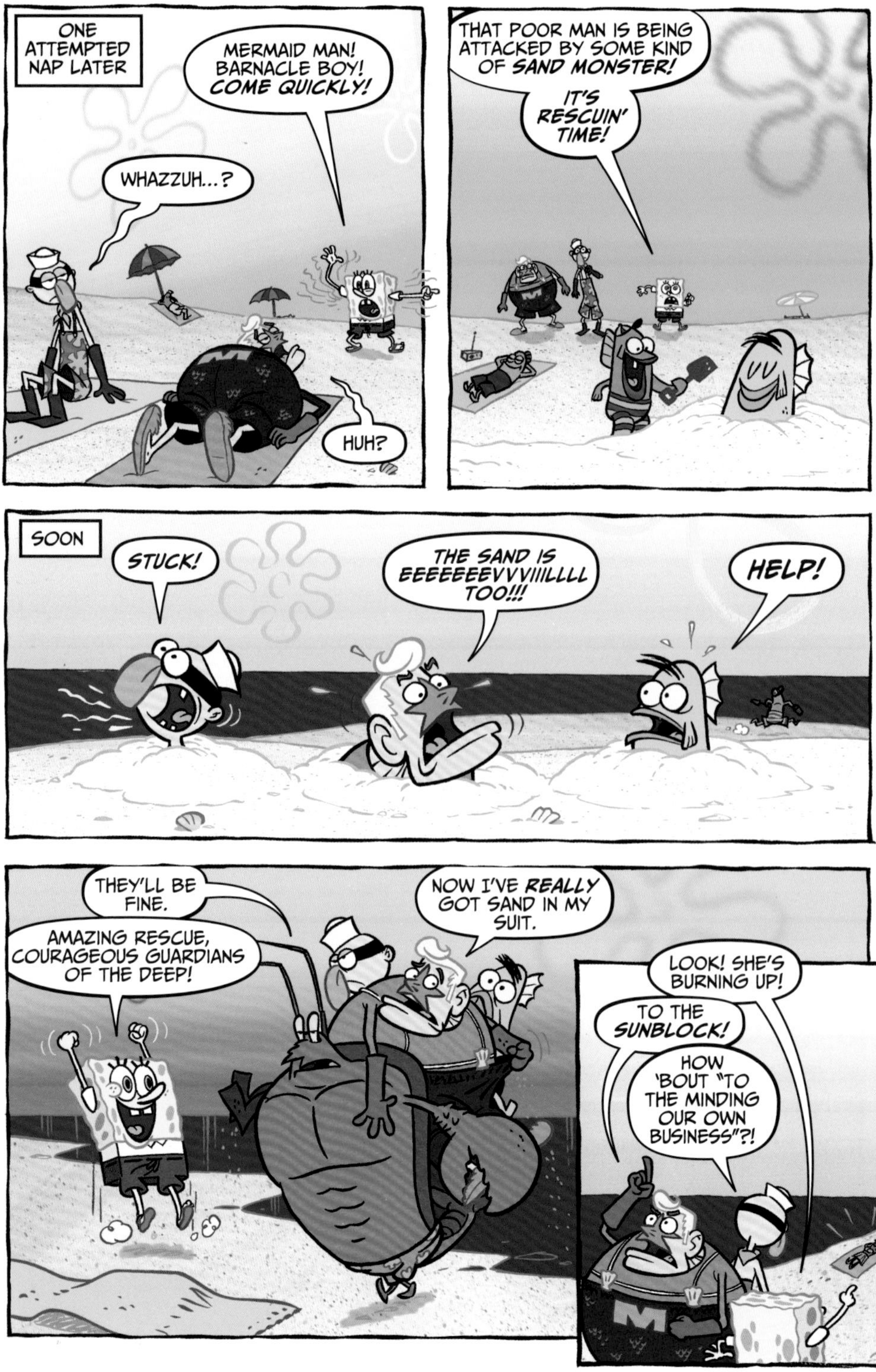
ONE ATTEMPTED NAP LATER
MERMAID MAN! BARNACLE BOY! COME QUICKLY!
WHAZZUH...?
HUH?
THAT POOR MAN IS BEING ATTACKED BY SOME KIND OF SAND MONSTER!
IT'S RESCUIN' TIME!
SOON
STUCK!
THE SAND IS EEEEEEEVVVIIILLLL TOO!!!
HELP!
THEY'LL BE FINE.
AMAZING RESCUE, COURAGEOUS GUARDIANS OF THE DEEP!
NOW I'VE REALLY GOT SAND IN MY SUIT.
LOOK! SHE'S BURNING UP!
TO THE SUNBLOCK!
HOW 'BOUT "TO THE MINDING OUR OWN BUSINESS"?!

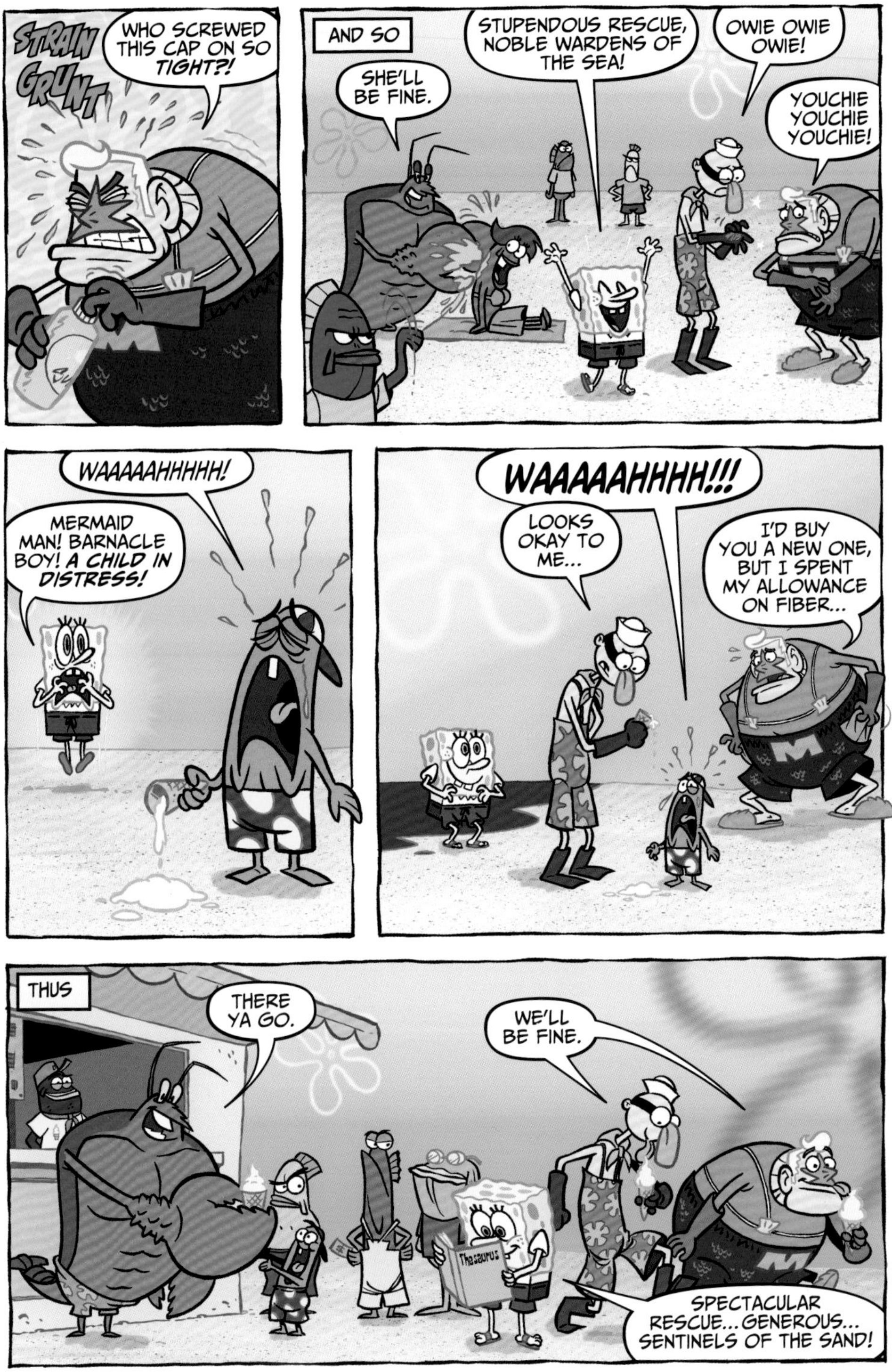
STRAIN
GRUNT
WHO SCREWED THIS CAP ON SO TIGHT?!
AND SO
SHE'LL BE FINE.
STUPENDOUS RESCUE, NOBLE WARDENS OF THE SEA!
OWIE OWIE OWIE!
YOUCHIE YOUCHIE YOUCHIE!
WAAAAAHHHHH!
MERMAID MAN! BARNACLE BOY! A CHILD IN DISTRESS!
WAAAAAHHHH!!!
LOOKS OKAY TO ME...
I'D BUY YOU A NEW ONE, BUT I SPENT MY ALLOWANCE ON FIBER...
THUS
THERE YA GO.
WE'LL BE FINE.
Thesaurus
SPECTACULAR RESCUE... GENEROUS... SENTINELS OF THE SAND!

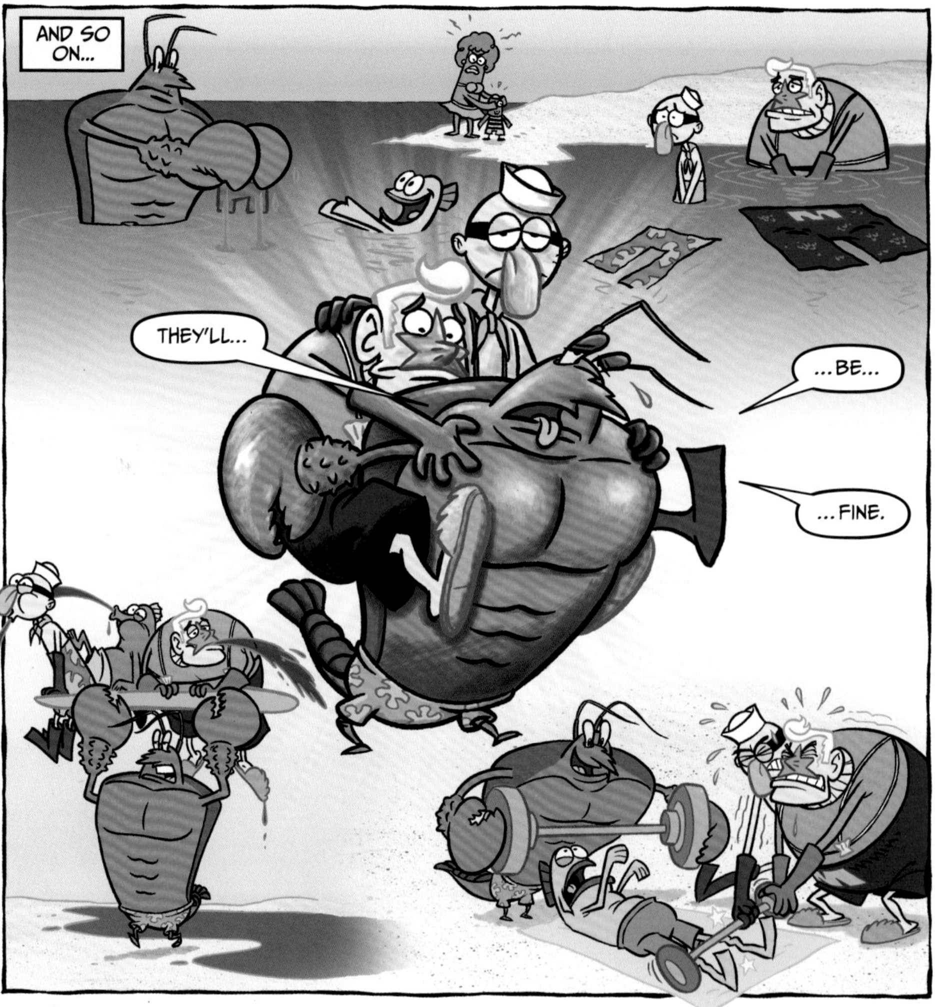
AND SO ON...
THEY'LL...
...BE...
...FINE.

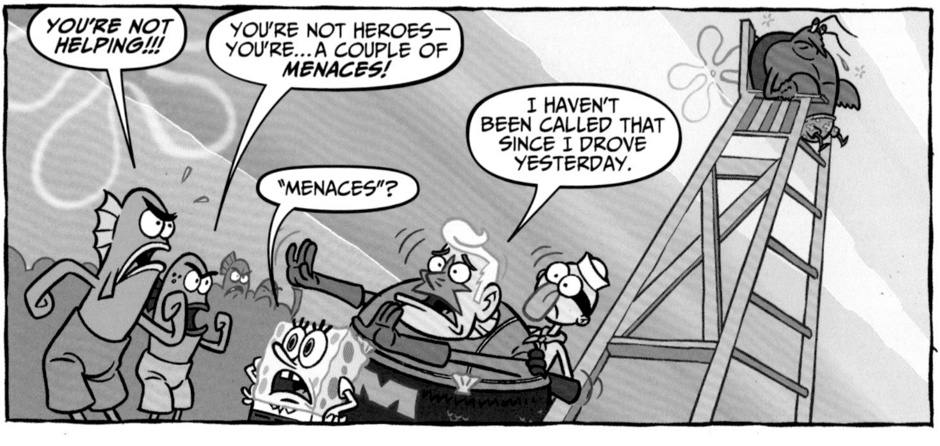
YOU'RE NOT HELPING!!!
YOU'RE NOT HEROES— YOU'RE...A COUPLE OF MENACES!
"MENACES"?
I HAVEN'T BEEN CALLED THAT SINCE I DROVE YESTERDAY.

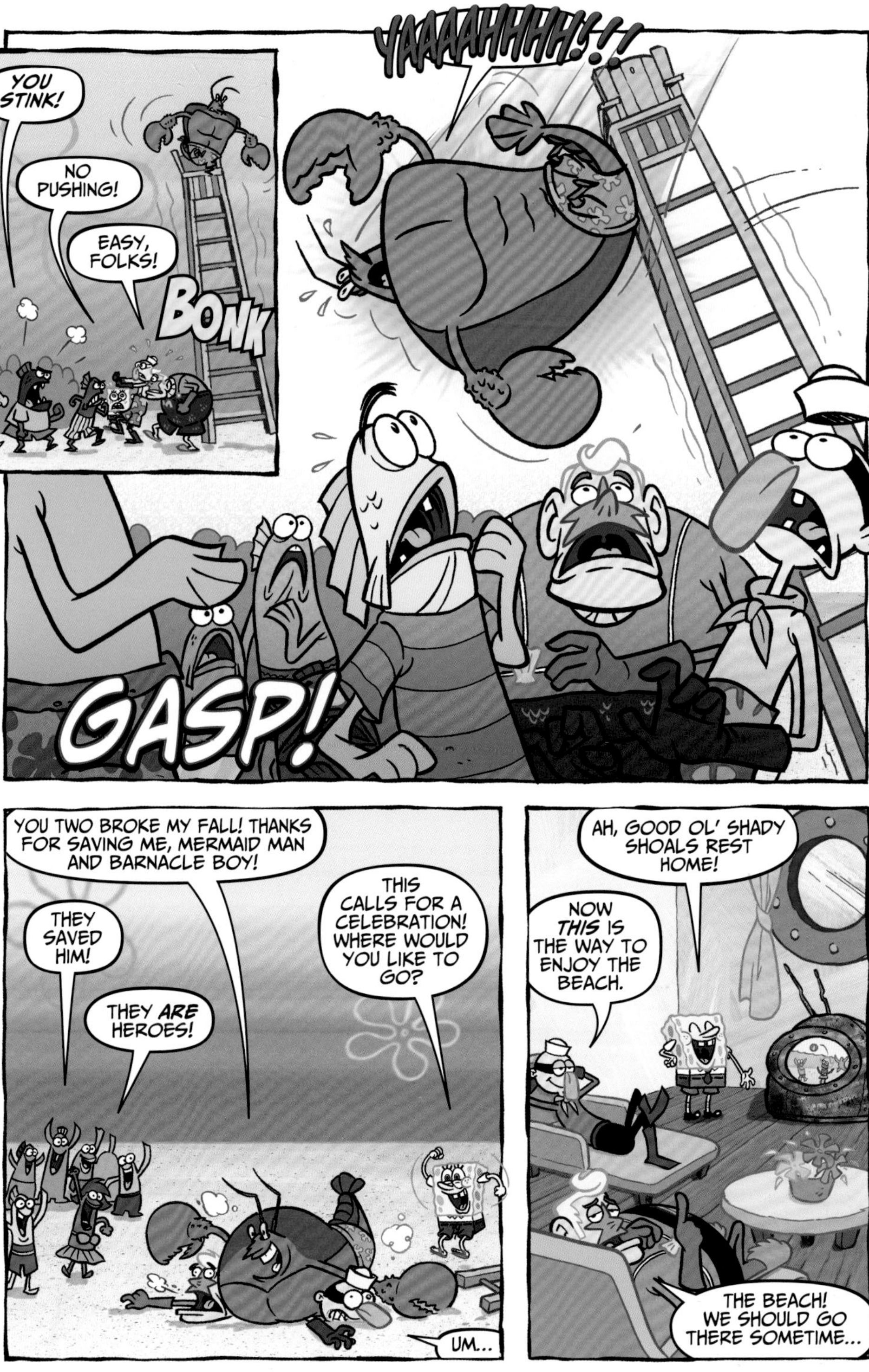
YOU STINK!
NO PUSHING!
EASY, FOLKS!
BONK
YAAAAHHHH!!!
GASP!
YOU TWO BROKE MY FALL! THANKS FOR SAVING ME, MERMAID MAN AND BARNACLE BOY!
THEY SAVED HIM!
THEY ARE HEROES!
THIS CALLS FOR A CELEBRATION! WHERE WOULD YOU LIKE TO GO?
UM...
AH, GOOD OL' SHADY SHOALS REST HOME!
NOW THIS IS THE WAY TO ENJOY THE BEACH.
THE BEACH! WE SHOULD GO THERE SOMETIME...
FINE.

Mermaid Man for
BLËK OF SCANDINAVIA

Barracuda $3

Catfish $3

Half-Gill $3

All three $6

IMPRESS! MYSTIFY! SEDUCE!

Give yourself any look you desire—any time you want!

Now for the first time—through the wonders of the breakthrough substance known locally as BLËK—you can transform your appearance easily and instantly. Turn heads and raise eyebrows every time you enter a room. People will be talking about you after you leave—we guarantee it.

BLËK is a substance so revolutionary it cannot be sold from within the borders of this country. Only here in Scandinavia can BLËK be made available, and only for a limited time.

How do you want to look? Hip? Cool? Psychedelic? Freakalicious? BLËK is an amazing shape-shifting substance specially formulated to mold to your face and features. And don't worry about embarrassing slips. BLËK can only be removed by a trained dermatologist—and even then with extraordinary effort.

BLËK is so lifelike that only someone with 20/80 vision is likely to notice that your new look is artificially applied. Take it from MERMAID MAN—he's not only a customer, he's a paid spokesman.

BLËK comes in a handy aerosol can pumped with extra fluorocarbons for ease of application. Just spray on and mold to the shapes shown here. But move fast! BLËK hardens within microseconds of leaving the container.

Order today using the handy coupon below.

BEGINNING FINNISH

FREE with each order:
Easy step-by-step language guide
BEGINNING FINNISH.

MAIL COUPON TODAY!

*Please allow up to 6-8 months for your order to be processed - - and twice that time to be packaged. Delivery times are additional.

Wear BLËK with complete confidence. You'll be envied and admired. Take it from Mermaid Man and Barnacle Boy. Barnacle Boy is now a lifelong customer, thanks to the adhesive qualities of

Blëk OF SCANDINAVIA

Blëk
OF
SCANDINAVIA

BLËK INTERNATIONAL
Dept. 2360
Scandinavia City, Scandinavia

Why should Scandinavians have all the fun? Yes, I want to change my appearance. Rush me a full canister of BLËK at your earliest convenience.* I understand that if I am not completely satisfied with this product my dissatisfaction will be guaranteed. Check items desired.

RUSH ME THE FOLLOWING ITEMS:
- ☐ Barracuda
- ☐ Catfish
- ☐ Neon Tetra
- ☐ Half-Gill
- ☐ Wear Any Combination

Name ....
Address ....
City ....
State & Zip ....

BLËK OF SCANDINAVIA is not officially affiliated with BLEK Industries, nor is BLËK OF SCANDINAVIA repackaged BLEK or ASTROBLEK. Any similarity in product's appearance or properties such as glowing, vibrating, or ability to be deep-fried and consumed is purely coincidental.

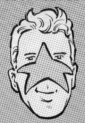

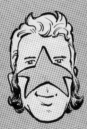

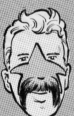

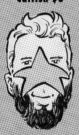

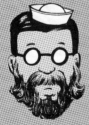

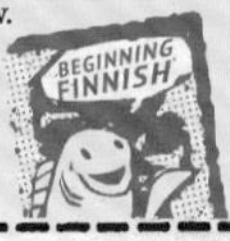

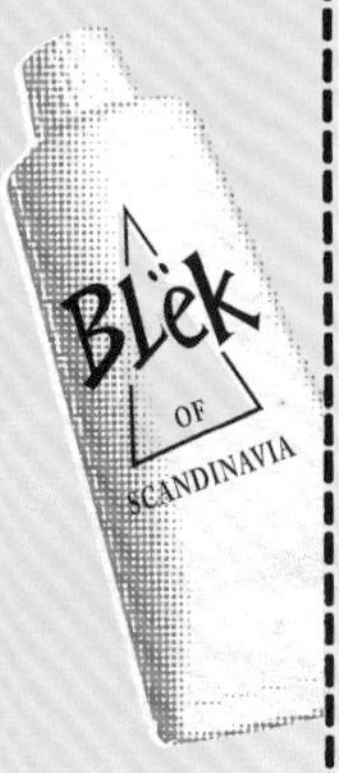

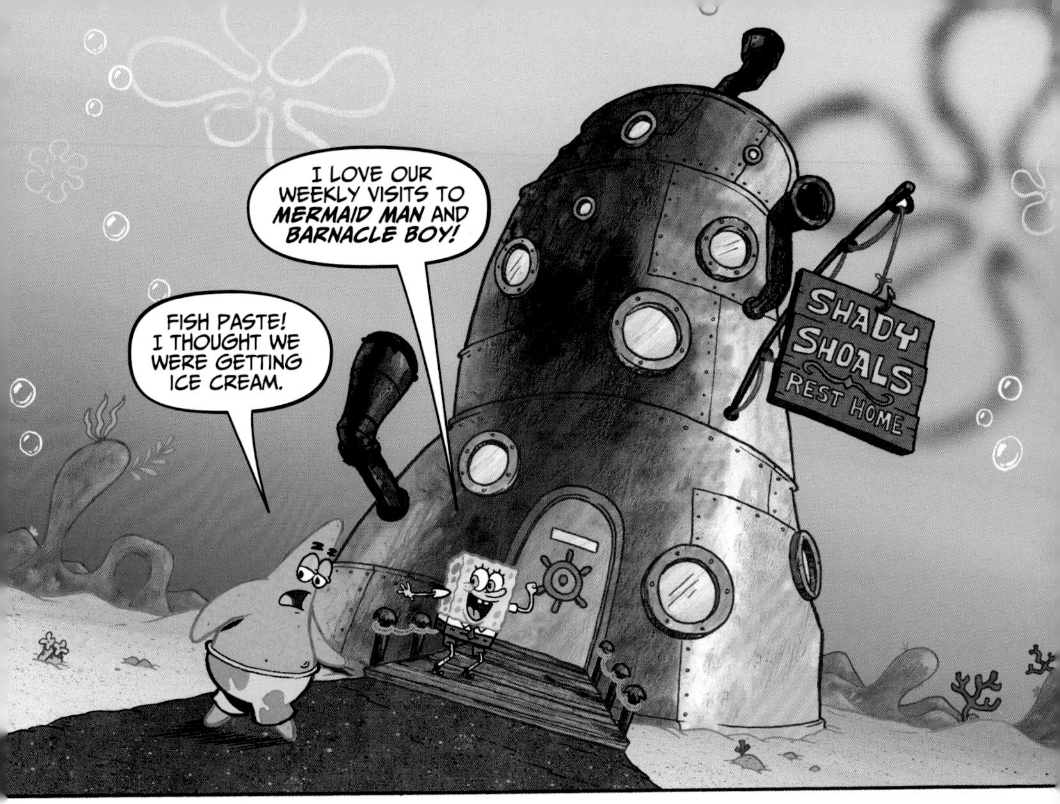
I LOVE OUR WEEKLY VISITS TO *MERMAID MAN* AND *BARNACLE BOY!*
FISH PASTE! I THOUGHT WE WERE GETTING ICE CREAM.
SHADY SHOALS REST HOME

MISSING MAN!

STORY: DAVID LEWMAN PENCILS AND INKS: JACOB CHABOT COLORING: MOLLY DOLBEN LETTERING: COMICRAFT

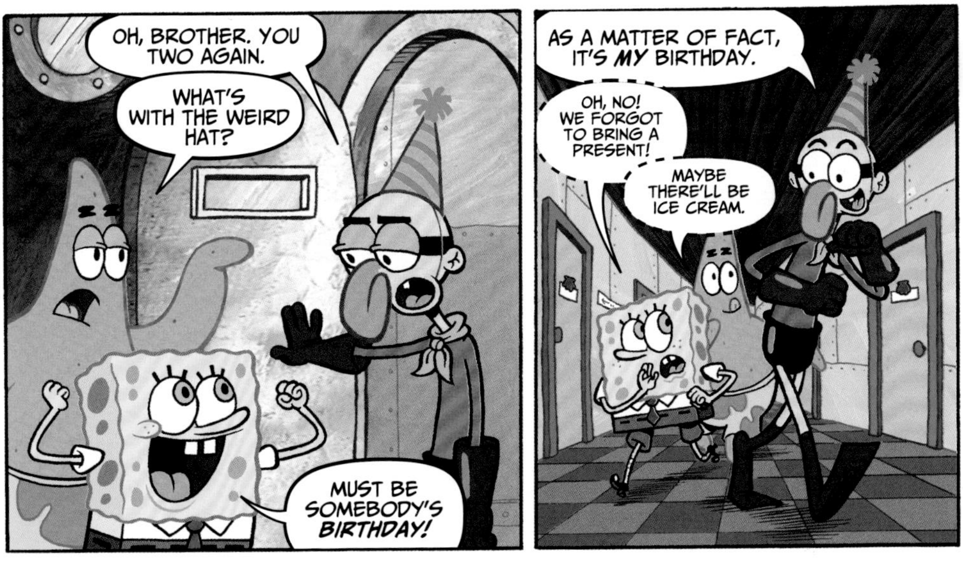
OH, BROTHER. YOU TWO AGAIN.
WHAT'S WITH THE WEIRD HAT?
MUST BE SOMEBODY'S *BIRTHDAY!*
AS A MATTER OF FACT, IT'S *MY* BIRTHDAY.
OH, NO! WE FORGOT TO BRING A PRESENT!
MAYBE THERE'LL BE ICE CREAM.

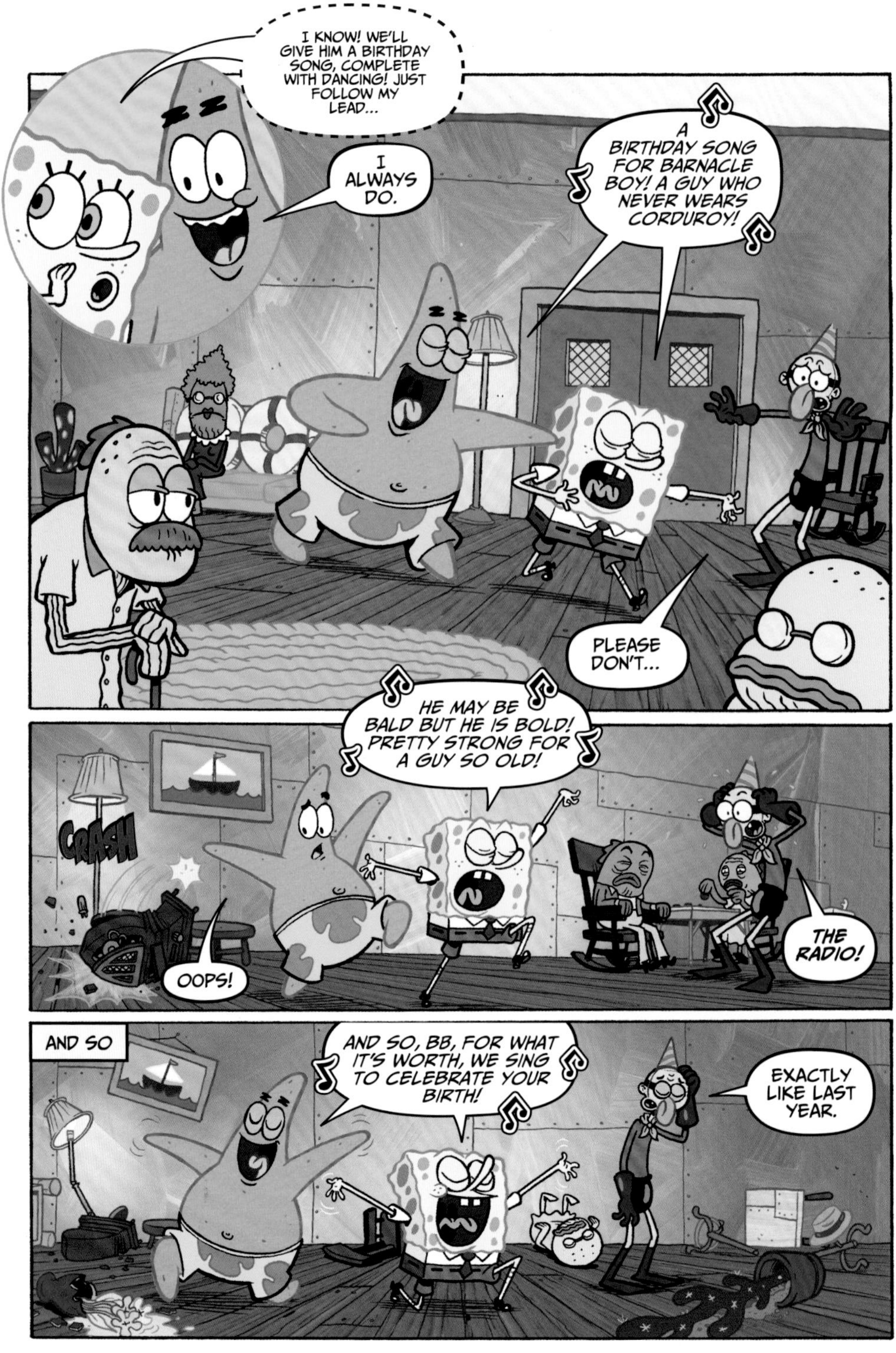

I KNOW! WE'LL GIVE HIM A BIRTHDAY SONG, COMPLETE WITH DANCING! JUST FOLLOW MY LEAD...
I ALWAYS DO.
A BIRTHDAY SONG FOR BARNACLE BOY! A GUY WHO NEVER WEARS CORDUROY!
PLEASE DON'T...
HE MAY BE BALD BUT HE IS BOLD! PRETTY STRONG FOR A GUY SO OLD!
CRASH
OOPS!
THE RADIO!
AND SO
AND SO, BB, FOR WHAT IT'S WORTH, WE SING TO CELEBRATE YOUR BIRTH!
EXACTLY LIKE LAST YEAR.

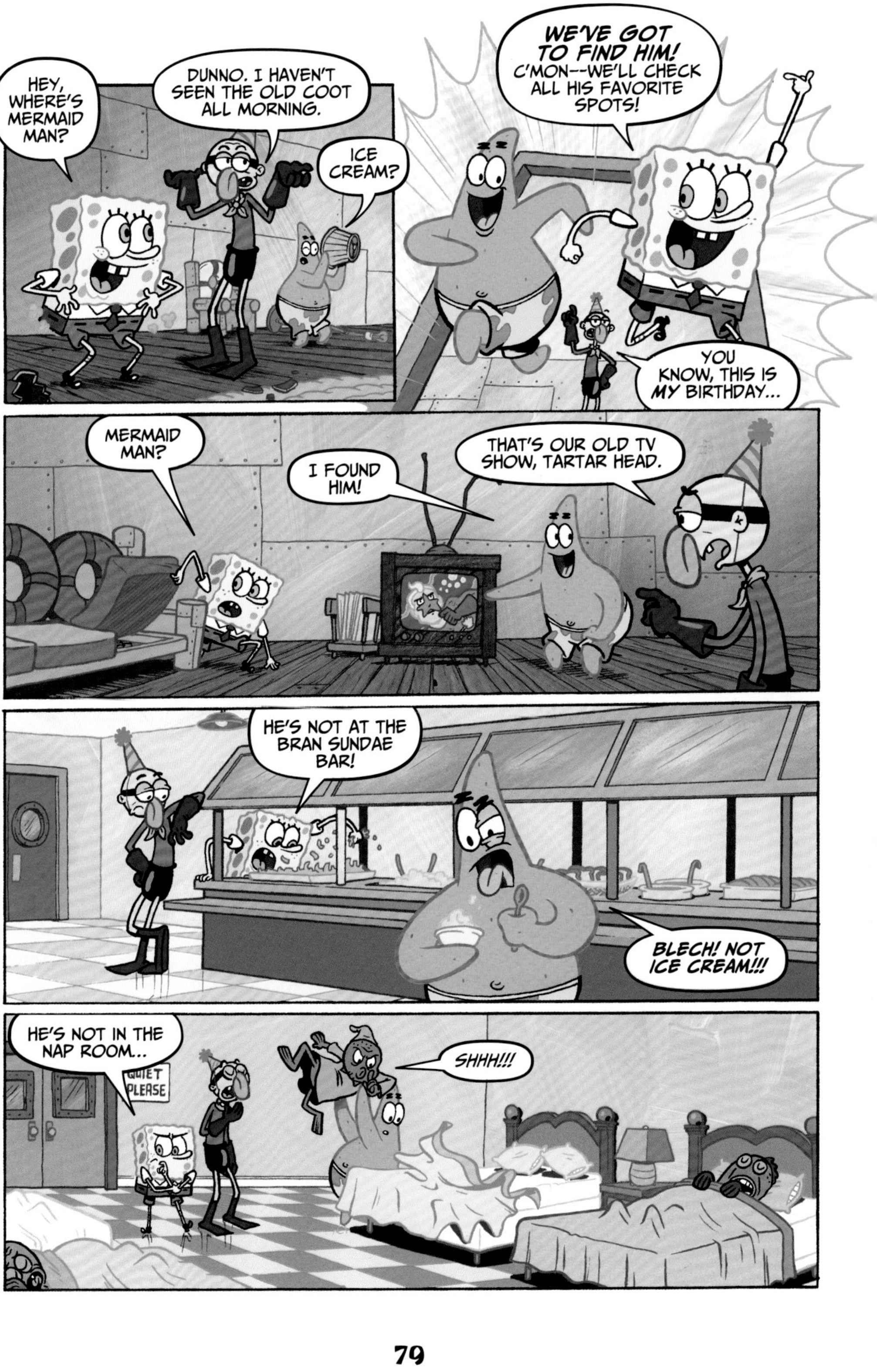
HEY, WHERE'S MERMAID MAN?
DUNNO. I HAVEN'T SEEN THE OLD COOT ALL MORNING.
ICE CREAM?
WE'VE GOT TO FIND HIM! C'MON--WE'LL CHECK ALL HIS FAVORITE SPOTS!
YOU KNOW, THIS IS MY BIRTHDAY...
MERMAID MAN?
I FOUND HIM!
THAT'S OUR OLD TV SHOW, TARTAR HEAD.
HE'S NOT AT THE BRAN SUNDAE BAR!
BLECH! NOT ICE CREAM!!!
HE'S NOT IN THE NAP ROOM...
QUIET PLEASE
SHHH!!!

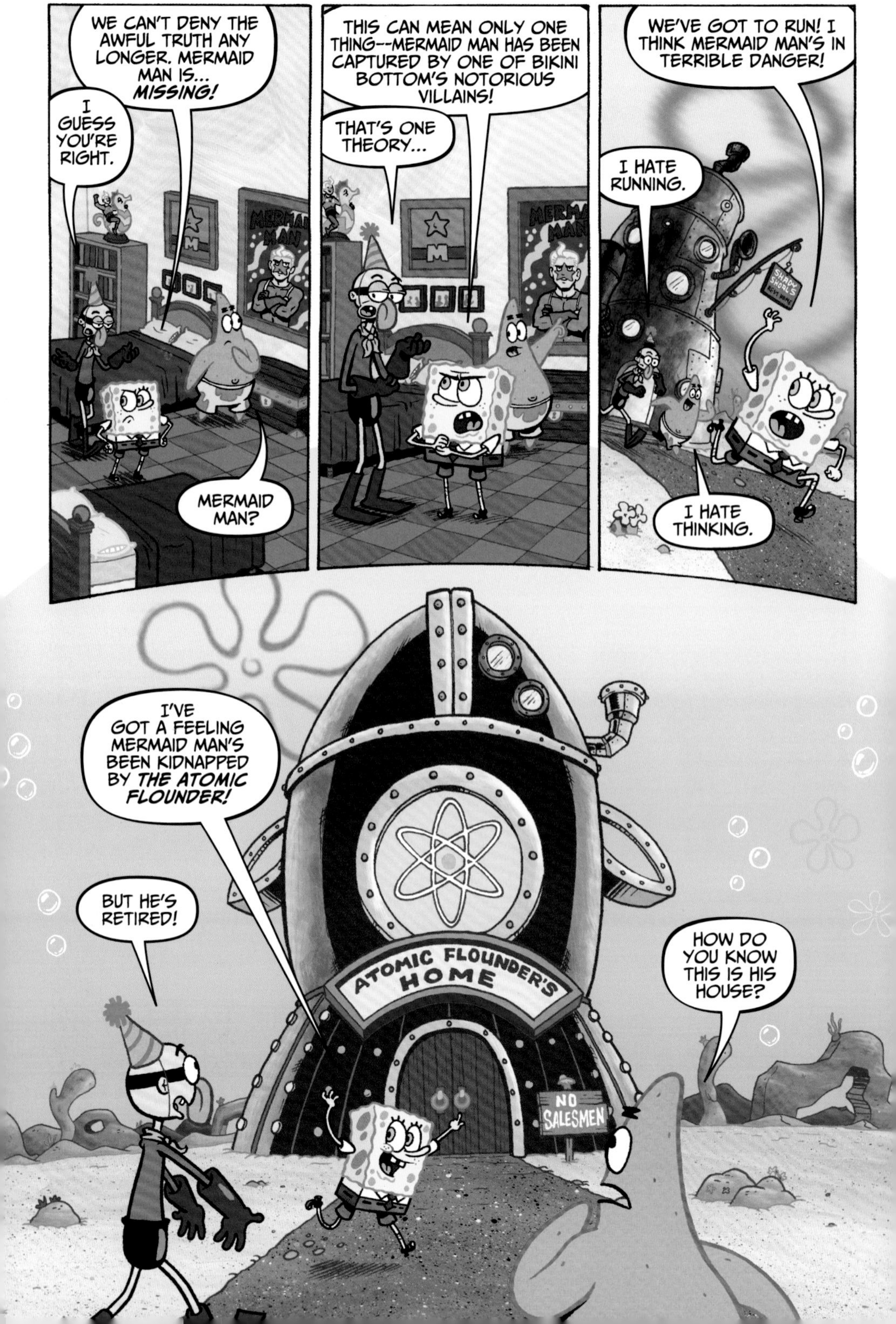
WE CAN'T DENY THE AWFUL TRUTH ANY LONGER. MERMAID MAN IS... *MISSING!*
I GUESS YOU'RE RIGHT.
MERMAID MAN?
THIS CAN MEAN ONLY ONE THING--MERMAID MAN HAS BEEN CAPTURED BY ONE OF BIKINI BOTTOM'S NOTORIOUS VILLAINS!
THAT'S ONE THEORY...
WE'VE GOT TO RUN! I THINK MERMAID MAN'S IN TERRIBLE DANGER!
I HATE RUNNING.
I HATE THINKING.
I'VE GOT A FEELING MERMAID MAN'S BEEN KIDNAPPED BY *THE ATOMIC FLOUNDER!*
BUT HE'S RETIRED!
ATOMIC FLOUNDER'S HOME
HOW DO YOU KNOW THIS IS HIS HOUSE?
NO SALESMEN

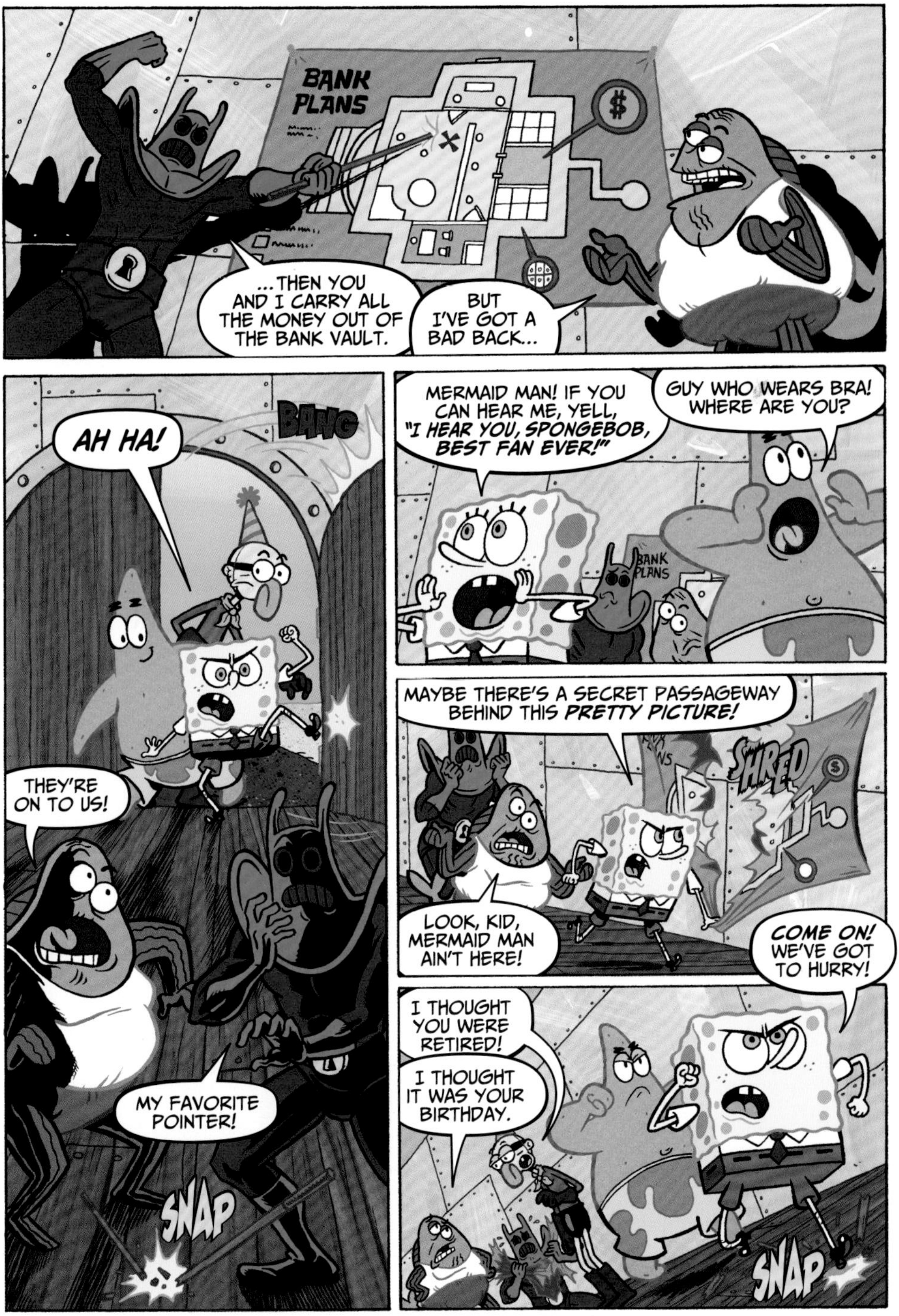
BANK PLANS
...THEN YOU AND I CARRY ALL THE MONEY OUT OF THE BANK VAULT.
BUT I'VE GOT A BAD BACK...
BANG
AH HA!
THEY'RE ON TO US!
MY FAVORITE POINTER!
SNAP
MERMAID MAN! IF YOU CAN HEAR ME, YELL, "I HEAR YOU, SPONGEBOB, BEST FAN EVER!"
GUY WHO WEARS BRA! WHERE ARE YOU?
BANK PLANS
MAYBE THERE'S A SECRET PASSAGEWAY BEHIND THIS PRETTY PICTURE!
SHRED
LOOK, KID, MERMAID MAN AIN'T HERE!
COME ON! WE'VE GOT TO HURRY!
I THOUGHT YOU WERE RETIRED!
I THOUGHT IT WAS YOUR BIRTHDAY.
SNAP

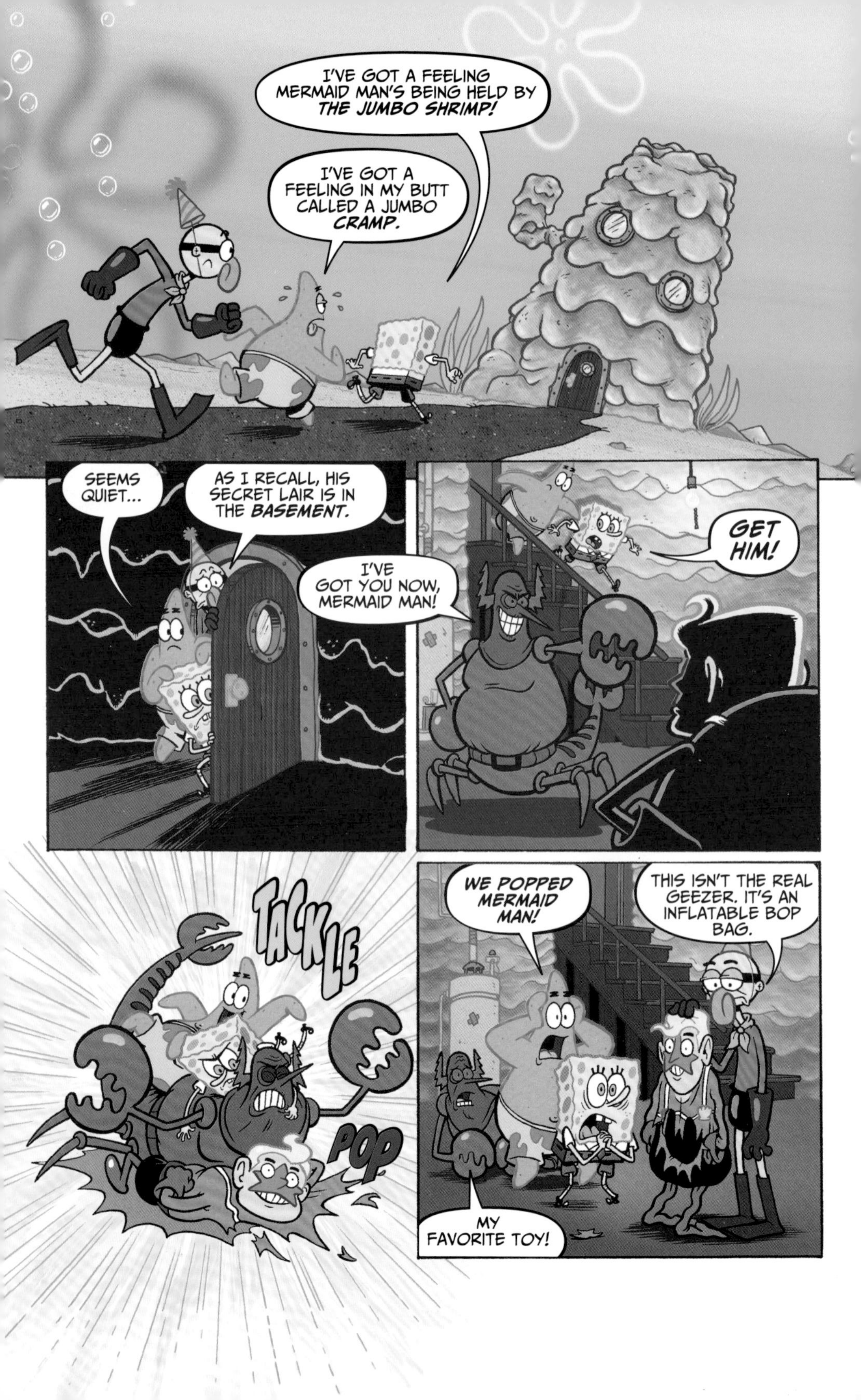

I'VE GOT A FEELING MERMAID MAN'S BEING HELD BY ***THE JUMBO SHRIMP!***
I'VE GOT A FEELING IN MY BUTT CALLED A JUMBO ***CRAMP.***
SEEMS QUIET...
AS I RECALL, HIS SECRET LAIR IS IN THE ***BASEMENT.***
I'VE GOT YOU NOW, MERMAID MAN!
GET HIM!
TACKLE
POP
WE POPPED MERMAID MAN!
THIS ISN'T THE REAL GEEZER. IT'S AN INFLATABLE BOP BAG.
MY FAVORITE TOY!

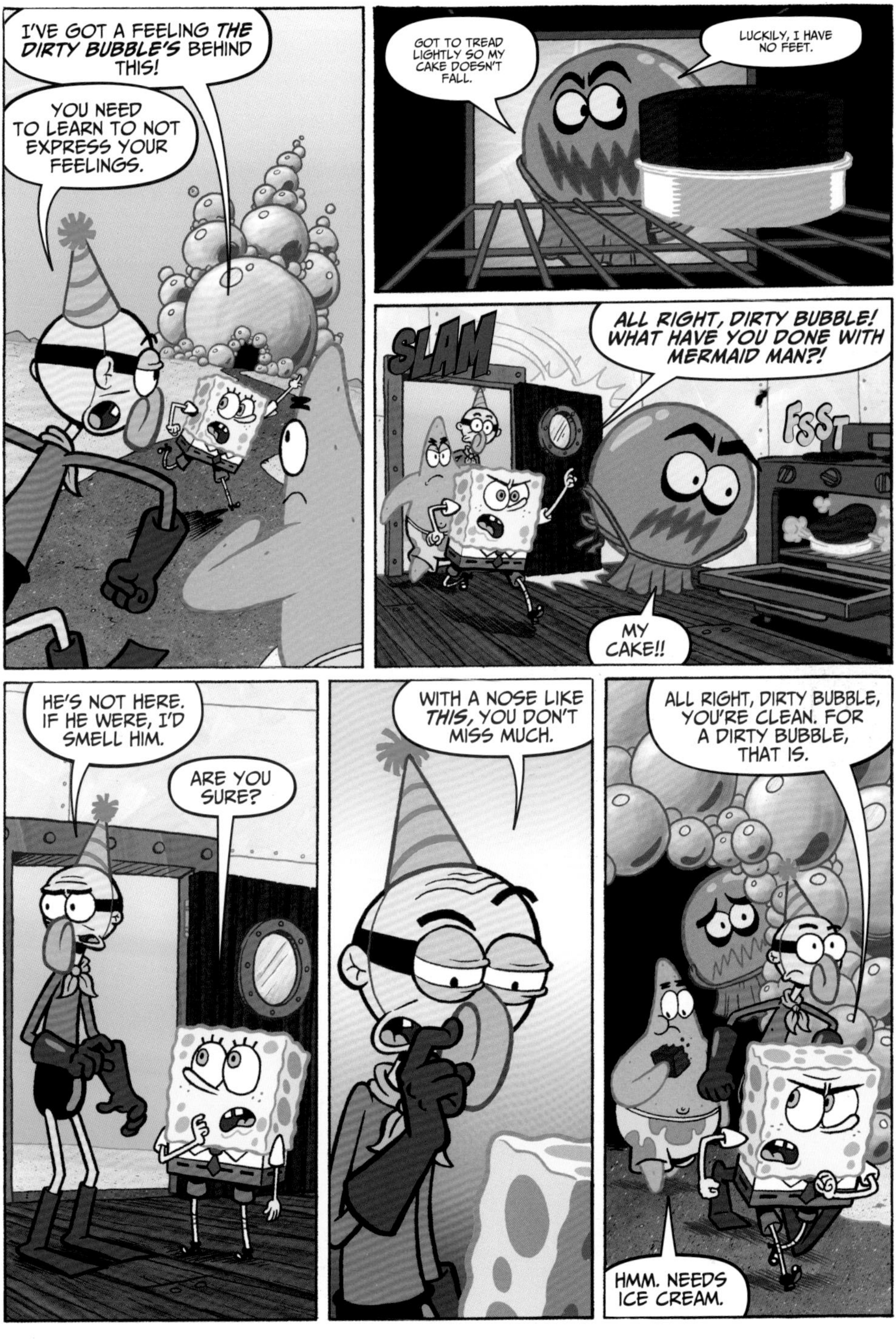
I'VE GOT A FEELING THE DIRTY BUBBLE'S BEHIND THIS!
YOU NEED TO LEARN TO NOT EXPRESS YOUR FEELINGS.
GOT TO TREAD LIGHTLY SO MY CAKE DOESN'T FALL.
LUCKILY, I HAVE NO FEET.
SLAM
ALL RIGHT, DIRTY BUBBLE! WHAT HAVE YOU DONE WITH MERMAID MAN?!
FSST
MY CAKE!!
HE'S NOT HERE. IF HE WERE, I'D SMELL HIM.
ARE YOU SURE?
WITH A NOSE LIKE THIS, YOU DON'T MISS MUCH.
ALL RIGHT, DIRTY BUBBLE, YOU'RE CLEAN. FOR A DIRTY BUBBLE, THAT IS.
HMM. NEEDS ICE CREAM.

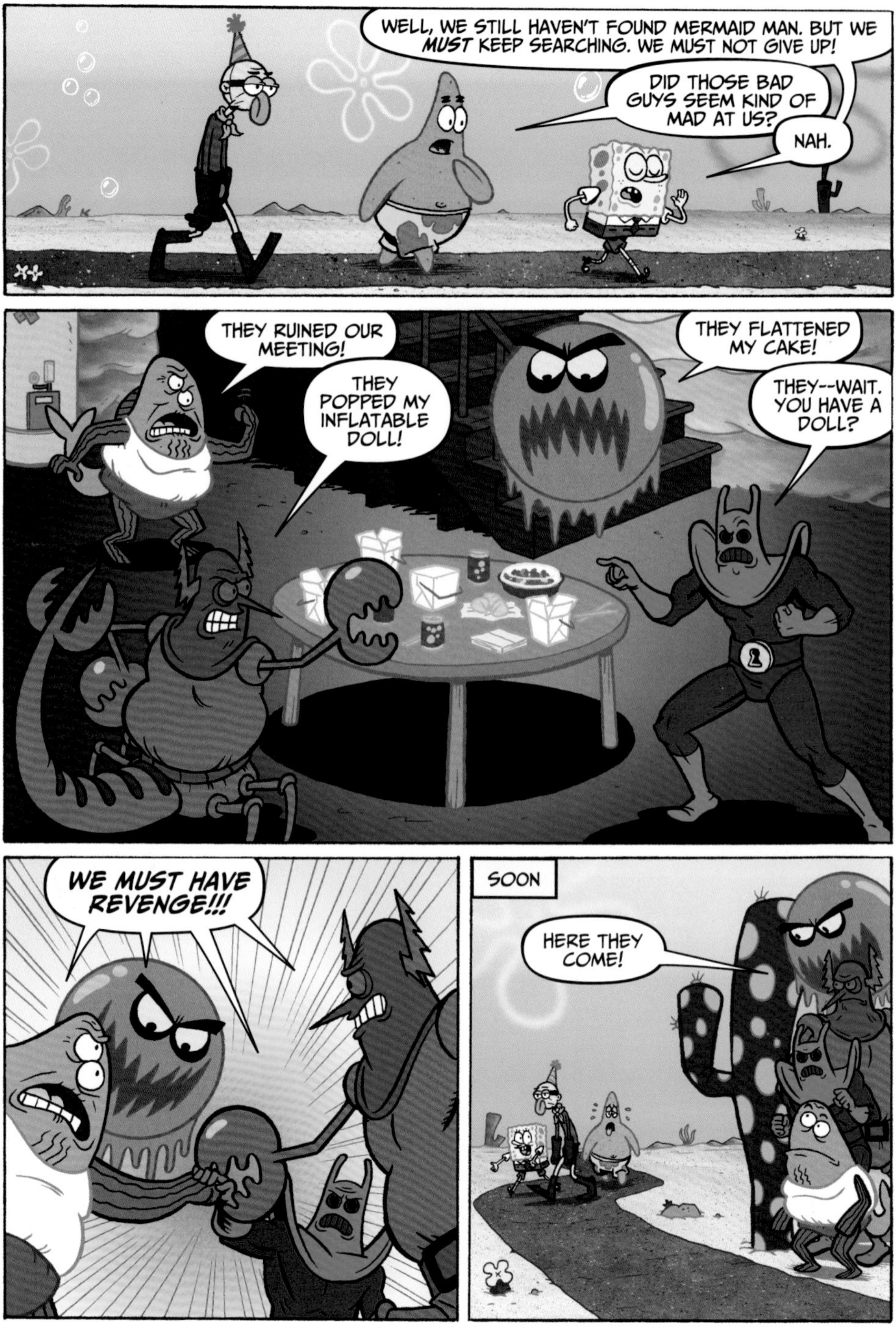
WELL, WE STILL HAVEN'T FOUND MERMAID MAN. BUT WE MUST KEEP SEARCHING. WE MUST NOT GIVE UP!
DID THOSE BAD GUYS SEEM KIND OF MAD AT US?
NAH.
THEY RUINED OUR MEETING!
THEY POPPED MY INFLATABLE DOLL!
THEY FLATTENED MY CAKE!
THEY--WAIT. YOU HAVE A DOLL?
WE MUST HAVE REVENGE!!!
SOON
HERE THEY COME!

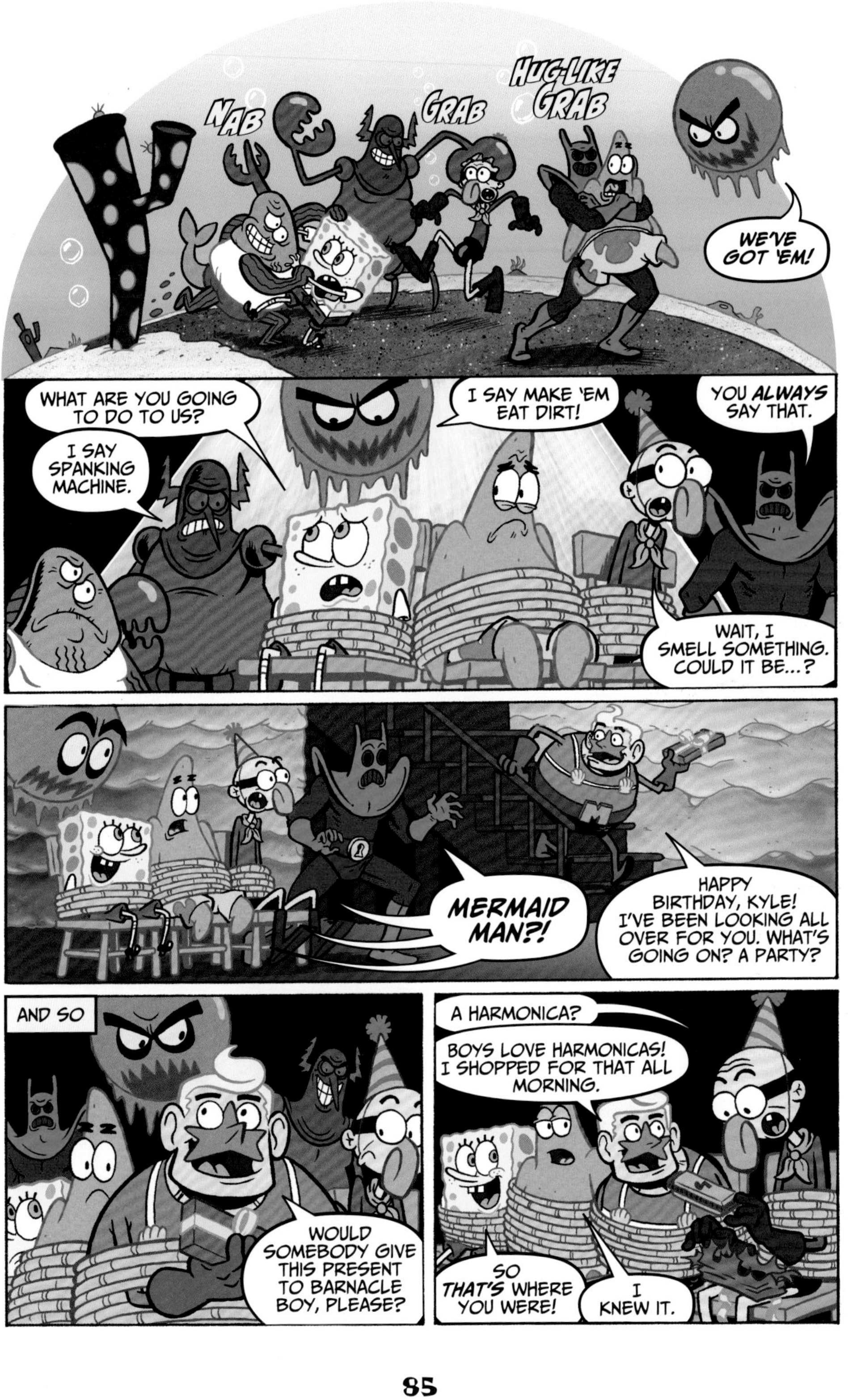
NAB
GRAB
HUG-LIKE GRAB
WE'VE GOT 'EM!
WHAT ARE YOU GOING TO DO TO US?
I SAY SPANKING MACHINE.
I SAY MAKE 'EM EAT DIRT!
YOU ALWAYS SAY THAT.
WAIT, I SMELL SOMETHING. COULD IT BE...?
MERMAID MAN?!
HAPPY BIRTHDAY, KYLE! I'VE BEEN LOOKING ALL OVER FOR YOU. WHAT'S GOING ON? A PARTY?
AND SO
WOULD SOMEBODY GIVE THIS PRESENT TO BARNACLE BOY, PLEASE?
A HARMONICA?
BOYS LOVE HARMONICAS! I SHOPPED FOR THAT ALL MORNING.
SO THAT'S WHERE YOU WERE!
I KNEW IT.

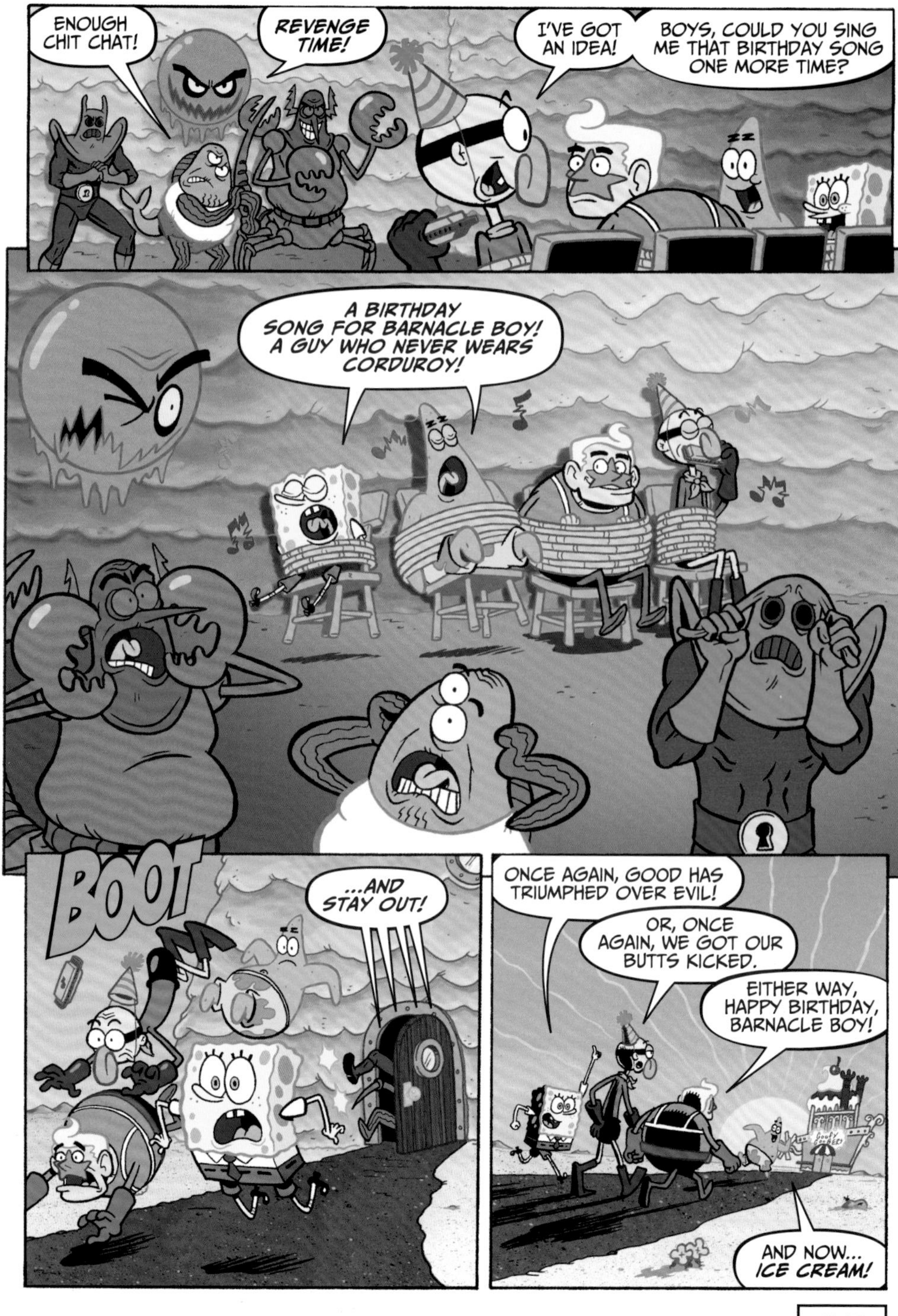
ENOUGH CHIT CHAT!
REVENGE TIME!
I'VE GOT AN IDEA!
BOYS, COULD YOU SING ME THAT BIRTHDAY SONG ONE MORE TIME?
A BIRTHDAY SONG FOR BARNACLE BOY! A GUY WHO NEVER WEARS CORDUROY!
BOOT
...AND STAY OUT!
ONCE AGAIN, GOOD HAS TRIUMPHED OVER EVIL!
OR, ONCE AGAIN, WE GOT OUR BUTTS KICKED.
EITHER WAY, HAPPY BIRTHDAY, BARNACLE BOY!
AND NOW... ICE CREAM!
END

FLOTSAM AND JETSAM OCEAN FACTS — TARDIGRADES — BY MARIS

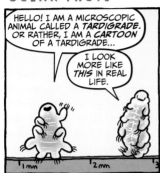

HELLO! I AM A MICROSCOPIC ANIMAL CALLED A *TARDIGRADE*. OR RATHER, I AM A *CARTOON* OF A TARDIGRADE...

I LOOK MORE LIKE *THIS* IN REAL LIFE.

1 mm   2 mm

ALSO CALLED WATER BEARS, THERE ARE MORE THAN 700 SPECIES OF US FOUND ALL OVER THE WORLD.

EVEN THOUGH WE'RE ITTY BITTY, WE'VE GOT SIMPLE EYES, A MOUTH, 8 LEGS, GUTS, AND A BUTT.

WE LIVE IN SALT WATER, FRESH WATER, MOIST MOSSES AND LICHENS... WHEREVER THERE'S WATER, WE'LL LIVE THERE.

ACTUAL SIZE

BECAUSE WE'VE BEEN FOUND ALL OVER THE WORLD--IN A VARIETY OF HABITATS--SCIENTISTS WANTED TO SEE IF WE COULD SURVIVE, WELL, *ANYWHERE*...

Scientists tried to freeze me all the way down to -458° F...

YOU CALL *THIS* COLD?

...they heated me up to 300°F...

MMMM... NICE AND TOASTY WARM.

...they subjected me to *6 times* the pressure found at the deepest part of the ocean...

OH, COME ON. YOU CAN DO BETTER THAN *THIS*.

...and even exposed me to the vacuum of *space* for 10 days!

I DON'T EVEN NEED A SPACE SUIT!*

WHEN MY ENVIRONMENT BECOMES *EXTREME*, I SIMPLY DRY OUT OR FREEZE...

...BUT JUST ADD WATER (OR WARM ME UP) AND I'M BACK TO NORMAL. IT'S A PRETTY AWESOME *SUPER POWER* TO HAVE.

SO, HUMANS: WHATEVER WACKY EXPERIMENT YOU WANT TO DO TO ME?

THIS LITTLE WATER BEAR SAYS *BRING IT ON!*

*Author's note: You can't hear sound in space. Also, tardigrades can't talk.

STORY AND ART BY MARIS WICKS LETTERING BY COMICRAFT

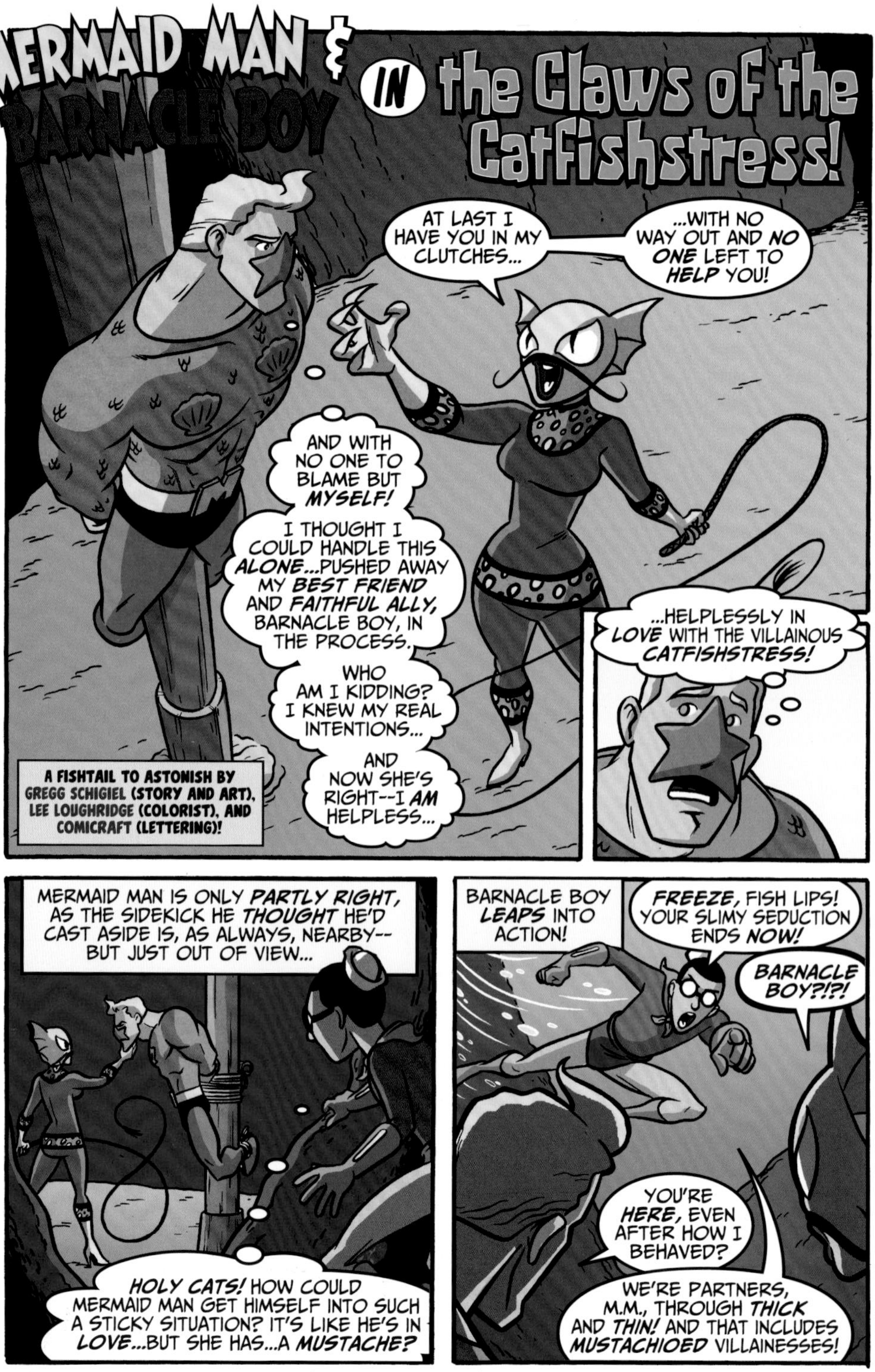
MERMAID MAN & BARNACLE BOY
IN
the Claws of the Catfishstress!
AT LAST I HAVE YOU IN MY CLUTCHES...
...WITH NO WAY OUT AND NO ONE LEFT TO HELP YOU!
AND WITH NO ONE TO BLAME BUT MYSELF!
I THOUGHT I COULD HANDLE THIS ALONE...PUSHED AWAY MY BEST FRIEND AND FAITHFUL ALLY, BARNACLE BOY, IN THE PROCESS.
WHO AM I KIDDING? I KNEW MY REAL INTENTIONS...
AND NOW SHE'S RIGHT--I AM HELPLESS...
...HELPLESSLY IN LOVE WITH THE VILLAINOUS CATFISHSTRESS!
A FISHTAIL TO ASTONISH BY GREGG SCHIGIEL (STORY AND ART), LEE LOUGHRIDGE (COLORIST), AND COMICRAFT (LETTERING)!
MERMAID MAN IS ONLY PARTLY RIGHT, AS THE SIDEKICK HE THOUGHT HE'D CAST ASIDE IS, AS ALWAYS, NEARBY--BUT JUST OUT OF VIEW...
HOLY CATS! HOW COULD MERMAID MAN GET HIMSELF INTO SUCH A STICKY SITUATION? IT'S LIKE HE'S IN LOVE...BUT SHE HAS...A MUSTACHE?
BARNACLE BOY LEAPS INTO ACTION!
FREEZE, FISH LIPS! YOUR SLIMY SEDUCTION ENDS NOW!
BARNACLE BOY?!?!
YOU'RE HERE, EVEN AFTER HOW I BEHAVED?
WE'RE PARTNERS, M.M., THROUGH THICK AND THIN! AND THAT INCLUDES MUSTACHIOED VILLAINESSES!

NO! YOU CAN'T HAVE HIM!
WELL, IF I CAN'T HAVE MY PARTNER BACK, CAN I BORROW YOUR WHIP FOR A SECOND?
BECAUSE IT'S JUST THE THING TO WRAP UP THIS CATTY CAPER!
WHAT? NO! HOW?!?
IT'S ALL IN THE WRIST!
WITH THE CUNNING CATFISHSTRESS CONTAINED, BARNACLE BOY FREES HIS CAPTIVE COHORT!
LET'S GET YOU OUT OF THESE BINDINGS...
GRRR...
TERRIFIC WORK, BARNACLE BOY! THANKS FOR NOT GIVING UP ON ME!
NEVER!
THOUGH, IN ALL FAIRNESS, CATFISHSTRESS'S MUSTACHE IS PART OF HER MASK...
OH, REALLY?
A...REAL MUSTACHE!!
MERMAID MAN, NO! WE...WE CAN STILL BE TOGETHER! YOU CAN HELP ME BE RID OF THIS MUSTACHE AND THIS LIFE OF CRIME!
NOT UNTIL YOU SERVE YOUR TIME FOR KIDNAPPING! THE POLICE WILL BE HERE SOON.
LET'S GO, MERMAID MAN!
RIGHT BEHIND YOU, CHUM.
WHY IS IT SO HARD TO SWIM AWAY? COULD SHE...REALLY CHANGE HER WAYS?

END

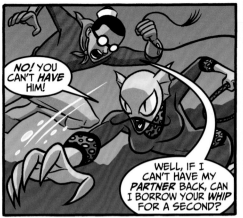

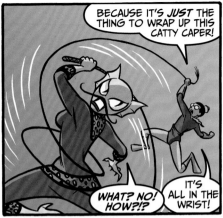

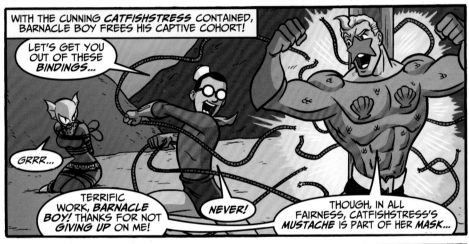

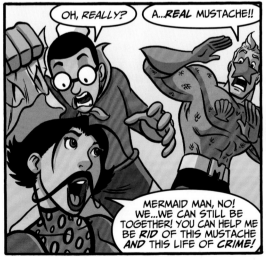

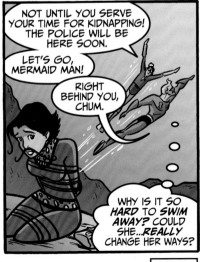

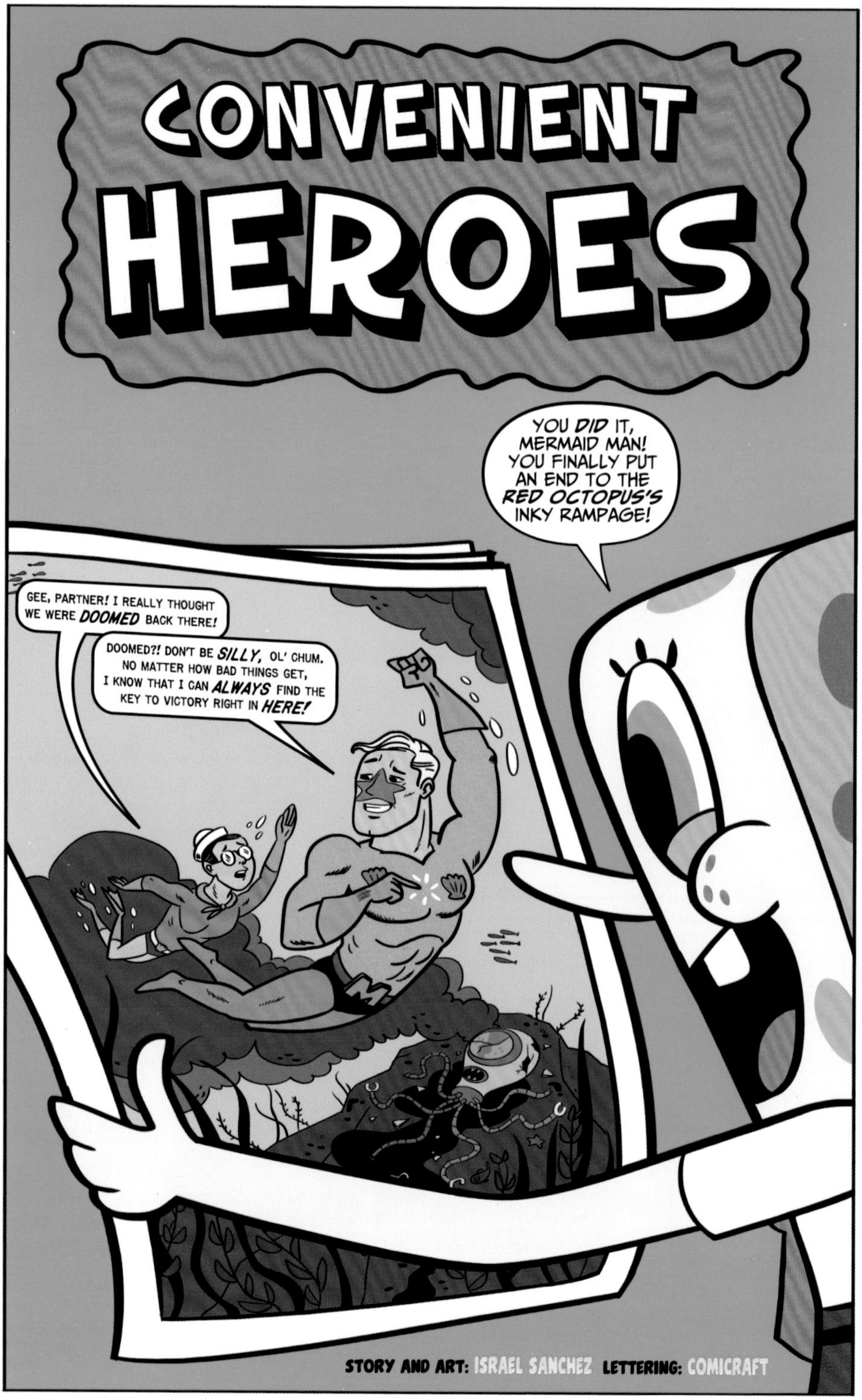
CONVENIENT HEROES
YOU DID IT, MERMAID MAN! YOU FINALLY PUT AN END TO THE RED OCTOPUS'S INKY RAMPAGE!
GEE, PARTNER! I REALLY THOUGHT WE WERE DOOMED BACK THERE!
DOOMED?! DON'T BE SILLY, OL' CHUM. NO MATTER HOW BAD THINGS GET, I KNOW THAT I CAN ALWAYS FIND THE KEY TO VICTORY RIGHT IN HERE!
STORY AND ART: ISRAEL SANCHEZ LETTERING: COMICRAFT

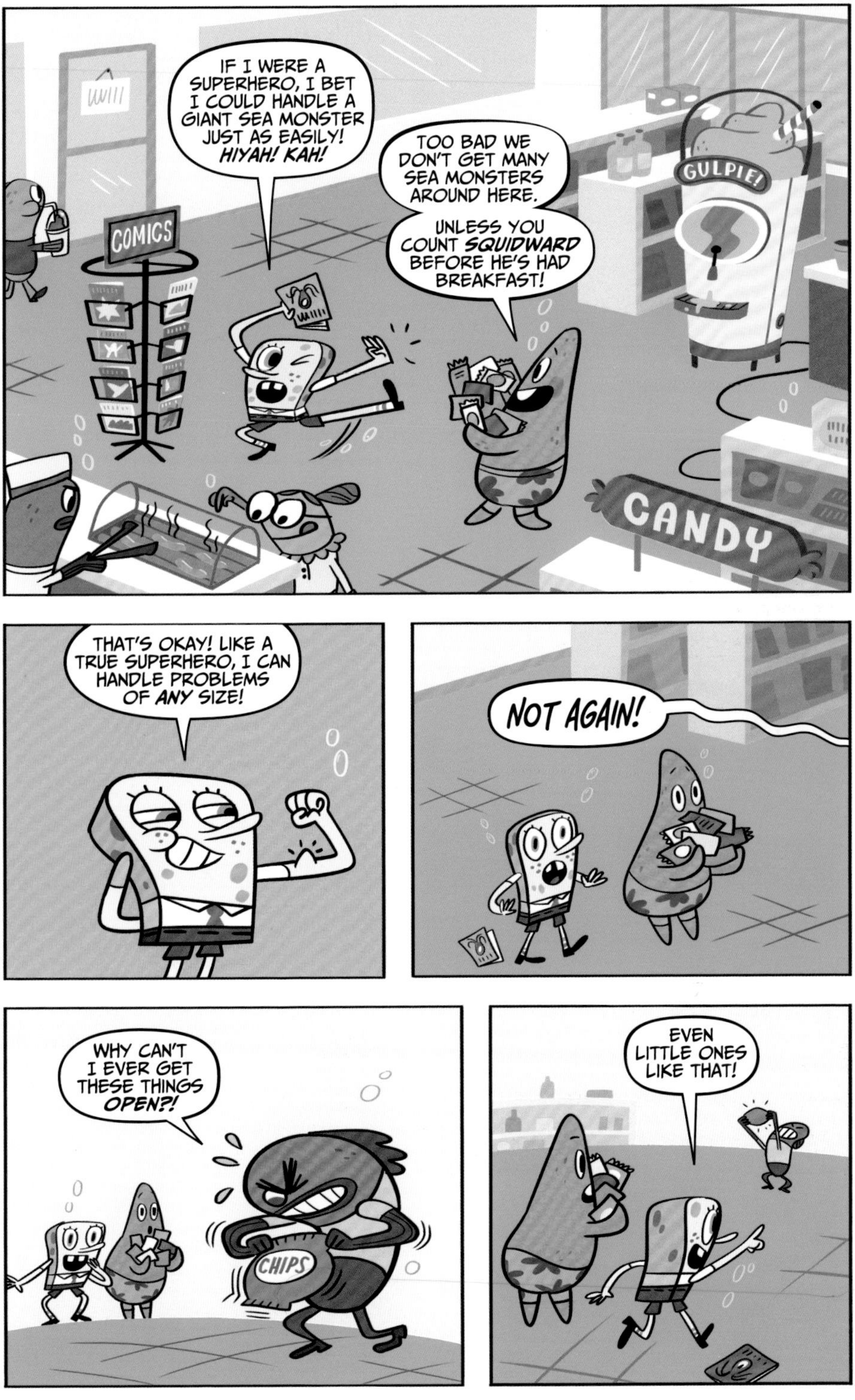
COMICS
IF I WERE A SUPERHERO, I BET I COULD HANDLE A GIANT SEA MONSTER JUST AS EASILY! HIYAH! KAH!
TOO BAD WE DON'T GET MANY SEA MONSTERS AROUND HERE.
UNLESS YOU COUNT SQUIDWARD BEFORE HE'S HAD BREAKFAST!
GULPIE!
CANDY
THAT'S OKAY! LIKE A TRUE SUPERHERO, I CAN HANDLE PROBLEMS OF ANY SIZE!
NOT AGAIN!
WHY CAN'T I EVER GET THESE THINGS OPEN?!
CHIPS
EVEN LITTLE ONES LIKE THAT!

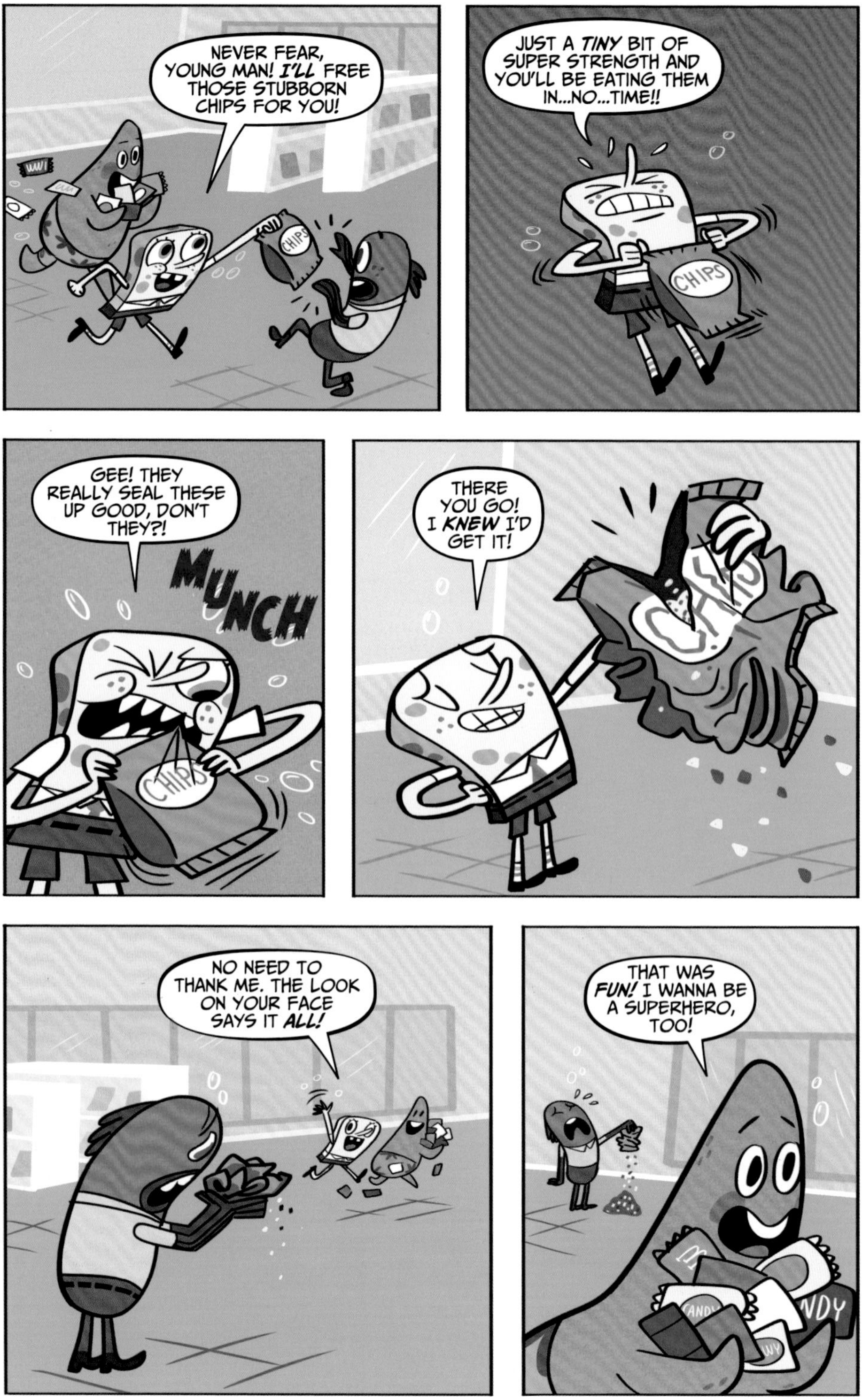
NEVER FEAR, YOUNG MAN! I'LL FREE THOSE STUBBORN CHIPS FOR YOU!
CHIPS
JUST A TINY BIT OF SUPER STRENGTH AND YOU'LL BE EATING THEM IN...NO...TIME!!
CHIPS
GEE! THEY REALLY SEAL THESE UP GOOD, DON'T THEY?!
MUNCH
CHIPS
THERE YOU GO! I KNEW I'D GET IT!
CHIPS
NO NEED TO THANK ME. THE LOOK ON YOUR FACE SAYS IT ALL!
THAT WAS FUN! I WANNA BE A SUPERHERO, TOO!

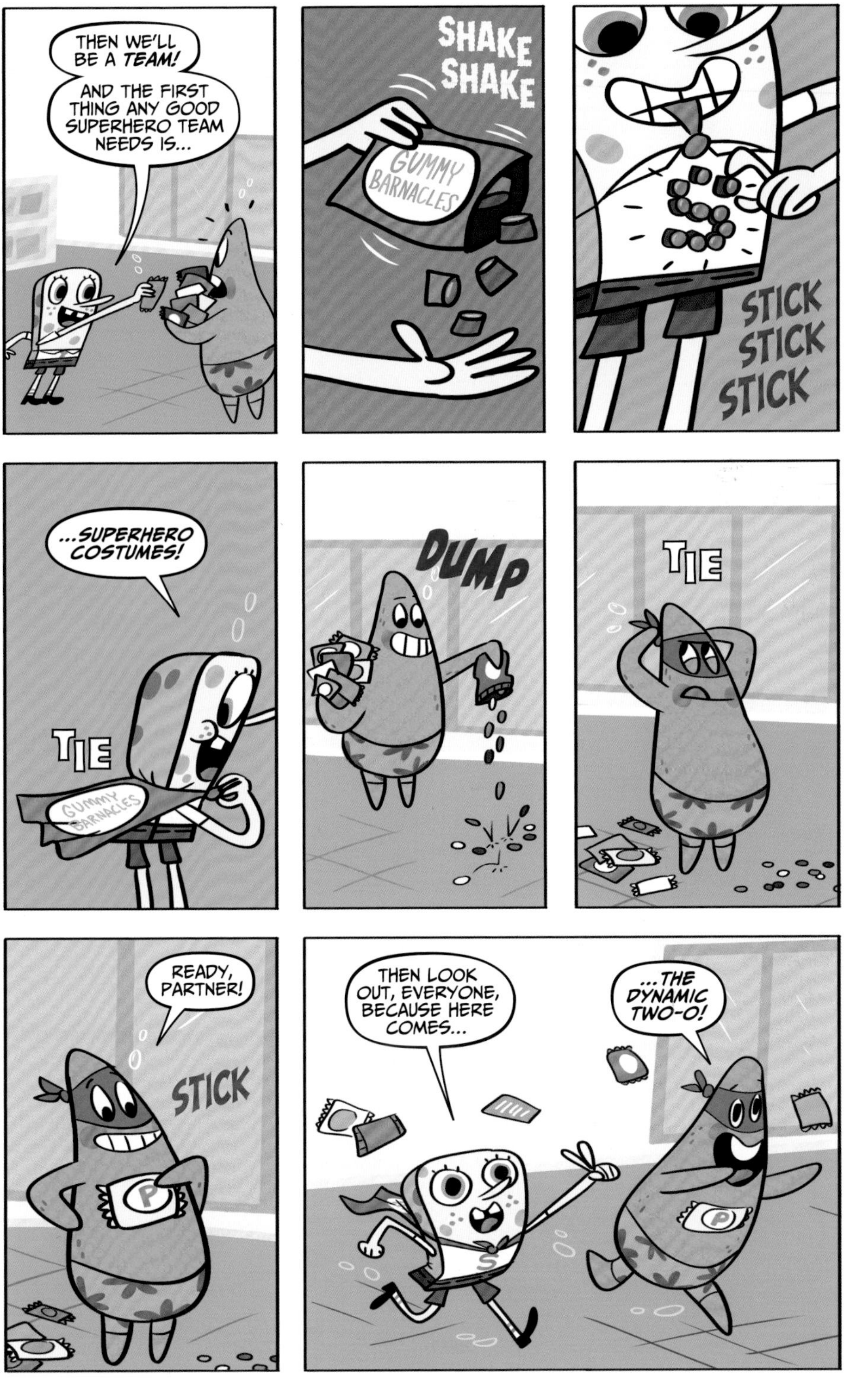
THEN WE'LL BE A TEAM!
AND THE FIRST THING ANY GOOD SUPERHERO TEAM NEEDS IS...
SHAKE SHAKE
GUMMY BARNACLES
STICK STICK STICK
...SUPERHERO COSTUMES!
TIE
GUMMY BARNACLES
DUMP
TIE
READY, PARTNER!
STICK
THEN LOOK OUT, EVERYONE, BECAUSE HERE COMES...
...THE DYNAMIC TWO-O!

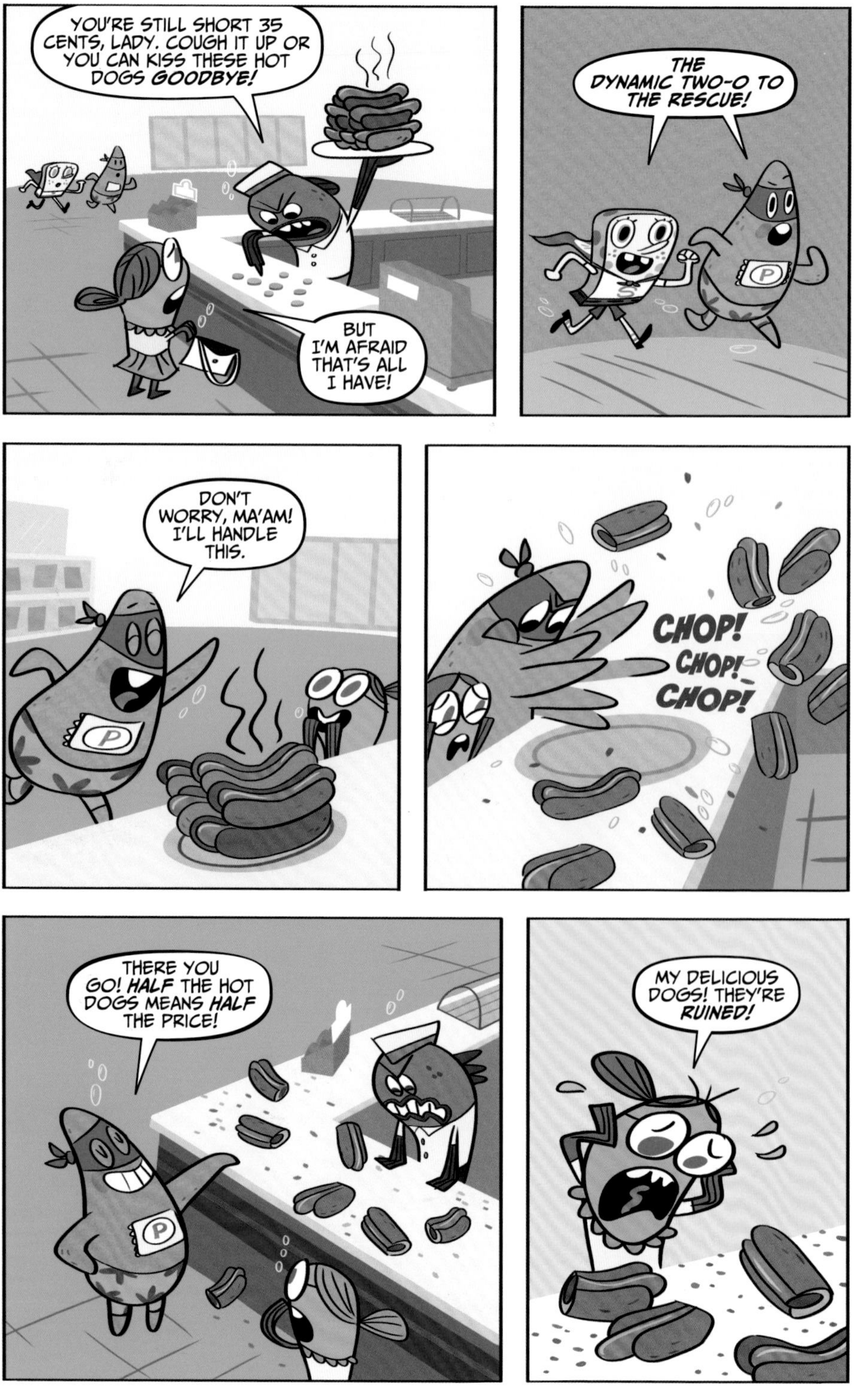
YOU'RE STILL SHORT 35 CENTS, LADY. COUGH IT UP OR YOU CAN KISS THESE HOT DOGS GOODBYE!
BUT I'M AFRAID THAT'S ALL I HAVE!
THE DYNAMIC TWO-O TO THE RESCUE!
DON'T WORRY, MA'AM! I'LL HANDLE THIS.
CHOP! CHOP! CHOP!
THERE YOU GO! HALF THE HOT DOGS MEANS HALF THE PRICE!
MY DELICIOUS DOGS! THEY'RE RUINED!

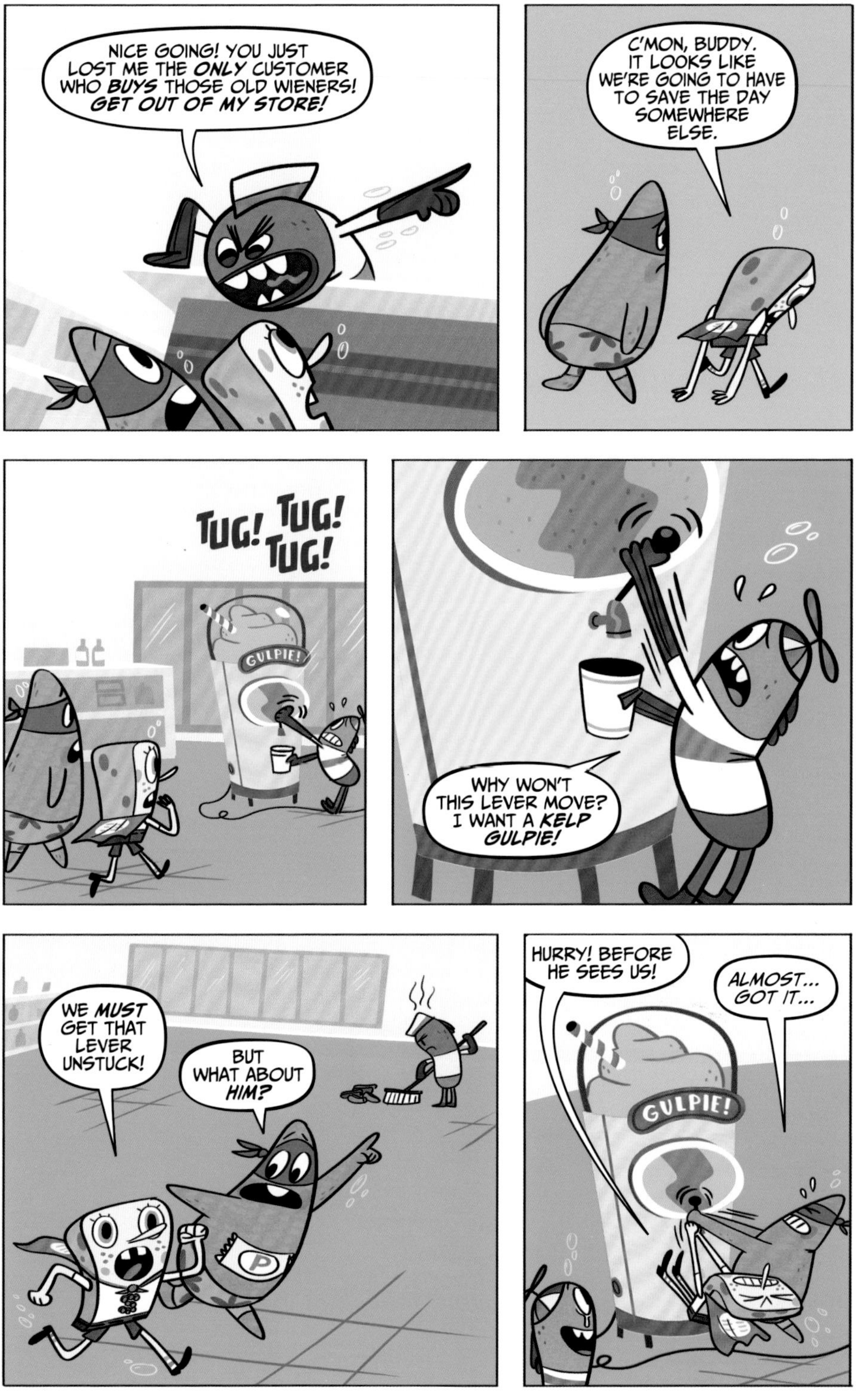
NICE GOING! YOU JUST LOST ME THE *ONLY* CUSTOMER WHO *BUYS* THOSE OLD WIENERS! *GET OUT OF MY STORE!*
C'MON, BUDDY. IT LOOKS LIKE WE'RE GOING TO HAVE TO SAVE THE DAY SOMEWHERE ELSE.
TUG! TUG! TUG!
GULPIE!
WHY WON'T THIS LEVER MOVE? I WANT A *KELP GULPIE!*
WE *MUST* GET THAT LEVER UNSTUCK!
BUT WHAT ABOUT *HIM?*
HURRY! BEFORE HE SEES US!
ALMOST... GOT IT...
GULPIE!

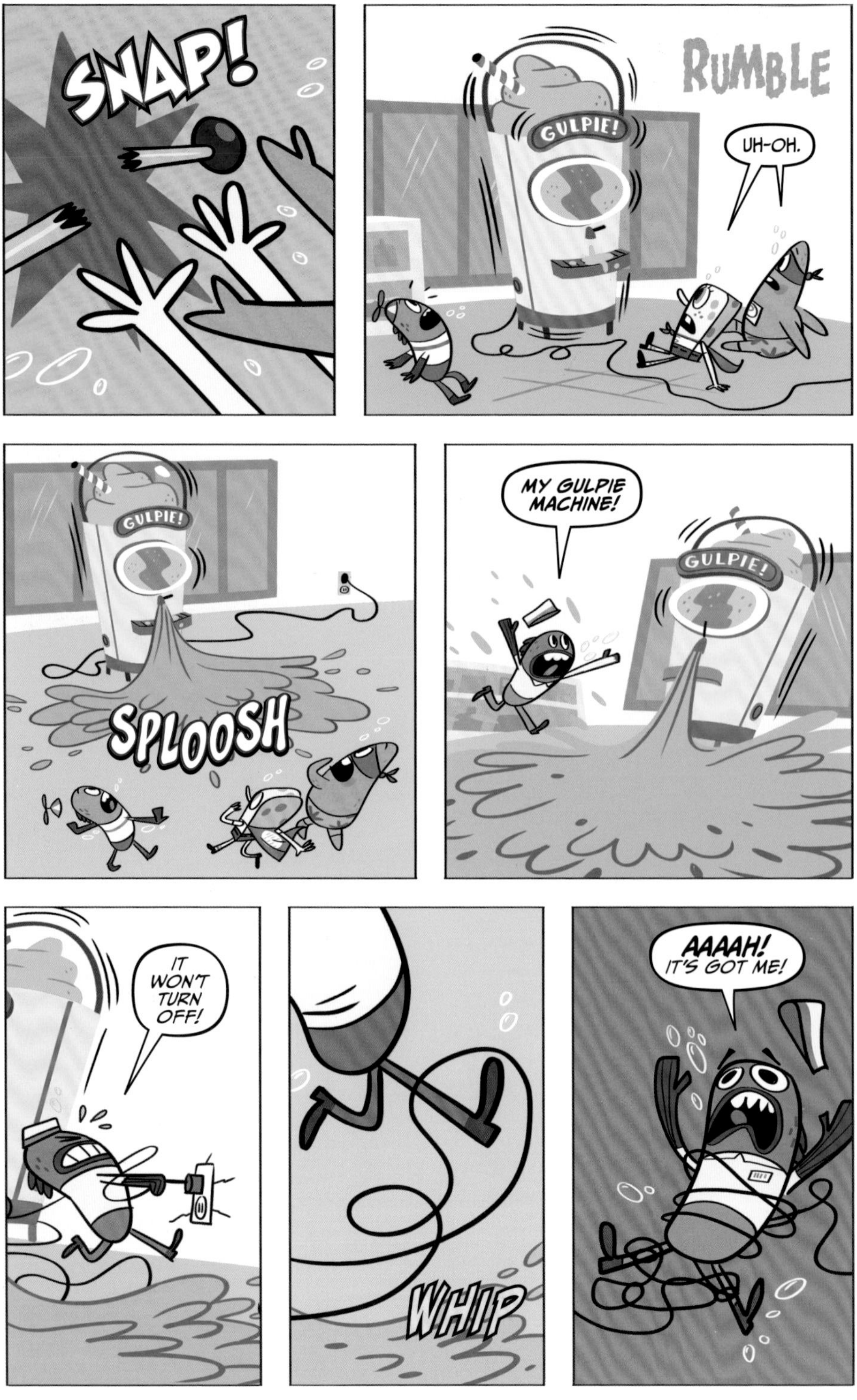
SNAP!
RUMBLE
GULPIE!
UH-OH.
GULPIE!
SPLOOSH
MY GULPIE MACHINE!
GULPIE!
IT WON'T TURN OFF!
WHIP
AAAAH! IT'S GOT ME!

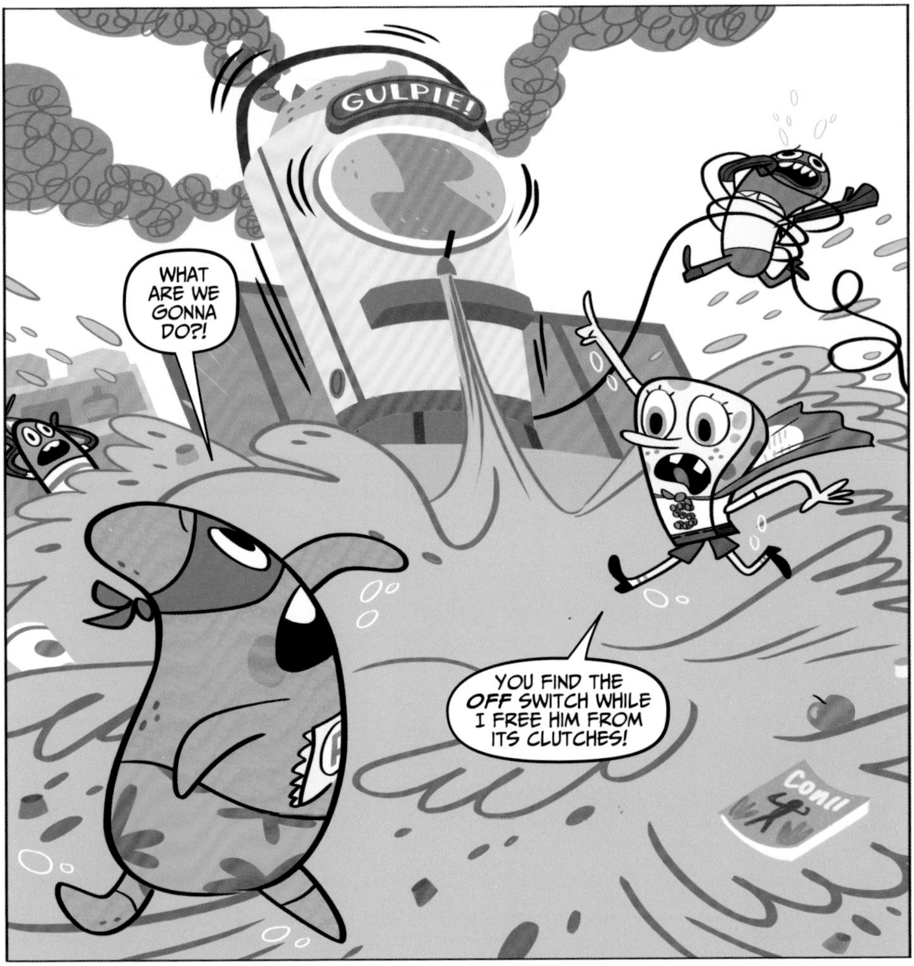
GULPIE!
WHAT ARE WE GONNA DO?!
YOU FIND THE OFF SWITCH WHILE I FREE HIM FROM ITS CLUTCHES!

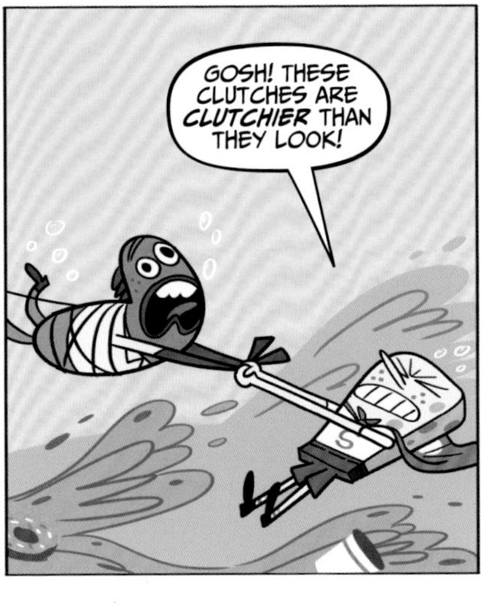
GOSH! THESE CLUTCHES ARE CLUTCHIER THAN THEY LOOK!

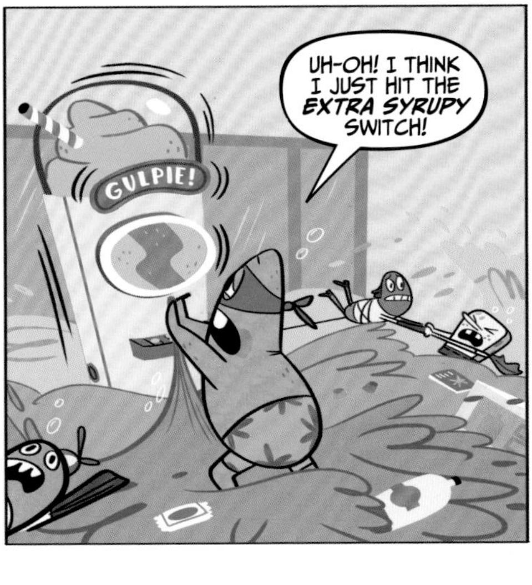
UH-OH! I THINK I JUST HIT THE EXTRA SYRUPY SWITCH!
GULPIE!

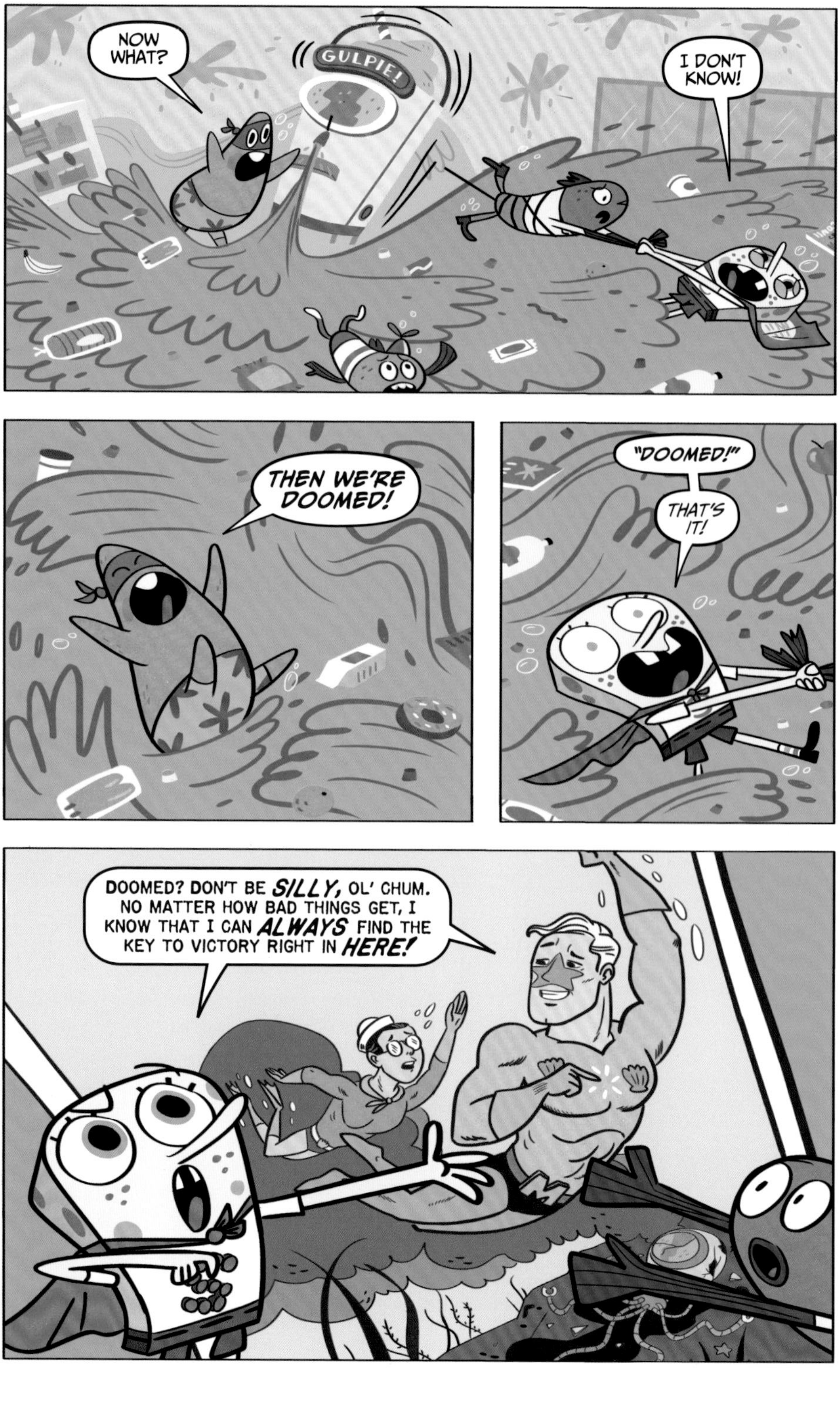

NOW WHAT?
GULPIE!
I DON'T KNOW!
THEN WE'RE DOOMED!
"DOOMED!"
THAT'S IT!
DOOMED? DON'T BE SILLY, OL' CHUM. NO MATTER HOW BAD THINGS GET, I KNOW THAT I CAN ALWAYS FIND THE KEY TO VICTORY RIGHT IN HERE!

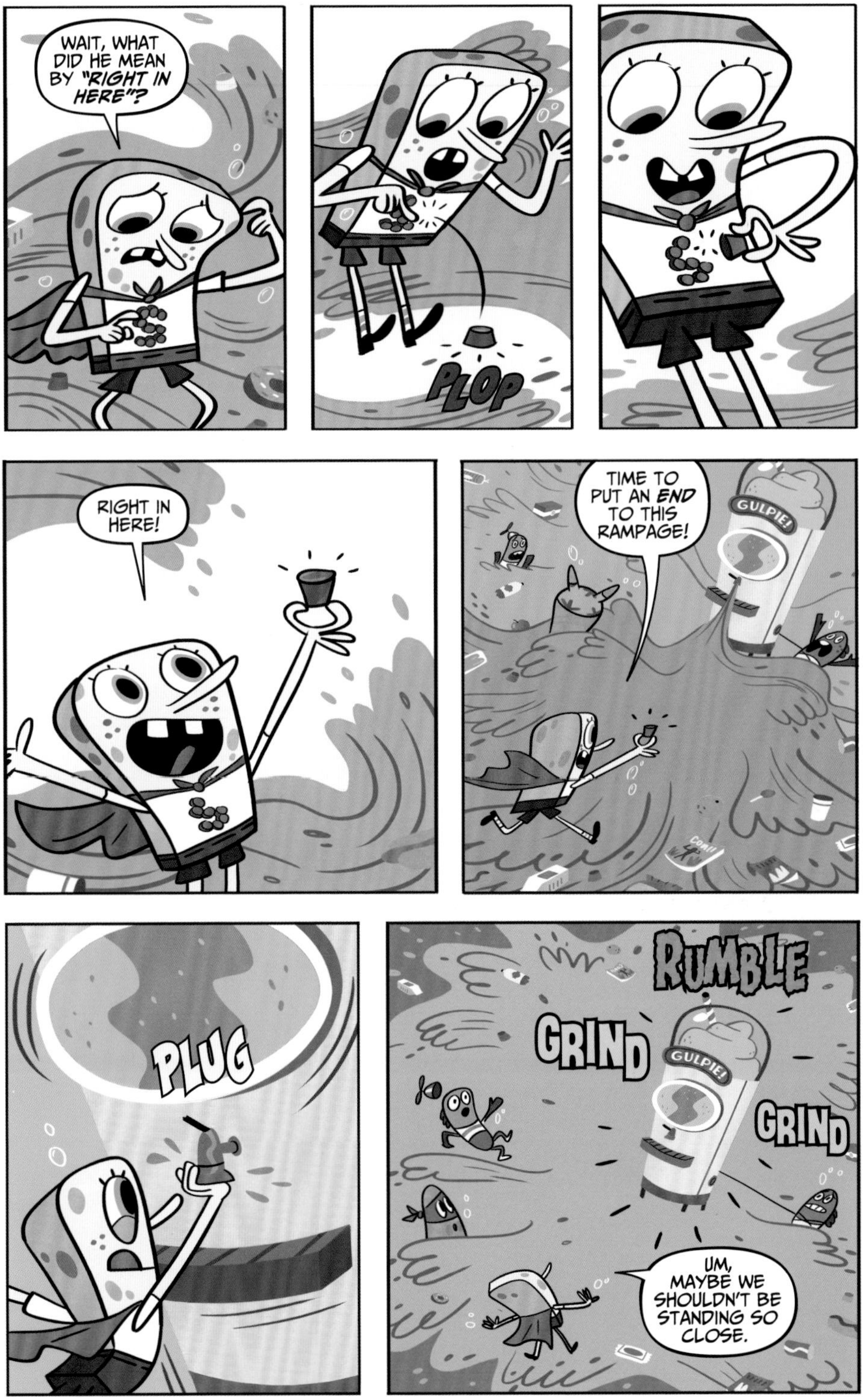
WAIT, WHAT DID HE MEAN BY "RIGHT IN HERE"?
PLOP
RIGHT IN HERE!
TIME TO PUT AN END TO THIS RAMPAGE!
GULPIE!
PLUG
RUMBLE
GRIND
GULPIE!
GRIND
UM, MAYBE WE SHOULDN'T BE STANDING SO CLOSE.

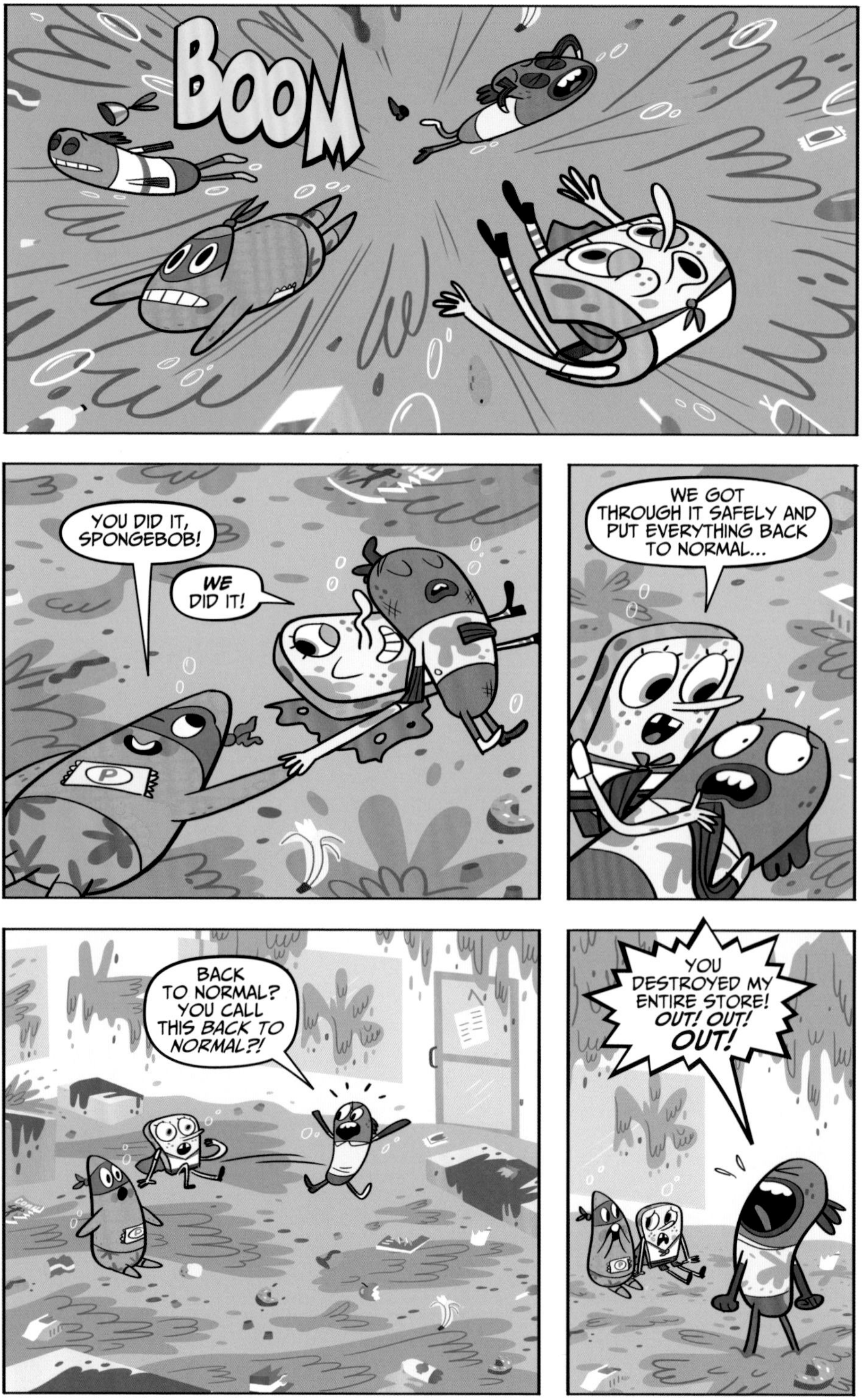
BOOM
YOU DID IT, SPONGEBOB!
WE DID IT!
WE GOT THROUGH IT SAFELY AND PUT EVERYTHING BACK TO NORMAL...
BACK TO NORMAL? YOU CALL THIS BACK TO NORMAL?!
YOU DESTROYED MY ENTIRE STORE! OUT! OUT! OUT!

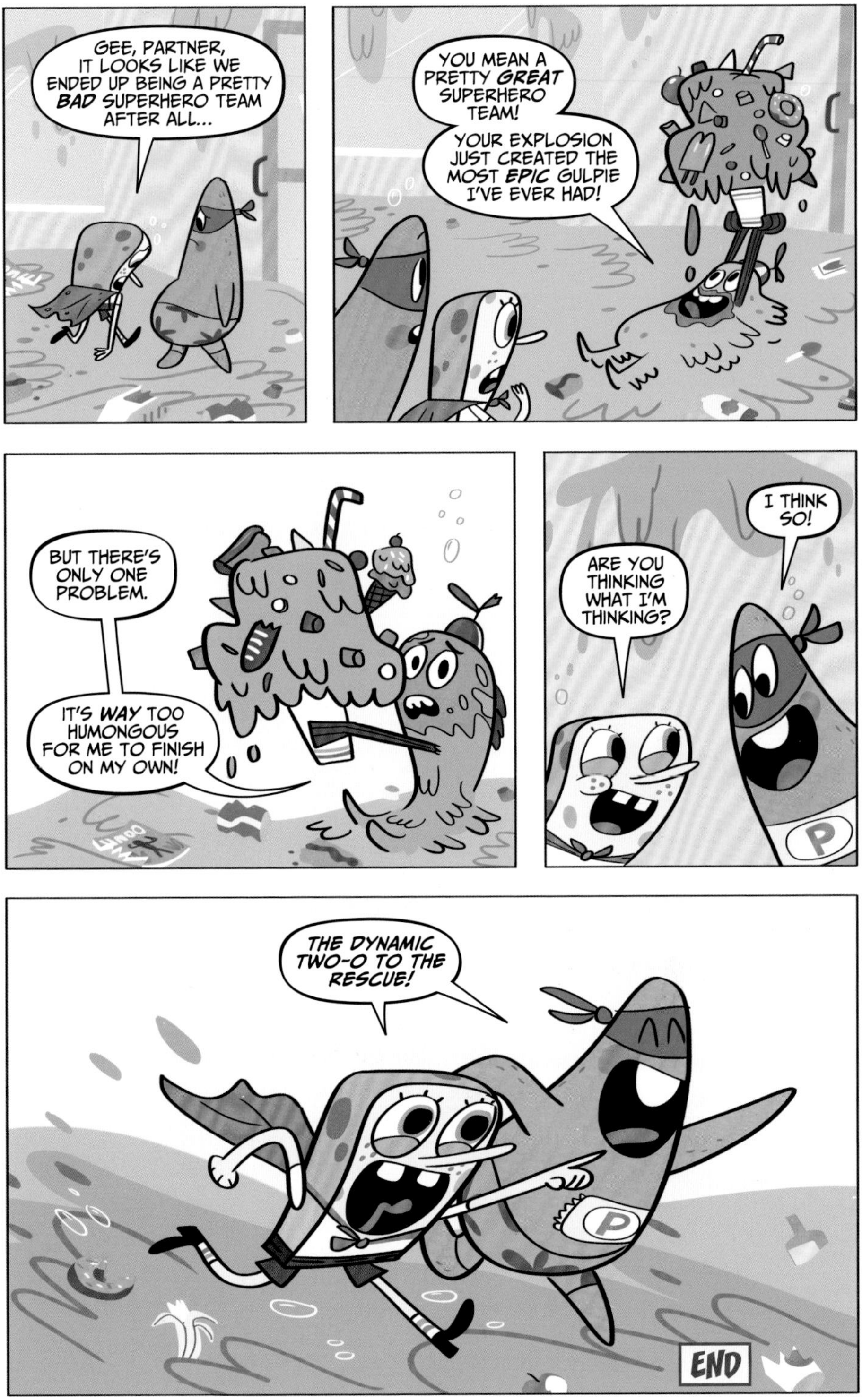
GEE, PARTNER, IT LOOKS LIKE WE ENDED UP BEING A PRETTY **BAD** SUPERHERO TEAM AFTER ALL...
YOU MEAN A PRETTY **GREAT** SUPERHERO TEAM!
YOUR EXPLOSION JUST CREATED THE MOST **EPIC** GULPIE I'VE EVER HAD!
BUT THERE'S ONLY ONE PROBLEM.
IT'S **WAY** TOO HUMONGOUS FOR ME TO FINISH ON MY OWN!
ARE YOU THINKING WHAT I'M THINKING?
I THINK SO!
THE DYNAMIC TWO-O TO THE RESCUE!
END

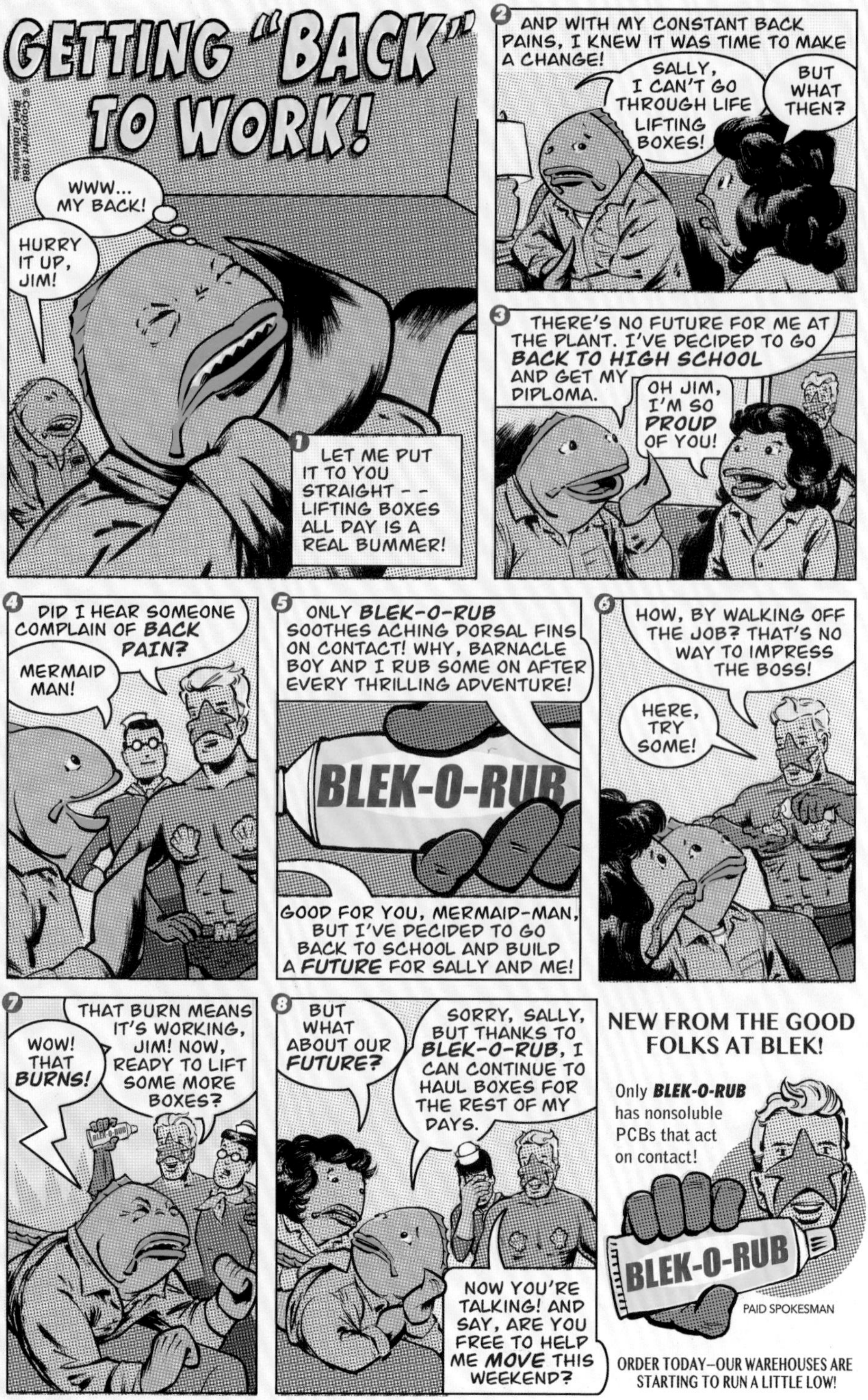
GETTING "BACK" TO WORK!
© Copyright 1986 Blek Industries
WWW... MY BACK!
HURRY IT UP, JIM!
1
LET ME PUT IT TO YOU STRAIGHT - - LIFTING BOXES ALL DAY IS A REAL BUMMER!
2
AND WITH MY CONSTANT BACK PAINS, I KNEW IT WAS TIME TO MAKE A CHANGE!
SALLY, I CAN'T GO THROUGH LIFE LIFTING BOXES!
BUT WHAT THEN?
3
THERE'S NO FUTURE FOR ME AT THE PLANT. I'VE DECIDED TO GO BACK TO HIGH SCHOOL AND GET MY DIPLOMA.
OH JIM, I'M SO PROUD OF YOU!
4
DID I HEAR SOMEONE COMPLAIN OF BACK PAIN?
MERMAID MAN!
5
ONLY BLEK-O-RUB SOOTHES ACHING DORSAL FINS ON CONTACT! WHY, BARNACLE BOY AND I RUB SOME ON AFTER EVERY THRILLING ADVENTURE!
BLEK-O-RUB
GOOD FOR YOU, MERMAID-MAN, BUT I'VE DECIDED TO GO BACK TO SCHOOL AND BUILD A FUTURE FOR SALLY AND ME!
6
HOW, BY WALKING OFF THE JOB? THAT'S NO WAY TO IMPRESS THE BOSS!
HERE, TRY SOME!
7
WOW! THAT BURNS!
THAT BURN MEANS IT'S WORKING, JIM! NOW, READY TO LIFT SOME MORE BOXES?
BLEK-O-RUB
8
BUT WHAT ABOUT OUR FUTURE?
SORRY, SALLY, BUT THANKS TO BLEK-O-RUB, I CAN CONTINUE TO HAUL BOXES FOR THE REST OF MY DAYS.
NOW YOU'RE TALKING! AND SAY, ARE YOU FREE TO HELP ME MOVE THIS WEEKEND?
NEW FROM THE GOOD FOLKS AT BLEK!
Only BLEK-O-RUB has nonsoluble PCBs that act on contact!
BLEK-O-RUB
PAID SPOKESMAN
ORDER TODAY—OUR WAREHOUSES ARE STARTING TO RUN A LITTLE LOW!

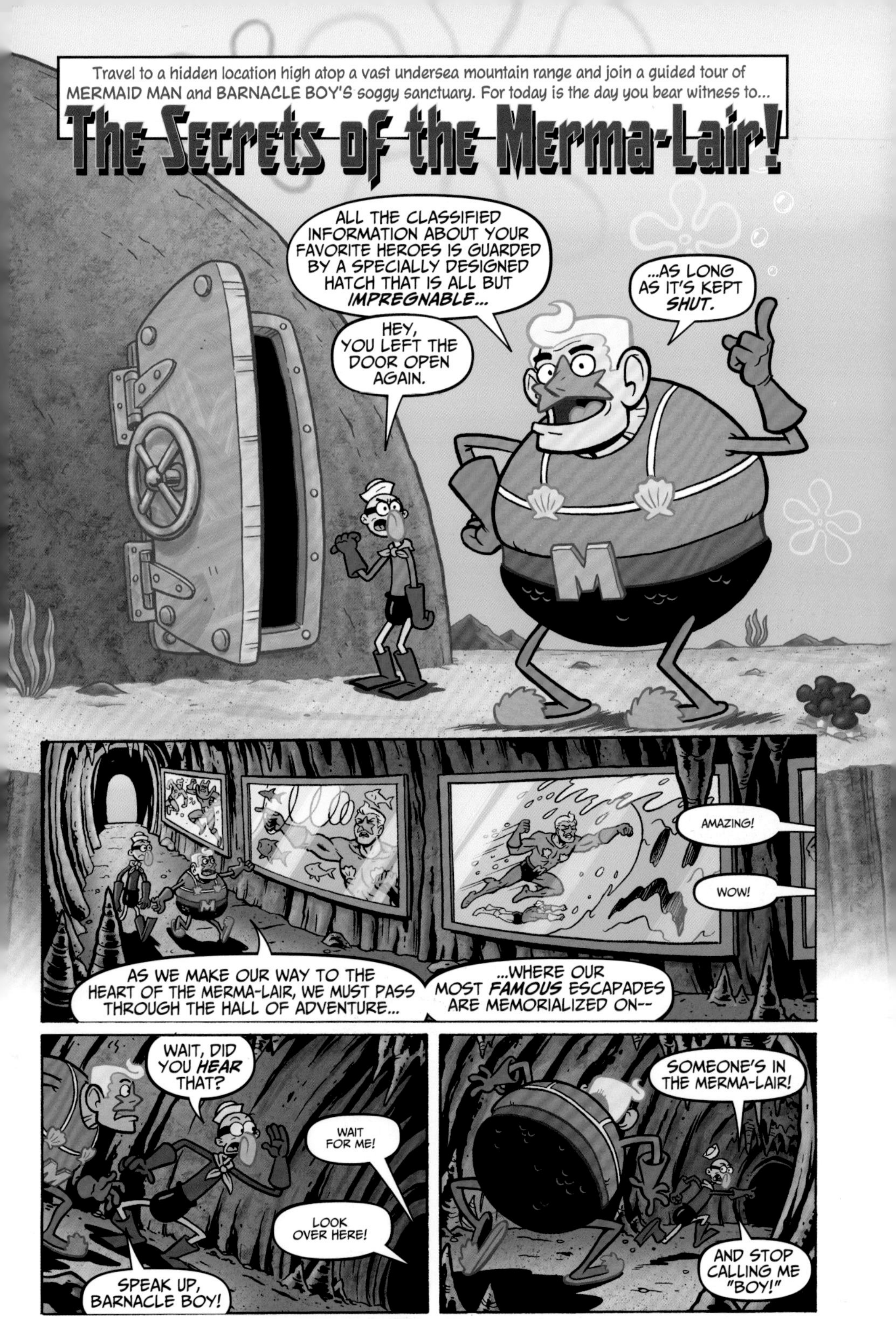
Travel to a hidden location high atop a vast undersea mountain range and join a guided tour of MERMAID MAN and BARNACLE BOY'S soggy sanctuary. For today is the day you bear witness to...
The Secrets of the Merma-Lair!
ALL THE CLASSIFIED INFORMATION ABOUT YOUR FAVORITE HEROES IS GUARDED BY A SPECIALLY DESIGNED HATCH THAT IS ALL BUT IMPREGNABLE...
HEY, YOU LEFT THE DOOR OPEN AGAIN.
...AS LONG AS IT'S KEPT SHUT.
AMAZING!
WOW!
AS WE MAKE OUR WAY TO THE HEART OF THE MERMA-LAIR, WE MUST PASS THROUGH THE HALL OF ADVENTURE...
...WHERE OUR MOST FAMOUS ESCAPADES ARE MEMORIALIZED ON--
WAIT, DID YOU HEAR THAT?
WAIT FOR ME!
LOOK OVER HERE!
SPEAK UP, BARNACLE BOY!
SOMEONE'S IN THE MERMA-LAIR!
AND STOP CALLING ME "BOY!"

STORY: DEREK DRYMON **PENCILS AND INKS:** JACOB CHABOT **COLOR:** RICK NEILSEN **LETTERING:** COMICRAFT

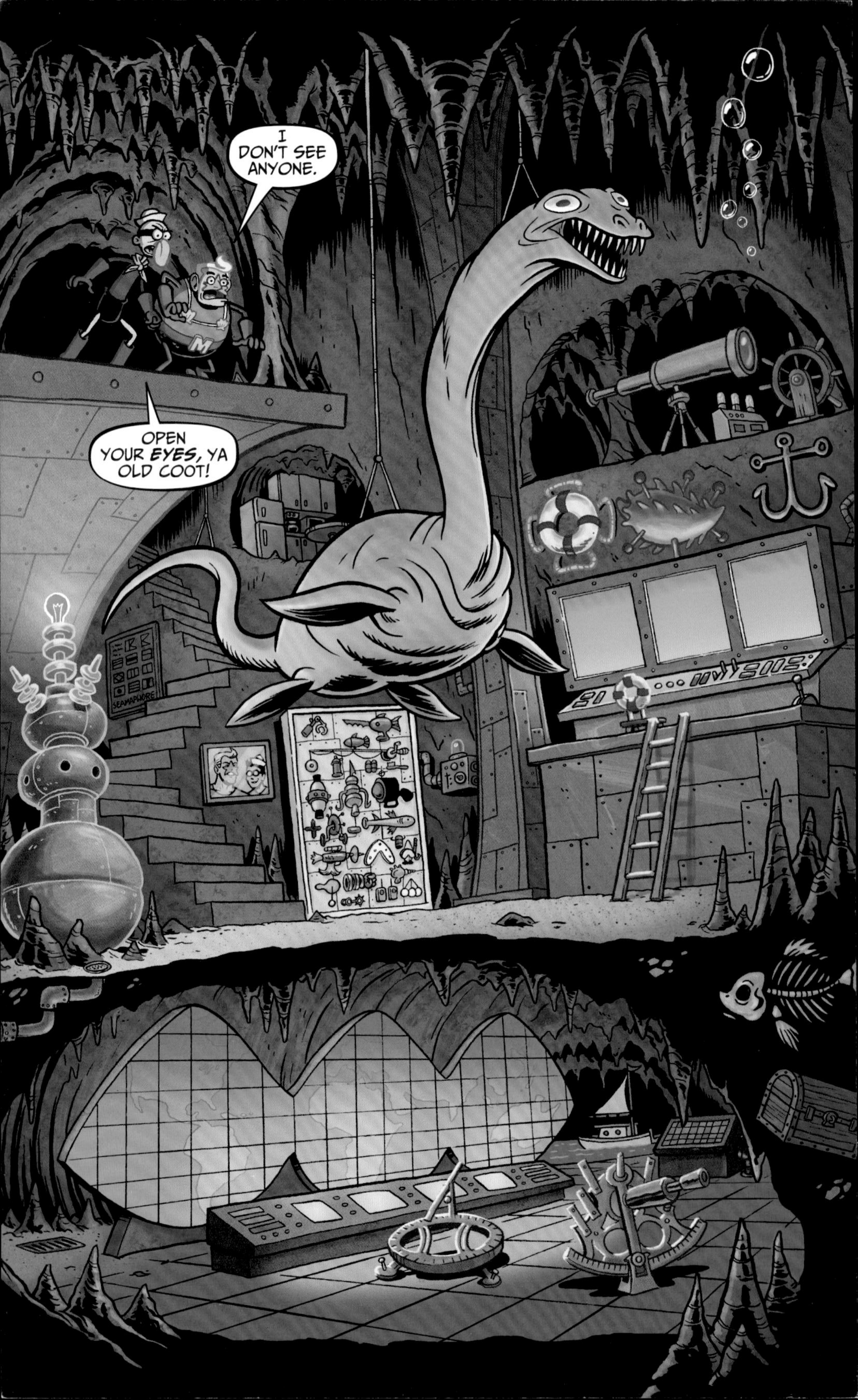
I DON'T SEE ANYONE.
OPEN YOUR *EYES*, YA OLD COOT!
SEAMAPHORE

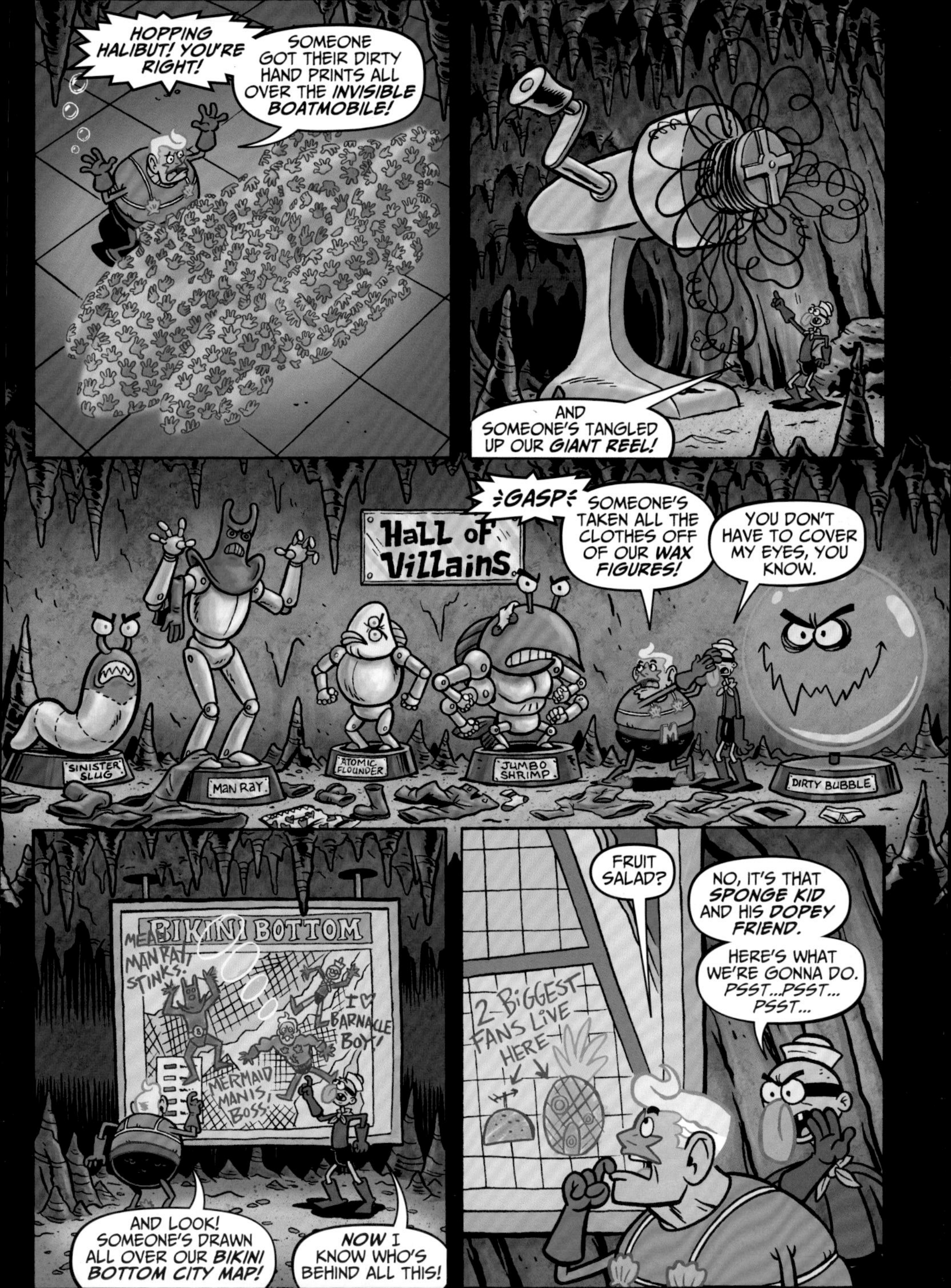
HOPPING HALIBUT! YOU'RE RIGHT!
SOMEONE GOT THEIR DIRTY HAND PRINTS ALL OVER THE *INVISIBLE BOATMOBILE!*
AND SOMEONE'S TANGLED UP OUR *GIANT REEL!*
Hall of Villains
GASP
SOMEONE'S TAKEN ALL THE CLOTHES OFF OF OUR *WAX FIGURES!*
YOU DON'T HAVE TO COVER MY EYES, YOU KNOW.
SINISTER SLUG
MAN RAY
ATOMIC FLOUNDER
JUMBO SHRIMP
DIRTY BUBBLE
BIKINI BOTTOM
MAN RAY STINKS!
I ♡ BARNACLE BOY!
MERMAID MAN IS BOSS!
AND LOOK! SOMEONE'S DRAWN ALL OVER OUR *BIKINI BOTTOM CITY MAP!*
NOW I KNOW WHO'S BEHIND ALL THIS!
FRUIT SALAD?
NO, IT'S THAT *SPONGE KID* AND HIS *DOPEY FRIEND.*
HERE'S WHAT WE'RE GONNA DO. *PSST...PSST... PSST...*
2 BIGGEST FANS LIVE HERE

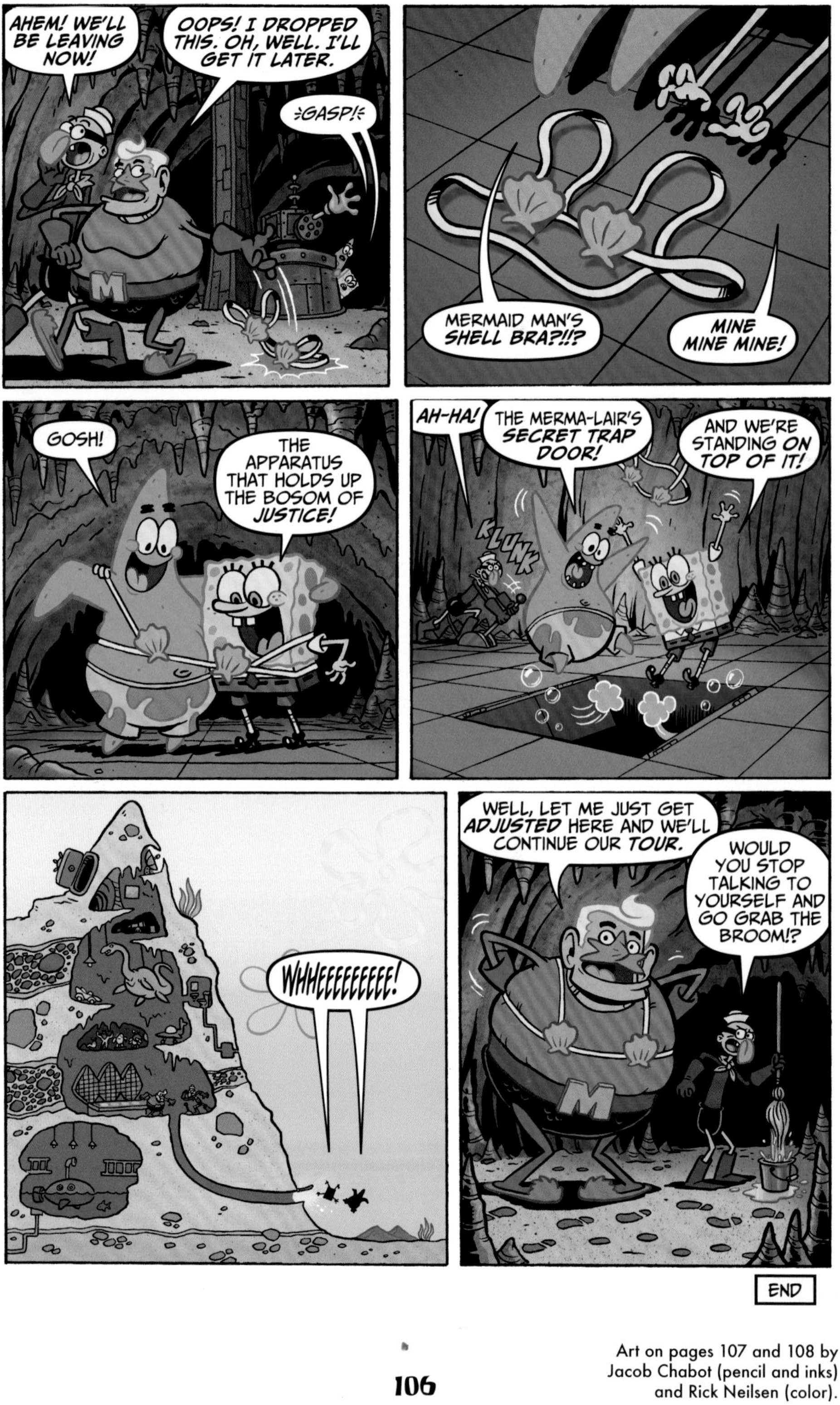
AHEM! WE'LL BE LEAVING NOW!
OOPS! I DROPPED THIS. OH, WELL. I'LL GET IT LATER.
GASP!
MERMAID MAN'S SHELL BRA?!!?
MINE MINE MINE!
GOSH!
THE APPARATUS THAT HOLDS UP THE BOSOM OF JUSTICE!
AH-HA!
THE MERMA-LAIR'S SECRET TRAP DOOR!
AND WE'RE STANDING ON TOP OF IT!
KLUNK
WHHEEEEEEEEE!
WELL, LET ME JUST GET ADJUSTED HERE AND WE'LL CONTINUE OUR TOUR.
WOULD YOU STOP TALKING TO YOURSELF AND GO GRAB THE BROOM!?

END

Art on pages 107 and 108 by Jacob Chabot (pencil and inks) and Rick Neilsen (color).

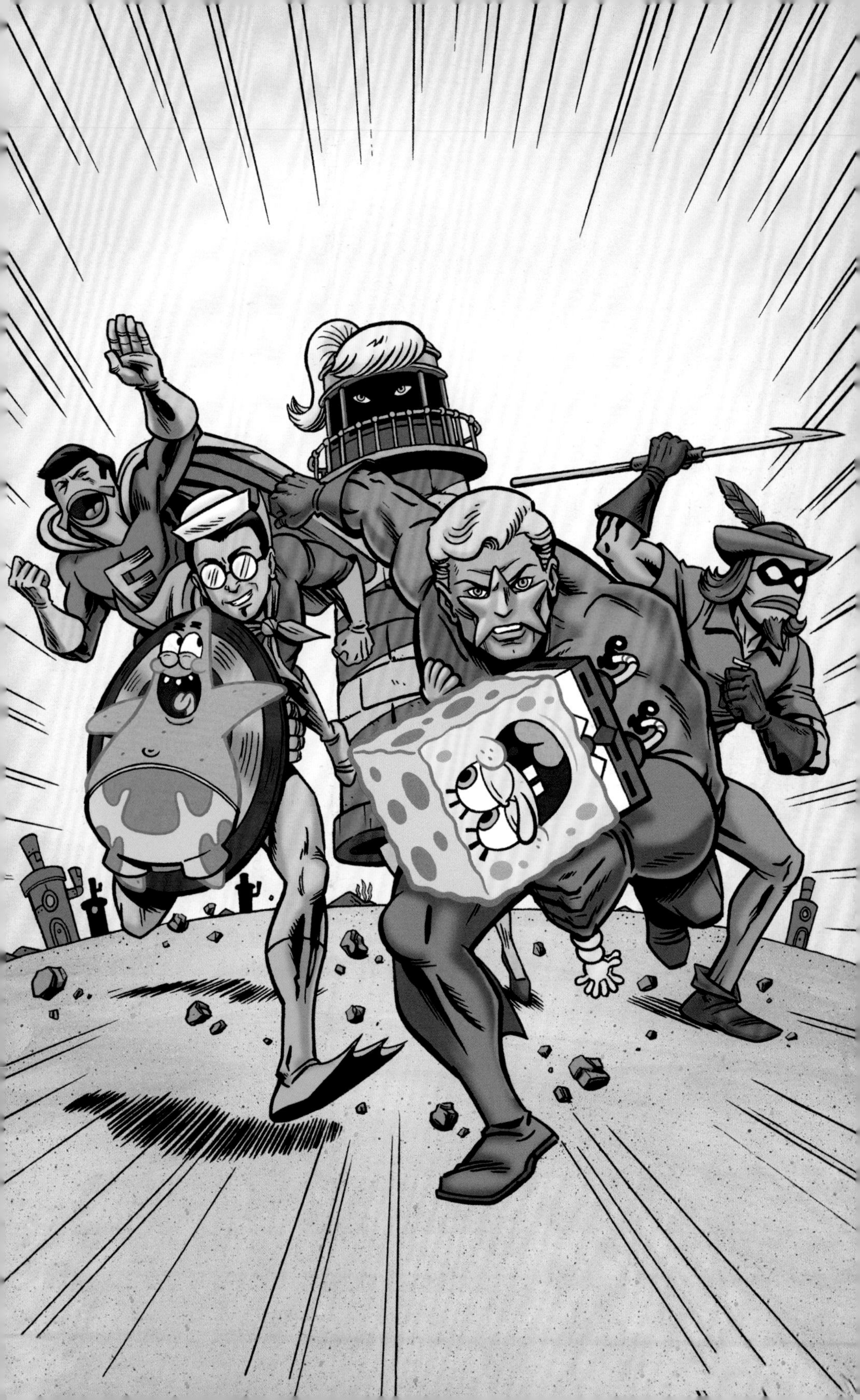

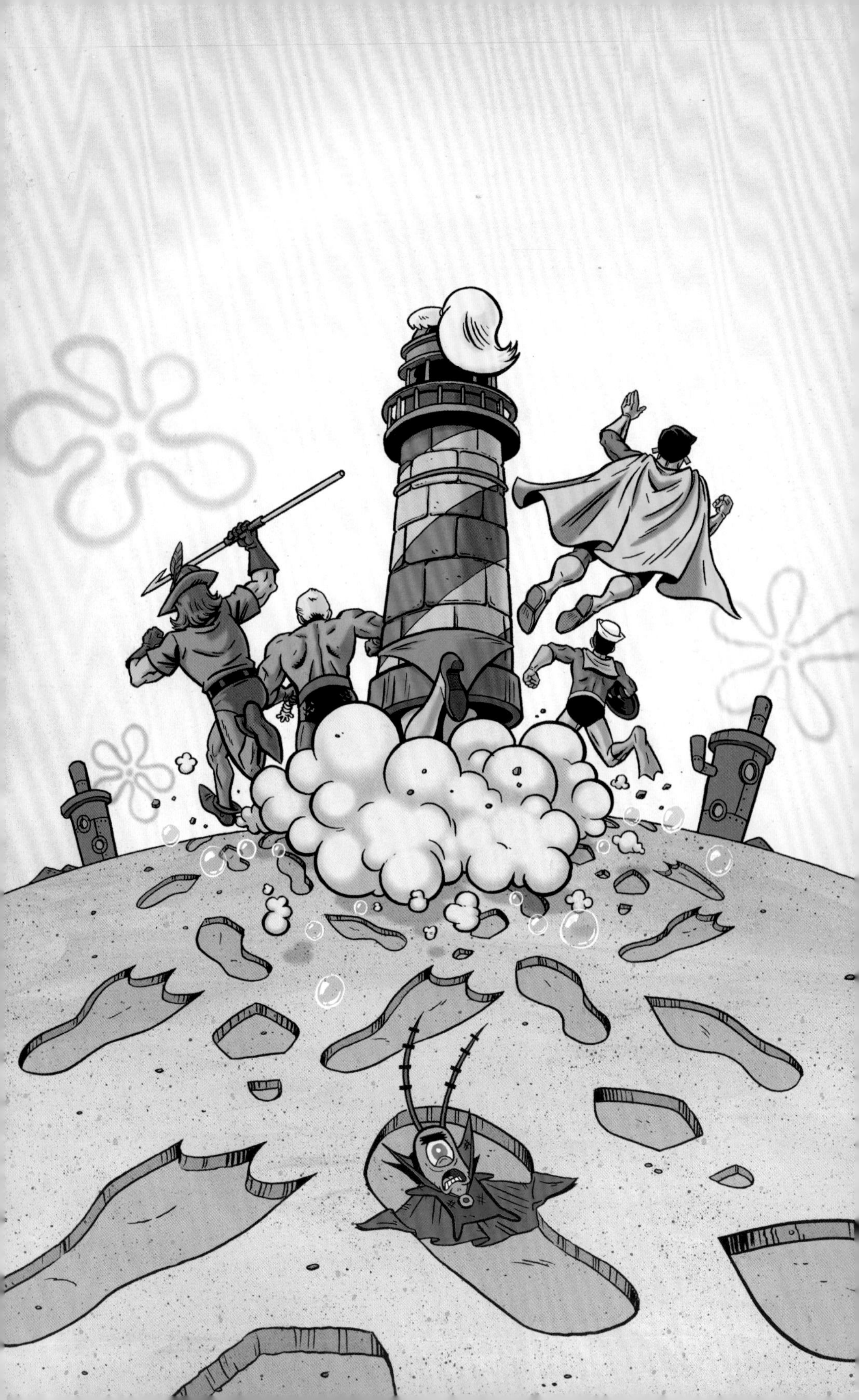